ONE WEEK'S NOTICE

T.J. BARTLETT

For my Family
I swear this isn't about you.

MONDAY

1

"Time to get up."

She must be kidding. The only thing it's time for is five more REM cycles. I can't have slept more than two minutes.

"Sean, you've slept more than two minutes." Christ Almighty, she can read my thoughts. I married a witch. "Though passing out hardly qualifies as sleep."

I bury my head in the pillow as something whacks me in the back. I muffle something unintelligible and blindly search the covers for the projectile.

"You're going to miss the girls again before they go to school."

A brush. Alex threw her fucking brush at me. That seems aggressive, even for a Monday morning.

I throw back the covers and sit up. My mouth tastes like ass.

"You're picking Claire up at practice tonight." She leans against the wall and slips her right foot into a spiked contraption Torquemada would have envied. She exhales sharply to blow a rogue strand of dirty blond hair out of her pale blue eyes. I ponder telling her it's time to stop dying her roots black, but it's a joke she tired of a hundred tellings ago. I opt for something less confrontational.

"How are you so awake?"

"I work," she says, no longer bothering to hide her disappointment as she slides her left foot into the torture device's mate. "So do you, which is why you should get your ass out of bed."

"My ass is far more comfortable in bed."

"There was a time when you loved your job and there was nobody better at it. What the hell happened to you?"

Before I can answer, she disappears into the closet.

"All I'm asking for is five more minutes," I whine.

She reemerges, a diamond earring now dangling from each ear.

"Don't be such a baby." She's moved from disappointment to disdain.

She stands by the door, hands on hips, and waits. I hold her gaze and in that moment, we fight a thousand unspoken battles. The preconceived notion of the ideal husband versus the man who has fallen hopelessly short. The dream giving way to reality.

For a flash, I consider telling her how unhappy I am; how, when she gets up each morning, puts on clothes more suited to someone ten years younger, jewelry we can't afford and makeup that, no matter how thick she cakes it on, never seems to hide the crow's feet that grow deeper with each passing day, she looks less like the successful businesswoman she hopes to project and more like the pathetic suburban mom she's trying to hide; how, when she leaves, I'm going to spend the next ten minutes willing myself not to beat off, not because I know it's sad and lonely, but because it's the only activity that gives me even a hint of joy and I'd rather keep it as something to look forward to for the rest of the day.

But it all sounds so exhausting. And if there's one thing on which we both agree, it's that I don't do exhausting. Surrender and capitulation are more my speed, the bedrock of any healthy marriage.

"I'm up," I sigh, swinging my feet to the floor. "Claire. Practice. I got it. You win."

She snorts as she turns to leave. "Yeah, I won the fucking lottery."

Happy Monday.

I WALK INTO THE KITCHEN, delicately checking the tissue covering the small canyon my razor carved out of my neck.

"You've got a stain on your tie."

I look down. A grease spot the size of a quarter stares back at me.

"Crap. Is it noticeable?"

"Not if you're Helen Keller."

My ten-year-old is in a Helen Keller phase. She gauges everything by whether Helen Keller could or could not see it, hear it, say it or do it.

"I'm already late, Jules," I say, pouring myself a cup of coffee. "I don't have time to tie another tie."

"Don't worry about it," she says brightly. "It's not really noticeable compared to all that blood on your collar."

"Shit."

I look at my reflection in the microwave and see an expanding pool of blood on my previously white shirt.

"Nice language, Dad."

"It's one of those mornings, Jules."

"Mom says you shouldn't swear so much."

"Mom should keep her fucking trap shut."

Julia cheerfully munches her toast and turns her attention back to her magazine.

"Is Claire still here?"

"Fees abut to leaf," she mumbles.

"What?"

She swallows hard and tries again. "She's about to leave."

"Try not to eat with your mouth full," I say, as I rummaging through the pantry for breakfast.

She giggles. "You mean talk?"

"What?"

"Don't you mean talk with your mouth full?"

"Yeah. What did I say?"

"'Eat with your mouth full,'" she answers with another laugh. "As if there's some other way to do it."

She leaves me to ponder that conundrum as Claire thunders down the stairs and into the kitchen. I see the scowl and brace myself. Fourteen years old and she has disgust and disdain down cold. At five feet four inches of pure fury, she is her mother's spitting image, right down to the blond hair, blue eyes and sharp, angular features.

We do not get along.

"You coming home after school?" I venture.

"I've got practice," she spits out, "or did you forget again?"

"Your mom reminded me," I say, scrambling to recover as she grabs her backpack and heads for the door.

"At least *someone* has a clue what's going on around here." She puts her hands on her hips and blows a strand of hair out of her eyes. Even her mannerisms are the same as Alex.

"Easy, Claire. Let's try to at least feign respect once in awhile, okay?"

"What's the point? We all know I'd just be lying."

"Nice," I respond, but she is already out the door. "I'll pick you up after practice!" I call after her.

"I'm sure she heard you," Julia says, grabbing her lunch and shoving it into her backpack. "I mean, it's not like she's Helen Keller.

"Where are you going? Your school doesn't start for another hour."

This stops her cold. "You're not suggesting I hang out here alone, are you?"

"You wouldn't be alone," I answer. "I'd be here, too."

"Please. It's not like I'm a child."

"Funny, because that's exactly what you look like."

"Not to Helen Keller."

I laugh. "You've got a point. Tell you what. Hang out for a little bit and help me pick out a new tie."

"Dad," she says with a heavy sigh, "why don't you just go to work? At least people there get paid to hang out with you."

Julia walks out the door, leaving me to sip my coffee and pick through the remnants of her toast. I look at the microwave and see that the reflection hasn't improved. If anything, it's even more disapproving than my daughters.

I take one last slurp of coffee before trudging back upstairs in search of a clean shirt and tie.

2

When I was ten, my dad let me skip school and tag along with him for Take Your Kid to Work Day. He didn't want to, mind you. He thought having me at his side while he did the work of our town's deputy assistant building inspector made about as much sense as him going back to elementary school. And he let my mom and me know in no uncertain terms he would never go along with it, never mind that all of the other fifth-grade parents eagerly let their kids participate in this annual rite of passage. I took the news as any ten-year-old would, which is to say I cried my eyes out. But no amount of begging, wailing or carrying on would change his mind. My father was unmoved.

I don't know why wanted to go so badly. It's not like I had a clue what a deputy assistant building inspector did, other than, you know, inspect buildings. But I was ten and no ten-year-old ever needed a reason to want to get out of school. More than that, though, it would have meant spending all day with my dad, which was practically too good to be true. Sure, I got to hang out with him at home, following quite literally in his footsteps as he puttered around the house on weekends, so much so that, on more than one occasion, he ran headlong into me when he doubled back quickly to get something he forgot in the garage. He would curse and laugh simultaneously as he picked me up, dusted me off and looked me over to make sure no bones were broken. And while I always appreciated the pat on my back as he sent me on my way, I nonetheless wished that look of concern in his eyes was more than the pity one would bestow on the animal they'd run over. Just once, I hoped I'd see something close to honest to goodness paternal love.

I guess that's how, in the mind of a ten-year-old, something as mundane as Take Your Kid to Work Day could be built up into the single most important happening this side of the Immaculate Conception (you know, assuming you believe in that kind of thing). I had convinced myself it was going to be special. Important. Life altering, even. It was my chance to spend time with Dad not just as father and son, but as two men doing men things. And at the office, no less. It seems silly in retrospect, but I remember wanting to go to work with him about as much as I'd ever wanted something in my life. I'm sure that made me insufferable but, like I said, I was ten. Ten-year-olds are built to be insufferable.

A week's worth of pleading went unrequited until Mom, the night before the big day, took my father in the back bedroom and gave him the business end of a hissy fit. I didn't catch all of it, and what stern snippets I did manage to overhear made little sense to me at the time. Sure, I understood the parts about the importance of being present and the tragedy of lost opportunities, but she completely lost me when she insisted that he not make me pay for her sins. But while the full meaning of her words wouldn't become apparent until years later when our family's disintegration was in full bloom, all I cared about was what he said to me when he emerged from the bedroom, ashen, humbled and, if I'm not mistaken, a little scared.

"We leave at eight."

Elated, I woke up early the next morning, brushed my teeth, scrubbed my face and donned my best clothes, which meant a pair of navy blue Toughskins and a clean but wrinkled button-up shirt I found balled up in the corner of my room. Catching a glimpse of my reflection in the mirror just before bounding downstairs for breakfast, I nearly exploded with pride. I looked exactly like what I imagined a professional would look like, notwithstanding the mis-buttoned shirt, which I quickly recti-fied as I barreled down the stairs to the kitchen.

I gobbled down a bowl of Life, taking care to forego my shirt-sleeve in lieu of a napkin to wipe the milk off my chin. I also made it a point to ask my younger brother, Kevin, several times in an excessively loud voice to let me know if I missed anything important at school while I was – AHEM! – at work with Dad.

I was a grade-A asswipe, even as a kid.

My father kept me waiting for what seemed an eternity, long enough for me to guzzle down some orange juice, clean my dishes and read the entire sports page. I couldn't imagine what was taking my father so long – wasn't he just as excited to get this day going as me? – so I kept myself busy reminding my little brother what an honor it was to accompany Dad to work, assuring Kevin that, if he did his chores, worked hard and got good grades, he, too, might one day be conferred the same august honor.

Like I said, huge asswipe. Gargantuan.

Finally, a full seventeen minutes after his supposed deadline, Dad slinked into the kitchen, poured himself a cup of coffee and eyed me the way a man looks at a dead rodent in need of disposal.

"Let's get this over with."

I nearly peed myself leaping to my feet. He met my excite-ment with a sigh and trudged towards the garage. My mom —

watching the scene with what I thought at the time was joy but years later realized was more likely satisfaction at having once more imposed her will on my father — kissed the top of my head and told me to have fun. I shrugged off her kiss like a big kid and bade farewell once more to my brother.

"See ya, Kev. Can't wait to hear all about school when I get home from work."

Someone should have kicked me right in the Toughskins.

No surprise, the day wasn't nearly as good as I hoped it might be, not that I would have admitted it at the time. From the meetings to the calls to the lunch with soda (real life Ginger Ale!), I thought then that the entire experience was a thin slice of heaven. But looking back, all of the harbingers of the soul-sucking professional life coming my way were present: the fluorescent lighting, the tired furniture, even the passive aggressive backbiting and stale-coffee breath of co-workers. I had always thought work was this mythically wonderful thing – why else would adults spend so much time there? – but one look at my dad confirmed that work was not all it was cracked up to be. He spent almost all of his time on the phone trying to answer people's questions about whether a deck constitutes a permanent structure or whether an inch encroachment on a setback really warranted getting the zoning board involved. Holding the phone in one hand, he would close his eyes and rub his scalp with the other, trying desperately to keep his cool. By the end of the day, I had a pretty good guess as to why he was going bald.

Other than the fleeting moments of joy — such as when I went through an entire box of staples trying to figure out how many I could shoot into the trashcan (it wasn't official, mind you, because Guinness wasn't on premises, but I'm pretty sure I got the world record) — work with Dad was dull. Excruciatingly so. Not even the Ginger Ale's sugar-induced high could save me. By four o'clock, I was dragging, having long ago concluded that work was nothing more than periods of drudgery interspersed with moments of mind-boggling boredom.

When the clock finally hit five, Dad turned off his computer and looked my way. I had just finished covering the window in his door with seven stacks of Post-It notes, and was pretty anxious to go home.

"You ready?"

"Yeah," I answered gratefully.

"So, what did you think?"

I paused, considering the question. "Seems like a hard way to spend the day," I said finally.

"How so?"

I chose my words carefully. "People call you because they have a problem. But when you try to help them, they don't seem to be all that nice to you."

He gave me a sad smile. "That's about the size of it."

He clapped me on the back and we walked out of his office. As he turned out the light, he wondered aloud whether a stop at the ice cream shop was in order.

Unable to hide my smile at this surprising turn of events, I told him maybe this work thing wasn't such a bad gig after all.

Christ Almighty, was I wrong.

3

I stare at the blank screen, the cursor's incessant blinking mocking me. I'm about to run my hands through what's left of my hair and then stop, remembering why Dad went bald. I glance at the empty glass to the right of my laptop. It's not even ten. Still too early for a drink, even by my standards.

I sigh and crack my knuckles.

Here we go. Time to write.

My fingers flicker above the keyboard, awaiting inspiration.

I wiggle my fingers again.

Any minute now.

Christ, this is painful.

"Hey."

I practically jump out of my chair. My heart pounding, I turn and see Naomi's familiar tangled mane of auburn hair. Her green eyes shine against her olive skin, the high cheekbones accentuating her broad smile. She could stop traffic, and regularly does when we go out for lunch.

"You okay?" she laughs.

"You scared the shit out of me."

"I gather. What are you working on?"

"Press release for the clinical manager conference." The annual meeting of Infirmus Health's clinical leadership – a bacchanalia of five thousand doctors, nurses and care managers known as CareFest – starts Friday. Ten years ago, the meeting started as a chance for clinicians to get together and share best practices. Since then, it has morphed into a self-congratulatory corporate lovefest where, instead of discussing patient care, senior executives congratulate each other for how much money they're making. But this being healthcare, we have to at least try to maintain a façade of caring about the patients we treat.

Hence this year's tagline: We. Care. About. Patients.

Of course, if you have to spend millions of dollars to demonstrate how much you care, chances are, you really don't.

"How's it going?"

"Almost done," I lie.

She looks over my shoulder at my laptop.

"There's an awful lot of white on that screen."

"I'm building momentum."

"Didn't you used to be known as the best PR man on the east coast?"

"Still am."

"You sure about that?"

"Just wait. I'm on the verge of greatness."

She nods to the glass. "Is that the booze talking?"

"I wish. Figured I'd try it sober."

"Why start now?"

"Got me," I sigh, pushing my chair away from the desk. "Christ, I can't seem to get it going."

"We still talking about the press release?"

"Screw you."

"That seems about right. I mean, given that you're so bad at it lately, me screwing me is all I'm left with."

I glance anxiously towards the door. "Naomi, can we please

do this somewhere else? Diane is right outside."

"You really think there's someone in this office who doesn't know you're screwing me?"

"According to you, I'm doing no such thing."

"I didn't say you're *not* screwing me," she corrects me. "I said you *suck* at screwing me. Big difference."

"One that is not readily apparent to me."

"It would be if you had to put up with you climbing all over you, only to pass out with a soft dick inside you."

"You need to work on your misplaced pronouns."

"Fuck you."

"Fuck me? Or fuck 'me,' the guy who's climbing all over me to fuck me?"

"You're an asshole."

"A point my wife, my two kids and now the woman I'm having sex with – badly, as it turns out – have all made crystal clear this morning."

"You should watch yourself."

"Or what? You were the one who seduced me, as I recall."

Instead of lashing back, Naomi stares at me with the same intensity that drew me to her when she first walked into my office three years ago. Finally, she curls a strand of auburn hair behind her ear and leans across my desk, so close that I can smell her. Hyacinth in the spring. I try to hold the gaze of her green eyes even as I catch a glimpse of her black bra against her bronze skin. I can hear my heart beat.

"I can fuck any man here," she says slowly, drawing out each syllable. She leans closer still, her lips tantalizingly close to my ear, her breath hot on my cheek. "Any. Man. I. Want."

She straightens up and stares defiantly at me. I struggle not to adjust my pants, which are suddenly tight in places I haven't felt in ages.

She turns and strides out of my office, passing my boss on

her way out.

"Morning, Naomi."

"Suck a bag of dicks, Tim."

Tim turns to watch her walk back to her office. He and I are not the only ones who notice her tight black pants making their way through the cube farm.

"Classy," he mutters, adjusting his frameless glasses awkwardly. In his mid-fifties with tightly clipped silver hair, strong jaw and sharp cheekbones, Tim Dwyer is the Hollywood version of what a general counsel should look like. Maniacal devotion to his rowing machine and a diet that borders on the monastic (with the notable exception of a fairly impressive bourbon habit) has ensured that there's not a soft edge to be found on him, whether on his face or anywhere under his tailored suit.

"She's got an edge," I admit.

"And then some." He pauses a beat. "She knows I'm your boss, right?"

"As far as I know."

"And she knows you're her boss?"

"That appears to be up for negotiation."

"You may want to start putting your foot down."

I refrain from telling him that current circumstances make that a bit of a challenge.

"What can I do for you, Tim?" I ask, trying to change the subject.

"Come with me."

"Do I have to?" Naomi's still on my mind. Besides, I think it would be a bit off-putting to walk down hall next to my boss with a raging hard-on. But since that won't do for an excuse, I do what I do best: I obfuscate. "I'm working on a press release for CareFest."

Tim squints at the blank screen. "You don't seem to have

made much progress."

"I, uh, just started."

He looks tired as he breathes deeply and pulls the starched white shirt cuffs of his shirt from beneath the gray sleeves of his worsted wool suit jacket. "Sean, how often do I come down to your office?"

"Not often," I admit.

"So when I do show up, don't you think there's a decent chance it might be important?" His tone brings back memories of my fifth grade teacher calling me up to the front of the class and asking me why I continued to pick my nose until it bled. Thirty years later and Ms. Sherman still gives me the heebie-jeebies.

"Seems likely," I concede.

"So don't you also think it might be prudent for someone in your position to drop what they're doing and do what I ask?"

Thankfully, his Socratic examination has gone on long enough to make even the horniest of thirteen year-olds — let alone a middle-aged PR flak — soft as a sponge, so I get to play magnanimous. "Of course, Tim," I say, rising up and practically bowing before him. "Lead on."

I follow Tim to the elevator and try to hide my annoyance when he presses the button for the fourteenth floor. As general counsel of the company, Tim has a large office on the top floor with the rest of the executive staff. I am merely head of external communications, meaning I am neither senior nor important enough to bask in such rarified air. Instead, I make do with the rest of the communications and marketing stiffs down on ten (though at least we're on a double-digit floor. Suck on that, Compliance). Every now and again, I'll get delusions of grandeur and ponder demanding an office with the big swinging dicks, but then I'll remember I hate those insufferable blowhards and the feeling will pass.

"We've got an issue," Tim says as the elevator doors close.

"Public?"

"Not yet, but it will be. That's why we need you."

Need. Please. They need me like they need a hemorrhoid. He and the rest of senior leadership want a scapegoat, someone to take the lumps while they count their money and tell themselves how smart they are. Why else hire an official spokesman? Still, I play along. It's why I get paid.

"Tim, you softie. I didn't know you cared."

He looks at me sideways and I wonder not for the first time why the head of communications reports directly to the general counsel. Tim and I have a decidedly different approach to communicating. By that I mean, I speak English and he speaks legalese. If I try to make a concept easy to understand using as few words as possible, he will complicate it with a long-winded explanation that confuses rather than explains. That may be why, after running my public statements past him for approval, I end up sounding like Orwell's bastard child.

For example, patients don't die in our care. Instead, we experience involuntary declines in patient census levels. And you'll never hear me say our revenues fell. Rather, I will tell you that clinical reimbursement levels from public and private sources show opportunity for improvement. And it goes without saying that none of our patients are fat. However, we may from time to time treat people who suffer from hypercaloric syndrome.

But it's hard to blame him. He's a lawyer; being abstruse is ingrained in his DNA. From what I hear, Tim's wedding vows were twenty minutes of caveats, provisos and stipulations. By the time he wrapped it up with an emphatic "I do, subject to the qualifications set forth above," the entire wedding party was asleep – everyone, that is, except his bride, a fellow lawyer who, by all accounts, was as wet as Niagara Falls.

The elevator doors open and it is immediately apparent that

all is not well. The usual hush and understated dignity of the fourteenth floor have been replaced by harsh whispers and manifest urgency. I look at Tim who responds with a raised eyebrow.

That's lawyer for "See? I wasn't fucking around."

I keep my smartass comments to myself and follow him down the hall. I try not to get caught up in the flurry of activity around me – midlevel minions scurrying about and secretaries whispering urgently into phones – and marvel instead at the surroundings. The furnishings are elegant but a little passé, if you'll pardon the Architectural Digest aside – a touch too 80s walnut for my discriminating palate. But what the place lacks in modernity, it more than makes up for in luxury. The carpet alone exceeds my entire net worth, though I suppose that's the wrong barometer, what with an upside-down mortgage and countless maxed out credit cards working against me. In fact, I'll bet a thousand dollars I don't have that my wife is applying for a new credit card as we speak.

As if on cue, my phone buzzes with a text from Alex.

DID U FORGET TO PAY BILLS?

The woman loves all caps. Nothing like being screamed at in written form. I text back while trying to keep pace with Tim.

No

MY VISA WAS DENIED.
U MISSED A PAYMENT

Really??

YES REALLY FUCKHEAD

There was a time she loved me, I swear.

                                              Sorry – will pay tonite

FORGET IT. ALREADY
GOT 2 NEW CARDS

Suddenly woozy with calculations of compounding interest dancing in my head, I steady myself at the nearest expanse of gleaming walnut. The secretary whose desk I'm groping eyes me warily.

"Sean," Tim barks impatiently. "Let's go."

"Give me a second," I pant, struggling not to vomit all over the carpet plush enough to have been painstakingly woven out of angels' vaginas.

"I know," he says, his tone softening. "I used to get nervous meeting with senior staff, too."

My hand shoots to my mouth. I can't believe he honestly thinks I give a rat's ass about whatever meeting he's dragging me to. Now, I really am about to puke. "I'll be okay," I stammer. "Just catching some air."

Then, something horrible happens. He takes a step towards me and, pinning my arms to my side, envelops me in what I can only imagine is a team-building embrace he learned at some senior exec retreat (because nothing says team-building like inappropriate touching). But instead of supportive and kind, it comes off as robotic and forced. And just when I think it can't get any worse, he whispers gently in my ear.

"I'll be with you the whole time."

I feel like a rape victim. There's nothing I can do except squeeze my eyes shut and wait for him to finish. After three long seconds, he steps back and looks at me with the proud eyes of a dad sending his toddler off to the first day of school.

"Let's go get 'em, shall we?"

I'm amazed he doesn't tousle my hair.

Humiliated, I follow Tim into the conference room, which appears to be filled with every member of senior management.

"Jesus Christ!" a voice thunders. "Isn't there anyone in this fucking company who can tell me what happened?"

The exasperated voice emanates from a bald head seated at the middle of the table. Its face is hidden behind two hands hand futilely rubbing exhaustion out of its eyes, but its identity is unmistakable. Vern Williams has been chief executive officer of Infirmus Health since its inception, single-handedly taking a single non-profit hospital and transforming it into the nation's largest chain of for-profit healthcare providers by acquiring rivals, crushing competitors, steamrolling regulators and buying off community activists. In little over a decade, he has gone from unknown and unrecognizable to infamous and in demand. He sits on every charitable board in town and is a fixture on the dais of all of the major healthcare conferences across the country. If the topic is healthcare and you're looking for an *éminence grise* to lend credibility to your cause, Vern Williams is your man.

His lone misstep? The company name and tagline: *Infirmus Health: We take the sick right out of you.*

Today, however, does not appear to be one of his good days. As he pulls his hands from his face, I can see his temporal artery bulging from across the room.

"There you are," he says, seeing us. "It's about damn time."

Tim knows better to answer. I follow his lead and take one of the two empty seats facing Williams across the enormous oval table.

Good lord, this seat is comfortable. Soft, supple and supportive in all the right places. They must have had extra carpet vaginas lying around and decided to make a few chairs with the surplus. I cinch my butt around to see if it's possible to be uncomfortable in the chair. Not a chance. With every movement, the leather gives a pleasing little burp as it readjusts to cup my ass just so. It's miraculous. I give it a few last butt shifts until I feel Tim's hand on my shoulder.

I look up. Williams and the rest of the execs are staring at me.

"Comfy?" Williams says finally, his eyebrows arched over piercing eyes. "Need anything else? A blanky? Some warm milk?"

Both would be lovely, but I suspect taking him up on the offer might cause that artery of his to burst. And while I'd do just about anything to get out of this meeting, being the proximate cause of my CEO's death is one step too far, even for me. Instead, I wave him off with my best 'No thanks, bro' face.

"I'm good," I assure him.

He holds my gaze for another beat and then turns to Tim, unimpressed. "Strong addition."

Luckily, the discussion quickly turns away from my idiocy and back to the cause of this august gathering. It's difficult at first to glean what happened, what with each department head deftly deflecting responsibility and parrying Williams' probes, but finally the picture emerges. A patient at one of our New York hospitals went into the operating room for what should have been a straightforward orthopedic procedure on his right knee. Unfortunately, and for reasons that are not yet clear, the surgeon – board certified and tenured chair of the orthopedic department at the local med school – decided to operate on the left knee, notwithstanding the fairly clear directive that the nurse had scrawled in red Sharpie on that leg not five minutes before the initial incision:

CUT THE OTHER KNEE, DUMMY!

The patient, an otherwise healthy man in his early thirties who had blown out his knee playing pick-up basketball, no doubt would have been miffed to learn that the hospital had gone to great trouble and expense to reconstruct his perfectly healthy left knee, while leaving the torn and tattered ligaments in his right knee untouched. He would have, that is, had he not almost immediately gone into septic shock after the surgery. The crack post-op squad failed to note his elevated fever or skyrocketing respiratory rate, so by the time an enterprising young intern asked whether it made sense to run a blood work-up (the results of which showed the poor sap's platelets had fallen through the floor), it was too late. The attending physician pumped every antibiotic known to man into the patient's system, but to no avail. He expired the next day, as did all hopes of remedying the surgeon's colossal fuck-up with a hushed apology, a hastily executed confidentiality agreement and a subsequent operation (which, had I been forced to spin it, would have been justification to laud the company for giving this nice man two reconstructions for the price of one. They don't call me the best PR hack in the business for nothing.).

"Good god," I whisper to Tim. "This is a disaster."

"Just wait."

"There's more?"

Unsurprisingly dismayed, the patient's widow immediately availed herself of the court system for redress. She approached local television stations to try to exact revenge in the court of public opinion as well. Meanwhile, local management did what they do best, which was ignore the problem and hope it went away. Of course, any fifth grader with a science project due date looming can tell you how well that's going to work. No surprise, local news had a field day. State regulators took note of the press coverage by increasing their "random" surveys of our facilities to ensure we were compliance with all applicable regulations.

I venture a glance at Williams. His head is redder than I remember and his artery has resumed pulsing at an alarming rate. No wonder. As the head of clinical services continues her summary, it is clear that our clinical and compliance folks knew about the increased surveys. They told local management to be on the lookout for surveyors and to redouble their efforts at running a tight operation.

To no avail.

Six weeks ago, a surveyor in New Jersey – just across the river from the hospital that started this whole mess – walked into one of our outpatient dialysis clinics and politely asked the clinic manager for a tour. Soon thereafter, as she silently took notes, the surveyor watched our staff lead a fifty-four-year-old man from the front door to a chair on the treatment floor and initiate dialysis. There was nothing particularly odd about the encounter, except for the fact that – from the time the man was brought into the clinic, ushered to his chair, cleaned, swabbed and stuck with a needle – the man was screaming at the top of his lungs that he was not our patient and did not need dialysis.

Fairly important information, if you ask me.

Not to the rest of the staff, however. Everyone — from the ambulance driver who drove the patient to the clinic, to the clinic manager who ushered him to his chair, to the nurse who stuck a needle in his arm to the social worker who tried to comfort him as he screamed bloody murder — apparently came to the same unspoken conclusion: why doesn't this patient just shut the hell up so we can do our job?

Never mind that the man had been receiving dialysis three times a week for the last four years. Never mind that – after more than *six hundred* dialysis treatments – he was in a pretty good position to know this wasn't his clinic and these weren't his usual caregivers. Never mind any of that because patients can't be trusted. We, on the other hand, are professionals. We know better, right?

Right?

The clinic staff knew better right up to the point when the patient went into catatonic shock (on the upside, he stopped complaining). Had they bothered to listen to his screams, they would have learned that the man had been dialyzed at his regular clinic the day before and that the absolute last thing he needed was to have more fluid taken out of his blood. As any first year med student can tell you, taking excess fluid out of the blood of a person with kidney failure is vital; taking too much out, however, can be fatal.

The patient tried telling us all of this, right up to the moment that we killed him. And did I mention this was happening all while the state surveyor patiently took notes?

"Wait a second," Williams says wearily. "We've got a man entering our clinic claiming not to be our patient and we still dialyze him? You mind telling me how that happens?"

The woman from clinical services shifts uncomfortably in her chair and considers her response. "Earlier that morning, the clinic had received a call from the patient's rehab hospital saying they were sending over a man for treatment. Clinic staff checked the man's ID upon arrival and his name was a match. Douglas Swanson."

"Okay..." Williams says impatiently, waiting for the punch line.

"The name was a match, sir, but the patient wasn't."

"Meaning?"

"Apparently, there are two Douglas Swansons at this rehab facility."

Williams folds his hands in front of him and looks squarely at the woman from clinical services. "Please tell me at least one Douglas Swanson is our patient."

"Yes, sir. Douglas P. Swanson is alive and well. He just received dialysis yesterday, in fact."

"And the dead one?"

"Douglas H. Swanson. He is – or was – a patient of River Partners Dialysis, a local operator."

"Any chance these two gentlemen look similar?"

"I beg your pardon?"

"Rebecca, you've just told me—"

"Rachel."

"Excuse me?"

"You called me Rebecca. My name is Rachel. Rachel Coleman."

Until now, I never realized there is no such thing as absolute silence. I always assumed that, in the absence of movement, there would be no noise. But sitting here, waiting for Vern Williams to unleash his wrath upon Rachel Coleman, I discover I am wrong. For even though not a soul in this walnut paneled room is breathing – let alone moving – all I can hear is the roar of a train. It is bearing down on us with such ferocity that I begin to sweat, my fingers sinking into the armrests of my chair as my eyes dart furiously around the room, struggling to find the source of the calamity.

And then it hits me. There is no train. There is no impending doom, at least, not for anyone not named Rachel Coleman. The roar I hear is the blood rushing through my ears. My fingers relax slightly and I chance a glance at Ms. Coleman. I say a silent prayer for her and wish her well in the afterlife.

But then Williams surprises us all. He unclasps his hands, leans back and smiles.

"My apologies, Ms. Coleman," he says. "It seems mixing up names is a corporate-wide malady." He lets the nervous laughter die down before continuing his inquiry. "Let me make sure I've got this right. Two patients: Douglas P. and Douglas H. Douglas

P. is ours and Douglas H. is not. Douglas P. is alive and Douglas H. is not."

"Correct."

"And we killed him."

At this, Tim perks up. "Excuse me, sir, but causation has not been established. We, of course, will be disputing this in court."

"Of course," Williams says, waving away the legal niceties.

"I remind everyone in this room," Tim continues, "that this entire conversation should be considered in anticipation of litigation and is therefore privileged. I further remind you not to discuss the subject matter of this meeting outside the presence of counsel."

"You finished?" Williams asks archly.

"Yes, thank you."

Williams turns back to Rachel. "Douglas H. comes into our clinic, says he's not our patient. Says he's just been dialyzed, but we plop him in our chair anyway, stick a needle in his arm and let her rip. Twenty minutes later, he's dead. Do I have that right?"

"Give or take, yes sir."

"So back to my original question. Do Douglas P. and Douglas H. look alike? That is, could any reasonable person mistake one for the other?"

She considers her answer for a moment. "No, sir. Not likely."

"Not even a little?"

"Douglas P. is an eighty-three-year-old white man and has been in a wheelchair for the last six years. Douglas H. is — or was — a fifty-four-year-old fully ambulatory African-American man."

"Louis," Williams says, turning his attention to the head of human resources, who had been doing his level best to sit unnoticed at the far end of the table, "when we hire clinic staff, do we administer an IQ test to ensure we only hire borderline retards?"

Louis has the good sense not to respond.

"They did check the patient's ID."

"Who said that?" Williams snaps, looking up and down the long conference table. There is no response.

"WHO SAID THAT?" Williams thunders, his temporal artery now on the verge of rupturing.

I see Tim remove his glasses and rub his eyes wearily as a voice pipes up from a chair against the wall behind me. A backbencher.

"I did, sir."

"WHO THE FUCK ARE YOU?"

"Randall J. Simon, deputy assistant counsel for litigation." No wonder Tim is dismayed. The backbencher works for him. "My point, sir, is that clinic staff did everything they could be expected to. They received a call the morning of the event—"

'The event.' We've already sanitized it. It's not The Day We Killed Douglas Swanson, or even That Time We Unfortunately Treated the Wrong Patient and He Tragically Died, Though on the Advice of Counsel, We Cannot Speculate as to Whether There Is Any Causative Link Between the Aforementioned Treatment and the Patient's Demise (though I hear CBS has a three-part miniseries in development with that as a working title). Instead, this poor man's death is now The Event. No mention of the deceased or our culpability, just an innocuous sounding reference to an amorphous concept eliminating all sense of emotional connection or moral responsibility from the record. Pretty soon, we will be speaking in the passive voice to further distance ourselves from the possibility that people with whom we work could have done something so horrific.

"— and a chair on the floor was prepared."

And there it is. You have to hand it to Randall J. Simon, attorney at law extraordinaire. He is hitting all of his marks. He presses on.

"When the patient came in, his ID was checked according to protocol. If anyone is to blame in this instance, it is the rehab facility."

"The rehab facility?" Williams sputters.

"Absolutely," Simon agrees, not realizing he is digging his own grave. "They should have known that the Douglas Swanson they put in the ambulance to be transported to our dialysis clinic was not the correct Douglas Swanson."

Williams sighs dramatically. "Well, thank Christ for that. Honestly, Mr. Simon, I am thrilled beyond words. I am so relieved that – wait, how did you put it? Oh, that's right: 'protocol.' I am so relieved that we did everything 'according to protocol.' You know, I feel a little foolish. I completely missed that. But not you. Not good ol' Mr. Simon. You saw the whole thing. I have to admit. I was a little worried. I mean, I wasn't sure we'd be able to explain why the people who treated Douglas P. Swanson three times a week every week for the last ... how many years?"

"Twelve," Rachel answers immediately, giving the young lawyer no quarter.

"Twelve years," Williams says to Simon, shaking his head in amazement. "That's a long time. That's longer than you've been having sex, by the look of you. And still, after all that time, the people in our clinic – the people we say in all those slick ads are the best trained and most compassionate people alive – turns out they can't be troubled to remember that their patient is thirty years older with a significantly lower melanin content than the guy they're dragging kicking and screaming across the clinic floor to certain death. And all the while, a state regulator stands watching, taking notes. Oh, hey, that reminds me, Mr. Simon. There's still one question that plagues my addled brain. Can you tell me, in your learned experience after working in this industry for ... how long has it been?"

"Four months," Simon says weakly.

"Of course it has. Tell me. What do you think that surveyor's notes will reveal? Do you think she'll say we should be absolved because we did everything according to protocol? Or do you think – and I'm just spit-balling here – she'll wonder why we never took the time to ask the poor man why he wasn't—" Williams stands and places his palms flat on the table, leaning forward as his face contorts menacingly. "—AN EIGHTY-YEAR-OLD WHITE GUY IN A FUCKING WHEELCHAIR?"

You know what? I was wrong before. Absolute silence does exist. I stand corrected.

Mercifully, Tim clears his throat to intervene. "Why don't we take a fifteen minute break?"

"That's a good idea," Williams says, recovering. "That'll give Mr. Simon a chance to clear out his office."

To anyone who thinks balding, middle-aged bureaucrats have lost their athletic ability, I offer up this conference room as evidence to the contrary. Heads down, hoping like hell not to be noticed, everyone not named Williams sprints towards the door in near world record time. I join in, throwing an elbow or two to try to get to the front of the pack.

"Not you, Reilly."

Shit. I can feel his glare burning through my back. I slowly turn around and see Williams staring at me.

"We need to talk."

I slink back to my chair and wait, a condemned man awaiting execution. I was this close to sneaking out of this clusterfuck, but now I'm about to have a one on one with the big man. Next thing I know, he'll expect me to do some actual work.

"Tim," Williams says once the room has cleared, "we have got to get some better people in this place. I don't know who is worse – the morons we've got in the field dialyzing the wrong patients or that fucktard in your legal shop defending them."

"Technically, that's his job."

"Of course it's his job. And of course we're going to blame the rehab hospital. But that's for the courtroom, not the boardroom. I don't need some wet behind the ears junior associate trying out his closing argument on me when we've got bigger problems to solve – like how to keep our hospitals and clinics open when we can't seem to stop killing people."

"That," says Tim, glancing at me, "is where Sean comes in."

"Me?" I ask dumbly.

"Of course," Williams chimes in. "The way I understand it, you're a public relations specialist. And this, to put it mildly, is a significant public relations challenge."

Tim jumps in. Mr. Nuts and Bolts. "We need a public statement, internal and external talking points – a complete P.R. strategy. The press is going to have us by the shorthairs on this one unless you can work your magic."

"I understand all that," I say cautiously. "And of course my team will jump on this immediately."

If by "team" you mean a mistress who currently wants to chop my dick off, a couple of interns who are still learning the difference between a dangling participle and a split infinitive and a secretary whose primary skill is ordering lunch, then yes, I have a team.

"We'll get the ball rolling on the P.R. front," I assure them.

"We'll need to move quickly," Williams adds.

"How quickly?"

"Preferably by the end of the week," Tim answers. "Care-Fest starts Friday. The board will be in town and it would be best if we had, uh, minimized any external distractions by then."

The dead patients are now 'external distractions.' I told you this guy had a flair for the mundane.

"Terrific," Williams says, rising to indicate the meeting is over.

"I haven't gotten any inquiries on this yet," I say, rising with him. "Have we heard from the patient's family?"

"Not yet," says Tim. "Nor have we heard anything from the regulators. But as we all know, that's only a matter of time."

"Which is why you're on the case," Williams says, much too brightly for my taste.

As they walk me to the door, I can't resist. "One last question, Mr. Williams."

"Anything," he says. Even as his lips smile wide to reveal perfectly capped and polished teeth, his eyes are dead. For the first time, I am truly startled. The bluster at the meeting was just that: theater designed to bludgeon us into complying with his wishes. But up close, it's clear that Williams doesn't give a damn about anyone that gets in his way. We are chattel, easily discarded to serve his needs. I stifle a shiver.

"We'll frame the public debate and start getting some surrogates to speak on our behalf. But as far as the regulators go, shouldn't our government affairs team take the lead on interfacing with the policy makers?"

"Oh, absolutely," he agrees, leaning in and clapping his hand on my shoulder. "This whole exercise is doomed to fail unless our government affairs folks play an active role. But Sean—"

He called me Sean. In the six years I have worked here, he's never once called me by my first name. Sure, you can count our interactions on one hand, but that's not the point. By calling me Sean, he's bringing me in. He's showing that we're on the same team. We're buddies. Compadrés. Equals.

I'd be honored if it wasn't complete horseshit.

"—they're not the real leaders here. Oh sure, they can make a few phone calls and open a few doors. But answer me this: who's going to do the talking once those doors are open? A bunch of lobbyists?" He makes a face like he just swallowed some bad fish. "Please. They don't have the first clue what goes on around here. No, it has to people like me. People," he says gravely, placing his other hand on my shoulder and looking me squarely in the eye, "like you."

He is so close I can smell his breath, which has the distinctive whiff of Listerine trying and failing to mask the smell of bourbon.

"I need you, Sean," he continues, laying it on thick. "We need you – *I* need you – to step up and run point on this. To be honest with you, Sean, there's no one else here we can trust to get this right."

Translation: you're the patsy and there's no one better suited to take the fall than you.

"Tell you what," he says, turning me once more towards the door. "After you put some thoughts down on paper, run them by me. You and I should work closely on this."

Translation: you take the lead so I don't have my fingerprints on any of this. But involve me just enough so I can look like I know what I'm doing.

"This is going to be fun," he says finally, the marionette smile returning to his face.

Translation: get out of my office and don't let me see you again until I fire you.

I shake his hand and turn to leave. As I walk out of the conference room, I hear the door click behind me. No Williams. No Tim. Just me, alone among the minions. I look at the desk across the hall and see Mr. Williams' secretary hard at work on the phone, politely declining an invitation for yet another charity ball. Between the stapler and pencil holder is a sign, a warning to all:

DON'T FUCK WITH DADDY

Now you tell me.

4

My computer screen is still blank but at least my glass is now full. I take a healthy sip and the familiar warmth returns.

"Better?" Naomi asks as she walks in my office.

"Have you ever knocked? Or is this new since we've been together?"

"Look at you, talking so freely about us in the office. Is that your first or are you already shitfaced?"

"First sip," I say, taking another. "And this isn't the booze talking. I've simply decided that I no longer give a fuck."

"In that case," she says walking around my desk and grabbing a glass out of the cabinet, "I think I'll join you." She plops down in the chair facing me and pours a glass. She drains half of it in one sip. The woman can outdrink a sailor.

"You know," I muse, "I suddenly can't remember why I didn't start drinking earlier."

"That press release must really be rocking your world."

I look at her quizzically and then remember the blank screen behind me. "Not even close." She raises her eyebrows and I continue. "I was summoned to the fourteenth floor."

"And?"

"And this company appears to have made a habit out of killing its patients."

"That doesn't sound good for business."

I nod. "Generally speaking, it's bad form to eliminate your customer base."

"Is this an across the board thing, or limited to a specific site?"

"One hospital and one dialysis clinic so far, but I'm sure there will be more."

"Meaning we're not cracking down?"

"Meaning the more we dig into this, the worse it will be. Reilly's Law: Be Careful What You Look For."

"This is serious," she says, ignoring me.

"Damn right. A serious issue that merits serious response. You see, my dear Naomi, there is nothing more important than the care of our patients. That is why we have implemented a detailed remediation plan across all our sites. Where we have fallen short, we will get better. Where we find errors, we will hold those responsible accountable. We will do everything necessary to ensure that we live up to the commitment we make each and every day to our patients and their families..." I trail off, suddenly more interested in my drink than in the drivel I'm spouting.

"At least you've got your talking points down."

"I better. I'm in charge."

"Come again?"

"That's what you said."

"Very funny."

"Not really, but I appreciate the sentiment."

"What the hell do you mean you're in charge?"

"Just what it sounds like. I'm in charge of the public response. Oh, the clinical and compliance folks will handle the investigation and remediation aspects, and I'm sure legal will be holding their hands all the way. But as far as the public face of the company," I say, holding my glass aloft, "well honey, you're looking at him." As I drink, I notice Naomi has put her glass down. Looks like I'm drinking alone. Again.

"What are you going to do?"

I shrug. "Just what they ask. Be the face of the company for the time being. Do some local press, toe the company line – you know, the usual. And, of course, get ready for the big clinic manager meeting on Friday. That's going to be the showpiece. All eyes will be on us, so we have to make sure we look good."

"You mean we have to make sure Williams looks good."

"That's what I said."

She rolls her eyes. "You really want to do press? You're not worried about tough questions?"

"Set up something local. Not the hospital. Use something out in the neighborhood – a dialysis clinic or one of our doc-in-a-boxes."

"Our urgent care clinics?" she corrects me.

"Whatever. Just as long as it shows us delivering high quality care when and where our patients need it most – that kind of thing."

"Walk and talk?"

"Yeah. Call Channel Five's consumer reporter, the one who always wears the leather jacket. What's her name?"

"Jane Collins."

"Right. She's always looking for ways to be a woman of the people. Plus, she owes me a solid."

"When?"

"See if she'll do it tomorrow. In fact, make it an all-out media blitz. Call those sniveling little shits at our P.R. agency. It's time they start earning their ungodly retainer. Over the next three days, I want every man, woman and child in every major media market getting the warm and fuzzies about Infirmus."

"You want anyone from corporate on camera?"

"Not a soul. This has to be local. Make sure our logo is plastered all over every shot, but don't have anyone in a suit within twenty miles of the joint. The only people on camera should be smiling patients and local caregivers."

"Don't we want someone higher up talking about our national footprint?"

"And make people think we're some kind of monolithic, uncaring behemoth? Come on, Naomi, you're better than that."

"Right," she says, catching herself. "We're the friendly neighborhood doctor."

"With nary a worry of gross revenue or operating margin."

"What else?"

"Keep prepping for Friday. Check in with the dickweeds in marketing, make sure the event is buttoned up tight. Something tells me we're going to have extra eyes on us. We've got to look like we know what we're doing for a change. Give me an update tomorrow."

"What about Williams?"

"What about him?"

"He's our CEO. Shouldn't he be doing something?"

"He is. He's keeping his head down."

"Okay," she says, exasperated, "how about Tim?

"He's no dummy. He's hiding out with Williams."

"So you can be the one on camera."

"If need be. But that's only if this blows up. And it's my job to see that it doesn't."

"Yeah, but why you?"

"Because I'm expendable."

"That is truly fucked up."

"That's the way the world works. Shit flows downhill." I raise my glass in a toast and take a sip.

She pauses to sip her drink contemplatively. "This all happened this morning?"

"Just after you stormed out. After accusing me of failing to get it up, as I recall."

"That was no accusation. That was a statement of fact."

"A fact that's in dispute," I countered, taking another sip.

"Keep drinking like that and there'll be no dispute."

"Well, then," I say, setting my glass down and looking squarely in her eyes. "I suggest you give me a shot at redemption before things get completely out of hand."

"Twenty bucks says you'll just pass out as usual."

"I'll take that bet," I counter. "But you better bring your A-game."

"I always do."

"Don't be so sure, my dear. My alleged failure to perform may be directly correlated to your failure to arouse me."

She laughs her wonderfully deep, throaty laugh. She knows I'm full of shit.

"Naomi, it's nothing to be ashamed of," I persist. "It happens to everyone at some point. So you've lost some off your fastball. Deal with it with dignity and move on."

She holds my gaze intently and I can feel the spark between us. My skin is tingling. It's a damn shame I'm married to another woman.

"You're a cocksucker, you know that?" she asks finally.

"Oh, that reminds me. You should probably stop accusing your boss and your boss' boss of fellatio."

It takes her a moment to remember this morning. "Tim complain?"

"Not so much of a complaint as a statement of surprise that a subordinate would suggest he suck – and I quote – an entire bag of dicks. That's an awful lot of penises for one sitting, even for Tim."

I stand and start for the door. Naomi doesn't move. "You coming?" I ask.

"You're serious?"

"Yeah, sure. Why not?"

"Didn't you just finish telling me how much work you have?"

I shrug. "It can wait."

She stands and I hold the door for her expectantly. "Williams is only half right. You're not just expendable, you're pathetic." And with a look of what I'd like to think is admiration, but what I'm pretty sure is revulsion, she walks past me, through the door and towards the elevator.

5

Sun streams across my face as I try to bury my head in the pillow. I open my eyes and see I forgot to close the curtains. God, if there's a more depressing place than a hotel room in the afternoon, I don't want to know. I close my eyes and try to imagine something less sordid. Nothing's coming to mind. I reach out to the other side of the bed and come up just as empty. No Naomi, just an empty pillow that's long gone cold.

I throw back the covers and sit up. Eight hours since I got up this morning and I don't seem to have made much progress. My mouth tastes just as bad now as it did then, but I've regressed to a shabbier bed and a smellier room. True, I woke this morning to a woman yelling at me, but at least she had the good grace not to leave without saying goodbye.

I swing my feet to the floor and stand up, discovering two things along the way: my head is pounding and my dick is rock hard. I look at the nightstand and see causes for both conditions: four empty miniatures of Seagram's and a bottle of blue pills. As if that's not enough to spark the shame spiral, I see a note under the pills. I pick it up, scrunch my eyes and try to make out the message scrawled on it.

You owe me $20.
Statement of fact, asshole.

Cute, but judging by my throbbing hard on, accurate. I look at the clock: still an hour before I have to pick up Claire. Fuck it. I walk into the bathroom to shower and beat off knowing full well I'm the only man in America who takes Viagra just so he can masturbate.

Twenty minutes and a bottle of mouthwash later, I feel at least moderately human. I'm in that netherworld between buzzed and hung over. As I cruise through lobby, I toy with the idea of stopping off at the hotel bar to tip the scales in the right direction, but a fatherly instinct I didn't realize I still possessed suggests that picking up my daughter completely soused isn't the best idea.

So instead of one big mistake, I decide to make two smaller ones. First, I check my email: Thirty-six messages, most of which are polite but firm inquiries from Tim about my progress or short but bitchy reminders from Alex about my shortcomings as a breadwinner and husband. I skim through these quickly, putting off my boss with vague allusions to bold steps forward and assurances of an in-person status update tomorrow morning. My wife I ignore. Engaging with her over email is roughly the equivalent of negotiating a hostage situation with a terrorist: a loud, emotional but ultimately fruitless process that can only end in blood.

I see a message from Naomi. Good news. Channel Five's Jane Collins will meet me at one of our dialysis clinics at eleven o'clock tomorrow morning. She'll get a tour of the clinic from one of our docs and interview a few patients who have been prepped to wax poetic about how caring our staff is and how convenient our clinics are. You know, bullshit. Our P.R. agency has followed in kind. Similar media hits are scheduled to run in fifty-three different markets across the country over the next two days. Home fucking run. I shoot Naomi an email with an attaboy and a promise that I'll make it up to her next time, though we both know that's a lie.

As I scroll through the last of the messages, one jumps out. Marcus Cannon, the *Times'* Pulitzer prize winning reporter who has single-handedly brought down nearly a dozen CEOs with his exposés on healthcare fraud, wants to talk. On its face, the message is benign ("Sean, I'd love to learn more about Infirmus. Give me a call...") but there is nothing benign about Marcus Cannon. If he reaches out, he's doing it to put a target on your back.

Naturally, I make my second mistake and decide to call him.

"Marcus," I say warmly when he picks up, "Sean Reilly from Infirmus, returning your call."

"Sean, thanks for calling." I can hear him shuffling papers to find his notes. He has notes on us. Not good. "I was hoping you could help me out with a few things."

"That's what I'm here for," I chirp brightly. Actually, I'm here to protect my boss and my boss' boss from getting ass-raped in the press, not help the great Marcus Cannon get another notch on his belt, but I seem to be getting ahead of myself. "Fire away."

"I was hoping you could give me some information about your star ratings."

For years, the federal government has collected data on nearly every hospital and outpatient facility in America on a variety of quality measures – everything from infection rates to patient satisfaction to death rates. But no one in government thought to make the information publicly available or, if they did, they did it in the least accessible way imaginable. Assuming an interested citizen managed to unearth the data, she would then have to wade through spreadsheet after spreadsheet (in non-searchable format, naturally) to find the information on the specific facility she happened to be looking for. It was like looking for a needle in a stack of needles.

And then, Yelp came along. Eager to jump on the consumer-friendly bandwagon, the government hired a few young programmers to develop a rating system for the healthcare industry. With a swiftness that shook the healthcare market-place to its core, these whiz kids built statistical models and fancy new algorithms rating every healthcare provider in the country, and wrapped it all in a glossy new website, search engine optimized to ensure top billing on Google. Hitherto undiscovered data was now searchable, digestible and – worst of all for providers like Infirmus – easily promulgated.

Thus was the Five Star System born.

It didn't take long before every healthcare provider saw their admissions fluctuate depending on the latest incarnation of the Star Ratings. After all, why would anyone looking for an ortho-pedist to fix their balky knee go to a one-star doctor down the street when they could see a five-star specialist across town? The government's new ratings system hit providers right where it hurt most: the pocketbook.

Not surprisingly, practice patterns for one and two-star providers started to change overnight. After all, there's no better way of getting a doctor to sit up and take notice than showing her a twenty percent drop in patient-related revenue. Only prob-lem, it's not entirely clear these changes have been for the better. Providers weren't interested necessarily in changing patient care; they just wanted to see their ratings improve. So they scoured the metrics used by the government and figured out the best way of adjusting their practice patterns to maximize their ratings, regardless of whether the changes actually improved patients' outcomes. And thus "Teaching to the Test" became the hallmark of medicine in America.

But Marcus Cannon knows all this. In fact, he has written extensively on the growing disconnect between providers' Five Star ratings and actual quality. Moreover, the scores for every one of our hospitals and clinics are available to anyone with an Internet connection. I have nothing to add to the debate and no new information to give him. He's fishing for something else, and it's my job not to give it to him.

"Not sure there's much to say," I tell him truthfully. "Our scores and everyone else's are online. That's why God created Google."

"I should have been more precise," he says smoothly. "What I really want to know is how a hospital with such a good ranking could kill a knee replacement patient by operating on the wrong leg."

"We've said all along those ratings can't be trusted," I answer without thinking. And then I actually laugh. What the hell is wrong with me? Have another Seagram's, you dumb fuck.

I can hear his jaw hit his desk.

"Is that the official position of Infirmus?" The son of a bitch is actually laughing.

"Of course not," I say quickly. Scrambling to recover, I go into talking point overdrive. "Patient care is our top priority. There is nothing more important than our patients and their families. We value the trust they place in us and we strive to improve the lives of every patient, every day. Providing our patients with the highest quality care is our mission."

I can hear him yawn. My only hope at this point is he doesn't mention me by name in the article. Maybe I can persuade him to attribute everything to an anonymous "spokesperson for the Company."

"So you're saying patient care is important," he says dryly.

"It's what drives each and every one of our employees, from our CEO on down."

"Speaking of your CEO," he says, perking up.

Shit. I've brought Williams into this conversation unbidden. He didn't even have to work for it. When did I become the single worst press flak in the history of press flaks? I used to be good at this job. Clearly, the gin isn't helping.

"What does Mr. Williams think of these developments?"

"Like everyone in the company he—" I catch myself. *These developments?* He has only mentioned the hospital patient and yet now we're talking about *developments*, as in more than one. He knows more than he's letting on. I need to be careful. Because so far, I've been the paragon of cautiousness. "I'm sorry, Marcus. To which developments are you referring?"

I use correct grammar to let him know I mean business.

"The orthopedic patient," he answers innocuously.

I say nothing, waiting him out.

"And," he adds finally, "the patient at one of your dialysis clinics. It's in – let me check my notes here—" I can't believe it. He actually ruffles his papers for effect. I suppose I should appreciate the effort, if not the theater. "Ah yes!" he exclaims (it must have killed him not to shout, "Eureka!"). "New Jersey. Says it right here on the surveyor's notes."

So there it is. He has the surveyor's notes. We don't even get those and we're the ones who went to the trouble of killing a man. All we'll see at the official inquest is a highly sanitized departmental report. But this son of a bitch has managed to put his hands on the surveyor's hand-written notes, which, I feel safe in assuming, won't be terribly sanitized. I can all but see the scrawled notes in the margin:

OH MY GOD!
HE BEGGED THEM NOT TO DO IT
BUT THEY FUCKING KILLED HIM!

This entire conversation has nothing to do with getting a statement. This is about sending a message: Marcus Cannon has us by the balls and he's about to squeeze. I remain silent, waiting for him to deliver the hammer.

"That's right, Sean," he says, menace creeping into his voice. All pretense of polite give and take between reporter and flak is gone. He smells blood – or at least another Pulitzer – and he's going in for the kill. "I've got the notes. I know everything."

"Bullshit," I say with a confidence that shocks even me.

"What did you say?" he asks, just as surprised.

"You heard me. This is bullshit. You don't know everything. If you did, you'd have written it already, or at least you'd be asking me for a final comment right before going to press. Either way, you wouldn't be fronting like this, trying to make me piss myself —" I look down, just to confirm that I had not, in fact, pissed myself. Yet. "—or say something stupid."

"That thing about how the ratings aren't to be trusted wasn't stupid?"

"Just feeling you out," I lie. "I can play the game just as well as you, Marcus."

"Is that right?" he answers, rising to the challenge. "I don't know who the fuck you are, but let me tell you who I am. I'm the guy who's blowing this wide open. I've taken down companies far bigger and far more prestigious than yours. Infirmus is dirty and I'm going to put it all on the front page. Someone is going down for this, Sean. Someone always does. The only question is who it's going to be."

The false bravado disappears and I realize that Marcus is

telling me what I've known all along: that someone is going to be me.

"Do me a favor, Marcus," I say wearily. "Call me when you have something."

I hang up the phone, hoping he can't tell that I have, in fact, pissed myself a little.

6

Dad didn't start pissing himself until much later, not until well after Mom died. The doctors told us it often happens in the later stages of Alzheimer's, but I was never sure if Dad's incontinence was a product of the disease or the fact that he just didn't seem to care anymore. When I went over to his house to check on him in the days right after Mom died, I would usually find him sitting in the dark with the blinds drawn, staring at the wall. Sometimes, he didn't even make it out of bed. But as the months wore on, he began to change. Instead of lying alone in the dark, I'd find him sitting contentedly on his favorite chair, watching television in a puddle of urine. Sure, he smiled more, but I still don't know if this was a product of happiness or just of not knowing any better.

Long before, when Kevin and I were just kids and words like Parkinson's and Alzheimer's were still decades away from entering our vernacular, Dad was a dependable, caring, if slightly aloof father. Aloof, that is, with me. With Kevin, Dad could be warm and goofy with a booming laugh that was infectious. But with me, he was always a shade more distant. Don't get me wrong. He was a fully capable and dependable father, always caring and supportive even when forced to discipline us, which, in my case, was often. As a father, he hit all his marks with me. But too often, that's all it felt like – like he was play-acting. With Kevin, Dad's parenting seemed effortless. With me, it was like he was reading someone else's lines.

But if he was easier or freer with his compliments towards my younger brother, it was easy to see why. Kevin was a model student, a gifted athlete and a supremely nice kid. I was techni-cally older, but as Irish twins separated by little over a year, it was only natural that we suffered comparisons to each other. And by most assessments, I came up short. Kevin was a parent's wet dream, which is why most of the moms in town desperately wanted their daughters to date him. Every semester, he topped the Dean's List and every season, he was a district all-star, no matter the sport. Humble to a fault, he was also polite, courteous and a hell of a good cook. Had our town's parents, teachers and coaches convened in a lab to construct the ideal teenager, Kevin is what would have emerged (to the accompaniment of all the choirs of angels, naturally).

Trouble was, not many girls at school shared their mothers' infatuation. Kevin wasn't ugly per se, but he didn't exactly have a face that made panties drop. I know what you're thinking. Looks, brains *and* brawn? Let's not get greedy. Kevin should have just sucked it up and dealt with it. Ordinarily, I would agree with you, were it not for the fact that our parents were pretty damn attractive. My dad's square face and aquiline nose were some-thing out of *GQ* (or so I was told by the ladies in the neighbor-hood), and my mother's luminescent green eyes and high cheekbones made heads turn long after she passed through middle age. But somehow, the combination of their features on Kevin's face didn't work. With Dad's nose and forehead looming over Mom's cheekbones and pointed chin, Kevin looked like something living on the island of Dr. Moreau. No surprise, then, that romance was the one subject in high school in which Kevin did not excel.

I, on the other hand, had a very different experience. I was neither the student nor the athlete that Kevin was. Academically, I was capable but never dazzling, good. Any measure of satisfaction I took in getting a B+ would quickly fade when I would register my teachers' faces. *Decent job*, they seemed to be thinking, *but you're no Kevin Reilly*. Athletically, it was the same story. Whether on the soccer field or the basketball court, I was serviceable, but never a star; a role player, reliable for hustle and some gritty plays, but never enough to carry the team. Not like Kevin.

He was the all-star. I was an also-ran.

Not that it was all bad. I may not have inherited the genius or athletic gene from my parents, but I got just the right combination of DNA in the facial department. In contrast to Kevin, my father's broad features were recessive in my genetic makeup. Instead, I inherited most of my looks from my mother, with my dark wavy hair falling over my green eyes and angular cheekbones in a way that made most girls look twice. And if circumstances ever conspired to bring me face to face with one of them, I had the good sense to talk about something other than me (because, let's be honest, there wasn't much to brag about in that department). Instead, I'd throw in the occasional witty remark, often eliciting a surprised but grateful giggle from the girl, as if she had no idea that it could be so easy to talk to a boy. Most of my friends became nervous and tongue-tied around girls, but for whatever reason, I was calm and relaxed.

I guess the best way of putting it is that I had game. Whereas other guys would come off as creepy when they started talking to a girl, I could walk up to a girl I had never met before and put her at ease. At more than one basement party, I would flirt endlessly with a girl, laughing and joking back and forth while my friends were left to clutch their plastic cups of warm beer in the corner and gawk at us. Before I knew what was happening, girls were actually interested in me — not because of what I did on the basketball court or the soccer field, but because of how I made them feel. When it came to sex (or the kind of furtive basement heavy petting that every teenage boy prays leads to sex), girls seemed to care far more about who looked good and talked even better. And that suited me just fine.

High school is when I first realized what I'm good at. I can connect with people. The less I know them, the better I do. Give me five minutes and I'll make a complete stranger think we're best friends. But people close to me? That's a different story. Whether it was Kevin and my parents back then, or Alex and the girls today, I've never been able to make the people closest to me feel nearly as good as some schmo I just met on the street.

Why is it we can be our best selves with those for whom we care the least and fail miserably with those for whom we care the most? It's the same reason that, when I see Claire through the windshield, glowering at me, I am not the least bit surprised to discover that I can't think of anything remotely loving or fatherly to say. Instead, I pull up to the curb and gird myself for her wrath.

"Could you *be* any later?" she seethes. As she throws her bags in the backseat and slams the door shut, I look at my watch. Five thirty-two. Two minutes late. In my book, that's early.

"Good to see you, too. How was practice?"

No response outside of an eye roll and disdainful sigh. The "Just drive, asshole," is implied.

Opting for resentful silence over volatile confrontation, I comply. I turn my eyes to the road and she turns hers to her ubiquitous phone, furiously scrolling through texts as she jams headphones into her ears, lest I try to break our brokered silence. Something catches her eye and she snorts disdainfully before tapping out a response that makes me wonder how the phone screen can withstand her fingertips' ferocity. Her contempt fills the car, and I start to feel more sympathy for the subject of her ire than for my own flesh and blood.

I shake my head and try to remember when revulsion wasn't the hallmark of our relationship. When she was born, I remember being awe-struck at the sheer fragility of her existence. Until I held her for the first time, I didn't truly understood how small babies are. As I watched her minuscule fingers grasp at air and her tiny lips purse at the newness of her world, I couldn't help but be consumed with the responsibility thrust before me. I was her father, her protector as she entered this world. I resolved with a fervor I didn't remember having felt up to then – nor have I felt since – to never to let harm come her way. I swore that, as long as I was lived, this nymph, this tiny angel, would confront no pain, feel no disappointment and experience no anguish.

The extent to which I have fallen short on all counts takes the air out of my lungs.

I steal a glance at the girl sitting next to me, her blond hair pulled back in a ponytail to reveal a woman in the making. Her pale blue eyes, so like her mother's, are luminescent. With each passing day, she retreats further into her own world, shutting me out so completely that the memory of the little girl who squealed with delight as she ran to escape my wrath as Tickle Monster is unrecognizable. But her eyes, those jade pools of limitless depth, are forever a reminder of what was and what I wish could still be again.

You know, assuming I don't fuck it up.

Instinctively, I reach out as if to smooth a stray curl. She recoils, meeting my desperate attempt to connect with her with a withering look of contempt. Once more, I see her mother.

I sigh and turn towards home.

We pull into the driveway and I see her mother's hulking Audi SUV has beat us home. Before I even come to a stop, Claire shoots out of the car, slinging a bag over each shoulder and slamming her door in a single, seemingly impossible motion. As she breezes past me and into the house without a look, I remember sadly how I used to be able to make her laugh. I'd be telling her a joke and she would hold my gaze, an expectant smile on her lips as she waited for the punch line. Then, her patience rewarded, she would throw her head back and laugh with her whole body. It was never clear who was more satisfied – Claire, cackling in delight, or me, delighted to revel in her joy.

For a moment, I consider saying something to try to bring that laugh back, but think better of it. That was a long time ago and that girl has long since disappeared. Instead, I grab my jacket and bag and follow the young woman she's becoming silently inside.

I step over the bags that have moved from my car to the mudroom floor and close the door behind me. Claire and Alex are in the kitchen, engaged in a blow by blow recitation of the day's events, complete with animated descriptions of who said what to whom at lunch and who might ask whom to the dance on Friday night. It's the kind of conversation I once thought I would have with my girls. But as I quietly put my bag in the cubby labeled "DAD" and walk into the kitchen to join them, I know it's an experience I'll never have. I wait a beat to see how – or if – I'll be greeted, but no one seems to notice or care that I'm there. Claire and Alex babble on as Julia does her homework on the kitchen island, her head bobbing to the music blaring through her ear buds.

I consider saying hello, but figure it's more trouble than it's worth. So I do what I always do, which is walk past the Carrera marble island towards the butler's pantry, trying not to remember how much longer I'll be paying for the second full-scale kitchen renovation ("But Sean, the honed granite looks so *tired!*"). I toss two ice cubes into a Simon Pearce tumbler whose price tag still makes my kneecaps float and cover them with three fingers of Hendrick's gin. I wave a bottle of tonic water over the glass for effect and throw in a slice of cucumber for good measure. Then I take a long, slow sip and pray for oblivion to come.

My prayers are not answered. Instead, I am summoned.

"Are you going to join us," Alex bellows sardonically, "or are you going to drink yourself into oblivion?"

"Can I do both?" I answer, walking back to the kitchen where I see her making a salad.

"Cute. Just once, do you think you might want to try being a role model for your kids by putting the put the booze down?"

"Just once, do you think you could be less of a bitch and stop deriding your spouse in front of the kids?"

"Stop making it so easy and I'll see what I can do."

She turns her attention back to the cutting board, where she slices a cucumber with such precision and – how else can I say this? – resentment that I shudder.

I raise my glass to Claire and Julia, who regard us both with resigned detachment. "Domestic bliss, girls. Don't let anyone try to tell you marriage is anything different."

Claire shakes her head in disgust while Julia returns wordlessly to her homework. I am once more an object to be tolerated rather than embraced.

My position at the bottom of the family food chain thus restored, I grab the stack of mail on the island and retreat to my study. I flop down in the overstuffed leather chair – not quite as comfortable as the chairs in Williams' executive conference room, but just as expensive – and toss the bills on my desk. As they splay across the reclaimed wood surface, all I see is red ink and words like "PAST DUE" and "LAST NOTICE." I close my eyes and gird myself before looking any closer. I try another healthy sip of gin, but I know it's no cure; it's merely anesthesia to help dull the pain of reality.

I take a deep breath and dive in. It's worse than I thought. Six credit cards maxed to their limit and long overdue. I do some quick math and realize that I'm fifty-two thousand in the hole, and that's just the credit cards I know about.

I rub my eyes and wonder if Alex rolled over the debt on any of the existing cards to the two new ones in her wallet. Doubtful. To her, it's free money, consequences be damned. I finish my glass and start to curse her, but the worst part is that I know it's not really her fault. Oh sure, when it comes to piling on debt, she has no peer. The woman simply has no governor. A few years ago, she came home from the mall with bags and bags of goodies. As she gleefully dumped Prada and Manolo Blahnik bags on to the bed, I looked at her incredulously, begging her to rein in her spending. She looked at me blankly and said, "But there was a sale. It would have cost money *not* to buy them."

To make matters worse, she has impeccable taste, and every salesperson, designer and contractor within a hundred square miles knows it. Whether it's shoes, jewelry or house renovations, she goes top shelf all the way. The contractor who did our house – twice – has sent three kids to college and bought a ski house, all on my dime. We've become welfare for the high-end service sector.

I rummage through the desk drawers and find the safety bottle of Hendricks. I refill my glass and wonder how we got here. When we first started out, Alex and I were frugal like every newly married couple. Walking the aisles of the discount supermarket, bare bulbs swaying overhead, we selected food based on its calorie-to-dollar ratio. We rented a studio apartment in the seedy part of town. We took public transportation. Our idea of splurging was name buying name-brand cereal instead of generic (But cookies? Never. Hydrox can suck it. A man needs his Oreos). It wasn't a fairy tale, but at least we were in it together.

Of course, as we grew older and progressed in our respective professions, our way of life improved. Our concept of savings evolved from a jar of loose change to a bank account. Our retirement plan graduated from the occasional lottery ticket to a 401(k). Out of the slums and into the suburbs, we had two kids, two cars and a mortgage. We were happy. We were content.

And then we weren't.

It started slowly at first. Occasionally, Alex would splurge on something new for the house or a bauble for her. I didn't mind. In fact, I welcomed it. We had busted our asses for years to get to a place where we could treat ourselves to something nice so why not enjoy it? My wife – who I adored the minute I helped her escape from the clutches of a neanderthal in a fraternity basement back in college – deserved to be happy. And if I could help make her happy, well, then dammit, that's what I was going to do.

But soon – much sooner than I expected or noticed – the occasional became the routine. Monthly became weekly. Weekly became daily. I remember walking in from the garage one day after work and not recognizing the kitchen. It was like waking up and realizing that you're suddenly living someone else's life. I talked to Alex about dialing back the expenses, but she just assumed we could afford it. After all, hadn't we always been able to pay our bills? Didn't we just take that Caribbean vacation? Truth is, I didn't have the balls to tell her everything was funded on the magic of debt: a revolving credit line here, a rolled over credit card there. One mortgage became two, which soon became three. As quickly as she could buy something, I would figure out creative ways of funding it. She may have pulled the trigger but I was the one loading the gun.

And thus I sit on a hand-crafted Moroccan leather chair I can't afford behind a vintage desk I haven't paid for in a wood-paneled study that's subject to a contractor's lien in a sprawling house that is in danger of being foreclosed.

I swig my drink and realize the gin isn't helping. Knowing I'm going to regret it, I grab the phone and call my accountant. Yes, it's late but he'll still be at the office. The guy gets paid by the hour and I'm pretty sure he's figured out how to bill 36 hours a day.

"Sean," he says brightly when he answers, "how the hell are you?"

"Aces," I blurt out, wondering why I sound like a 70s British spy movie. "Listen, Carl, I need your help with something."

"Name it."

"Uh," I stammer, not sure how to put this. "How bad is it?"

"I'm sorry, Sean. I'm not sure I understand. How bad is what?"

"Me. My situation. Financially, I mean."

"Let me see," he says cheerfully as if dire financial straits are something to be embraced. I hear him bang a few keys on his computer and then he utters a satisfied, "Ah yes. Here we are."

I brace myself and then he launches into it.

"Sean, my boy, I'll give it you straight. I've seen worse, but not much. You've got three mortgages on your house, which appears to be worth a lot less than what you paid for it. You bought it for one point five million subject to a principal mortgage of one million and a secondary of 450."

Son of a bitch. Who the hell puts fifty grand down on a one point five million dollar house? There should be a law against that. Come to think of it, I'm pretty sure there is.

"Market's been down, as you well know. And if I have to guess—" He taps his keyboard to check an up-to-the-minute quote precisely so he doesn't have to guess. "—I'd say your house is worth something around a million. So you're under on your primary residence by at least 450.

"Now then, you are the fiduciary for your parents' house but you've mortgaged that three times already."

"That was for my dad," I interject. Not that it matters what the mortgages were for. The point is they exist and they're pulling me under.

"Yes, well," Carl answers vaguely. He doesn't give a shit what I used the mortgages for. All he cares about is telling me how much I owe. That and getting paid. "You've taken out almost nine hundred on a house that's worth ... let's see here ... about 430 if this website is to be believed."

"What? I've mortgaged my parents' house more than twice its value? How is that even legal?"

"They got you on a teaser."

"What the hell does that mean?"

"The bank gave you attractive initial terms on both mortgages. Of course, the interest rates have increased a touch since then."

"Do I even want to know?" I ask, rubbing my eyes and wondering if I have anything in the house stronger than gin. Like a gun.

"Probably not," he concedes. "Moving on..."

He walks through the credit cards, car loans and bank accounts. All told, we are well over a million dollars in debt. I gasp. It's insurmountable.

"Sean, are you okay?" he asks sympathetically.

"What about our retirement?" I ask hoarsely.

"What about it?" There's something unsettling in his tone.

"Alex and I both have 401(k) accounts, right? They must have something in them, right?"

He loses all pretense of discretion and bursts out laughing. "Are you kidding?" he says, gasping for breath. "You've borrowed against those three times already! You took a vacation and then financed two separate house renovations with it. I can take a look but I'm quite sure those have been empty for a long time."

"Is there any good news?" I stammer, trying to sound optimistic.

"There's a little insurance."

"How much?"

"Not a lot."

"So it's possible I'm worth more dead than alive?"

"I'm not sure I'd go that far," he hedges. "There may be enough to send the girls to college for a couple of years – *state* school, mind you. Nothing fancy."

"But there's something? I mean, that's good, right?"

"Sean, it's not even close to being enough to righting the ship. Breathing or not, you're in debt up to your eyeballs."

Carl keeps talking, but I don't hear him. He is still mixing his metaphors when I hang up the phone. I lean back in my chair and try to absorb it all.

Over a million dollars in debt. We're millionaires, only in the wrong direction.

I can't breathe.

I need a drink.

I need many drinks.

I need many drinks and an oven to stick my head in.

"Sean!" Alex calls from the kitchen. Her shrill level is off the charts. "Dinner!"

Food is the last thing I want, but not showing up is going to cause more problems than it's worth. I stumble down to the kitchen and wordlessly scarf down whatever Alex has thrown on the plate. I'm a zombie. I say nothing and react to nothing. I am vaguely aware of the looks of hatred emanating from my wife and daughters and I'm fairly certain I deserve all of them and more. I give them nothing so I suppose I deserve nothing in return.

I don't know what to do. I only know I can't stand to be here anymore, surrounded by people I have failed in so many ways I can't begin to count. I get up from the table and dump my plate in the sink.

"So drunk you're going to stumble away without a freaking word?" Alex seethes. "God, you're an asshole."

I don't respond. I merely stagger out of the kitchen towards the garage, grabbing my phone and keys on the way.

"DON'T EVEN THINK ABOUT DRIVING—"

I slam the door closed before Alex can finish her thought. I know Alex is right. Driving is the absolute last thing I should do, but I need to clear my head and going for a walk seems so ... pedestrian.

I stumble to the driver's side door and yank it open, forgetting the garage's tight quarters and watching with dismay as the door slams into the cinderblock wall. Great. I haven't even started the car and I'm already a thousand bucks in the hole. I toss my phone on the passenger seat and wedge myself into the driver's seat and take a deep breath. First things first. I rummage around the center console and am rewarded with the last piece of Wintergreen Extra. Then I reach back and click the seatbelt into place. I may be driving drunk, but at least I'll have minty breath if I get pulled over and my seatbelt on if I plow into a bridge abutment. You have to love the logic of a drunken man.

I ease out of the garage, taking care to open the garage door first, something (I'm ashamed to admit) I haven't always done. A few turns later, I'm barreling down the highway, my windows open and what's left of my hair blowing in the wind. I put the car on cruise control (a drunk driver's best friend) and take stock of my current predicament:

A mountain of debt fueled by financial mismanagement that makes a rap star look fiscally prudent.

A wife whose disdain for me is matched only by her exasperation at my spineless griping.

A mistress who reviles me.

A dick that can't satisfy either of them.

Two daughters who don't respect me.

A job that doesn't inspire me.

Co-workers who loathe me and whom I loathe right back.

A boss who's setting me up as the patsy.

And, unless I'm misreading the rumbling intestine, an acute case of diarrhea.

I try to figure out how things got so bad but my head is too fuzzy. All I see and hear are flashes from the day: Williams' shiny teeth and dead eyes; Alex and Naomi's revulsion; the menace in Marcus' disembodied voice and the disgust in my daughters'.

I lean back and close my eyes. I never want to open them again. I want to drive off this road and die in a mangled mass of metal.

My eyes flash open as I sit up straight.

Holy shit, that's it. I can die. I can remove myself from this hellish existence and never have to feel like this ever again. I wouldn't have to field debt collectors' calls, endure my daughters' disdainful stares or suffer my wife's harping. I wouldn't have to clean up Williams' shit, parry Marcus' attacks, navigate Alex's sexual barrenness or manage Naomi's depravity.

I would be free. Physically, emotionally and economically free.

More to the point, everyone else would be free of me. I would be doing virtually every person I've come in contact with a huge favor by removing myself from their lives. The sheer number of people whose lives would improve by my death is staggering. It's utility maximization on a global scale. Now, I know my economics is a little rusty, but I'm pretty sure that kind of self-sacrifice would put me in line for the Nobel Prize.

For the first time in I don't know how long, I find some sliver of resolve.

I will do it. I will bring this shitty life to an end.

I need to figure out how to do it, of course, but I resolve to have it done by the end of the week. I smile as I imagine calling Tim to give him my one-week's notice.

I take a deep breath and exhale slowly. I can feel the tension leave my body. Thirty seconds ago, I was wound tight as a drum but suddenly I feel relaxed. I've found a calmness that usually comes only after a dozen cocktails. Tonight, it took a dozen cocktails and the realization that my life isn't worth living. Who knew?

I turn on the radio and *You Can't Always Get What You Want* by the Stones is on. I laugh. Ain't that the pot. Sounds like the music gods have a sense of humor. I grip the wheel and press the accelerator, pushing the car past eighty. I wonder if I shouldn't just end it all now. Find the closest bridge abutment and take aim. Given the amount of gin I've consumed, it would probably the safest course for everyone.

But I hesitate. There's no one on the road and, truth be told, I feel better than I have in a long time. I decide to let myself enjoy this, even if I know driving drunk is about as irresponsible as it gets. But there's a freedom that comes from no longer giving a fuck that I'm starting to enjoy.

I lean my head towards the window and let the air wash over me, as close as I'll get to being a Labrador retriever. A dog, that's where it's at. What's there to worry about other than eating, shitting and lounging in the sun? Throw in the occasional car ride with your head out the window, tongue flapping in the breeze, and you've got the makings of a damn good life. As long as you do an occasional trick and keep the indoor shitting to a mini-mum, you've got it made. Everyone loves you. And it's not like there are any predators to worry about, not anymore, anyway. You're inside, comfortably curled up in your three hundred dollar L.L. Bean TempurPedic doggie bed, dreaming of doggie bones and fire hydrants. Not a care in the world, certainly not one about whether the glowing eyes staring at me in the road ahead belong to friend or foe.

Those eyes. They're hypnotic. They bore right through me. The way they tilt slightly to the left, it's as if they're waiting for me to stop and—

Stop. I need to stop.

Son of a bitch, I need to stop because THERE'S A FUCKING DEER IN THE ROAD!

Without thinking, I yank the steering wheel to the right to avoid a collision. The wheels respond more aggressively than anticipated and the car shudders as it begins to skid sideways. My heart now racing in earnest, I jerk the wheel back to the left, over-correcting the over-correction. In a bizarre moment of clarity as I scramble to regain control, I realize that the car is drifting, the front wheels pointed in the opposite direction of the turn.

Suck on that, Vin Diesel.

The pride at having replicated a Fast and Furious stunt quickly evaporates as I realize that I have no idea what to do next. The front of the car whipsaws back to the left even as the rest of it skids wildly to the right and I find myself sliding side-ways down the highway, looking straight into the eyes of the creature that caused this misadventure. As Mick Jagger wails on about me getting what I need, the deer regards me calmly, chewing grass and wondering why in the world this dumbass is sliding sideways down the highway doing eighty. I start to scream an obscenity at him – because everyone knows how receptive deer are to profanity – but it is drowned out by the screech of my tires as I careen off the road. I look frantically to my right, and am distressed to see a bridge abutment approaching at an alarming rate.

The irony is not lost on me that the instrument of my demise I once coveted, but then forsook, will not be denied. Oblivion is destined to arrive whether I want it or not. God, it seems, isn't all that troubled by my decision to take my life. In fact, He apparently thinks I need a push.

With milliseconds left, I succumb, flinging the steering wheel back to the right to try and take the abutment head on. Shockingly, the car obliges and swerves headlong towards the concrete mass, leading me to wonder whether I had the ability to regain control of the car all along.

Pushing this depressing realization out of my mind in favor of acceptance, I take my hands off the wheel and accede to my fate.

And then, there is nothing. Silence and darkness envelop me.

I AM CONSCIOUS, which is a feeling I did not expect, though, now that I think about it, I'm not sure whether any feeling could be expected after death. I never gave it much thought but, if pressed, I suppose I would have guessed that just as nothing existed before birth, so, too, would nothing exist after death. I would never have sworn to it, of course, because I've never died, let alone experienced anything close to a near-death experience, but no amount of experience or philosophical musing could have prepared me for the sensation of consciousness after death. That, in and of itself, is something that I never would have expected.

I take a moment to relish the feeling, not wanting to rush

whatever comes next. I inhale deeply (at least, I think I'm inhaling. That's certainly what it feels like. But do our disembodied souls need air? That doesn't make any sense at all. Maybe I'm not breathing. But if not, what the hell am I doing? Damn, I should have paid attention in that introduction to theology course I took in college. Fucked by my intellectual shortcomings, even in the afterlife.).

Finally, I open my eyes. All I see is white. There are no shapes or discernible forms – only an oppressive whiteness that pushes against my skull (or the disembodied portion of my form that was formerly referred to as my skull but now of course is something that none of us have seen, let alone can describe. You know what? I'm going to stop qualifying all of this and assume that you get the fact that my skull is no longer a skull and my lungs are no longer lungs, but something far greater, more profound and utterly indescribable. I'm ethereal. You get the picture.).

I'm not religious, but of course I've always hoped there would be a heaven and that somehow I'd sneak in. I take stock for a moment. I remember skidding out of control and trying to tell that assclown of a deer to go fuck himself. I remember the car skidding back the other way and seeing the concrete abutment bearing down on me. But I don't remember seeing St. Peter or any pearly gates. I don't remember hearing strings or choirs of angels, either. Not so much as a goddamn peep from cherubim or seraphim, come to think of it. That's disconcerting, but not overwhelmingly so. I mean, this HAS to be heaven. Nothing in this world is this blindingly, impenetrably white. Maybe I got in through a loophole.

Oooh – I wonder if I'll get to see any of the angels whose vaginas made the conference room chairs!

And then, in an instant, all sound returns with a deafening roar as I am thrown backward by a blast of air. Good lord, what an entrance! I am humbled beyond measure, awed at the power of whatever celestial body has come to visit me. I open my eyes once more, anxious to be dazzled by its glory.

Instead, I see a shattered windshield and a crumpled hood. A deflated airbag hangs limply from the steering column, looking more like a used condom than the magnificent celestial body I took it for. You'll have to trust me that it seemed a lot more impressive when it was inflated and pressed against my skull. The engine block hisses its disapproval as oil, radiator fluid and wiper fluid spray wildly within the labyrinth of twisted and mangled metal.

I look down and realize that I've pissed myself.

So much for ethereal.

I hear a buzzing and look to my right. Miraculously, my phone has survived the crash and sits pleasantly on the passenger seat, its screen illuminated as a text comes in. Not knowing what else to do, I pick it up.

It's from Alex. Naturally.

DID WE GET LUCKY AND
U KILLED URSELF IN A
FIERY CRASH OR R U
COMING HOME TONITE?

Fucking airbag.

TUESDAY

7

I open my eyes. It's dark and I'm lying down. In my bed.

Better than I would have expected.

I try to piece together how I got here. I remember work and I remember dinner, though I'd rather forget both. I remember becoming morbidly depressed by, well, everything, and then I seem to recall—

Ah, yes. The driving. I can see it all. The car, the deer, the airbag and the sirens. Lots and lots of sirens. I remember an extensive physical exam by the EMTs and an even more intrusive mental one by the boys in blue. I remember being certain I was going to get arrested for any of a number of offenses, not the least of which was smelling like a distillery, but then being flabbergasted when I was neither admitted to a hospital nor thrown in the clink (the relief was short lived after overhearing one of the detectives tell no one in particular they shouldn't worry about locking me up. "Just look at him," he practically giggled. "I've seen dozens like him. His wife is gonna be way worse than anything we could throw his way." No wonder he made detective.) I also remember a young patrolman with Sampson engraved on his nameplate who looked to be reevaluating his

career choice as he drove me home and dumped me unceremoniously on the front porch. And I remember going inside and
downing half a bottle of whiskey to celebrate not being in jail,
which I suppose is what passes for good fortune for me these
days.

And now I'm here. Lying in the dark with my tongue
cemented to the roof of my mouth. I struggle to free it but there's
not an ounce of saliva to help. Finally, it peels off with an
audible pop and I exhale contentedly. Big mistake. I have
unleashed an unholy smell so far beyond morning breath as to
defy categorization. I gag, bringing my stomach into the fray,
which responds by sending a sampling of last night's
debauchery back up my throat. The gag intensifies, threatening
to turn into full-scale reverse peristalsis. I'm caught in a vicious
gag-churn-gag maelstrom that cannot end well. If I think Alex
hates me now, just wait until I hurl a pint of bourbon and God
knows what else across the bed. Forget suicide. She'll murder
me on the spot.

I swing my legs to the floor and struggle to beat my stomach
into submission. It's futile. My entire body is in a state of rebel-
lion, desperate to exact revenge for my callous and continuous
disregard for its wellbeing. Every organ system joins the revolt.
Even my kidneys hurt. As I sit up, my head chimes in, spinning
wildly and sending me tumbling out of bed. My stomach retakes
the lead in this vengeful dance, shooting a highball of gastric
juice-infused whiskey up my gullet. Things are officially dicey.

I clamp my mouth shut and lurch to the bathroom, barely
making it to the toilet before violently depositing everything I
drank last night and more. By the time I finish, I cannot
imagine there is an ounce of fluid left in my body. I flush the
toilet and gingerly turn around to the sink. I brush my teeth
and greedily slurp mouthfuls of water. I stand up and belch,
which I take as a (hopeful) sign of thanks from my stomach. As I

see my reflection in the mirror, though, my hopefulness is dashed.

I look like shit.

My nose is swollen and red, my teeth are brown and my day-old beard is splotchy and gray. I'm still wearing my undershirt from the day before, which is threadbare and yellowed with age, to say nothing of being splattered with the detritus of my recent battle with the commode. But my eyes are the crowning achievement. One is cemented shut with sleep while the other is an alarmingly bright shade of crimson. It's practically glowing. I wonder whether I popped a blood vessel slamming my head against an airbag or hurling my guts out. If eyes are truly the windows to one's soul, then mine is cracked, bleeding and irreparably broken.

I glance out the window hoping to take solace in the darkness, but the first hint of dawn appears obstinately on the horizon. I stagger back to bed, nearly tripping over the clothes that I must have peeled off a few hours earlier. I nestle back beneath the covers, hoping for a few minutes more slumber.

Sleep doesn't come. Instead, as I stare at the ceiling, I hear Alex snort next to me. It's just a snore, but it's hard not to hear an undercurrent of scorn in her breathing. I sigh. There will be plenty of time for contempt when she and the girls wake up. For now, it's just me and the ceiling. The goddamn ceiling. The one we went twelve rounds over. Popcorn or smooth. Textured or flat. I don't even remember which side I was on. I just know I lost. When Alex and I attended the engagement retreat foisted upon us by the Catholic Church in which my mother-in-law demanded we be married, the prelate counseled us that there's no scorecard in marriage.

What an asshole.

Of course, there's a scorecard in marriage. How else do you know who's winning? Every fight, every argument, every freaking *grocery list* produces a winner and loser. It's human nature. And it's healthy – it keeps us on our toes and makes sure we are always striving to do better. No, the problem isn't keeping score. The problem is making sure the score doesn't get out of hand. If one side goes up or down by too wide a margin, there is imbalance, and with imbalance comes instability. Instability, as I've discovered, brings uncomfortable conversations and agonizing silences.

Trouble is, I stopped keeping score a long time ago. I know who's winning, but it's been a hell of a long time since I knew how far behind I am. Even worse, I no longer care.

A number flips on the clock next to me and the radio comes on, a hipster and his banjo joining my thin slice of heaven. He sings about leaving the world the same way we come into it: alone. I smile sadly.

If only.

I hit the snooze button and close my eyes.

Alone.

It's a shoe this time. Yesterday, she threw her brush at me. Today, it's her shoe. She's the Nikita Khrushchev of the bedroom.

"You getting up or are you spending the whole day in bed?"

"I'm up," I mumble as I bury my face in the pillow.

"You're awake," she counters. "Up implies you're ambulatory."

"It's six-fifteen and you're a fucking thesaurus."

"Did you just say I'm fucking a thesaurus?"

I laugh and lift my head from the pillow. "No, you idiot. I said you are a fucking thesaurus." I look at her and though it hurts to admit it, she looks terrific. But judging by her sharp intake of breath, I'm guessing she doesn't think the same of me.

"What the hell happened to you?"

"What do you mean?" I ask, knowing exactly what she means.

"Your face. It's ... grotesque."

"That tends to happen when it slams into an airbag."

"You didn't."

"I did, indeed."

She puts her hands on her hips and eyes me with what I'm sure she views as justifiable disdain but it comes across more as loathsome bitchiness. Of course, that may just be the romantic in me talking. I struggle to sit up in bed as she continues the inquisition.

"How bad is the car?"

"It didn't seem to enjoy being wrapped around that bridge abutment."

"Dammit, Sean."

"I'm fine, by the way. Some scrapes and a busted nose, but otherwise safe and sound. Thanks for asking."

"I wouldn't be lucky enough to hope for anything more."

"Good one."

"Where is it?"

"Where's what?"

"The car."

"Some salvage yard. Mac's or Mick's or Mike's. I can probably find the number."

"Didn't they give you a business card?"

"From the look of the guy in the truck, they didn't exactly strike me as the kind of establishment that would go to the trouble of printing up business cards."

"Well, did you talk to him?"

"The EMTs wouldn't let me. They seemed to think making sure I wasn't bleeding internally was slightly more important."

"Clearly, they don't know you."

"Another good one. I think you're ahead on points."

"So are you?"

"Am I what?"

"Bleeding internally."

"Unfortunately not."

"Lucky me."

"I knew you'd be thrilled."

"The only thing that could thrill me is, right after you clean up the puke in the bathroom, you slip, hit your head on the tub and put us all out of your misery."

"But then I'll be a corpse who will shit and piss myself and stink up the bathroom all over again. You know, Alex, you really have to think through these fantasies of yours. They're not even the least bit realistic."

She doesn't find this nearly as funny as I do, which is probably for the best given how much it hurts to laugh.

"I'm headed out. See if you can make an appearance downstairs before the girls leave. It would be nice for them to know their father is alive, even if he is a fucking drunk."

She turns to leave. I know I shouldn't but I can't help engage.

"Can you blame me?"

She stops and turns around slowly. "Excuse me?"

"You heard me. No self-respecting human being would want to live like this."

"Like you have any respect for yourself."

"Thank you for proving my point."

"So you want to kill yourself." A statement, not a question.

"Why not, especially when the alternative is living with Alex the Ice Queen and the two princesses she's raising in her image?"

"Nice."

"Fuck nice, Alex. You haven't been nice since Claire was born. It's like a badge of honor with you."

"I'm plenty fucking nice," she snaps.

"Oh yeah," I say with a rueful laugh. "That's why the neighborhood kids hang you in effigy every Halloween."

"Don't make this all about me," she snarls. "You're not exactly a joy to live with. You think it's easy to be upbeat and fun with you moping around all the time? It's hard enough cleaning up your empty bottles so the girls don't see what a fucking lush you are."

"Don't confuse cause and effect, Alex. I drink so I don't have to deal with you, not the other way around."

"So being a fall down drunk is now a source of pride?"

"Momma always said if you're gonna do something," I say, standing and stretching, "do it well." I fart for good measure.

Hands on her hips, she glares at me. Insults pass silently between us, each more vitriolic than the last. Finally, she sighs as her arms fall limply by her side. This morning, she is the one to capitulate.

"I'm tired, Sean," she says with a sigh. "I'm sick and tired of your bullshit."

"You used to find it charming."

She shakes her head wearily. We both know that's a lie.

"Jules' dance recital is Thursday and Claire's first playoff game is Friday. If you manage to stay sober – and alive – that long, it would be a nice change of pace for you to actually take part in your daughters' lives. For reasons that completely escape me, they still seem to care about you."

"They've got a funny way of showing it," I snort.

She ignores me. "After that, I don't give a shit if I ever see you again."

"Don't worry," I say brightly. "Come Saturday, you won't have to."

"Careful, Sean. Don't make promises you can't keep. You might start disappointing people."

She turns and walks out the door.

I don't bother rushing downstairs to send Claire and Jules off with a kiss. They don't want to see me, and if I tried to kiss them, they'd probably call social services. Instead, I take my time, enjoying the shower and relishing the time alone. I'm not sure how much of it I'll have today.

I had several dozen texts and emails from Tim last night. I dare not think of how many he has sent in the interim. I start plotting out the day. First, I need to get to the office. I don't want to, but I realize something as the water beads gloriously down my face. One benefit of working at Infirmus is the life insurance policy the company takes out on our behalf. It ain't much – one and a half times my annual salary – and God knows it won't take care of all of our debt. But, together with the life insurance policy I took out with Carl's help, it might get the girls within spitting distance of respectability. You know, assuming being destitute is the same as being respectable. Still, it's one of the few assets I haven't leveraged to the hilt, so I might as well do everything I can to not piss it away. I figure not getting fired before killing myself is the least I can do for Alex and the girls.

The very least.

But that brings me to my next conundrum. I make it a point of pride not to read fine print of any sort, but I'm reasonably certain one of the primary exclusions to any life insurance policy is the taking of the insured's own life. If I'm serious about offing myself – and this morning's cheery sendoff from Alex has done nothing to dissuade me – then I need to figure out how to make that happen. It can't be that hard. I mean, I'm not the only person who's faced this problem. It's the age-old chestnut:

Boy meets girl.

Boy marries girl.

Boy finds creative way of killing himself to escape a life of unending torture with girl, but still provide some meager economic payout to girl and girl's offspring.

As I rinse the soap out of my eyes, I tick through the usual methods: gun to the head, slashing of the wrists, plummeting off a building. I shake my head. They all seem so obvious, so clichéd and so ... violent. Hell, I came close last night with the whole fiery car crash thing last night, but even that was too much to bear. Every method I can think of sounds like it would hurt. A lot.

I lean against the tile wall and feel the water beat down against my scalp. Life is too painful to bear, but death is would hurt too much.

God, I'm a pussy.

In a pique of anger, I twist the shower handle hard. Too hard, as it turns out. The handle comes off in my hand, and instead of turning the water off, I've transformed a soothing hot shower into an icy waterfall. I shriek and hop around the shower in a ludicrous and vain attempt to avoid the Arctic blast. I try forcing the lever back on the valve, but it's no use. I've broken it well and good. I can't turn the water off and I can't make it any warmer. My head is searing from the cold and all air has left my lungs. Gasping, I throw open the shower door and jump out. Naturally, my wet foot slips on the tile and I botch the dismount completely, my bare ass landing hard on the cold floor. Naked, frigid and soaking wet, I lie on the bathroom floor wondering just how this could get any worse.

I had to ask.

My youngest daughter walks in.

"GROSS!" she shrieks. "You're naked!"

"That I am," I groan.

She runs back into the bedroom and slams the door closed. I can hear her on the other side of the door, chanting, "Oh my God! Oh my God!"

"Calm down, Jules."

"OH! MY! GOD!"

I can imagine her on the other side of the door, trying to shake the image out of her body. I've got bad news for you, sweetheart. Your Mom has tried unsuccessfully to do that for the last twenty years.

"This is so ... REVOLTING!"

"Thanks."

"Dad! This is no time for sarcasm. I'm dealing with severe emotional trauma here."

"Now who's being sarcastic? It's just your father."

"Yes. And you're naked!"

"I was in the shower."

"You ever hear of a towel?"

"You ever hear of knocking? It's *my* bathroom," I remind her.

She considers this. "Are you okay?" she asks finally.

"I'll live." For now.

"Um, I was about to leave for school, but I heard someone yell. I thought it was Mom."

"Nope. Just me." Your manly old Dad, shrieking like a schoolgirl.

"And then I heard a crash."

"That was me again."

"It sounded like Helen Keller trying to ice skate."

"I bet." What is it with this girl and Helen Keller?

"That's why I came to check." She pauses. "Are you alright?" Apparently, she's not convinced.

I stand up gingerly and assess the damage. No broken bones. Just a bruised ego and a really sore tailbone. "I'm fine."

I grab a towel and make a late stab at dignity.

"You need any help?"

She has no idea. "No, honey. I've got it. You go on to school." I start drying off, careful to go easy on the nether regions.

"You sure?"

"Yeah, I'm sure." She waits a moment. Even over the din of the shower, I can still hear her doubt. "Hey honey?" I call after her.

"Yeah?"

"There might be a plumber here when you get home from school. Just didn't want you to be surprised."

"Okay."

"Have a good day at school. Love you."

No answer. Just the sound of footsteps retreating down the hall. Suddenly the pain of dying seems a lot less daunting.

9

I finish drying off and try to make the shower handle as conspicuous as possible on the counter. I throw on some clothes and a reasonably clean tie and run to the basement to cut the main water supply. I'm sure there's a better way of turning the shower off, but I can't think of it. I call the contractor that Alex has on speed dial, and he agrees to send his plumber over later this morning. As he starts to hang up, I can hear him stifle a laugh. Not for the first time, I wonder whether my wife has been schtupping the hired help. Bully for her.

I leave a note for Claire letting her know there's no water and consider calling Alex to give her an update. The thought of trying to describe what happened, between my meek explanation and her furious reaction, is too much to bear so I opt for a text instead. Just one more dysfunctional marriage powered by modern technology. A grateful nation is indebted to you, Steve Jobs.

My mess (reasonably) cleaned up, I order a Lyft and get a ride to the office because God knows that shitshow is just what the doctor ordered. Walking in, Diane gives me the hairy eyeball, which doesn't bode well. Of course, she can't be bothered to get off the phone and give me a clue as to why I am on the business end of such a look, so I'm surprised to see Tim sifting through the papers on my desk as I walk in the office.

"Something I can help you find?" I ask as evenly as I can.

He looks up, not the least bit embarrassed.

"Good lord," he says. "You look awful."

"I got into a car accident last night."

"Are you okay?"

"It looks bad," I allow, "but at least I'm moving around. My car was not so lucky."

"Airbag?"

"Saved my life but smashed my nose."

"Do you need to go home?" He tries to sound like a concerned boss looking out for my wellbeing but ends up sounding like a douche for whom only work matters.

"I'm fine," I assure him.

"I just thought because you hadn't returned my calls or emails..."

"That I had fallen down on the job?"

"Of course not." He tried to smile but it's clear that's exactly what he thought.

"Listen, I was under the distinct impression you had no desire to be involved."

"How do you mean? Didn't Mr. Williams make it clear that we should all work closely on this?"

"Those were his words," I agreed. "But what he didn't say spoke even louder."

"Enlighten me."

"He didn't schedule a follow-up meeting. He didn't schedule a daily update call. Hell, he hasn't even sent an email wondering how my day is going. He's washed his hands of this entire exercise."

"I called. I emailed. Don't I count for anything?"

"Oh, Tim. I'm touched. Really."

He holds my gaze and his eyes narrow. Apparently, this is lawyer for 'I'm a shark and you're swimming perilously close to danger.' I consider upping the snark level, but the only thing that would do is prolong this conversation and my head hurts enough as it is. I sigh and opt instead for the path of least resistance.

"What can I do for you, Tim?"

"An update would be nice."

"Fair enough. In about five minutes, I've got to run to one of our dialysis clinics across town for a human-interest piece Channel Five is doing. Walk and talk with a doc and a patient – local company brings high quality healthcare to the people, that sort of thing."

"I like it."

"We're doing the same thing today and tomorrow with local affiliates in over 50 cities. With any luck, the six o'clock news in almost every major media market will end up looking like a paid advertisement for Infirmus Health."

"I'm impressed."

"Yeah, well, don't be. It's basic P.R. shit. This why we pay agencies 100 large each month."

"Still, nice job."

"We'll see. It's a long week, which reminds me – the *Times* is sniffing around. You ever hear of Marcus Cannon?"

"Mike Wallace wannabe? Has a hard-on for bringing down CEOs and politicians?"

"That's the one, and he's pointing his hard-on our direction."

"Fuck."

"Fuck indeed."

"What do we do?" Now he's asking me. These assholes are all the same – all bluster and bombast until shit turns real. Then they're all about expert advice and second opinions, just so they don't have to put their asses on the line.

"*We* don't do anything," I answer. "I, however, will continue to work the press, as ordered. Let me run with this for the next couple of days and we'll see how it plays out."

"Think we'll get a pass?"

"We'll know by CareFest."

"That's what I'm afraid of." He turns and walks out, with decidedly less swagger than when he walked in.

I am banging away on my laptop with my head down when Naomi pokes her head in.

"He offer to help?"

"He walked in practically demanding to run the show," I answer without looking up.

"And now?"

"His enthusiasm cooled considerably when he heard Marcus Cannon is poking around."

"So much for hoping this would blow over."

"I'm never that lucky." I look up and note she looks as amazing as ever. She is wearing a black pencil skirt with black stockings. Her stylishly unkempt hair tumbles over a cream silk blouse. My heart quickens and I consider if she wants to give me a shot at redemption after yesterday's rendezvous. Until I see her face. Mouth agape, she looks horrified.

"What?" I ask.

"Your face! What the fuck happened?"

"I got in an accident."

"What kind? Industrial?"

"Auto."

"Really? Because that looks much more like something in the chemical spill family."

"I broke my nose."

"Slipping on spilled chemicals?"

"Funny."

"Seriously, what happened?"

"I told you. I got in a car accident."

"With your face?"

"The airbag broke my nose."

"Ouch. I've never heard of that. Does it happen often?"

I shrug. "This is my first time."

"First car accident?"

"First broken nose."

"It hurts?"

"Like a motherfucker. Doesn't it look like it hurts?"

"It looks repulsive."

"Good. That's what I was going for."

"Well, then, you hit it out of the park."

I try to smile but even small muscle movements hurt too much.

"You know you're supposed to go on camera in an hour?"

"I was about to head out," I agree. "But I'm not going on camera."

"Damn right, not with that face. You'd scare mothers and small children."

"You're on a roll."

"Seriously, Sean. Have you looked in a mirror?"

"Unfortunately."

"Are you okay to do this?"

"I'll be fine."

"You and that reporter have a history?"

"Why do you ask?"

"You said something yesterday about her owing you a favor."

"Yeah, so?"

"Well, make sure you cash in that favor by keeping you as far off camera as possible."

"Got it."

"Who is this woman, anyway?"

"It's no big deal." I check my reflection in the screen of my laptop. Swollen nose, red eye and scratched forehead. Nailed it. "I knew her when she was a struggling reporter and I was a young PR flack, that's all."

And yet now you're checking your look like you're headed to the eighth grade dance."

"Do I detect a hint of jealousy?" I ask, headed to the door.

No response. Just a raised eyebrow as she sips her coffee and follows.

I shrug. "I made her see God."

"I beg your pardon?" she blurts out, spitting out her coffee on a passing intern.

"You heard me. The lovely Ms. Collins and I were known to have rustled a few sheets back in the day."

"What day was this?" She's laughing.

"A day long, long ago," I assured her.

"When the plumbing worked a little better?"

"Easy, tiger," I say quietly, turning to face her. "That reminds me. About yesterday..."

"What about it?"

"We need to talk?"

"Not unless you want to explain to me why I'm wasting my time with a guy who can't satisfy me."

"I satisfy you plenty."

"Is that right?

"Sure," I say, as we turn back towards the elevator. "The witty conversation, the tender moments."

"The limp dick."

It's my turn to laugh. "God, you talk perty."

"Just calling it like I see it."

"You want to tag along and compare notes with Jane?" I ask, pressing the elevator call button.

"Like some lovesick puppy? Please. Besides, I've got work to do. You go do your one press hit. I'll stay here and manage the other fifty-two."

"God, you're impressive." The elevator chimes twice and I get on while Naomi remains behind.

"I run this place," she says, tucking her hair behind her ear, knowing it will get a rise out of me. "You'd be fucking toast without me."

"How would I fuck toast with a limp dick?"

I can hear her laugh even after the elevator doors close. I chuckle to myself and smile at the woman next to me.

She is horrified.

10

My dad always thought he was better than his station in life indicated. It's not that he minded being a deputy assistant building inspector per se. It's just that he thought he was smarter and more qualified better than the assistant building inspector above him. And the building inspector above her, for that matter. Heeding the lessons of his Northeastern puritanical ancestry, he tried to keep his disenchantment to himself, usually burying it beneath layers of shame, guilt and Johnnie Walker. But there were times when he couldn't help himself and his dissatisfaction with his lot in life would shine through.

One Friday during the fall of my senior year in high school, my English teacher, a lovely but eccentric woman named Cynthia von zur Muehlen who was fond of dressing in black every December 8 to commemorate John Lennon's passing, told us to put J. Alfred Prufrock's love song to the side so we could have some fun. "Fun" in this instance was a personality test, the Myers-Briggs test, to be specific. My teacher was a big fan of the test — never mind that study after study have shown it to be of poor validity, poor reliability and entirely devoid of any predictive value — and believed emphatically in its results, going so far as to sit us in groups the rest of the year according to our prescribed personality types. Thus I spent the next winter and spring huddled with my fellow ENTPs as we parsed through Dickens, Faulkner and Melville.

No surprise, Ms. von zur Muehlen quickly pivoted from our Myers-Briggs results to life planning. Now that we had a better handle on our inner selves, she argued, we were much better positioned to make the hard choices that would shape the rest of our lives, such as which careers to pursue. For too long, she explained, the youth of America had been told that they could do anything. Hogwash. Not all of us were suited for each and every job. To think otherwise was folly, for it stood to reason that not every personality type would thrive in each and every situation. Take an INTJ. Visionaries and schemers, INTJs are always looking for ways in which to improve a system. Once they decide on a plan of action, they see it through to its completion. Their introspective, intuitive, thinking and judging personalities are the last people you would want to have as an actor or performer on stage. But a corporate titan or criminal mastermind? Well, then, INTJs are just what you're looking for.

As I said, I was an ENTP, an extroverted, intuitive, thinking preceptor. Frankly, I didn't know what the hell any of that meant, but Ms. von zur Muehlen was convinced that my ability to see the big picture and argue any and all sides of an issue with equal passion (according to the test, anyway) made me ideally suited to become a lawyer. Or a stockbroker. Or an inventor. Or even – and I still don't know whether to thank or blame her for everything that was to follow – a public relations specialist. I remember coming home and asking my dad what he thought.

"About what?" he asked, sipping his beer and not bothering to look up from the Sox game. And why would he? The Sox were only down eight.

"About a career. About whether only certain people can do certain jobs."

He shrugged.

"Well, do you think I could do anything?"

"Anything you put your mind to." No feeling. Just the rote recitation you'd expect to hear from an actor running through his lines.

"Is that what you thought when you were my age?"

He put his beer down and forgot about the game for a moment. Good thing. The A's had just taken the Sox bullpen deep. Again.

"What's all this about?"

"Just what I told you. Ms. von zur Muehlen gave us this test a little while ago."

"Did you flunk it?"

"It wasn't that kind of test. It was a personality test. After we answered a hundred questions, it told us our personality type."

"It can do that?"

I mirrored his shrug. "She says it can. In fact, she swears by it."

"And?"

"And it says I'm an ENTP."

"Like one of those guys in the ambulance?"

I smiled. "Not an EMT. An ENTP. 'E' is for 'Extrovert,' 'N' is for 'Intuition.'"

"Intuition starts with an 'I.'"

"Yeah, I know it does, it's just—"

"What kind of test doesn't know that intuition starts with an 'I?'"

"I think the people running the test know intuition starts with an 'I.' It's just that they already used 'I' for 'Introvert.'"

"So they went with 'N?'"

"Well, yeah. What else would you use?"

He took a sip of his beer and turned back to the game as he pondered this conundrum. I watched with him as a new reliever came in, only to serve up a triple on his first pitch. The Sox going to the bullpen that year was like throwing gasoline on a fire.

"What about 'T?'"

"What about it?"

"You asked what else I would use for intuition. What about 'T?'"

"Well, there are more 'Ns' in intuition than 'Ts.' Besides, 'T' is for 'Thinking.'"

"Thinking?"

"Yeah, 'T' is for 'Thinking' and 'F' is for 'Feeling.'"

"This test sounds complicated."

"Yeah."

"And full of shit, if you don't mind me saying."

I laughed. He had me there.

"Ms. von zur Muehlen doesn't think so. In fact, she thinks it can help us pick a career."

"Hence all this talk about you becoming a stockbroker."

"Among other things."

He turned back the game. "Stockbrokers are just used car salesmen. Is that what you want to do?"

"I don't know what I want to do."

He groaned in what I thought was disdain for my indecision. I quickly realized, however, that the Sox had just given up another run. Apparently, our catcher had decided it was no longer necessary to catch the pitches headed his way – a curious strategy, especially with a man on third.

"These guys suck," my dad said to no one in particular.

"And yet you keep cheering for them."

"Product of bad upbringing."

"That's why I stick to hockey."

"The Bruins aren't much better, you know."

"Dad, you cut me deep."

At long last, he smiled. "So you know you're a Bruins fan but you don't know what you want to do with your life."

"That's about the size of it."

"There are worse predicaments."

"I guess."

"You're a junior in high school, Sean. You've got all the time in the world to figure things out."

"How did you do it?"

"Do what?"

"Figure things out?"

"Who says I have?" he asked quietly, as the A's drew another walk. The game, and the Sox's season, seemed to be circling the drain.

"I thought you liked your job."

"I like my job fine," he said unconvincingly. "It's just that..." He shifted in his chair, suddenly uncomfortable.

"It's just what?"

"My whole life, I was told I could be anything I wanted."

"You just said the same thing to me," I reminded him.

"Yeah, well, just because I repeat something someone once told me doesn't mean I believe it."

"So I can't be anything I want?"

"Of course you can," he said irritably. "You've got time on your side. Just realize that all those paths that are open to you now will close over time. If you're not careful, you'll only have a single, dimly lit path in front of you by the time you're my age."

This didn't sound at all like the advice I wanted when I started this conversation.

"Are we still talking about me, Dad?"

He looked at me sourly. "You started this conversation. Don't blame me if you don't like where it ended up."

I tried a different tack. "So what do you think I ought to do?"

He shrugged again. It was his go-to move that I found myself adopting as my own.

"Honestly, I have no idea. Go to college. Have fun. Take a wide variety of classes and see what's out there. Find what drives you. Then find a job and do your level best not to poke your eyes out when it becomes stultifying."

It was my turn to look at him crossly. "Your bedside manner could use some work."

He raised his beer in my direction. "Reason number 684 why I'm a building inspector and not a doctor."

"Building inspectors keep us safe," I offered, "thereby obviating the need for doctors."

He tilted his head and looked at me, like he was trying to figure out who I was. Then laughing sadly, he said, "Maybe that test isn't bullshit after all."

"What do you mean?"

"You could put lipstick on a pig. You're made for public relations." The way he said it made me wonder if it was public relations he was insulting or me.

He grew silent and we both turned back to the television just in time to watch the Red Sox second baseman let a tailor made double-play roll between his legs.

"Goddammit," Dad muttered. "If it ain't one thing, it's another."

For some reason, this is the memory bouncing around my head when I get out of the taxi in front of our dialysis clinic. As I grab the change from the cabbie, I see Jane has already set up her shot outside the clinic. It's just her and her cameraman, and judging by the resigned and haggard look on his face, I can tell they've worked together awhile. As he silently acquiesces to every bark of every order, shuffling his feet from one task to the next, I see a broken, pathetic and hopeless human being, one who has long since given up on the joy of having an idea, an opinion or a life of one's own.

In short, I see myself.

As he and I make eye contact, we have the good graces not to acknowledge the agony we see in each other. Instead, he lets me off the hook with a curt nod. Duty bound as his compatriot in misery, I return it with one of my own.

Oblivious to the morality play going on around her, Jane bounds over and wraps me in a bear hug. She gives me a sloppy kiss on the cheek, giving me a smeared residue of lipstick and foundation for my trouble. I worry for a moment she's ruined her makeup for the shoot, but my concerns are misplaced. She's caked so much on, she could walk through a carwash and she'd emerge unscathed. I start to wonder how badly she needs this segment. I know it's been awhile since I've seen her on TV, but now that I think of it, I can't remember how long exactly. Come to think of it, she might be the only person who needs this segment to go well more than me.

"You look fantastic!"

I laugh. "Only if you're into guys with broken noses and popped blood vessels."

She had the good graces to laugh back. "What happened?"

"Bar fight this morning. You should see the other guy."

"Good to see nothing's changed."

"I wish."

"Well, you still look great."

"So do you," I gush, lying right back.

"This is going to be terrific! The clinic looks amazing." White lies about a friend's appearance are one thing, but now she's gone too far. We're standing outside a strip mall, the tenants of which include a liquor store, a massage parlor, a payday lender and a dialysis center. It's a *pu pu* platter of depravity where locals can get a slug, a rub and a tug, all at a cool 28 percent interest.

And, if they're still feeling randy, they can swing into the dialysis clinic and Infirmus will flush their system clean (provided you've got adequate health insurance, of course. We're not running a charity here, people.).

We go through the run of show, which she swears will be your standard local clinic does good puff piece. And sure enough, Jane is as good as she promised. After a quick stand-up outside the clinic, some B-roll footage of patients being dialyzed inside, and two quick (and mercifully benign) interviews with a patient and a doc, Kurt the cameraman is packing up and Jane and I are catching up back outside by their truck.

"How are things?" I ask.

"Can't complain," she answers, lighting a cigarette and inhaling deeply. "I mean, I *could* complain, but no one gives a shit, you know?"

"All too well."

"You?"

"Muddling through." That seems as rousing an endorsement of current circumstances as I can muster.

"I appreciate the call, Sean. Really." She takes another deep drag. Her cigarette is wearing almost as much lipstick as she is.

"No worries," I shrug. "Glad it worked out."

"You wouldn't believe what it takes to get on air these days. Unless you're a bobbleheaded teenager with plastic tits or standing in front of a burning building, you don't get on camera."

"We could light the clinic on fire," I offer.

"Not necessary," she says without the trace of a smile. "Of course, if you could arrange to have one of your patients to die on camera, I certainly wouldn't ask any questions."

I change the subject. "How'd you manage to stay in the game so long?"

"I suck the station manager's cock."

"Ever the hopeless romantic."

"How come you and I didn't work out?"

"As I recall, you started fucking your co-anchor."

"Right." No shame or embarrassment. Just another deep drag. The cigarette is now crimson. "How long ago was that?"

"Almost twenty years." Shortly after my fifth wedding anniversary, I don't add. Jesus, I've been a bastard for so long, I've completely forgotten what it was like to feel human.

"Back when I was the bobbleheaded teenager."

"Minus the plastic tits."

"Don't be so sure," she says with a rasping cough, blowing smoke in my face. I laugh politely, trying not to cough back in hers. I look at Kurt, who is making a big show of wrapping up cables and fussing over his camera.

"You guys are national, right?"

"Infirmus?" I ask, startled by Jane's abrupt change in topic. "Yeah, we've got hospitals and clinics in every state."

"How many employees?"

"Well over 100,000."

"Jesus. You're a fucking monster."

"Providing the highest quality care in your neighborhood, and every neighborhood." I may be a lot of things, but off message is not one of them.

"God, you're a shill."

"And you're a media whore."

"Damn straight." She wears her whoredom like a badge of honor. "Say, you mind doing an interview yourself?"

"Me? What for?"

"Just what we're talking about. Your national presence."

"No, we're good. We want to keep this local."

"That's exactly what I mean. Local company does good not just here, but all across the country. People eat that shit up."

"We want to make it about the patients," I demur.

"It will be. Just what you said – highest quality care for patients in every neighborhood across the country."

It does have a nice ring to it. "Jane, I don't know..."

"Sean, please. We go back a long way. I'm not trying to screw you. I just want to make it a better piece."

"You mean longer."

She smiles. "If my face happens to get on camera a little bit more, who's to complain?"

"The bobbleheaded teenager?"

"Fuck that bitch." She takes another drag on her cigarette for emphasis. "Listen, Sean. You saw what we did here. It's practically a paid advertisement for you guys. I'm not looking to jam you. I just want to round this thing out and make it a better story."

"What, do it here?" I ask, waving to the front of the clinic. I can feel myself caving.

"Why not? We can frame you by the company logo on the front door. It'll be a nice shot."

"Except I look like death warmed over."

She waves my objection away. "Nothing a little make-up can't fix."

I feel myself waffling but keep up the fight. "I don't want to bother Kurt. You guys are all packed up."

"Kurt will be fine. He'll do whatever I tell him to."

"Today is all about the company, Jane. I don't want to make this about me."

"Sean, you're the company spokesman. Do your job and tell the world how great a company you are. You'll be a hero."

The last thing I need to be is a hero. I just need to get by. But for some godforsaken reason, I feel myself leaning yes. Maybe it's that I owe Jane for being here at all. Maybe it's because we've got some history. Or maybe it's just that I can't stop making bad decisions. Whatever the reason, I look at Jane and say seven words I know instantly I'm going to regret.

"Okay, you got me. Let's do it."

Before I know what's happening, Jane slaps some make-up on me and Kurt wires me for sound and frames me against next to the company logo. As he checks the f-stop and makes some final adjustments to the light stand that miraculously appeared moments after I assented to the interview, it dawns on me that maybe Kurt isn't the rube I took him for. The look I saw in his eyes a few minutes ago wasn't commiseration; it was deception. He was playing the fellow simp. He was the grifter and I was the mark.

As I count to ten to test sound levels, it hits me.

He and Jane have played me like a fucking fiddle.

Which is why I shouldn't be surprised with Jane's first question.

"For a company that purports to provide high quality care, can you explain to our viewers why your Star Ratings are so awful?"

"Excuse me?" I stammer.

"The dialysis clinic you're standing in front of has a one star rating. None of your seven other clinics in a ten-mile radius has a rating higher than two. And your hospitals aren't any better. The three metro-area Infirmus hospitals have some of the lowest ratings in the state."

"We stand by our quality." I don't sound convincing, even to myself. I'm so pissed I can hardly think straight. How the fuck did I let her convince me to do this? We had a nice little story about local patients at a local clinic and then I go and ruin it by letting her take me down the quality care rabbit-hole. I'm an assclown. But she's a twat of the highest order. I clasp my hands together, lest I lose control and wrap them around Jane's throat.

"How can your patients be so sure? The government's rating

system – which, I should add, is based on data your company provides – suggests your quality is substandard at best."

"We stand by our quality," I say again. I need a new talking point.

"Is size the problem?"

"I've never had any complaints." Jesus, what the fuck is wrong with me? That better not make the final cut.

"What I mean," she says, stifling a laugh, "is that Infirmus has over 100,000 employees in 50 states across the nation. With so many people and facilities to manage, has quality fallen by the wayside?"

"Absolutely not. Whether you're at an Infirmus clinic in this neighborhood or any neighborhood across the nation, the one constant is high quality care." That was marginally better. But I'm still going to kill her. I'm torn between strangling her with my mic cord and bludgeoning her with Kurt's camera.

"So you disagree with the government ratings?"

"Absolutely. We are on record describing the numerous methodological flaws in the so-called Star Rating system. And we are not alone. Countless others in the industry – from patient groups to physicians to other providers – have been saying for years that this program is flawed." There we go. That was definitely better. Positive, aggressive, unapologetic and on message. I feel like I'm finding my footing.

"Years?"

"Yes, years."

"So you've had these low ratings for *years* and still you haven't found a way to improve them?" Shit. Walked right into that one. What was that thing I said about footing?

"We are constantly working with our physicians to devise better ways of caring for our patients. In fact, we have won awards—"

"I'm glad you brought up your physicians," she interrupts.

Shitbird won't let me get one positive sound byte in. Maybe I can push her into traffic, claim she slipped and fell in front of an oncoming bus. "Recently, your company was sued for medical malpractice by the widow of one of your patients. She claims that, when one of your orthopedic surgeons performed a complete reconstruction of her husband's knee, the doctor operated on the wrong leg. To compound matters, when her husband went into shock after the surgery, your hospital staff failed to diagnose the problem properly, leaving the patient to die a painful and agonizing death."

Please. He didn't feel a thing. He was in a coma the whole time, though that's probably not the best tack to take just now.

"Is there a question?"

"My question is, how to you respond to these claims?"

"We cannot comment on ongoing litigation, you know that." I gamble and give her my best concerned smile, knowing there's a fine line between concerned sincerity and creepy smarminess.

"Well, can you comment on whether this kind of case is how Infirmus treats its patients, generally?" From her tone, it's pretty clear I lost the gamble and went full smarm. Time to double down.

I take a deep breath and look deep into her eyes. If I go any deeper, I'd be skull-fucking her eye sockets. In my most compassionate, sincere and corporately concerned voice, I say, "While I can't comment on any particular patient, I can say that we take every comment, every complaint and every allegation very seriously. No one is perfect. But that doesn't mean we can't still strive for perfection. Have we gotten there yet? Unfortunately not. But we're trying. We owe it to each and every one of our patients to be better. To do better. And to treat you as we would treat our own family. Because that's who you are. You're family."

With my best Boy Scout look of earnestness and determination, I hold Jane's gaze and dare her silently to ask another question. I'm done backpedaling. I'm done apologizing.

Bring it on, bitch. I fucking dare you.

But she doesn't. Instead, she turns to Kurt and says simply, "We're done."

I wait for Kurt to click off the camera and take off my mic before turning to Jane.

"What the fuck was that?" I fume.

"That's called good TV. You ought to try it sometime."

"The hell it was. That was an ambush!"

"What are you talking about?"

"What am I talking about? How about 'I'm not looking to jam you, Sean?' 'I just want to round this thing out, Sean.' You didn't just round it out. You blindsided me, you cunt!"

"I did no such thing."

"Fuck you, you didn't! You whipped your dick out, bent me over and fucked me in the ass!"

Her voice is cold as she looks me in the eye. "You fucked yourself, Sean. You did it the moment you asked me to do this ridiculous puff piece."

"I did you a favor!"

"Fuck you and your favors, you condescending little shit! I don't need a thing from you. I didn't twenty years ago when you were a snot-nosed kid who couldn't get it up, and I sure as shit don't now from some tired, balding has-been hack."

"At least I'm not a washed up beauty queen whose only skill is fucking her way on camera."

"Those days are long gone. I'm a serious reporter. You better get used to it."

I burst out laughing. "If I wanted a serious reporter, I wouldn't have called you."

"I said I wanted to make it a better story," she says, ignoring me. "Now it is." She turns and walks to the truck where Kurt, the ostensible beaten and battered sidekick, smirks as he climbs behind the wheel. Jane opens the passenger door and, just before she climbs in, turns back to me. "Who knows? Maybe I'll even leave in your line about not getting complaints in the size department. Even though we both know that was your biggest lie of all."

She slams the door shut and they drive off, leaving me standing on the side of the road, seething and alone.

11

As I walk into my office, Diane hands me a stack of messages. Two calls from the marketing department to talk about CareFest, three from Alex and one from Marcus at the *Times*. Deciding they can wait, I stuff the pink slips into my pocket. None of them can wait, of course, but my impending mortality has given me a new perspective on life. I'm all about the big picture. That, and I'm trying not to give a shit.

"Any update from Naomi?"

"Like she'd ever tell me," she huffs.

Diane and Naomi do not get along. Not hard to understand why. There can only be one Alpha Woman in a nest, and Naomi is more alpha than any four women I've ever known. Never a match for Naomi, Diane has resented the hell out of her since the day they met. Actually, it wasn't so much a meeting as it was an unspoken confrontation in which Naomi shot Diane a look of clear disdain and Diane retreated meekly back into her shell. Complete and utter defeat in under a second.

"But she's in the war room if you want to see for yourself."

Before you get excited, the "war room" is just a conference room down the hall with a hi-def camera and satellite link-up for media hits – complete with a plastic plant and a backdrop plastered with the Infirmus logo. Beyond that, there's not much to write home about: just a table, some chairs, a Polycom phone and a few LED televisions to monitor press coverage. Besides, this is the tenth floor. Getting excited about a nice room on the tenth floor is the equivalent of getting jacked up about snagging a cute little pied-à-terre in Detroit. Dress it up all you want, it's still Detroit.

I turn down the hall to see how Naomi is faring. Diane calls after me, letting me know that Williams and Tim have asked me to join them on fourteen.

"When?" I ask, turning around.

"As soon as you get back. They seemed insistent."

"Let them know I'll be up in forty-five minutes."

"So you're not back yet?"

"Not for another forty-five minutes."

I can't bear them just yet. Instead, I continue down the hall to check on Naomi. But as I enter the war room, it's clear that I needn't have bothered. She has everything covered. On two screens, I see live feeds of ongoing interviews. Two of our physicians – hair professionally coiffed and teeth freshly whitened – are extolling the virtues of our fair company. To hear them tell it, there's not a patient we can't treat or a disease we can't cure. On a third screen, a clinic manager runs through her sound test, over-enunciating as she nervously counts to ten. Naomi, ever the puppet master, seethes into the Polycom on the table in front of her.

"Someone get that woman a Valium. We're trying to project confidence, not incompetence. Christ, she looks like she's about to shit herself."

I smile as I imagine two junior flaks scrambling off camera to see which one of them packed the Valium.

On a whiteboard across the room, someone with a severe

case of OCD has charted every interview in glorious detail. Fifty-three rows, one for each interview, each with column after column of data – location, media outlet, interviewer, interviewee, duration, expected airtime. The last column – labeled EVALUATION – contains no words, just colors. Scanning quickly, I see twenty-two greens, one yellow and twenty blanks. One blank, I am dismayed to see, has my name next to it.

"How did it go?" Naomi asks without taking her eyes off the screens.

"What are the colors?" I ask, ignoring her.

"Standard stoplight. Green is good, yellow needs improvement, red is ... well, you don't want to be red."

"So things are good so far?"

"Everyone's on time and on message." She leans towards the Polycom. "How are we coming with that Valium?"

"I gave her a Xanax," comes a disembodied male voice from the field. "She'll be fine."

"Damn well better be, Steve." Naomi snaps in return. "It'll be your balls on a platter if you're wrong."

"Your management style could use some work," I offer.

"Ask me if I give a fuck."

Duly silenced, I watch as the clinic manager does her interview. What she lacks in nervousness, she more than makes up for with detached indifference. I feel like I'm watching a Stepford wife give a eulogy. Still, she hits all of her talking points and leaves the interviewer complimenting us for our steadfast dedication to patient care. As the screen goes black, Naomi stretches and looks at her watch.

"Seventeen minutes until our next hit. I'm going to get some coffee." She motions for me to join her. On our way out the door, she turns to the intern at the whiteboard who, green marker in hand, is about to register another successful interview. "Don't you dare. That one was yellow. Someone better make sure that woman never steps in front of another camera as long as she lives."

Somewhere, Steve just swallowed his tongue.

I follow Naomi out the door. Just before we get to the kitchen, she pulls me into a storage closet and locks the door behind us.

"What the—"

"Take off your pants," she breathes just before shoving her tongue in my mouth and sliding my suit jacket down to the floor.

I pull back. "Are you serious?"

She pushes me against a stack of shelves and I see an avalanche of Post-It notes just before my head slams against a stack of copy paper.

"Deadly," she answers as she starts unbuckling my belt for me.

"I didn't realize the effect some good press had on you."

She pulls my pants to the floor and grabs my ass. "I'm so fucking wet."

"I think they have a salve for that."

Standing up, she shimmies out of her skirt and panties. She sucks my earlobe and breathes into my ear. "I want you inside me." She slides her hand down between my legs and grabs my dick. I'm rock hard.

"Well now," she purrs with a devilish smile. "Looks like someone else is ready to play."

"I'm as surprised as anyone," I moan, now completely at her mercy.

She isn't listening. She turns us both so her back is to the shelves. Then, wrapping one leg around me, she guides me inside. I grab her ass and lift her up so she can lift her other leg around me. She grabs the shelves with both hands and rides me. It quickly becomes apparent that I am a sideshow in this sordid little excursion, a means to her end. She tightens her legs around me and begs me to go deeper. With each thrust, she screams and pulls harder on the shelves, sending office supplies down like some ridiculous outtake from a porno shot at the local office supply store. I don't know whether to laugh, come, or dodge toner cartridges. So I do all three.

Thankfully, she climaxes at the same time, screaming bloody murder and wrapping her arms around my head as she pulls me into her chest so I can't breathe. To hell with killing myself. She's about to do it for me. I'm moments away from oddly erotic asphyxiation.

Panting, she dismounts and gives me a wicked smile. Not for the first time, I wonder what the hell she is doing with me. There are dozens of guys who would gladly fuck her at a moment's notice. Why she bestows this honor on a pudgy, married, alcohol-dependent loser is completely beyond me. That I'm her boss is doubly mystifying.

And then it hits me. She picked me precisely because I am her boss. And married. Sure, the pudgy alcoholic thing is less than ideal, but an acceptable tradeoff in the grand scheme of things. She doesn't want complications or entanglements; she is in it for pleasure, pure and simple. As I button my pants and watch her slide back into her skirt, her auburn hair tumbling down her shoulders, I realize nothing about this is real. We have no meaningful connection. She's with me simply because I'm easy, available and easily manipulated.

She tucks in her blouse and sees me looking at her.

"What?"

"So this is all it takes. A few good press hits and you're ready to go?"

She doesn't catch the gloom in my voice, or if she does, she chooses to ignore it. Instead, reaches up on her toes and kisses me tenderly. Her soft lips linger on mine and, for a moment, I think I must have it all wrong. We do have something. She does care.

Then, just as quickly, the moment is gone. She pulls back and smiles, hitting me playfully on the chest.

"That reminds me. You never told me how your interview went."

"Oh, right," I answer, grabbing my jacket off the floor and trying to sound as carefree as she does. "Let's just say I have good news."

"Went well?" She suddenly looks like she could go another round. Her hand actually flutters towards her blouse, ready to rip it off if my news is as good as she hopes. I'm just beginning to understand the depths of this woman's emotional problems.

"Not exactly." And just like that, her hand drops to her side. Any hint of sexual energy has evaporated. "But on the upside, that fancy whiteboard of yours just got a little more colorful."

"You didn't."

"I did."

"Please say yellow."

"I could, but you always say not to lie to you."

"Shit. How red?"

"Crimson."

"I thought you two had history."

"We did. Apparently, that was the problem."

"There's a surprise."

"It's not my fault not everyone finds me as charming as you do."

Unlocking the door and leaving Naomi before she can respond, I ignore the dirty looks from the secretaries huddled just outside the closet – apparently, our exploits attracted a crowd – and make my way to the elevator. Seeing Williams is the last thing I want to do but I suppose it's perfect timing; nothing follows getting raped by a subordinate quite like having your boss shove his fist up your ass.

My phone rings as I walk out of the elevator and curious heads pop out of cubicles like prairie dogs at the sudden disturbance. I am tempted to ignore the call until I see the 212 area code. Marcus. Nothing good can come from taking his call, but I've put him off long enough. It's time to sack up and deal with him. Plus, there's the added benefit of making Williams wait a little longer. If there's one thing I've learned in my forty-four years on this planet, it's this: if I'm miserable, everyone else might as well be miserable too.

I tap my phone and hope like hell this isn't a mistake.

I am not, however, optimistic.

"This is Sean."

"Hey, Sean. It's Marcus."

"Marcus!" I exclaim like we're long-lost college buddies. "What's going on?"

"You told me to call when I have something. Well, I have something."

"Let me guess," I sigh. "The patients' families want to go on record?"

"Please. I had the patients' widows weeks ago."

"Okay. You've got pictures."

"Of course I do. Pictures of the patients, pictures of your docs. I've even got a picture of one of the corpses on the slab. Your only hope there is someone in legal gets squeamish and tells me not to run it."

"Not those pictures."

"What?" For the first time, he seems off balance.

"You mean you haven't found the cache of pics of Vern Williams prancing around in women's underwear?" The prairie dogs pop their heads up again. Phones ringing is one thing, but slandering their venerable CEO is something else entirely. They start looking for the lightning bolt to strike me down. "Well, that's a relief. For a second, you had me worried."

Silence.

"You there, Marcus?"

"Are you certifiable or do you just not give a shit?" he asks finally.

"Aren't those the same thing?"

"I don't know if there's a method to your bullshit," he says with a laugh, "but I have to hand it to you. You're one of a kind."

"Marcus, please. I'm blushing."

"That's what I mean. I'm about to destroy you on the front page, and all you want to do is joke around."

"I'm dead serious. I am blushing."

"And that thing about cross-dressing?"

"If there's one thing I never joke about, it's women's underwear. Some things are sacred."

"Alright," he says with the exasperation of someone used to dealing with pathological liars, "guess I'll have to look into that too."

"Hey Marcus?"

"Yeah?"

"Front page?"

"Sunday. Above the fold."

"So you've got the hook?"

"I do indeed."

"What is it?"

"You mean aside from two patients dying in your care?"

"People die all the time. Under far grislier circumstances, believe me. What makes this any different?"

"Three little words."

"Suck my dick?"

"You talk to every reporter like this?" he asks with another laugh.

"Only the *Times*. And occasionally the *Journal*, but only 'cause they like the rough stuff."

"You do know we're on the record, right?"

"When are we not?"

"Guess you do know your shit."

"So what are the three magic words?"

"Dialysis Support Network. You want to comment?"

"Let me get back to you."

"You've got two days. Then I lock the story down."

I hang up with an unsettled feeling. A Pulitzer Prize winning reporter at the *Times* thinks he has the drop on us.

And that can't be a good thing.

12

"Don't bother getting up," I say as I walk into the conference room. Williams and Tim look up, surprised. Apparently, unescorted visitors to their sanctuary are not kosher, but fuck it. I'm feeling frisky. After talking to Marcus, I'm fairly certain these two jackwagons haven't been entirely forthcoming with me. So I think a certain amount of insubordination is warranted. Besides, I've got less than a week to live, so I really don't give a fuck.

I help myself to a Diet Coke from the credenza and take a chair next to Tim and directly across from Williams.

"Sorry to be late. Been busy burnishing the public image of this fine institution." I crack open the soda and take a loud slurp. "Damn, that's cold! On ten, we make do with tepid soda from the machines. But this? This is glorious. Membership has its privileges, eh gents?" I take another sip and wipe my mouth with the back of my sleeve.

Williams is not amused. "You look like shit."

"I'm fine," I say, answering a question he didn't ask. "I got in a bit of a car accident yesterday."

"Who won? The car or your face?"

"It looks bad," I allow, "but at least I'm moving around. My car was not so lucky."

"Airbag?"

"Saved my life but smashed my nose."

"Are you okay to work?" he asks without a hint of concern for me. Just wanting to make sure I can work. What a douche.

"I'm fine," I assure him.

"You mind telling us what you've been doing since yesterday? I thought I was clear that I wanted regular updates."

I sigh, trying not to dwell on the fact that I am about to replay my conversation with Tim earlier this morning nearly word for word. It's clear he didn't brief Williams or, if he did, he wants me to defend myself directly to the head honcho. Either way, there's not an ounce of sincerity in anything he and Williams are doing.

"Mr. Williams," I begin slowly, "it doesn't take a genius to figure out that you don't want to be within a hundred miles of this mess. We've got two dead patients on our hands, both of whom died because your staff fucked up."

Your staff. See how I did that? I may be the odds-on favorite for fall guy, but that doesn't mean I can't remind these two asshats they're the ones who should be on the hook for it, not me.

"Now we can and should feign all the compassion and contrition we can muster," I continue, "but it's been clear that your singular priority from the jump has been to make this problem go away."

"Of course we want this issue resolved," Tim interjects. "That's clearly in the best interest of all stakeholders."

"Stakeholders? You mean stockholders, don't you Tim? Because, with all due respect, the kind of resolution you're talking about sure as shit isn't in the best interest of the widows. They want to make this mess as big and ugly as possible so Mr.

Williams here will have no choice but to sign two checks bearing unholy sums of money."

Tim bristles. "These matters may well end up in litigation, but that is all the more reason that we remain up to speed if these issues metastasize."

"Are you for real?" I'm dumbfounded. "Look, you guys wanted me to try to control the situation, so that's what I'm doing. Like I told you this morning, we're going to get the press equivalent of a blowjob tonight in over fifty markets across the country. We're talking five to seven minute segments on the local six o'clock news showing our doctors and staff in action as they care for patients. We'll also have patients fawning about the care they get at our facilities. Every single person who will appear on camera has been pre-screened and each talking point was vetted in advance. My team is controlling the whole operation downstairs as we speak.

"In every market we care about, people are going to sleep the sleep of kings knowing their healthcare needs are in good hands, never mind that we apparently can't operate on the right limb or dialyze the right patient. And if that's not enough for you, when three-quarters of this country sits down to breakfast tomorrow morning and open their local paper, they're going to read an op-ed from a local physician waxing poetic about all of the great things going on here at Infirmus."

"Nicely done," says Tim begrudgingly.

"I'm not saying we'll be completely insulated if regulators start sniffing around, but at least we'll have the makings of a firewall."

"Looks like we put our trust in the right person," says Williams with a small smile.

"I'm not sure about that, sir," I answer sheepishly, wondering how it's possible a guy who has already decided to kill himself can still be manipulated with some fairly obvious flattery. Oh, that's right. I'm shameless. "I'm just doing my job."

"Oh, you've done more than that. By keeping me out of it, you've done exactly what I asked, even if," he says with another smile, "I didn't exactly ask for it."

I sip my Diet Coke and try not to get completely sucked into Williams' flattery wormhole. I came in here fuming, ready to take a flamethrower to the place. Now, enjoying my ice-cold beverage and basking in the adulation of my superiors, I realize I've done the complete opposite: I'm sucking up. Time to shift gears.

"There is something else we need to discuss."

"What's that?" asks Williams genially.

"The *Times* is going to write about the dead patients."

"When?" asks Tim.

"Sunday. Page one. Above the fold."

"Why the front page?" asks Williams, alarm seeping into his voice. "Isn't this a local story?"

"It should be," I agree. "But Marcus Cannon is the reporter."

"Pulitzer Prize winning reporter with a bug up his ass, right? Likes to take down CEOs after exposing them for healthcare fraud and corporate malfeasance."

"That's the one," I agree. Williams has done his homework. "He's thorough, accurate and ruthless."

"Tim said he was sniffing around."

"That's right. But what worries me is that Marcus Cannon wouldn't be interested if this was just a story about two patients dying under our care."

"And yet," Williams says impatiently, "that's *exactly* what this story is."

"But that's not big enough to really get our panties in a bunch, is it?" I ask pointedly. I can't see the outlines of the story yet, but I'm starting to get a sense that I've been handed a bill of goods from the jump.

"What are you talking about?" Tim interjects.

"There's something else going on here. I can smell it, and you can be damned sure that Marcus Cannon smells it, too. Someone like him doesn't really care if a patient or two dies in our care. No, what he cares about is something more. Something like ..."

"A lack of institutional control," Tim offers.

"Exactly. The death of two patients in the care of their healthcare providers is tragic. But that's ultimately a human-interest story, better suited for the metro section of the local paper. The good news is that the blitzkrieg my staff is conducting downstairs will inoculate us against most of that. But that's not the only fight we should have been fighting, is it?"

The two of them are quiet so I plow on.

"The first time we spoke, Marcus said something interesting. He said Infirmus is dirty and he's going to take us down for it. I always he assumed he was referring to our lousy patient care, but I'm starting to think he meant something different. Killing those two patients the way we did makes us a lot of things – wildly incompetent and appallingly stupid, yes – but dirty? I don't think so."

"Is there a point to all of this?" Williams asks impatiently.

"Marcus asked about the Dialysis Support Network."

His face is impassive, but his eyes have taken on an intensity that unnerves me.

"Sean, do you have any idea how little the federal government pays for dialysis care in this country?" I look closely at Williams, trying to make sense of this non sequitur, but he simply carries on. "As I believe you know, kidney failure was the first disease state to confer automatic Medicare eligibility on Americans regardless of age. Any American – whether they are five or sixty-five – can sign up for Medicare once their kidneys fail."

"Yes, sir," I offer dumbly, not sure why I'm being treated to a history lesson. "It's the Medicare benefit for end stage renal disease. It's been in existence since the early seventies."

"1972, to be exact. Congress passed the law after a kidney patient from New York by the name of Shep Glazer dialyzed while testifying before the House Ways and Means Committee. However, I don't think Mr. Glazer, or anyone on that committee, could have anticipated what transpired over the next forty years."

"What do you mean?"

"When Congress passed that law, there were very few people receiving dialysis. You see, dialysis was a new therapy. Before the late sixties, a diagnosis of kidney failure was tantamount to a death sentence. That all changed with outpatient dialysis. Suddenly, a machine could take the place of patients' kidneys. It was remarkable. Quite literally, we had the ability to give the gift of life. But there was one problem."

"Cost," I interject.

"Precisely. When the Medicare benefit for dialysis patients was first enacted into law, no one could have predicted how costly it would become. Part of that had to do with the aging of the baby boomers, and part of it had to do with the way we eat."

"Too many Big Macs."

"Indeed. We went from 14,000 new dialysis patients a year in 1978 to 120,000 today. And the tragic fact is that the federal government simply doesn't have enough money to pay for all of those patients. It costs over thirty billion dollars to provide dialysis to the U.S. Medicare population. *Thirty billion*. That's an awful lot of money to pay to one sector of healthcare."

"Which is why Medicare keeps reducing our rates," Tim

interjects. "Medicare reimburses us $240 for every dialysis treatment. That's not enough to even cover our costs."

"I'm well aware of this," I counter. "And so is Marcus. He knows we lose money on every one of the 90 percent of our patients that are covered by Medicare. But he also knows that all of our profit comes from the other ten percent – the ones with private health insurance."

"So what?" Williams says impatiently. "These stories have been around as long as I can remember."

"You're right," I concede. "In fact, I've spent the last six years spiking story after story about our economic model. We don't want to publicize the fact that we charge private insurance companies an average of four times more than what Medicare pays us."

"God bless private insurance," Williams chortles. "We positively *kill it* with those patients."

Important side note: I don't profess to know all that much about the business of healthcare, much less the public policy that underpins it. I may not even be the world's best communications professional, but I've been around long enough to know this: if you're in the business of caring for people, you may want to refrain from referring to a successful business model as, and I quote, "killing it." This guy is such a douche, I'm no longer sure whether it's me I want to kill or him. Maybe a murder-suicide is in order.

"Any chance you can kill this story like you've killed the other ones?" asks Tim.

"Not likely. Marcus is like a dog with a bone."

"Doesn't he know commercial insurance subsidizes Medicare in virtually every sector of healthcare?"

Williams adopts a professorial tone. "Precisely. It's the public-private partnership that makes the whole system work."

I gag. Once someone says 'public-private partnership,' whatever comes next is a complete and utter snow job. I know because I've worn out that phrase every time I speak to the press.

"Yeah, but I'm pretty sure he also knows few, if any, sectors of healthcare have commercial rates that can be as high as ten or twenty times Medicare like we do. Listen, Marcus is no dummy. He knows we cry pauper every chance we can about Medicare rates. But he also sees us opening new dialysis clinics each year across the country, so he knows we must be doing just fine financially. He wants to know how."

Tim runs his hands through his hair. "And he thinks the Dialysis Support Network is the answer."

"Apparently."

"Goddammit," Williams says petulantly. "Charities like DSN fill a necessary gap in the system." Here comes the snow job. "They provide much needed funding for patients on the lower end of the socioeconomic spectrum to find the coverage of their choice."

Time to admit ignorance. It's not my strategy of choice, but sometimes there are no better options. "Listen, I know DSN pays health insurance premiums for poor people who need dialysis. And I know we support the DSN with contributions."

"The Infirmus Foundation has been a proud supporter of the DSN's mission for many years." Gotta love Tim. Always there with an anodyne talking point when you need him.

"A point I'll make clear to Marcus. What I don't know, though, is how much we support it."

"What do you mean?" Williams asks.

"Well, we make all of our money on patients with commercial insurance. And DSN is a charity that helps patients obtain commercial insurance."

Tim sees where I'm going and interjects before I can get

there. "DSN is a charity that supports dialysis patients in dire economic straits. We are a proud supporter of their mission."

"Yeah, but we don't just do it out of the goodness of our hearts. We love DSN because more commercial patients means higher reimbursement for us."

"And higher profits for shareholders," Tim agrees reluctantly.

"And bigger bonuses for senior execs." Judging by his wicked smile, Williams is not so reluctant.

"Right. So what I need to know before talking to Marcus is how much."

"How much?"

"How much do we give?"

Tim answers exactly as I don't want: as a lawyer covering his corporation's ass. "Our donations are not linked to DSN's decision on which patients to support. Moreover, what an insurer pays us for dialysis is irrelevant to the DSN's decision on whether to pay premiums to that insurer."

"And yet," I goad him, "we still support their mission financially. And so I'll ask again, how much do we give?"

"It's substantial," Tim demurs, now fully dug in.

I sigh. "You guys want me to do my job fending off the *Times* and the hatchet job that's coming? Fine. But force me to do it with one hand tied behind my back and we'll all go down. In flames."

They stare back blankly.

"Nothing?" No one blinks. "Fine," I answer, starting to get up to leave. "Have fun explaining the article to the board."

True to form, Tim equivocates. "It's not exactly a secret. All you need to do is pull DSN's tax filings."

I sigh. This is becoming tedious. "Let's assume for the sake of argument I haven't. But we can be sure Marcus will. What do you think he'll find?"

"One hundred and fifty million," Williams says finally.

"Excuse me?" I plop back down in my chair.

"Last year's donations were one hundred and fifty million dollars."

I'm stunned. For Marcus Cannon to be interested, I gathered our involvement had to be significant, but this kind of scale is – or was – unimaginable.

"Gets the heart racing, doesn't it?" Tim asks needlessly.

"Not as much as the benefit we get in return," Williams replies. He's practically licking his chops.

"How much?" I press.

Williams can hardly contain himself. "Over one point eight billion last year. That's 'billion' with a 'b.'"

I shake my head. "Holy shit. We give DSN 150 million and get more than ten times revenue back in return?"

"That's not revenue," Williams cackles. "That's pure profit!"

The shit is indeed quite holier than I could have ever guessed. This is a shell game that even a Three-Card Monte dealer would say is over the top.

Step one: Donate tens of millions of dollars to a charity.

Step two: Watch as the charity uses that money to pay premiums for health plans for your patients – and not just any plans, but plans that pay top dollar for dialysis.

Step three: Lie naked in a bathtub full of money because you just made over a billion dollars in profit.

I have to admire the simplicity, if not the outright avariciousness, of it all. These magicians have figured out a way to take people who are otherwise entitled to cheap government healthcare and force them on to high-paying insurance plans. By no means am I an apologist for insurance executives who are among the slipperiest eels that ever slithered across the face of the Earth, but I'm beginning to realize why they might be ripshit over this arrangement. I cover my face with my hands. This story is going to be explosive.

"Sean?" I look up and see Tim looking at me with concern. "You okay?"

"Yeah, sure. Just trying to formulate a response to Marcus."

"I don't suppose you can tell that nosy fuck to fuck off?" Williams asks, his reptilian smile still firmly in place.

"That may be one too many 'fucks' for the *Times*' discriminate readers."

"We'll leave it to you to formulate a response to Mr. Cannon," Tim says, signaling this conversation has run its course. "Suffice it to say that we wholeheartedly endorse the DSN's mission and are proud to be recognized as a supporter. Beyond that, I'll let you put the right words together."

"While we're talking press," I say, taking his cue and getting up to leave, "I suppose I ought to mention that the local coverage tonight may not be quite as rosy as some of the other markets across the country."

"What do you mean?"

"I did a stand up this morning in front of one of our local clinics and got blindsided by the reporter."

"How so?"

"She started in with our star ratings. She wanted to know why our hospitals and clinics are ranked lower than the competition."

"And how did you respond?"

"I told her the truth. That our scores are not where they should be and that we will get better." I pause. "That is the truth, right? I mean, we will get better, won't we?"

"Indeed we will," Williams assures me. "I'm glad you answered with such candor. That's exactly how we need to portray ourselves – as honest brokers who are doing our best. It makes us sound ..."

"Almost human?" I offer.

"Exactly," he says with satisfaction, conveniently ignoring how much closer we hew to the 'almost' side of that equation than the 'human' one. "I'm impressed. Tim told me you would fit the bill, but clearly we underestimated you. You're a lot smarter than any of us had given you credit for."

"Thanks, Mr. Williams," I answer with a laugh.

"What's so funny?"

"Well, I'm sure you meant it as a compliment, but it sounds a lot more like an insult."

"Like I said," he says, chuckling in response, "you're smarter than we thought."

I turn to go but as I reach for the doorknob, I hear him call after me.

"Sean, one other thing." I turn and see his oily smile. "Given everything that's going on and how well you did with that news report yesterday, I think we need to make a major change to CareFest."

"Oh really?"

"Yes. It's clear we need a seasoned professional at the helm. You know, someone with the communications and messaging chops to keep the focus on our quality agenda and draw attention away from any ... distractions."

I wait, knowing what's coming but hoping nonetheless it doesn't.

"I know how much you've got on your plate, but with the board coming to town and all the press attention we're about to receive, nothing is more important than making CareFest is unadulterated success."

Funny. Here I thought there was nothing more important than actually taking care of patients.

"Which is why—"

Here it comes.

"—I want you to be the host. Do me a favor and sit down with marketing tomorrow morning. CareFest is only three days away, so there's a lot you need to catch up on."

He smiles again and I can't help feeling I stepped into a trap he set long ago. Remind me never to be good at my job again. Nothing good ever comes of it.

"I hope you don't mind."

"Not at all," I answer, feigning gratitude. "Besides, it wouldn't matter even if I did."

"Goddamn right."

I turn and leave. I could be wrong, but it I swear it looks like he's licking his chops.

13

My senior year in high school, I took a class called Introduction to Eastern Philosophy. I took the course not because it would set me on the path to righteousness (it wouldn't) or because it could teach me how to find inner peace (it couldn't). I took it because it was the only way I could think of to be near Jennifer Nieb.

A senior like me, Jenny was one of the few girls in my broad circle of friends I hadn't yet taken a run at. It wasn't because she was ugly. Far from it. Jenny had long blond hair that was invariably pulled into a ponytail, showing off her permanent suntan and bright white smile. And if that wasn't enough, she had the kind of tight body that fomented murderous thoughts in the minds of women ten years older. She was also incredibly nice. So nice, in fact, that I often thought she wouldn't take to a guy like me, which probably is what led to my reluctance in making a pass at her. But that didn't stop me from admiring her from afar or, in the case of any class where I could wrangle it, from the seat right behind hers. The way her underwear snuck out from under her jeans when she sat down probably had something to do with that.

When I overheard her telling a friend just before opening bell on the first day of senior year that she was taking Intro to Eastern Philosophy, I ran to my counselor and rejiggered my schedule. I told my counselor I was just looking to fulfill my non-western class requirement. In reality, of course, I wanted to spend every third period over the next nine months hoping like hell Jenny's shirt would cinch up a little higher so I could catch a glimpse of her cotton panties.

Obviously, I was dealing with a lot of shit back then.

Two hours later, I followed her into class. She took a seat on the aisle, about halfway back. Luckily, the seat behind her was vacant and I slid into it just before a femi-Nazi sporting a do-rag and smelling of patchouli oil could appropriate it (no judging people. This was the 90s. It was a different time). I unpacked my backpack and tried to look like I belonged as the femi-Nazi sulked away in search of another seat, mumbling something about the tyranny of the penis and the objectification of the vagina. Pencil in hand and notebook at the ready, I looked up to see, projected on a screen in front of the class, a picture of a man who bore a striking resemblance to Uncle Fester sporting a Stalin mustache. Below the picture was a series of letters that I never would have thought could be strung together: G-U-R-D-J-I-E-F-F.

As I pondered the connection between Uncle Fester and the incomprehensible string of letters, I realized that I had no interest whatsoever in philosophy of any sort, and certainly not any of the Eastern variety. But no matter. I was willing to stick it out so long as Jenny and her underwear remained firmly planted in the seat in front of me. In Jenny's panties I trusted.

As I stared at her backside the morning in question (and yes, the panties made an appearance, thank you for asking), a thirty-something man with a thick beard, plaid flannel shirt and jeans rolled up to reveal stylishly rugged construction boots, ambled to the front of class, put his hands on his hips and took us in with a look of bemused detachment. It was the late nineties, mind you, which meant it was too soon by about a decade to call this guy a hipster, yet that's exactly what he was: the world's first ultrasensitive, socially conscious, environmentally responsible, fully in-tune with his emotions, Grade A hipster. Wilson High, it seemed, had expanded its hiring criteria in the offseason. Finally, after a long moment, he broke the expectant silence with a deep baritone.

"G. I. Gurdjieff."

After an equally long moment in which the class began to look at each other, confirming that no one had the faintest idea what this impeccably coiffed mountain man was talking about, he spoke again.

"That's not my name, mind you. My name is Steven Pfeiffer and I'll be your guide this year into the fascinating and illuminating world of Eastern Philosophy. I have the privilege of introducing you to a way of thinking about life and the world in which we live that is entirely different than anything you've been exposed to thus far in your short, sheltered lives. This year, you'll be introduced to thinkers who will challenge everything you think you know and read philosophers who will make you question how you ever thought those things in the first place. You lucky few get to be exposed to the ideas of people like this man—"

Here, he turned to the board and pointedly reverently at Uncle Fester.

"—George Ivanovich Gurdjieff. Born in Armenia in the late 19th century – the date is uncertain because, well, it was late 19th century Armenia – died in France in 1949. There's no reason you should know who he is. Indeed, precious few remember his name, let alone know how to pronounce it. It's a shame, really. Not just because he created the Fourth Way. Or even that he survived two car accidents and fathered seven children by seven different women. No, the real crime in you of all people not recognizing his brilliance is that this man — this forgotten thinker of the early twentieth century — captured the essence of the people sitting before me this fine September day: you, the denizens of Introduction to Eastern Philosophy."

Mr. Pfeiffer paused, assessing the entire class. I looked around with him, and saw that some students were listening, others were daydreaming and a few were teetering on the edge of restful slumber. He smiled, shook his head slightly and continued.

"'Man,' Professor Gurdjieff wrote, 'lives life in his sleep.' And judging by your heavy eyelids and listless response this morning, I'd say he was on to something."

We had the good form to laugh. Twenty-six years later — sitting in the back of a Lyft, stuck in traffic after having fled Williams and my god-forsaken job — I remember that we laughed. Even Jenny, who, I would later find out, wasn't the sharpest tool in the shed, giggled softly and shifted in her seat, her pink panties shifting with her.

But now, sitting in the back of a car with countless brake lights strung out before me and my driver, my mind wanders not to Jenny and the disaster she would help me wrought, but to Gurdjieff's postulation that we are all asleep. In this perpetual state of slumber, trudging like zombies through each day of our existence, we are easy to manipulate. We are automatons, at the mercy of those who have the discipline and determination to awake from this reverie and regain the higher consciousness of which we are all capable, but are otherwise too lazy or too indifferent to achieve.

Christ, did Gurdjieff have me down to a T. As the driver eases the car forward, the Camry's brakes whining in protest, I realize I am no more human than the shiny metal box in which I ride. I am a tool for people like Alex, Tim and Vern Williams, a pawn to be directed, deployed and disposed of without a moment's hesitation. And the worst part is I can't even blame them. I let them take advantage of me. I practically beg them to do it.

Frustrated but powerless (a perfect name for my memoir, if I ever have the stones to write one), I glance to my left and see a man in his early thirties with tortoise shell glasses, feathery hair and a smart Windsor knot barking into his BMW's Bluetooth, no doubt closing a deal that's highly leveraged with equitable debt ... or indebted equity ... or whatever the hell happens when people with a lot of money get together and decide to make more of it. Jesus, I don't have the first clue what I'm talking about. Well, here's what I do know. That guy's an asshole. I don't even need to talk to him to know he's a world-class fuckwad. It practically oozes out of him.

I turn to my right and see a nineteen year-old kid sitting in a beat-up Kia leaning his head against the headrest, mouth agape. He's asleep – and not in the Gurdjieff 'we're all automatons,' kind of way, either. I mean, actual physical asleep, with REM cycles and everything. Just to be a cock-knocker, I ask the driver to honk the horn. He looks at me questioningly until I nod to my right. Seeing the kid dead asleep, the driver smiles like I just made his day. And why not? As he leans on the horn, the kid jumps like someone just shot a cattle prod up his ass, sending me and the driver into hysterics. I may be suicidal, but I know funny when I see it.

The moment passes and I turn back to the line of brake lights in front of us. It dawns on me that, while the kid may be a slacker now, at least he's got time to turn things around. He hasn't made any irredeemable mistakes yet, like marrying a shrew, signing up for a dead-end job or plummeting into a chasm of debt. I start to get oddly excited about his prospects, thinking that if he goes back to get his G.E.D., he can make something of himself. Just as I consider shouting a word of encouragement to him, he does something that throws it all to hell.

He picks his nose.

I don't mean he scratches his nose and offhandedly throws a digit up there to quickly clean things out. No, I mean, this kid Picks. His. Nose. He digs like he's going for a world record. He goes nearly two knuckles deep, for Christ's sake. I start to worry that if he jams his finger any higher, he's going to hit gray matter.

To hell with the G.E.D. This kid isn't going anywhere.

The Volvo in front of us creeps forward and we dutifully follow in its wake. We slowly round a curve and I see the reason for the traffic jam. Beyond the swirling lights from a phalanx of police cars, fire trucks and ambulances on the other side of the highway, a tractor-trailer lies on its side next to an SUV that smashed into the Jersey barrier, its safety bags deployed and its windshield spidered. A third mangled mass of metal, barely recognizable as a car, sits upside-down and smoking, one of its wheels dangling from its axel like an eyeball wrenched from its socket. Two firefighters frantically use the Jaws of Life to extract someone from inside. As I turn to gawk at the carnage, I wonder if they'll be too late. I find myself envious of the corpse they'll find.

Predictably, the traffic begins to clear as we pass the carnage. The driver sighs contentedly as the speedometer clears fifty.

"Next exit is ours," he offers.

"Sounds good."

He eyes me in the rearview mirror. "You sure this is where you want to go?"

"Google says this is the address."

"And God knows Google's never wrong," he says, laying the sarcasm on thick. We take the exit and I begin to understand his skepticism. We are in a part of town I've never been to, and for good reason. We pass a series of hollowed out warehouses and vacant lots until the driver finally slows and turns into a gravel driveway.

"You sure you trust Google?" the driver asks, looking at me sideways in the mirror.

I pick my phone in response to pay him, leaving a hefty tip. I figure I can use all the karma I can muster.

"You want me to hang out for a second, make sure this is the right place?"

"No, I'm good," I answer, not sure where my confidence is coming from.

"You're sure?"

"Yeah, I'll be fine."

"So says 80 percent of all rape and murder victims."

"I've already been raped today, so I think I'm good. What are the odds of getting murdered, too?"

"You really want me to answer that?" he asks, eyebrows arched.

I laugh. "You're an awfully considerate driver, you know that? Most people would have driven off as soon as I opened the door."

"Not everyone is most people," he says with a shrug.

"Still, I appreciate it."

I grab my bag, get out of the car and am about to shut the door when the driver responds. "You'll appreciate it all the more when you're left for dead out here."

I lean back into the car. "Believe me, I'm not that lucky."

He shrugs. "Suit yourself."

I shut the door and the car pulls away, its tires crunching on the gravel driveway, a cloud of dust billowing behind it. As its brake lights grow distant, I begin to wonder if I've made a mistake.

I turn and survey my destination. It's everything I would

expect a junkyard to look like. Used up and abandoned, their wheels long since lost or removed, burned out cars are piled like corpses in an unmarked grave. A mongrel, its fur patchy and gray, limps across the path that snakes its way through the stacks of automotive carcasses. Lining the perimeter of this vehicular mixing bowl is a chain link fence at least twelve feet high topped with spirals of razor wire. The whole place screams 'GO AWAY.' Naturally, I walk right in.

I follow the path, taking heed to give the mongrel a wide birth – he's breathing in a way that doesn't sound friendly, let alone healthy – and wind my way past countless crushed and unusable cars. I've heard of scrapheaps, but this is beyond imagination. I cannot fathom anything is worth salvaging in these aging, rusted out piles of steel. Finally, after passing a dozen signs notifying me that there is unequivocally NO TRESPASSING, I find myself facing a wooden building that is one strong wind away from collapse. Standing next to the ramshackle structure is a flatbed trailer with four steel pneumatic columns at each corner supporting a wide, flat piece of steel. In stark contrast to the crumbling building next to it, the trailer's high gloss blue paint is gleaming, with the words CANDI THE CRUSHER etched in yellow on the side. Candi may look clean and nice, but I'm pretty sure she packs a punch.

"Can't you read?" a voice thunders to my left.

I'm too startled to answer. Instead, I nearly drop my computer bag as I jump back four feet.

"Do the words NO TRESPASSING mean anything to you?" The voice's volume has come down, but its viciousness has held steady.

"I'm just trying to find my car," I reply unsteadily.

"Ain't no cars here worth finding." A man in a faded jeans, dirty white t-shirt and unbuttoned mechanic's shirt ambles out from behind a crumpled Buick LeSabre. His beard is unkempt and his belly hangs over his belt buckle. The name patch on his shirt says 'Mac.' He is exactly what I would have expected to find in a place like this. I'm beginning to wonder if I have wandered on to a Hollywood lot instead of a junkyard.

"It was in an accident yesterday. They told me I could find it here."

"Who told you?"

"The police."

"And you believed them?"

"Didn't have any reason not to."

This seems to amuse him. For the first time, there is a crack in his menacing veneer. "No, I s'pose not."

"So is it here?"

"Is what here?"

"My car."

"That depends." Here we go. The shakedown.

"On what?"

He looks at me quizzically. "On what kind of car it is."

I feel like a dumbass. "Oh. Right. It's a black Infiniti."

"It was."

"I'm sorry?"

"You said it came in yesterday. A black Infiniti. Only thing that came in yesterday was a useless hunk of scrap. May have had an Infiniti logo on it, but that don't make it a car."

I stare at him, at a loss for how to respond.

"You want to see it, check it out for yourself?"

"Uh, yeah. That would be great."

"Come on." He sounds like a man calling wearily to a clueless puppy, which in some ways I suppose I am. I hug my bag close and trot after him, struggling to keep up with his lumbering strides. We walk past Candi and the smell of spilled motor oil and despair fills the air. This is a place cars go to die and Candi is the instrument of their demise.

"Is Candi what I think she is?" I ask warily.

"She's my baby," Mac responds proudly.

"She crush all these cars?"

"Candi? No. She's just a li'l thing. She's portable so I can hitch her to a semi and take her around on jobs."

"You never know when or where you'll need to crush a car." Mac stops and looks at me, one eyebrow arched, trying to see if I'm clueless or an asshole. Time to backtrack. Quickly. "I mean, I didn't realize there was a need for portable crushers."

"More than you know," he grunts. "For big jobs, I use Sammy."

He continues on and I follow. I know I shouldn't ask but I can't help myself. "Sammy?"

"Sammy the Shredder."

Ordinarily, I would make fun of someone's predilection to give cute names to machines of death and destruction, but there's a playfulness to Mac that – despite the initial fear of God he instills – is endearing. Besides, he could kick my ass and feed me to Sammy in a heartbeat, so I tread lightly.

"I bet he's impressive."

"He's a beast," he agrees. "That's him, there."

We turn a corner and I see a monstrous ramp leading up to a four-story tower. Sitting next to the tower is a metal goliath with a giant V-shaped opening at the top and a crane hovering over-head. From where I stand, it looks like the ramp ends where Sammy's mouth begins.

"Whaddya think?" he asks proudly.

"It looks like a monstrous baby bird waiting to be fed by its mom."

Mac guffaws. "That's closer than you think. You got time? I can show you."

Without thinking, I nod, and quickly find myself following Mac as we trudge our way up the tower stairs. Following Mac's lumbering steps, I can see that the V-shape I saw below does indeed resemble a mouth, both in form and function. Cars are loaded on to the ramp below, where a motorized belt sends them slowly up an incline until they are dropped into the funnel, where Sammy can do his work. Both of us wheezing, we climb our way to a platform next to the top of the ramp, where a beat up Chevy Impala sits facing backwards, perilously close to the edge of Sammy's gaping mouth, blissfully unaware of the danger below. I lean over and see two rows of metal teeth at the bottom of Sammy's gullet, ready to gnash their way through the Impala or anything else unfortunate enough to fall into his clutches.

"What's the crane for?" I ask.

"When something doesn't fit on the ramp, we'll use the crane to drop it directly into Sammy's mouth."

"Let me guess. Mama?"

Mac smiles broadly. He's missing three teeth. "You're not as dumb as you look, mister. But we're not going to need her today."

He leans across my body and presses a green button on a control panel I didn't realize is there. With a shudder, Sammy roars to life. Its teeth –interlocking metal rotors that grab and then rip their prey to shreds – begin to turn. I look at Mac and he's nearly shaking with excitement.

"Buckle up."

With that, he reaches across once more to press a different button. The belt on the ramp begins to move, inching the Impala closer to Sammy. As the rear bumper and then the trunk clear the edge of the belt, the entire car begins to teeter over the chasm below. For a moment, the Impala looks suspended in air, as if it night be spared Sammy's wrath. But physics quickly take over and the car slips downward, landing with a thunderous crash on the funnel walls where it slides to Sammy's waiting, gnashing teeth.

It takes a little over three minutes for Sammy to devour the Impala and I'm not exaggerating when I say I feel like I'm watching snuff porn. It's like a National Geographic video about life in the veldt, and although this Impala is made of rubber and steel instead of flesh and bone, its demise in the jaws of the more powerful hunter is no less dramatic. Or gory. The air is fetid as each crunch of the rotors sends the Impala's bodily fluids spattering across the insatiable shredder. By the end, Sammy has ingested nearly the entire car. Only the engine block remains, bouncing on top of Sammy's rotating teeth, gamely trying to avoid the rest of the car's grizzly fate. But Sammy's determined patience is rewarded when a stray coil gets caught in its teeth, pulling the engine into the rotors toward the same crushing end.

I don't know whether to feel exhilarated or nauseous.

Mac, the proud papa, channels his gargantuan son and lets loose a barbaric belch. There's no doubting where he stands.

"Did my car go through this already?" I ask queasily.

"Nah, Sammy doesn't get to eat until everything of value has been stripped off and sold."

"So my car is alive?" I ask hopefully.

Mac shrugs. "In a manner of speakin'."

Once more, he leans over to press a button on the control board and the rotors slow to a stop. At first, I hear only distant ringing. It takes me a moment to realize it's just my ears registering their complaint over the din of Sammy's destructive appetite. Without a word, Mac walks past me and begins retracing his path down the stairs. I follow, taking one last look at Sammy and the oily blue sheen covering his teeth, motor oil and hydraulic fluid the only vestiges of the Impala's existence.

The walk down the tower is decidedly easier than the one up

and before long, we stand in front of a mangled mass of metal. Mac looks at me expectantly and I realize with a start that this is my car. Or, at least, it used to me. The front end is collapsed on itself, like an accordion that can no longer extend. The front left wheel, twisted at an obscene angle, has been pushed so far back that the driver could use it as a stepping stool to climb in the car. The windshield is gone completely and, poking my head inside the passenger compartment, I see that the airbag still hangs limply from the steering column, exactly as it had two days ago. But despite the devastation to the exterior of the car, the interior seems remarkably intact, albeit covered in bits of broken glass. I'm amazed to still be alive.

"Makes you thank your lucky stars, don't it?"

I said amazed, not thankful.

"Pretty remarkable," I say. "Guess that airbag saved my life."

"That and the engineerin'. I'm guessing you were doing, what? Sixty? Sixty-five?"

"Probably."

"Slammed head first into a concrete wall and the cockpit barely has a scratch. Say what you will, but those designers know their shit."

"That they do," I answer, not knowing what else to say. I look around and suddenly wonder why I've come. My car is totaled beyond repair and now I'm stranded with a man who seems distressingly excited to feed it to a grotesque eating machine that I am certain he believes is his offspring. "Guess it's dead after all," I say finally.

"Just a pile of spare parts," Mac agrees.

"How does this work? Is there something I need from you for my insurance?"

"Nowadays, most companies will accept a picture from your phone."

"Of you?"

"Of the car."

"Right." Trying to hide my embarrassment, I fumble for my phone and take a couple of pictures of the car. "Sorry," I say. "I don't know how this works."

"Most people don't," he answers with a shrug. "Sometimes, they still want to send out an adjuster to take a look first-hand. Depends on the company. If yours does, just give 'em my name. They'll know where to find me."

"And then what? Another meal for Sammy?"

"Depends on what the insurance company wants to do with it. But yeah, that's usually the way it works."

I look at Mac, who is looking at me expectantly. "Usually?" I ask finally.

Mac inhales deeply and hooks his thumbs in his waistband. He tries to strike an air of gravitas and look less like a salvage yard operator and more like a thriving auto salesman, or at least what a salvage yard operator imagines a thriving auto salesman to look like. I have the strong suspicion he is wishing he had a pair of suspenders so he could snap them and shout, "Have I got a deal for you!" As it stands, he opts for something only slightly less predictable.

"We could always make a deal."

"What kind of deal?" I ask warily.

"That car of yours won't never drive again. But that don't mean it ain't valuable."

Dammit. I always forget – do two negatives make a positive in grammar as well as math?

"How valuable?"

"I'm not sayin' it's top of the line, but there's some parts that might fetch a fair price."

Mac smells blood. There's a deal to be had and I am fresh meat. I casually put my hand in my pocket to make sure my wallet is still there.

"How much?" I ask, trying to cut to the chase.

"I'll give you two hundred."

"Dollars? I paid fifty thousand for this car."

"That's when it drove," he shrugs.

"Okay, but you said yourself some of the parts are still valuable. They've got to be worth at least a thousand."

"Like what?" he asks, a gleam in his eye.

"What do you mean, like what?"

"You said there are parts worth a thousand. Which ones?"

Goddammit. The fucker called my bluff.

"I don't know which ones," I say, exasperated. "Parts. Stuff. You know, engine type things." Jesus, I'm a moron.

He leans on the hood and the car groans audibly. "Don't take much to see that there ain't nothin' worth nothin' in here."

"Windshield?"

"Could be worth something," he allows. "If there was one." Shit. I forgot.

"Headlights?"

"Smashed."

"Axel?"

"Snapped."

"Bumper?"

"Totaled."

"Not that one, the other one."

"Rear one's totaled, too. The wrecker did a number on it."

"That's not my fault!"

"Don't mean I'm gonna pay for it," he shrugs.

"What about the airbags?" I ask, scrambling. "I've read stories about thieves stealing cars just for the airbags."

"That's for bags that haven't deployed." He points to the limp bag that looks surprisingly like a used condom. "This one's worthless."

"Okay, how about the passenger side? That one's still intact."

He nods, graciously granting a minor victory to me. At last. "Give you two hundred for it."

"Okay," I agree, "that's more like it. What else is there?"

"A/C unit looks decent."

"That's got to be worth at least five hundred."

"To who?"

"Whom."

"Huh?"

"It's 'to whom.' You said 'who.'"

"Yeah? Well, I don't give a fuck. Ain't no who or whom gonna give you more than a hundred for it."

He has a point, tortured grammar and all. "Fair enough. What about the seats?"

He makes a big show of inspecting the rest of the car, inside and out.

"I'll give you a thousand."

"So that's thirteen hundred total?"

"Not extra. All in. One grand, take it or leave it."

I don't have a leg to stand on, let alone two to walk away with, so I simply nod in agreement. He reaches into his pockets and pulls out two rolls of cash, one in each hand. He tosses them to me in quick succession and I manage to catch them in the least graceful manner possible, batting them around like a kitten surprised with two balls of yarn. Only rather than looking cute and cuddly, I look sad and pathetic as I fall on my ass and let the cash bounce off my lap and roll harmlessly in the dirt. I pick up the money and the shreds of whatever dignity I have left, and stand up, not bothering to dust myself off. A perfect ending to a fucked up day.

"It's all there," he says, trying to be helpful.

I look at the cash, worn twenties wrapped in rubber bands. It dawns on me that he knew all along he'd get the car for a thousand. He had the money with him the whole time. I try not to feel completely taken advantage of.

"Makes you feel any better, we don't need to report this."

"To whom?" See what I did there? I may be down but that doesn't mean I can't still be a prick. Who knows? If I really amp it up, maybe he can put me out of my misery. He's bound to have a gun somewhere on his person.

He smiles and I see the gaps in his teeth once more. He's definitely packing heat. "The insurance company. This transaction is strictly off the books."

"Won't they figure it out if they send out an adjuster?"

"I'll tell 'em the parts were stolen. This is a tough neighborhood. Shit like that happens all the time."

"They'll buy that?"

"Don't have much choice. Long as you keep your mouth shut."

"You don't need to worry about me." Most dead men have no problem keeping quiet.

He smiles again. "Well, then. Looks like we have ourselves a deal."

He sticks out a meaty paw and I take it.

"Excellent. I can't think of anyone I'd rather engage in insurance fraud with than you."

"Don't you mean 'with whom?'"

It's my turn to smile. "Well played."

"Seventh grade English. Mrs. Wish was a real ball buster."

I laugh. Mac is full of surprises.

"She must have been."

We start to walk back to his dilapidated shack of an office when I realize I'm stranded.

"Hey, Mac. I don't suppose you have a car I can borrow."

"Borrow? No."

"Buy?" I offer, knowing Mac has thought of this already.

"I might be able to help you out. What did you have in mind?"

Of course, it's not what I have in mind, but what Mac does. And that happens to be a beat to shit 1970 Chevelle SS parked on the other side of Candi. Its front end is barely held together with Bondo and the inside reeks so badly of bleach that I'm certain it's a crime scene gone bad. The paint job is a combination of metallic gold and what looks like Sharpie pen, and the rear window is held in place with duct tape. Meth heads would be embarrassed to be caught dead in this car, which, I realize, one probably was.

"Anything I should know about this car?"

"She's got 450 horses and goes like a bat out of hell."

"Let me put it a different way. Are the police looking for this car in connection with a recent violent crime?"

"Violent? No."

"Non-violent?"

"You know," he practically whines, "there's so much crime today, it's hard to say. I mean, who *aren't* they looking for these days?"

"Me. And I'd like to keep it that way."

"You'll be fine. Trust me." And if you can't trust a guy with half his teeth whose closest personal relationship is with car shredding equipment, who can you trust? "Besides," he continues, "the price is right."

"How much?"

"Five hundred."

"You just paid me a grand for spare parts, and now you're telling me I can get the whole car for five hundred?"

"It's priced to move."

"Exactly. You wouldn't be fencing this for someone, would you, Mac?"

"This car isn't hot."

"Luke warm?"

"That's fair," he allows.

I make a show of thinking about it, but my mind is made up. I only need the car for a couple of days and Mac is right. I can't beat the price. At five hundred, it's a decent two-day rental. After that, it's somebody else's problem. And if someone kills me in the interim, they'll only be beating me to the punch.

I reach into my pocket and pull out one of the rolls of bills. I toss it to Mac, who catches it cleanly.

"Keys are in it," he says, flashing me another toothless grin. Everything is going just as he planned. Throwing my bag on the passenger seat as I climb into the car, I wonder what that feels like.

Ten minutes later, I'm driving down the highway with no particular destination in mind. I know I should go home, but I can't bring myself to it just yet. There's only so much disdain I can handle being thrown my way in a given day. Alex and the girls will have to wait.

Besides (and I can't believe I'm admitting this), I am loving this car. Sure, the Infiniti had a smoother ride, a better sound system and more comfortable seats (the spring digging into my coccyx is particularly distressing). And yes, "smells like a morgue" is not a description that most people would hope to see applied to their auto interior. But all that said, the SS has something that today's antiseptically bland, halogen head-lighted, Soft Rock cookie-cutter sports sedans can't come close to matching: attitude. This car is badass, plain and simple. In fact, it's an absolute monster. When I put my foot on the gas, it sounds like fifty Hell's Angels thundering down the road. A little old lady is puttering in the right lane in her Subaru and I decide to have a little fun. I ease up on her left and, trying not to smile, I drop the hammer. All 450 horses roar to life and the Chevelle lurches forward. I have just enough time to see the old lady jump out of her seat, whipping her head around so fast, her wig falls off.

The giggles end, however, when I catch myself in the rearview mirror. I'm a middle-aged man in a beat to shit Chevelle wearing make-up to hide two black eyes and a broken nose. I look like a guy trying to make it in the underground backyard wrestling circuit, only it's not going too well. I'm sleeping on the couch in my parents' basement and haven't spoken to a girl in months, outside of the checkout girl at the local Market Basket who is skeeved out every time I show up at her register with nothing but an onion, a Lean Cuisine or a box of spoons. She looks over her shoulder nervously, making sure her manager has an eye out because she is convinced I am stalking her, which, of course, I am. When I'm not rifling through her mail or hiding in the bushes outside her house, I spend my time beating off to low rent porn and sniffing oxy whenever I can get my hands on it.

My phone rings, sparing me any further introspection, though it's not a call I want to hear. I listen to the woman on the other end of the line and murmur my thanks for calling, assuring her that I'm on my way. I put my blinker on and move into the right lane to take the next exit.

14

I should be used to the smell by now. After six years working at one of the largest health providers in the country, you'd think I would have become immune to it. But I haven't, not by a long shot. Every time it hits me – the sharp mixture of ammonia, floor polish, lemon extract and death – I have to stop for a moment and gather myself. It's like taking the first punch in a boxing match. You know it's coming, but it'll still knock you on your ass if you're not careful.

Sure enough, as soon as the automatic doors slide open, the aroma hits me and my gait falters. My eyes start to water and my nose runs. I stagger to the front desk and see a friendly face waiting for me, a tissue box in her outstretched hand. I gratefully pull out two tissues and blow my nose.

"Thank you, Chandice," I say, unapologetically wiping my nose. "You're a godsend." I deposit the tissues in her other outstretched hand.

"Years of exposure. I'm practically immune." I could listen to her Jamaican accent all day.

"You should get hazard pay."

"We tried. Without evidence of physical harm, we ain't got no case."

"Try emotional. This smell hurts the soul."

She smiles and her white teeth shine against her smooth dark skin. "How many rich white men you know are jus' handing out money?"

"Not many," I allow.

"Yah, well, if you find one who does, lemme know. Chandice will come callin'." She pulls herself out of her chair and walks around the desk to give me a hug. I wrap my arms around her generous curves and let myself get lost in her embrace, her dreads cascading across both our shoulders. I breathe deeply and something breaks inside me when I realize her smell is as close to home as anything I've felt in a long time. I pull away and her sad eyes belie her smile. She has the good graces not to say anything about my appearance.

"Where is he?" I ask finally.

"By the nurses' break room. We tried to take him back to his room, but he kept getting more an' more agitated."

"Worse than usual?"

"Yah, or I wouldn't have called. When he gets like 'dis, you be the only one he listen to." She laughs again and warmth returns to her eyes.

"I lived eighteen years under his roof, and the son of a bitch never once listened to me. But he loses his marbles and suddenly I'm the one he takes orders from. How is that funny?"

"It's sad as hell, if you ask me. But if you can't find reason to laugh, you ain't gonna find reason to live, 'specially round here."

I consider her point. "You're pretty good at this."

She nods. "I got my name for a reason."

"Chandice? What does it mean?"

"Talented one."

"No argument here."

She smiles. "I'll walk you down there." She slides her arm into mine and walks me down the hall. As we pass each room, I peak inside, but each time, I wish I hadn't. Each room is decorated with relics of the occupant's life before the nursing home – a plaid BarcaLounger, a patchwork quilt, perhaps even a crystal lamp or collage of grandchildren's artwork – but no matter of outside influence can mask what this place really is: a holding place for the dying or forgotten. And most of the residents know it. I stop looking at them. I can't handle seeing another old man or woman sitting on a chair, staring vacantly at the wall.

"How about yours?"

"Huh?"

Chandice playfully slaps my shoulder with her free hand. "Your name. What's it mean?"

"Oh. My mom told me Sean means God is gracious."

"That He is," she answers with a satisfied smile.

"Not from where I sit."

We turn the corner and she ushers me to a different wing of the nursing home. The rooms look the same, but the feeling inside them has changed. Resignation has given way to confusion, desperation to mania. We are in the dementia ward.

Chandice feels my arm tense and pats it gently.

"Come on, child."

We continue past the guest rooms – that's what staff has been instructed to call them, as if the occupants still have a choice in the matter – until we turn a corner and she runs headlong into a tall, thirty-something African-American nurse I've met at least six times but whose name escapes me. The tall nurse, with a broad face and broader shoulders, envelops Chandice in a bear hug and lifts her off the ground – no mean feet given her curves – causing her to squeal in equal parts alarm and delight. He puts her down and she slaps him playfully on his enormous bicep.

"Oooh, you're a bad man, Julius—"

Julius, that's it. I make a mental note to remember his name, knowing I'll probably forget it as soon as I walk out the front door.

Julius laughs at Chandice's teasing, his eyes shining and his entire face alight with joy. But when he turns and sees me, his smile disappears.

"Well, if it isn't the son of Satan." I can't tell if he's joking.

I offer a conciliatory smile. "That bad?"

"Let's just say he's not winning Patient of the Week."

"I thought they were 'guests.'"

Julius looks at me crossly. Now is not the time for semantics. It's also probably not the time to ask whether the red stain on his uniform shirt is blood.

I try a different tack. "What did he do?"

"Threw his dinner at me."

"So that's ketchup?" I ask hopefully, nodding towards his shirt.

"Stained as a motherfucker," he says, visibly annoyed. "This shit better come out or it'll be the third one ruined this month. These scrubs may not look good but that don't mean they're cheap."

"Try warm water and vinegar," Chandice offers.

"Thanks, baby. I will." The words practically slide out of him and wash over Chandice like a warm bath. It dawns on me that these two would make a hell of a couple. I find myself silently rooting for them.

"I'll pay for the shirt," I offer.

Julius looks at me and tilts his head, wondering if this white guy with the beat-up face is serious.

"Naw," he says finally, waving the suggestion away with one enormous hand. "Occupational hazard. Your dad doesn't know what he's doing. None of these poor folks do. Come on, I'll take you to him."

"This is where I leave you two," Chandice says. I detect a note of sadness in her voice. "Best be back at my post in case the boss man come round."

As Chandice turns and walks slowly back to the front desk, Julius calls after her.

"I'm coming after you if that vinegar don't work!"

The squeal and subsequent cackle lead me to believe that's exactly what she's hoping for.

Julius smiles and tilts his head, beckoning me to follow. I assume we are headed to my dad's room, which is four doors down the corridor to my left, but we we instead turn right towards the nurses' station. It's a slow day, so no one is there, save for a skeleton of a man sitting awkwardly in a wooden chair against the wall. His skin is sallow and his cheeks are hollow, as if he hasn't eaten in days. His body is slack, leaning awkwardly to the side so much that I'm surprised he hasn't fallen over. We walk closer and I realize two things.

First, the reason he hasn't fallen over is that he's strapped to the chair with zip ties.

Second, it's my dad.

I stop in my tracks and look at Julius.

"Not one of his better days," he says apologetically.

"What did he do?"

"He's skipped his last four meals, so I was trying to convince him to eat. Needless to say," he says, eyeing his scrubs again, "he didn't take too kindly to that."

I look back at Dad. His eyes are wild, fully dilated and darting back and forth, on the lookout for demons of some sort, known only to him.

"Has he hurt anyone?"

"No, but he swears he's going to rip all of our arms off."

I look at Julius, alarmed. He raises his eyebrows and smiles. I get his point. My dad can barely lift his arms in this state, let alone pose a serious threat to the likes of Julius.

"What can I do?"

Julius shrugs. "He's pretty far gone at this point, but see if you can talk some sense into him. More to the point, see if you can talk some food into him."

"Can we cut these ties off?"

Julius thinks for a moment. "He was pretty agitated. Talk to him first. If he stays calm, we can take it from there."

I nod and look back at my dad. Mouth open, his eyes dart from me to Julius to the far wall and back again. I walk slowly towards him, careful to appear as nonthreatening as possible. When I'm two feet away, I kneel down in front of him and look at him with a smile. There's no recollection in the eyes that look back at me.

We're quite a pair: one is lost inside his own head and the other is just lost.

"Hey, Dad," I say softly.

He picks up his head sharply and tries to focus. It's a struggle. He takes my features in and his eyes narrow. I know the look. He knows he knows me but doesn't know how. Still, I'm an ally. He thinks.

"I won't do it!" he snaps.

"You don't have to do anything you don't want to," I respond, careful not to ask what 'it' refers to. Never good to engage in an argument with a madman on his terms.

"Don't these bastards know it's Lent, for Christ's sake?"

So many problems with this statement. In the first place, Julius may be a lot of things – a nurse, a black man, a broad shouldered saint – but a bastard certainly isn't one of them. Second, while it is, in fact, Lent, he only got that right by virtue of dumb freaking luck. That's like giving the proverbial broken clock credit for being right two times a day. Third, so what if it is Lent? We're not Catholic. At least, we're not practicing Catholics, not since my brother and I were confirmed and my parents got tired of waking up early on Sundays. And finally, invoking the name of Christ as an epithet while claiming to be pious enough to observe whatever Lenten ritual is at issue is just hypocritical in the extreme.

Although, now that I think about it, hypocrisy is something I can get behind. I decide to let it slide. In fact, just for shits and giggles, I decide to engage. It's a gamble, but one I'm betting is worth it.

"Sons of bitches. What did they try to make you do?"

His eyes narrow and he emits a low grumble. "Eat meat on Friday," he seethes.

I stifle a smile. I have two options. One, I can tell him it's Tuesday, not Friday. But this is a losing battle. While factually accurate, this argument has the disadvantage of directly countering his version of reality. And if there's one thing this shit stain of a disease has taught me, it's never tell an Alzheimer's patient they're wrong. My only other option is accept his delusion as holy writ but change the parameters in a way he doesn't see coming. After banging my head against the wall far too many times trying to convince him that black was white or left was right, I decided long ago it was easier just to come up with delusions of my own.

"Haven't you heard?" I ask earnestly.

His eyes widen. Someone is finally talking to him on his terms. "Heard what?"

"The Pope issued a dispensation for the entire Eastern seaboard earlier this week."

"Really?"

"Yeah, I can't believe you didn't hear about it. You know about that massive offshore mercury spill last month, right?"

"Yeah," he offers cautiously. Now, you and I know there was no such spill but he doesn't, which is absurd if he gives it two seconds of thought. I mean, who's shipping mercury in such copious amounts these days as to cause such a big spill? Pretty sure the whole mercury thermometer industry went tits up with the rest of the analog world years ago. But my old man will be damned if he admits ignorance about anything. So I run with it. Besides, it's nice to be able to turn the famous Reilly obstinacy in my favor for a change.

"Well, because of that, there's an acute shortage of fish. It's really bad. We haven't seen anything like this since—"

I look at Julius, searching for inspiration, but he just smiles, enjoying the show.

"—the *Exxon Valdez* spill in the eighties."

I sneak another look at Julius. He looks impressed.

"Anyway, the Pope doesn't want anyone eating contaminated fish, so he issued a dispensation for the rest of Lent. We can eat whatever we want, though of course he asks that we say an extra prayer acknowledging the disaster and asking God for his Providence in helping us clean up the environment."

"Of course," Dad says solemnly.

"I thought I told the staff here about it, but it must have slipped my mind. I'm so sorry about that."

"It's not your fault," my dad says thoughtfully. "Now that you bring it up, I seem to remember hearing something about it. But with everything going on, I must not have said anything to the staff either."

I stifle a smile. Yeah, he's got lots going on. "Naturally."

Dad's suddenly face darkens and he nods in Julius' direction. "Not that these *heathens* would have had any idea what I was talking about."

I try to ignore his none too subtle racial overtones and move on. "How about we have some dinner? You must be starving."

Dad pauses before a small smile creeps across his face. "I do their like pudding."

I smile. "Me, too."

I stand and make my way over to Julius, who smirks in admiration.

"Well done."

I shrug. "Got lucky."

"No, I've seen luck. That was skill. You've can read people and get them to do what you want. Plus, it doesn't hurt that you love him."

I don't have the heart to tell him that he's one for two.

"You mind grabbing another dinner for him?"

"Sure thing." He turns to leave then looks back at me. "Catholic, huh?"

"First I've heard of it," I say with a laugh. "I know he went to Catholic school but he never seemed to care much about religion when we were growing up. That was more Mom's thing."

"It's amazing the shit that comes to the surface when your brain is fighting this disease. Those nuns must have done a number on him."

And he did a number on me, I want to say. But instead I nod sadly and walk back to my dad.

15

I park the Chevelle in the garage and walk quietly into the kitchen, hoping its empty. No such luck. Alex is sitting at the island, flipping through home magazines and plotting our next renovation. Judging by the empty glass and wine bottle, she's been here awhile.

"Where have you been?" she asks without looking up.

"Nursing home. Dad had a bad day."

She looks at me and I see what I think is concern in her eyes. Leave it to Alex for somehow liking my parents more than I did.

"How bad?"

"The usual," I shrug. "Thought it was Lent and swore up and down the nursing staff was trying to poison him."

"How?"

"By making him eat meat."

"It is Lent, you know."

I sigh. "I know that and you know that, but he definitely doesn't know that."

"And yet it's still Lent."

"Yeah, but that doesn't mean he's right."

She raises her eyebrows. "I didn't realize there was right and wrong when it came to Alzheimer's."

"No right," I conceded, "just wrong."

"Is he okay?"

"He's fine. A well placed lie and he was eating meatloaf with the best of them."

"So you lied to make him eat?"

I can't help but laugh. "Are you seriously suggesting I did wrong by getting my dad to eat?"

"If it goes against his belief system—"

"His *belief* system? Are you shitting me? Right now, he believes he's St. Jerome. Tomorrow, it will be Jerry Rice."

"I'm just saying—"

"You're just saying I'm wrong, as usual. Jesus, Alex, it's like I can't do anything right with you."

"Now you know how the girls and I feel."

"Exactly. I've singlehandedly fucked up your lives and now I'm fucking up my dad's life, never mind that he doesn't know what life that is from one day to the next."

She stands and starts to say something but catches herself. Instead, she takes a breath and chooses her words carefully.

"Sean, why does it have to be like this between us?"

"I don't know," I answer with a sigh, pulling a glass from one cupboard and a bottle of bourbon from another. "Probably because I'm such a son of a bitch." I pour fill the glass and drain it, then fill it again. "Or maybe it's because I just can't seem to do anything right."

"Maybe it's because you drink so much."

"See what I mean?"

She grips the countertop and closes her eyes. I bet she's counting to ten. Her new life coach is big on counting to ten. Of course, he charges five hundred bucks an hour, so he must know something I don't.

Her counting done, she breathes deeply and looks at me. "When did you become so angry at everyone and everything?"

"I'm not angry at everything. I still like hockey. I really like it when they beat the tar out of each other."

"Okay, when did you become so angry at me?"

"Probably around the time when you started hating me." I'm torn between holding her gaze for effect and downing the bourbon. I once tried both at the same time, but I ended up inhaling half the bourbon and spilling the rest on my shirt. Instead of a dramatic moment, all I had to show for my efforts was a stained shirt and a burning esophagus. Tonight, I decide to forgo the drama and gulp the bourbon. What it lacks in showmanship, it makes up for in symbolism.

"I don't hate you, Sean. I hate what you've become."

"This may be the bourbon talking, but I'm pretty sure those two things are the same thing."

"It's too bad you can't see the difference."

"That sounds like something your life coach and fuck buddy would say."

"His name," she says, bristling, "is Todd."

She turns and walks out of the room, leaving me to clean up her mess. It's hard not to notice she never corrected me on the whole fuck buddy thing. I grab the bottle and refill my glass. It's going to be a long night.

WEDNESDAY

16

My head hurts worse than usual, which is saying something. Most mornings, it feels like an evil sprite spent the night taking a ball peen hammer to the inside of my eyeballs. This, however, is far more intense. Even my teeth hurt. I'm no doctor, but I'm starting to think I haven't fully recovered from the car crash. I wonder if I have a concussion. Then again, the bottle of bourbon I took down last night probably isn't doing me any favors either.

I open one eye and take notice of two things: one, I'm still in bed, which means I haven't pissed or puked the bed. Two, Alex is still in bed, which means ... well, that I haven't pissed or puked the bed.

I know. I'm a credit to men the world over.

Emboldened, I open the other eye. It's still dark outside. I start to lift my head to check the clock, but abort when my bladder registers its objection. It is well beyond maximum capacity.

I weigh my options. A bathroom run is definitely in order, but that would mean throwing back the covers and braving the cold. And if there's one thing that must be obvious by now: I don't do brave. On the other hand, I could lie still and chance it, but I'm not sure how long my bladder can hold out. I decide a test is in order. Delicately, I roll on to my back and feel my distended bladder roll with me. I stifle a gasp as my urine balloon sloshes against my spine, sending a small spurt of urine out of the exit spout.

That clinches it: structural integrity has definitely been compromised.

As a dark spot seeps across the front of my boxers, it is clear that I'm going to piss imminently. The only question is where said piss is going to take place. I steal a glance at my wife, who remains blissfully ignorant of the danger in which she slumbers, and decide that being doused with a urine geyser is no way for anyone to be awakened, no matter how much she may deserve it. I take a deep but cautious breath and steel myself. I can do this.

I throw the covers back and swing my feet to the floor. But as I stand and ready myself for the dash to the bathroom, I misjudge the additional momentum brought on by the nine pounds of urine weight I'm carrying and lurch awkwardly forward, thus learning the hard way that Newton was right: a body in motion does indeed want to stay in motion. But with each step necessitated by Newtonian physics, I learn there is a distressing fluid dynamical consequence. That is, as each step shifts my weight and compresses my bladder, the pressure of the fluid inside increases, forcing it to look for an escape valve. While I'm sure my bladder is relieved that such a valve just happens to be close at hand, I am decidedly less so, as the spot on the front of my boxers is growing larger and darker with each step. In a futile attempt to defy the laws of physics, I clamp my dick with my fingers like forceps and quicken the pace. Of course, this only exacerbates my dilemma, so much so that by the time I reach the bathroom, my boxers, hands and torso are soaked with piss. I'm just hoping I managed I kept most of it off the carpet.

I take a look at the toilet and make a quick calculation: I'll never make it. It's only six feet away, but it might as well be six miles judging by the pressure I feel on the inner walls of my bladder. Plus, the toilet seat is down. Just thinking of the bladder constriction brought on by bending over to lift the seat is enough to make my kneecaps float. Between that and the time it will take me to tear these wet boxers off, I can't envision any scenario that doesn't end with me unleashing a wild stream of piss with such velocity that it threatens to separate the wallboard from the studs.

For the first time in I can't remember how long, I make a good decision: a quick detour into the shower. I face the wall, release my vice-like grip from my dick and let loose.

Sweet Mary Moses, that feels good. Sure, I'm now soaked to the bone with my own urine, but I can't remember feeling happier. I'm pissing and I didn't burst my bladder or incur any significant internal injury. What's more, I didn't piss the bed, the floor or the bathroom. For once in my life, I didn't make a mess of anyone or anything other than me. Plus, I get to wash off immediately after finishing, which, judging by the flow, is going to take awhile. I'm not sure I could have done this any better.

"What the hell are you doing?"

Scared out of my mind, I whip my head around and see a disheveled and disgusted Alex staring at me. As I slowly turn around, I catch my reflection in the mirror and see what she sees. Two black eyes, a nose as big and as red as Ted Kennedy's and a torrent of piss streaming down my leg.

I may have only made myself a mess, but damn, what a mess indeed.

I start to say something, but she only she shakes her head in dismay and walks towards the toilet, ready to do her business where all respectable humans do.

I see with relief that Alex's contractor came through and had his plumber fix the shower valve. Ignoring for the moment that his industriousness was likely fueled less by his good nature and more by his desire to (continue to) get in my wife's pants, I turn on the water and peel off my boxers. Just as the shower begins to heat up, Alex flushes the toilet, transforming the soul-nurturing streams of hot water into daggers of ice and sending my muscles into a paroxysm of pain. I scamper to the corner of the shower stall, contorting my body to avoid any more of the arctic blast. I hear a snicker and turn to see Alex watching me with a malevolent smile. Fuck her.

"You look like shit," she sneers.

"I was in a car accident," I remind her.

"That was two days ago."

"So?"

"So any pity garnered from car accidents lapses after 48 hours. It's in the rules."

"What rules?"

"The rules of marital engagement."

"Yeah, well, the accident was only 36 hours ago. I still have twelve hours of pity left."

"There's an important codicil that says the 48-hour window is shortened one hour for every year of marriage. We've been married eighteen years."

"Which means?"

"Which means any and all pity for you evaporated overnight. You're shit out of luck."

I'd challenge her math but my ability to do complex algebra evaporated overnight along with my ability to control my bladder. Again, I suspect the bottle of bourbon may have something to do with both developments. I change tactics.

"You know, most spouses would express concern if their loved one just missed getting the business end of a bridge abutment."

"Most spouses aren't married to you."

She wasn't always like this, you know. At our wedding, I distinctly remember her looking deeply into my eyes when she said her vows and giving me a long, slow, soft kiss afterward. Of course, now that I think about it, she skipped the part about in sickness and in health. She also seemed to linger a bit longer than necessary on the 'death to us part' part. Probably not the best omen.

"So you wanted me to die."

She shrugs. "I can't see how it would have made things any worse."

A pungent whiff of urine smacks me in the face and I realize I'm in the shower for a reason. I pick up my boxers, rinse them out a few times and then wring them out before flinging them over the shower door to drip dry. Then I grab the soap and shampoo, and clean myself off. But as I turn off the water, I realize I don't have a towel. I was too busy not spraying down the entire bathroom with urine earlier. I catch Alex's eye in the mirror as she brushes her teeth. She stops brushing and eyes me warily, toothpaste dripping down her chin.

"What?"

I stand naked and dripping, my arms extended pathetically. "You mind...?"

She shakes her head and spits in the sink. Then she turns to the wall, grabs a bath towel off the rack and throws it to me without looking. A perfect strike. I begin to towel off as she goes back to angrily brushing her teeth.

I throw the towel over my head and hear her spit in the sink again. "So did you?"

I pull my head out from under the towel. "Did I what?"

"Try to kill yourself."

"Why do you care?"

"I don't." She pauses. "I just need to know what to tell the insurance company."

I laugh and dry off my legs. "It won't matter what you tell them."

"What's that supposed to mean?" For the first time in this conversation, there is genuine feeling in her voice.

"It means..." I trail off, standing up straight. Do I really want to get into this right now? Telling her about our financial maelstrom is the absolute last thing I want to do. But seeing the alarm seep into her eyes, I know I should tell her something. I just I can't imagine where to begin.

"What's that supposed to mean?" she says again, her pitch higher this time.

"It means you should lay off the credit cards for awhile."

I make a big show of wrapping the towel around my midsection, which is increasingly reminiscent of cottage cheese wrapped in cellophane. The towel histrionics leave me breathless. Now I'm emotionally embarrassed and physically revolting. In fact, I'm beginning to wonder whether I actually have to kill myself by the end of the week or if I'll just be done in by general lack of health before then. It's a fucking wonder they let me work at a healthcare company.

I look up and see Alex staring at me, incredulous.

"What are you talking about?"

"I'm saying solvency is not a word one would use to describe our finances."

"What?"

Judging by her face and the toothbrush still dangling in her hand, I don't seem to be getting through.

"Any chance you're going to let me get dressed before having this conversation?"

Forgetting she is still holding the toothbrush, she folds her arms petulantly, stabbing herself in the rib with the toothbrush and smearing toothpaste on her midsection in the process. Guess that's a no.

"Things are bad," I say finally, leaning against the reclaimed wood and soapstone vanity that contributed significantly to our current financial straits.

"How bad?"

I think for a moment. "On par with the Hindenberg. Slightly less loss of life but just as flammable."

"You're serious?"

"As a heart attack."

There is a crack in her usual haughty veneer, as if she is seeing clearly for the first time.

"How much?"

"More than you and I will make in this or any other lifetime."

"How much?" She will not be put off.

"Over a million."

"DOLLARS?"

"Unfortunately. I offered the bank pesos, but they didn't think that was funny."

She pauses, struggling with the enormity of the problem.

"You're sure about this? You didn't make some stupid arithmetic mistake? Add a zero when you weren't supposed to?"

I inhale slowly. She's not trying to insult me, I remind myself. She's just trying to come to grips with this for the first time.

"The numbers are real. I can put you on the phone with Carl, if you'd like."

"Who the *fuck* is Carl?"

"Our accountant."

"Let me guess – he has a comb over and an office in a strip mall?"

"He prefers to work out of the local Denny's."

"You're shitting me?"

"Yes," I sigh. "Just trying to add a little levity to the situation."

"Fuck you, Sean. Fuck. You." She throws the toothbrush at me. Now we both have toothpaste on our midsections.

I stay quiet, trying to give Alex time to process the information. I could go put clothes on, but I worry that she'll interpret my departure as an attempt to flea the conversation. And as appealing as that may sound, I know it will only make things worse, so I content myself by brushing off the toothpaste and picking lint out of my belly button. Christ almighty, how does so much build up in there? I don't remember this ever being a problem, but then I hit forty and my belly button turned into a fucking lint factory. Is it the increased body hair? The larger waistline? A combination of the two? I'm telling you, every time I look down, I've got a tuft of God knows what poking out of there.

"You digging for gold?"

I look up and see her staring at me with equal parts revulsion and amusement.

"Just a little personal maintenance," I shrug.

"God, you're disgusting."

"It's only going to get worse," I answer. "Have you seen my ear hair?"

She laughs morosely, but at least it's a laugh. Then she catches herself and looks at me accusingly.

"What the fuck happened?"

"It's pretty simple. We've spent a shitpile more than we've earned."

"I thought we had things under control."

I do everything can not to laugh. "Are you kidding me?"

"What? We don't spend that much."

"Alex, we put professional athletes and rappers to shame."

"We're not that bad."

"Let me ask you a question. You're renovating your kitchen – granite or Formica?"

"That's not fair. *Everyone* does granite."

"Maybe, but not everyone re-does their kitchen every Olympiad."

"I didn't hear you objecting at the time."

"How could I? You were too busy screaming at the contractors to hear me. There's a reason every tradesman in the tri-state area calls you Queen of the Change Order."

"Don't make this all about me!" she screams. "This isn't all my fault!"

"I know," I agree, even though I'm not sure I do. "I was there too. It all adds up. The house, the cars .. the house again." I leave out the crystal, the shoes, the dresses, the pearls...

She pauses, trying to keep her composure, but her trembling lip and the tears welling in her eyes give her away.

"We don't have any savings?"

Fighting off the laughter is starting to hurt. "None to speak of. We spent every last penny on the house, renovations, furniture and cars. We borrowed against the equity, we took out advances our life insurance and when that wasn't enough, we levered up on the credit cards." A practice she is all too familiar with, I need not remind her.

"What about the kids?" she asks plaintively, her voice breaking.

"I don't think they have any money either, at least, none that they'd be willing to give us."

"What I mean is, don't we have any money set aside for them to go to college?"

This time I can't help it. I burst out laughing. "Are you kidding? The only thing we've got is the loose change hiding between the couch cushions. We talked about starting a 529 plan a few years ago but we both agreed that could wait."

"For what?"

"For the day we had money to save. Which never came."

She swallows a sob then looks at me coldly. "How the fuck could you let this happen?"

"Me?"

"Yes, Sean. You."

I've tried to be conciliatory, but now my dander is up.

"Look, Alex. I know this is tough to hear and I'm sorry to drop this on you like this. But you can't really believe this is all my fault."

"The hell I can't."

"I see. And the fact that you spend money like a sailor on leave has absolutely nothing to do with it."

"I don't spend any more than any of my friends."

"Friends? You mean the Housewives of Whore Island that you hang out with? Comparing yourself to them is like an addict comparing his coke habit to Keith Richards' and saying 'Wow, that guy is really out of control.'"

"Says the biggest drunk in four counties."

"I may be a drunk, but I'm a damn good one. I have to be to escape this emotional wasteland, you self-absorbed twat."

It's one thing to insult my fiscal responsibility, but cast aspersions on my alcoholism and I'm going to bring the noise. For a moment, Alex looks visibly shaken. But she recovers quickly for one last salvo.

"Why don't you do us all a favor today and get in another car accident? Only this time, make sure it actually does the job. Maybe then, we'll all be better off."

With that, she grabs a brush off the counter and throws it at the mirror over the vanity. With a loud crash, the mirror spiders and a thousand reflections, broken and battered, stare back at us.

By the time I get downstairs, Alex is gone and Claire is headed out the door. I tell her to have a great day but she slams the door behind her without responding, either not hearing me or ignoring me. I'd like to think it's the former, but I am well past deluding myself into believing that my family has anything other than contempt for me. This morning's fight has no doubt reinforced the kids' already dim view of me. Only Jules remains, cheerfully munching on cereal and listening on her iPhone to what sounds like two cheetahs being rhythmically beat to death to a solid bass line. She doesn't look up – how could she? The cheetahs are still a couple of verses away from being put out of their misery – leaving me to rummage through the fridge for something to eat. I settle on an English muffin and an espresso, popping the muffin into the toaster and turning to our $5,000 Jura espresso machine for my morning indulgence.

Alas, there's not coffee in sight, only a Post-It note left behind by Alex.

We need more coffee.
Unless you think we can't afford it.
Asshole.

"Did you get Mom's note?" Jules looks at me expectantly, Requiem for the Cheetah having apparently run its course.

"I thought it was nice. Usually, the 'asshole' is implied."

"Thought you'd like that." She returns to her cereal and dials up another song to bludgeon her eardrums.

I crumple the note into a ball and throw it on the granite counter just as my muffin pops out of the Dualit toaster. I grab the butter out of the Sub Zero and slather it on thick. I'm about to take a bite when I realize I need something to drink, so I pour some orange juice into a glass.

Realizing my mistake, I start laughing.

Jules looks up and eyes me quizzically. She even pauses her iPhone to devote her full attention to what I'm guessing is her desire to witness firsthand her dad (finally) having a breakdown.

"You ever notice that all of our stuff has names?"

She furrows her eyebrow and cocks her head like a dog.

"It's not a glass," I say, holding up my drink. "It's a Simon Pearce tumbler. And if I want more juice, I should probably look in the Sub Zero, not the refrigerator."

"We don't get in the car," she answers thoughtfully. "We jump in the Audi.'"

"Exactly. And you and Claire never get in trouble for putting your shoes on the couch."

"But God forbid if we put our Toms on the Mitchell Gold!"

"Do that, and you can kiss your iPhone goodbye."

It feels good to laugh, even if there is a sadness to it, as though we both know it can't last.

"Are things as bad as you and Mom were saying this morning?"

I look at her mournfully. No ten year-old should have to listen to the vitriol that Alex and I throw each other's way.

"You heard our fight?"

"Don't you mean the frank exchange of ideas?"

I laugh. Alex would never tell the girls we were fighting, even after one of our most vicious screaming matches. Instead, she would always say that Mommy and Daddy were just having a frank exchange of ideas. I love that Jules remembers.

"Things have been better," I admit finally.

"Is it all about money?"

"Things rarely are, sweetheart."

"Are we going to be okay?"

"I imagine you and Claire will be just fine."

"What about you and Mom?"

"We'll figure something out," I say with a shrug. "I'm not sure we have much choice."

"You're pretty good at answering questions without really answering them, you know that?"

I laugh. "With my job, I guess I ought to take that as a compliment."

I clear her cereal bowl and put it in the dishwasher.

"Thanks for putting that in the Bosch for me." My heart breaks a little as she tries to cheer me up. A daughter shouldn't have to do that for her father.

"Come on," I say finally. "I'll drive you to school. We can take the Infiniti." And then I remember that my car has likely been swallowed by one of Mac's automotive torture devices. The only car I can offer my daughter was most likely the scene of a grisly crime not too long ago. So much for providing the best in life for my offspring.

Seeing my eyes cloud over, Jules reaches over and gives me a hug as I try not to cry.

17

Growing up, I tried not to expect too much out of life. It wasn't that I didn't want good things to happen to me. I just knew that good things happened so rarely, it was best not to hope for them. Expect too much out of life and you're bound to be disappointed.

Take Eastern Philosophy and Jenny Nieb, she of the peek-a-boo underwear. Two months into senior year, I was content to spend every third period ignoring the lessons of Rumi, Lao Tzu or Mulla Sadra and focusing all of my efforts on her Jenny's sublime ass. I know it was shortsighted. It would have been far more productive to pay attention and learn a few things that could broaden my horizons as a student and educate me about my place as an inhabitant of this planet.

But in my defense, it was a really, really great ass. And it's not like I was missing out trigonometry or particle physics something that (arguably) could have served me well in the future. This was Eastern Philosophy. I'd be damned if I could figure out what Rumi, Lao Tzu or Mulla Sadra could teach me about how to make a buck in today's world.

Of course, now that I think of it, maybe I missed the point of that class.

The point being, I could have asked Jenny out. I could have taken a chance and moved our relationship beyond a pure stalker-stalkee vibe. Who knows? As much as I loved her body and cherished her posterior, maybe I would have been similarly wowed by her intellect and soulfulness. To my way of thinking, however, that was too much of a risk. Her ass was the bird in the hand for which I was willing to sacrifice access to her bush (or however that saying goes). So I waited. Rather than risk losing everything, I took pleasure where pleasure could be taken and for me, that meant a safe distance of about four-and-a-half feet every third period.

There was a downside to my inaction, of course. By not asking her out, I left open the possibility that someone else would swoop in and do just that. And then where would I be? Actually, I'd be right where I was every day – sitting behind her in Eastern Philosophy wondering where her mom shopped for underwear. And you know what? I was okay with that.

At least, I was until she and I walked out of class together one day that fall. The soccer team had won its first playoff game earlier that week. I was on the team but warmed the bench – as usual – which meant I had a front row seat to watch Kevin rack up a goal and two assists, even setting up the game winner on a gorgeous ball through the teeth of the defense, leaving our striker with nothing to do but tap the ball past the goalie for the win. Wilson High was not known for its sports, so the entire school had lost its mind. Suddenly, school colors were in vogue and banners lined the halls urging students to come to the game the following night to watch our team MAUL MADISON or POUND THE PATRIOTS, or what-ever other alliterative slogan the student government geeks had come up with. Like the rest of the team, I was decked out in my uniform, in part to help get people psyched up for the game but mostly because we thought it was a good way to snag the ladies. Again, it's important to remember that we were teenaged boys, so our thought processes were not yet fully formed (that said, I had managed to hook up with two different girls that postseason, so maybe there was something to the whole fan girl thing. Who was I to quibble with results?).

So there I was, chatting Jenny up with some harmless but patently false horseshit about class ("For our final project, I was thinking about showing how Mohism's theory of impartial care formed the basis of socialism more than two thousand years before Marx's *Das Kapital*. What about you?"), when my brother walked up.

"Hey, Kevin," I said, surprised to see him. His next class was French, which was at the other end of the building. "What's up?"

But he didn't respond. In fact, he didn't even look at me. Instead, he stared right at Jenny with no inkling that I was there. At first, I thought nothing of it. I mean, it was hard not to stare at her. It wasn't until she opened her mouth and responded with a sing-songy "Hey, Kev," that the hair on the back of my neck stood up.

Kev? Who the hell is Kev?

"Hey, Jenny," he cooed. "What's up?"

What's up is that I'm trying to figure out when the hell my brother got the stones to talk to a girl. And not just any girl, mind you, but Jenny Freaking Nieb.

"Nothin'," she cooed back. "Whatcha doin'?"

"Nothin'. What are you doin'?"

Holy lord. These two doe-eyed morons would have gone all day like this. I had to intercede.

"You need something, Kevin?"

My entry into the conversation seemed to stun my brother

back to reality. He looked at me, eyes wide, as if unsure as to how or why I was standing before him.

"Huh?"

That was more like the Kevin I knew. Smart as hell but utterly inarticulate, especially when girls were present. It might have been cute had it not been so pathetic.

"Jenny and I were just talking about our class projects. What's going on with you?"

"I, uh, nothin'."

"Well said."

"I mean, I was just wonderin' if, um, you wanna, you know, like go out sometime."

"Kevin, I'm honored. Really. But as much as I'd like to take our relationship to the next level, I don't think this town is ready for that kind of incest. At the very least, Mom and Dad would have something to say about it."

He laughed nervously as he ran his fingers through his hair and shifted from one foot to the other. He couldn't have been more awkward had he been standing there stark naked.

"Not you," he said with another forced laugh. "You."

He looked at Jenny, who blushed in response and pawed at the dusty floor with her Keds. I was aghast. Unless I was grossly misreading adolescent mating rituals, my brother was asking Jenny out. And this is where it got really weird – she looked like she was about to accept.

What the hell was happening?

"Me?" she asked coyly, tucking a strand of blond hair behind her ear.

Oh, please. This was quickly moving from surprising to nauseating.

"Mm-hmh," Kevin grunted. He couldn't even form words at this point.

In one of the more shameless flirting displays I'd ever seen –

and I took pride in the fact that I'd seen quite a few – Jenny took a step towards my brother and, standing on tiptoes, whispered in this ear. "I'd love to."

And unless I wasn't mistaken, she brushed her lips against his cheek as she pulled away from him. As she practically skipped down the hall, Kevin turned a bright shade of crimson and brought his hand to his cheek, delicately touching the spot where her lips had just been.

Shit. I wasn't mistaken.

I wasn't sure what I was more pissed at: the fact that he had asked her out, the fact that she said yes, or the fact that Kevin and I both struggled to adjust our hard-ons at the way she had said it.

18

I walk into my office with my head down in a vain attempt to hide my increasingly hideous face. I give my assistant a wave, but Diane is too busy munching on Funyuns and catching up on TMZ to notice. I hang my jacket behind the door and toss my bag onto the couch. I'm in the process of firing up the laptop so I can check the morning clips when Naomi barges in.

"Can you believe it?"

"By all means, come in," I say without looking up.

"Hard to imagine, given your crack security team," she answers snidely.

"Diane?" I ask, still fumbling with my computer. "She's not the world's best gatekeeper, I grant you."

"If you weren't such a pussy, you'd fire her ass."

"That would mean getting H.R. involved and believe me, it's not worth the effort."

I finish entering my fifth log-in ID and password and finally look up.

"Jesus Christ!"

"What?"

"Your face! It's getting worse!"

"Really? I hadn't noticed."

"So the accident affected your sight, too?"

"You come in here to bust my balls or for something else?"

"I came in to talk about the clips. Busting your balls is just a bonus."

"How are they?"

"How are what?"

"The clips."

"Haven't you seen them?" she asks incredulously.

"I was about to take a look," I say, nodding at my inert computer.

"Are you shitting me? I sent them to you four hours ago."

"What time is it?"

"Almost nine."

"Jesus. Do you sleep?"

"It's called doing my job. You should try it."

"Why bother when I've got you?"

"What's that supposed to mean?" she asks, a little too defensively.

"How about you openly gunning for my job for the last five months?"

"Have I been that obvious?"

"Subtlety was never your strong suit."

"Yeah, but I thought I was hiding it better this time."

"H.R. called last week wanting to know whether I had set a departure date."

She winces. "They weren't supposed to do that."

"Oh really?" Finally, I have found something to cheer me up. I'm genuinely enjoying watching her squirm. "What were they supposed to do?"

"There *may* have been a hypothetical conversation about

what would happen if – and I do mean *if* – you decided to leave. They should not have called you."

"That's okay. But that reminds me. Facilities called asking what color drapes you want once you move in here."

"They didn't."

"They did indeed."

She is mortified. This is going even better than I expected.

"I'm sorry, Sean. Everyone got out a little too far over their skis on this one."

"Some would say the same thing about you."

"I just wanted to understand whether there was a succession plan in the event you leave, Sean. There's nothing nefarious going on."

"I see. You are aware that most succession plans are not put in place by the successor, right?"

"I'm ambitious, Sean. I make no bones about that."

"Nor should you. I mean, we're already fucking. Why not fuck me over as well?"

"That's not fair," she says defensively.

"Oh no? And here I thought undermining your boss was frowned upon."

"Are you shitting me? It's practically part of the corporate culture around here."

"So you're not looking for me to leave?"

"I'm not pushing you out the door, if that's what you're asking."

"Just making sure the door is open in case someone else does the pushing?"

"Can you blame me?" She smiles impishly and I remember suddenly why we're sleeping together.

"So how are the clips?" I ask, our little dance having played itself out.

"Fucking brilliant."

"Naomi, you're among friends. You can dispense with the modesty."

"Go on," she says, ignoring me and handing me her iPhone, "take a look. I defy you to read that and not get hard."

I scroll through the clips. While not sexually arousing, they are pretty terrific. In fact, we killed it. In market after market, there are glowing newspaper articles, op-eds and evening news hits. In most cases, we have all three. It's enough to make someone believe Infirmus actually cares about its patients.

I take it back. I am getting hard.

"Has Williams seen these?"

"I had Diane send them to him from your email account."

"Looking out for your boss? Naomi, I'm touched."

"Chalk it up to a moment of weakness. Besides, I had just finished diddling myself. I wasn't thinking straight."

"I'm starting to worry about you. Do you have anything in your life other than work and sex?"

"No," she answers without a trace of irony. "Does anyone?"

I go back to the clips and notice there's only one market missing.

"I don't see anything local in here."

"I left that one out," she says, taking the phone back. She makes a few swipes and then hands it back to me. I watch as the Channel Five News chyron fills the screen and my heart skips a beat.

"How bad?"

"Just watch."

An impeccably coiffed man with impossibly white teeth fills the screen. His tie is knotted perfectly and there is not a wrinkle to be seen on his shirt, suit or face. He opens his mouth and it sounds like a cello is making sweet, sweet love with a French horn. It's gorgeous. He's gorgeous.

"Is he taken?" I ask.

"Trust me, you couldn't handle him."

I raise my eyebrow but know better than to question her. Instead, I look back at the screen.

"Now we take a look at a local company that's looking to single-handedly change the way we think about healthcare – sometimes with surprising results. For that, we turn to Jane Collins and tonight's HealthBeat. Jane—"

"Thanks Vance...

My new least favorite local TV reporter fills the screen and I inhale sharply, trying to brace myself.

"At nearly 3.5 trillion dollars, it's no secret that U.S. healthcare spending is spiraling out of control. But even though nearly one out of every five dollars spent each year in this country is used for healthcare, it is not clear that Americans are getting their money's worth. In fact, most U.S. health outcomes are not demonstrably better than many other industrialized nations. And in several key categories – including life expectancy and infant mortality – the U.S. is well below the international average, leading many experts to ask, is it time to do things differently?

"At least one local company thinks it is. And they think they've found the cure to what ails us. By focusing on the total health of the patient instead of an individual episode of care, Infirmus Health, based right here in our own backyard, thinks it can not only help patients feel better, but also reduce how much it costs to care for them. To learn more, we went out to an Infirmus dialysis clinic in Arlington."

The scene shifts from the studio to the inside of our dialysis clinic. Jesus, was that only yesterday? It feels like ages ago. We see patients sitting in treatment chairs getting dialyzed as nurses and care techs flit about. As I look at what almost looks like a professional operation, I hear Jane's voice.

"Half a million Americans suffer from kidney failure, leaving them only two options for survival: a kidney transplant or regular dialysis.

Given the lack of available kidneys, the vast majority of these Americans – over 400,000, in fact – come to a center like this one three times a week to receive dialysis."

The camera zooms in on an elderly black lady in a treatment chair who is knitting a blanket while a red tube snakes out of her arm into a dialysis machine.

"Because their kidneys have failed, dialysis patients are unable to urinate, leaving excess fluid and toxins to build up in their bloodstream. For nearly four hours a session, three times a week, patients are hooked up to a machine to remove that excess fluid and toxins. Without dialysis, none of these patients would survive."

We cut to an older man, with a tight crewcut and a facial sore, who sits in his chair during dialysis. A kind-looking, if overweight, Hispanic nurse stands beside him.

"I know I can't live without it," he says. *"But that don't make it easy. Most days, I go home feeling like I've just been run over by a truck. Still, it's a blessing. Without people like Carmelita,"* he says with a nod to the nurse, *"I wouldn't be alive."* Carmelita smiles beatifically.

"Nearly 90 percent of dialysis patients in America are treated at centers like this one," Jane's voiceover continues. *"And many observers argue that there has been precious little in the way of innovation in recent years. But the people here at Infirmus Health—"* the camera cuts to the sign on the outside of the clinic – *"are trying to change all that."*

Images of an ambulance with its lights flashing and a busy hospital emergency room flash across the screen.

"For too many people, the American healthcare system is confusing and disjointed. It can be particularly harrowing for dialysis patients, who average almost two hospital visits each year and take more than nine prescription medications on any given day. With so many specialists involved in their care – from nephrologists to cardiol-

ogists to endocrinologists – just trying to coordinate all of their appointments can be overwhelming."

The man with the crew cut returns to the screen. "*Sometimes, it can be too much. I go to one doctor, and he says 'Here's what we're going to do.' Trouble is, another doctor tells me the complete opposite the next day. I know everyone is trying their hardest, but it sure would be easier if they could all just talk to each other.*"

Cut to the knitting grandmother. "*It's like they expect me to be the one to keep everything straight. It doesn't help that, half the time, I have no idea what anyone is saying!*"

For the first time, we see Jane inside the dialysis clinic. She does the classic Walk and Talk routine, speaking directly to the camera as she saunters amiably through the clinic floor.

"*Here at Infirmus, they're trying something new. With their CompleteCare program, Infirmus physicians and caregivers adopt a more holistic approach. For example, rather than focus solely on dialysis, Infirmus clinics are also taking care of their patients' primary care needs. That means fewer trips to a doctor's office and less burden on the system as a whole. And Infirmus is putting their money where their mouth is. Working with the government and commercial insurers, Infirmus is creating new payment models where they don't make a dime unless the total cost of care for their patients is reduced.*"

"Do we actually do any of that?" Naomi asks skeptically.

"I dunno. I fed her the usual crap during the pitch about integrated care. I even waxed poetic about that government pilot we won last year. But I didn't think she was listening."

"*According to a company spokesman, initial results have been positive—*"

"Is that right?" Naomi asks archly.

"As far as you know."

"*—but it hasn't been without a few bumps in the road.*"

"Here we go." I look at Naomi but she gives nothing away.

"*The federal government recently announced a quality program that ranks dialysis clinics according to an easy to use star system – five stars for the best clinics and one star for the worst. The idea is to give patients and families more information about their clinics so they can make the best decision possible about their care. Of course, not all dialysis providers are thrilled with the system, including Infirmus."*

With that, the scene shifts to a man with salt and pepper hair and way too much make-up standing in front of the clinic. He looks like he once might have been handsome but he's got no sharp edges and it's clear that his best years are behind him. It's only when I see the words "Sean Reilly, Infirmus Spokesman" plastered beneath the man that I realize I'm staring at me.

"Fuck me."

"I've tried," Naomi answers. "You wouldn't like it."

"Cute."

"We are on record describing the numerous methodological flaws in the so-called Star Rating system," the screen version of me says. *"And we are not alone. Countless others in the industry – from patient groups to physicians to other providers – have been saying for years that this program is flawed."*

We cut to Jane at the end of her Walk and Talk inside the clinic. *"This Infirmus clinic received only one star under the government's latest rankings. And there have been allegations of medical malpractice at other Infirmus facilities that have led to serious adverse events, including death. But every one of the patients we interviewed here gave the clinic high marks for the staff and their attention to detail. So it's possible that the company's objections may have merit. And when asked directly about the other quality concerns, Mr. Reilly had this to say."*

Cut to me back in front of the clinic.

"No one is perfect. But that doesn't mean we can't still strive for perfection. Have we gotten there yet? Unfortunately not. But we're trying. We owe it to each and every one of our patients to be better. To

do better. And to treat you as we would treat our own family. Because that's who you are. You're family."

We cut back to Jane and Vance in the studio, who look distinctly like they just got back from the editing room after sneaking out for a quickie. Jane wraps up.

"And when you get right down to it, that single concept may end up being what determines whether Infirmus is successful in their audacious endeavor. Fixing the U.S. healthcare system will be a long journey, but by treating their patients like family, Infirmus hopes they can get one step closer. Vance..."

The screen fades to black. I look up at Naomi. I'm in shock.

"That's it?"

"Are you kidding? It's terrific. What more could you want?"

"Nothing. It's just that ... I'm surprised. I didn't think the interview went all that well."

"It didn't."

"No, it didn't."

"No, I mean I wasn't asking if it went well. I know it didn't."

"Yeah, 'cause I told you."

"That and because Jane sent me this late last night." She makes another swipe on her phone and hands it back to me.

It's a rough cut of our interview and I see me staring angrily at the camera.

"We stand by our quality." I sound like a sociopath copping to rape and murder charges on the grounds that the woman enjoyed herself. Off camera, Jane says that data suggests that our quality is substandard and I hear myself say it again. *"We stand by our quality."* This time I sound like I'm about to rape and murder the reporter, which I was.

Well, the murder part, anyway.

"Is size the problem?"

"I've never had any complaints..."

Mercifully, the screen goes black and I hand the phone back to Naomi.

"Told you it was bad," I say weakly.

"When you flame out, you flame out *hard*," she says with a laugh.

"Why didn't she include any of it? She could have destroyed me. Destroyed the company."

"She didn't say. All she said in the message was that I should tell you that she's come to terms with her inner bobblehead. That make any sense to you?"

I laugh the laugh of a condemned man who's just received a stay of execution. I'm not dead but that doesn't mean I'm innocent. "Just that she's about to get a lot more airtime on Channel Five."

"Williams and Tim have this as well," Naomi says, waving her phone. "I sent it to them separately so they wouldn't miss it. It's the best piece of press we've gotten in ages."

"Dumb fucking luck."

"Don't tell them that."

"Not a chance in hell."

Diane pokes her head in and says Williams wants to see me upstairs.

Naomi waits for Diane to go back to her desk and then asks, "You going up there now?"

"I go when beckoned," I answer. "Something wrong with that?

"It's just that…"

"Spit it out Naomi. You were never good at being coy."

She laughs. "You may want to do something about that face before you go up there. You really do look like something out of a horror movie."

Now it's my turn to laugh, though my nose throbs with each breath. "How the hell do you propose I do that?"

"I've got some cover-up in my office. You could try that."

"Naomi, my dear. There's a certain freedom that comes from not giving a fuck. That includes not having to don makeup when meeting with your boss."

"When did you gain this newfound perspective?"

I shrug. "Let's just say, I'm not living for the long term."

"Carpe diem?"

"Something like that."

"Whatever it is, enjoy the accolades."

"They're as much yours as they are mine."

"You better believe it, which is why you better share some of that fat bonus you're about to get."

"Are you kidding? The only people the C-suite gives bonuses to are other people in the C-suite."

"You're the hot piece of ass right now. Use it while you got it."

"Isn't that your theory of life?"

"Damn straight." She lifts up her blouse and I see she's not wearing a bra. She looks at me brazenly for a beat and then turns to walk out the door, leaving me to wonder why life keeps repeating itself.

And trying to remember how to breathe.

19

Things turned out different once Kevin and Jenny started dating. Not necessarily bad, mind you, just different. Whereas our respective specialties had been pretty well established – I did well with girls; Kevin did better at everything else – those lines blurred significantly once his relationship with Jenny bloomed. Similarly, our relationship with our parents changed.

My father had always been aloof and distant with me, but effusive and doting with my brother. But once Jenny entered the picture, my dad's behavior changed subtly. He still went on and on about how great Kevin was; in fact, now that Kevin had demonstrated prowess with the fairer sex, Dad wouldn't shut up about it. It was a little off-putting, I have to tell you, to hear my dad brag about what a piece of ass his son's girlfriend was. True, but off-putting. But with me, Dad was different. Once he saw Kevin succeed where only I had shown promise, his aloofness with me seemed less personal. It's hard to explain, but he almost seemed to take pity on me, as if now that my singular advantage over my brother had evaporated, it was no longer good sport to overtly favor Kevin over me. Thankfully, Mom seemed the same;

she continued to dote on Kevin and me both as fervently as ever. The terms on which she loved her sons remained unconditional and unmoved. Not so for Dad.

As for Kevin and me, we muddled through. Fact is, while there was always a sibling rivalry between the two of us, we always remained brothers. When it mattered most, I knew he would have my back and he knew I would have his. Sure, it was a blow to my ego that Kevin was able to add lady-killer to his already crowded resume but, to be honest, I was proud of him. It took balls for him to ask Jenny out. I couldn't do it. I just had to swallow hard and deal.

Not that it was all sunshine and roses. Every time Jenny came over to the house was a swift kick in the groin. Kevin would open the door to reveal Jenny in all her perky glory, and the two of them would retreat to his room to "study." The only saving grace was they had the good form to keep whatever else they were doing back there extremely quiet. Not once did I hear the thump of a headboard or a stray cry of passion, and for that I was incredibly grateful.

And as long as we're being honest, I have the two of them to thank for a far more productive senior year. As frustrating as it was to see Jenny and Kevin retreat to his room each day, I had to come up with ways to channel that frustration, especially since there are only so many times a kid can surreptitiously beat off to his brother's girlfriend in the hall bathroom (add the complicating factor of having my brother's face constantly pop up in my fantasies, and you can see why I needed a different outlet. Quickly.). I dabbled in TV and videogames, but was shocked to discover that constructive pursuits – like homework – fit the bill better than anything else. For hours, I could lose myself in calculus or physics Faulkner and not once think of how much I'd give to swap places with Kevin.

Sports also helped. I'd go outside and practice my jump shot in the driveway or throw the lacrosse ball against the pitchback for so long that I'd often be surprised to see Jenny waving goodbye as she walked out the front door on her way home. But I don't think anyone was as taken aback as my teachers and coaches. To a person, they were dumbfounded to see my grades shoot upward and my performance on the basketball court and lacrosse field improve markedly. I wasn't winning any scholarships, mind you, but I was suddenly a reliable option, good for a right answer in class or a few minutes of solid playing time to rest the starters.

Even my parents were impressed. Well, Mom was, anyway. Every time I would show her a grade, she was effusive in her praise. Dad? He was more muted. In customary fashion, he would do his best to ignore me. Only when that became absolutely impossible would he grudgingly look at the report card. In years past, that had been met with a frown and a shake of the head. But that winter and spring, he usually raised one eyebrow and nodded his head slowly. For him, that was high praise. I was so happy, I couldn't sleep for a week.

All in all, I had no complaints. Not only had I dealt with the supreme disappointment of watching my crush date my brother instead of me, I had come out the better for it. I was growing. I was maturing. I was becoming a better human being.

And then April 19 happened.

It was a beautiful spring day, the brilliant blue sky auguring warm weather to come. I took advantage by whizzing a lacrosse ball against the pitchback in the front yard, working on my off-hand cradle and mixing in a few razzle-dazzle behind-the-back throws for good measure. I must have been out there for over an hour when I saw Jenny coming out of the house. She didn't look as good as usual – come on, who am I kidding? She looked fantastic. Still, something was off. She didn't have the usual skip in her step. So after a few more behind the back passes (impressive) and something that was supposed to be a fake pass followed by a 180-degree spin but was instead something more like an epileptic seizure followed by a 90-degree spin, trip and fall to the ground (decidedly less impressive), I put the lacrosse on hold and walked over to see how she was doing.

"Hey," I said, casually dusting dirt and grass clippings off my shirt.

"Hey," she said softly.

"You guys done ... studying?" I figured I'd be a team player and stick to the script.

"Yeah."

We stood there looking at each other like idiots. Actually, that's not fair. She looked like a normal, if slightly somber high school student. I, on the other hand, looked like an idiot.

"Hope it was ... productive." Productive? What the hell did that mean? *Hey, Jenny, I hope making out with my brother was productive. Hope it progressed to some heavy petting and a happy ending for Kev.* What happened to the Sean Reilly who had game? Christ, I was an idiot around this girl.

She didn't respond. Instead, she looked into the distance, her face hard to read. "Just once," she said finally, "I wish we didn't actually study so much."

"That's my brother," I said with a forced laugh, hoping like hell my brother's girlfriend didn't just tell me he wasn't putting out. "Ever the diligent student."

"I try to fool around," she pouted, "but all he ever wants to do is study."

I couldn't believe this conversation was happening, though at least I finally understood why everything was always so quiet back in his room.

"Uh, have you tried telling him any of this?"

"I practically throw myself at him but nothing works."

"Maybe he's just missing the signals," I offered lamely. "Kevin's never been good at reading people.

"I took my shirt off today but he just stared at me like I was a cancer patient. Then he turned away and started doing more math problems."

I swallowed hard, partly because I felt bad for Kevin, who was clearly in way over his head, but mostly because I now had the image of a half-naked Jenny Nieb seared on my brain.

"I'm sure he didn't mean anything by it."

"That's the problem! He never means to do anything."

"Kevin's shy," I explained. "He's probably still trying to figure out how all this dating stuff is supposed to work."

"Well, he better figure it out quick because I'm not going to wait around forever."

Ugh. Poor Kevin.

"You headed home?" I asked, anxious for this conversation to be over.

"Yeah. Unless..." She looked down sheepishly at her Keds.

"Unless what?"

Jenny looked up at me and curled a strand of hair behind her ear.

Wait a second. I'd seen that move before. These were the same flirtatious shenanigans she pulled on Kevin, right before he asked her out. What was next? The whole whisper in my ear and brush her lips across my cheek thing? This harlot had some nerve dating my brother and flirting with me. Some nerve indeed.

I just hoped I wasn't drooling.

"Unless *you* want to do something..."

This girl wasn't playing fair. Not one bit. I had to watch myself.

"I can't," I replied with a nod to my lacrosse stick. "I have to work on my shot." Nice one. Simple, straight-forward with the added benefit of being true. Let's see you come back from that, you little strumpet.

"Oh, okay. Maybe we can hang out some other time. I'll let you work on anything you'd like." Before I could respond, she leaned in close and whispered in my ear. "Anything."

As she pulled away, her lips brushed up against my cheek and she giggled softly. Then she looked at me brazenly and said, "Maybe you'll think of something to do with these."

She lifted her shirt. She wasn't wearing a bra. My chest tightened and my breathing stopped. Good lord, I never realized reality could be better than imagination.

As she turned and walked down the driveway, I thought of defending my brother's honor by indignantly rejecting her overture, but opted instead to silently recite my multiplication tables in the hopes that the swelling in my pants would subside and I could go inside for dinner.

20

A fter Naomi leaves and the shock of being flashed by a beautiful woman for the second time in twenty-six years wears off, I still have to give myself a minute to let my heart rate and hard-on subside. Finally, with a deep breath, I get on the elevator for the ride up to the fourteenth floor. I take out my phone to send Jane a well-deserved thank you.

> I owe you big time

She must be glued to her phone because she writes back instantly.

Goddamn right u do

> U had me by the balls.
> Why let me off the hook?

Bobblehead anchors make
more $$$ than investigative

journos

No Dan Rather for you?

Fuck that shit

Anchors do happy stories
not mean ones

The door opens and I follow a nervous intern down the hall. It must be his first time on fourteen because he is trembling noticeably. He should try not giving a fuck. I turn back to my conversation with Jane, taking an inordinate amount of joy knowing that I'm breaking some unwritten rule by walking and texting at the same time in these hallowed halls.

You making a play
for the desk?

I'm not sucking Vance's
dick for nothing

HA! It looked like you guys
had been messing around
when the piece cut back to
the studio

U noticed? LOL

It wasn't subtle

I never am

> Thx again. Lemme know
> how I can pay u back

Don't u know never
to be indebted to member
of the press?

> I like to live on the edge

Careful – I'll be sucking
your dick next

I laugh out loud and draw stern looks from most of the secretaries. Jesus, the matrons of the executive suite need to get laid.

I head to Williams' office but his secretary redirects me back to the conference room. Apparently, I don't rate a visit to his private sanctuary just yet. I open the door and see that he and Tim are waiting for me.

"I see your face hasn't improved." Williams chuckles good-naturedly. I'm glad I'm a never ceasing source of enjoyment for him. The gift that keeps on giving.

"Mildly better than yesterday, sir."

"Could have fooled me. Not that it seems to have had any impact on you. What you and your team have accomplished this week has been nothing short of remarkable."

"That Channel Five piece last night was a work of genius," Tim adds.

"Genius enough to merit a bonus?"

Williams laughs even harder, this time with feeling. "That accident may have wrecked your face, but it clearly didn't impact your balls!"

I'm putting that down as a hard no.

"I'm glad the piece worked out," I say, changing the subject.

"It was phenomenal," Williams gushes, his broad smile still plastered in place. His veneers really are flawless. If I was going to stick around – and if I had any money – I'd ask his secretary for his dentist's number. "That kind of story shows us exactly as we are – a company trying to do the right thing. How you got them to focus on that integrated care bullshit is beyond me. Increasing quality and lowering costs. Jesus, we came off like saints! That reminds me – do we even have something called CompleteCare?"

Tim answers. "It's a pilot with the feds and some of our private payers. Nothing big – just a few of our centers. Capitated payments based on total cost of care, that sort of thing. The profit margins will be smaller than our traditional fee-for-service business, but we view it as a chance to get our toes wet in the move towards value-based care. But again, we're keeping it small."

"With lower margins? Let's hope it stays that way!" Williams says with another laugh.

His disdain for the program is comically predictable. Our dialysis business is obscenely profitable, as he was so helpful in pointing out yesterday. By accepting capitated payments – essentially, getting reimbursed for how we perform against a patient's expected total cost of care, whether due to dialysis, a hip fracture or a hangnail – we are assuming all of the financial risk of that patient's healthcare needs. Reduce costs against a predetermined spending baseline and we get to keep the savings. But if we have a particularly sick patient with higher than expected costs, we will lose money. In other words, we are effectively becoming an insurance company for the patients treated at centers in the pilot program. Williams' gripe, no doubt, is that insurance companies have profit margins of three or four percent, whereas our traditional dialysis business generates margins many times that. Looking at his insincere smile, it's clear what he's thinking: *Greater good, my ass.*

"That said," Tim chimes in, "we certainly can't argue with the press it's generated."

"True," Williams answers, "but I'll take a couple of hundred million in extra profit over a blowjob from some reporter any day of the week."

I shrug. "Depends on the blowjob, I guess."

Williams eyes me. "Do you have any idea how many blowjobs two hundred million bucks will get you?"

I'm feeling frisky, so I figure what the hell. "I'm sure you know better than me, but I'll take a shot." The withering glare Williams shoots me is worth it in and of itself. Still, I press on. "A lot depends on geography. Take New York. I'm guessing a high-class escort in Manhattan will run you a thousand minimum. But your run of the mill Brooklyn whore might go for as little as fifty bucks. The price points are significantly different. So that's..." I pause, doing the math in my head.

"Three point eight million more hummers in Brooklyn than Manhattan," Tim interjects. It's my turn to whip my head around in surprise. Tim's face is impassive, but I swear there's a glint of enjoyment in his eyes.

"As long as we're arbitraging fellatio," Williams chimes in, "we could significantly up the spread if we go with the Staten Island ten dollar special." I admit it, I'm stunned. Who knew these guys had a sense of humor?

"All do respect, sir, that's a huge hit in quality. I'm all for slumming it from time to time, but you have to ask yourself, is it worth it?"

"It's an extra nineteen point eight million blowjobs," Tim says, as if to sweeten the pot.

"I don't know about you guys," I respond, "but sometimes less is more."

"Only sometimes," Williams says. He's smiling, but the coldness in his eyes signals that the time for joking has ended. It's tempting to think that we are developing a bit of rapport, but there is no question that, when the chips are down, he'll cut me to pieces and sell me for scrap. A shiver goes up my spine as Tim turns back to business.

Tim picks up on his boss' cue. "We've asked you here, Sean, because the recent good press may have given us an opportunity."

"Indeed." Williams' deep baritone is back. "As you know, we are facing the prospect of some rather serious litigation."

"In the case of Mrs. Wheeler—" Tim begins.

I look at him quizzically and he rolls his eyes at my ignorance. "The widow of the patient allegedly killed by removal of the wrong leg. She has actually filed suit. You may recall that she has been rather aggressive in taking her claims to the press. In the case of Mrs. Swanson—"

I look at him quizzically again and he is disgusted with me once more.

"The widow of the patient killed by mistaken identity. Allegedly. She has not yet filed suit. We think she wants to negotiate a big settlement before incurring significant legal fees. But there's no doubt she'll file as soon as it looks like we won't deal."

"Clearly, it is not in our best interest for either case to proceed," Williams adds needlessly. "Trouble is, the Swanson woman doesn't seem to be the least bit interested in settling. It's as if this is her own personal jihad."

I can't imagine why. I mean, we only killed her husband.

"She's definitely got religion on this one," he continues. "And the other one ... what's her name ... Wheeler...?"

I'm no stickler, but I think it's good form to remember the name of the woman who is about to fleece you for millions.

"Yes, sir."

"Well, whatever her name is, it looks like she's holding out for a number that simply isn't reasonable."

Because reasonable is definitely what this case is all about. Because reasonable is what we were all about when we dialyzed a man who wasn't our patient.

"The bottom line," Tim continues, "is that negotiations with both women are at a particularly sensitive juncture."

"Meaning they've got us by the balls."

"It would seem so," Tim concedes.

"So where do I come in?"

"Sean," Williams says, laying on the benevolent paternal baritone a little too thick, "you are the lynchpin to getting these women to see reason."

"I beg your pardon?"

"You worked your magic with the press the last twenty-four hours, burnishing our image to a high gloss. If you can that, I can't think of anyone better to convince the two widows to accept our very generous offer."

"Which is?"

"Two hundred thousand dollars and the standard waiver of claims," says Tim.

"And a promise never to open their mouths again," adds Williams.

"Let me get this straight," I say, shaking my head. "You want me to look these women in the eye and tell them we fucked up. Tell them our staff was both moronic and reckless—"

"You should stay away from making any kind of legal conclusion," Tim cautions. "That could be deemed an admission, which we definitely want to avoid."

I ignore Tim, else I'm going to slug him. "—and that we killed their husbands."

"That's definitely something to steer clear of," Tim persists.

"But despite this raging incompetence and appalling disregard for human life," I continue, "I can't admit that we did anything wrong. Oh, and I'm also going to insist these women drop all of their claims and not utter a single word about this to anyone for as long as they both shall live. Do I have that right?"

Before they can answer, I press on.

"And then, you want me to tell them – presumably with a straight face – that in exchange for absolving us of guilt and keeping their cakeholes shut, we're going to pay them a measly two hundred thousand?"

"Phrase it however you want," Williams says, "but that's about the size of it."

I hear him but I don't believe him.

"You want me to tell them –face to face – that they're husband's lives were worth as little as that?"

"There's your bonus, P.R. man," Williams says wickedly as he rises and walks over to a credenza where he has set up a make-shift bar. Damn if the fucker didn't get me on that one. His back is to me as he makes himself a drink. It's a little early, but I'm not judging. In fact, I find myself hoping he's making one for me as well.

"Mr. Williams," I say, trying to keep my voice in check, "if you need me to meet with these women, I will. I'll put on my best face—"

"Not easy to do in your current circumstances," Williams says, clinking another cube of ice into his glass. The old man is just full of witty asides this morning.

"—and convey our heartfelt condolences at their loss. I'll express our sympathy that such a horrible thing happened to such good people. But at the risk of overstepping my bounds, sir, I really think we need to reconsider what we're offering them. Our incompetence tore these women's lives apart. The least we can do is give them something meaningful, something that will help ease the pain. But what we're offering ... well, frankly, sir, it's an insult."

Williams turns and eyes me coldly. The man who was joking around a few moments ago is gone. In his place is the same clear-headed and cold-hearted businessman I saw in this same conference room two days ago. I can't see him, but I can feel Tim shifting uncomfortably in his seat.

"You know, Sean," Williams says evenly as he clinks the ice in his glass of what looks like bourbon. "Technology is a funny thing. It's made a lot of things a lot easier. Whether it's a device in our pocket with the computing power of something that would have filled a room fifty years ago, or a doctor performing laser surgery to give someone the gift of sight, we are doing things today that were completely unimaginable just a few years ago. Banking is the same way. You can go anywhere in the world, stick a stick a piece of plastic in a machine, and money comes out. Think of that! Think how easy technology has made people's lives."

He pauses to take a sip. I don't know where he is going with this non sequitur, but it can't be good. And I know better than to interrupt him.

"And yet, for all the convenience that technology has given us, there is a downside. There has to be, right? I mean, nothing comes for free. There's always a price to be paid. Always."

Here we go.

"As wonderful as technology is, it has made us forget who we are. Look at any kid on the street and, chances are, they've got their head buried in their phone. They could be standing in front of one of the world's seven natural wonders and they'd miss it. Shit, I bet if had a naked supermodel shake her tits right in front of sixteen year-old boy's face, he wouldn't flinch. He'd be too busy tapping away on Snapchat or Instagram to even take notice.

"I remember, back when I started out, we used to get real paychecks. I still remember getting my first one. It was only a couple hundred dollars, but man, I felt like a millionaire. I remember opening that envelope and staring at the check for what felt like hours. I had done a job that I loved and they paid me for it. How much better could it get?

"But today? Today you don't even get a check. Instead, money is automatically deposited into your account. You don't get the satisfaction of holding the check and seeing in black and white what your labor has been worth. You don't get to flip it over, endorse it with your signature and hand it over to the bank teller so she can deposit it in your account. And you definitely don't get to stare at the bottom of the check and see who values your time and effort so much that they're willing to sign their name and pay you for your trouble.

"Don't believe me? I'll prove it. Do you know who signs your paycheck?"

I wait, unsure if this is a rhetorical question.

"Do you?" he asks again.

Damn. An actual question.

"Uh, no sir," I stammer. "I don't."

"You've never even seen your paycheck, have you?"

"No, sir, I haven't."

"That's a shame," he says earnestly, sipping his drink. "It really is." He puts the glass on the conference table and takes a step towards me. His voice is lower, with an undercurrent of menace. "Because if you had seen it, you would have noticed that it's *my* signature on the bottom of your paycheck. And do you know what that means?"

I take a chance and answer. "It means you're the boss."

"You're goddamned right I am," he snarls. "It means you do whatever the fuck I tell you to do, understand? I don't give a flying fuck what you think of our settlement offer. In fact, I don't care what you think about anything. You're here only because I allow it. And when I get tired of you, you'll be out on your ass so fast, your head will spin. So do yourself a favor, Sean. Stop thinking for yourself and just do what the fuck I tell you to do. You understand?"

"I think so, sir," I mumble.

"Do you?" His snarl has turned into a growl.

"Yes, sir," I answer, louder this time.

"Good. Now, don't you fucking forget it."

He turns and walks out the door. I look at Tim, who musters a conciliatory smile.

"Why don't you come to my office for a bit?"

Sensing I don't have a choice, I follow him out the door. As we walk down the hall to his office, secretaries peer over their cubicles for a look. Word has traveled fast: Williams the Magnificent has crushed another minion's soul into dust. The Fourteenth Floor vultures want to spy the carcass before they feed.

"Try to ignore them," Tim says quietly, reading my mind. "Reacting only spins them into more of a frenzy."

We walk the rest of the way in silence. I follow Tim into his office and he mercifully closes the door behind me.

"Grab a seat."

I flop down on the microfiber couch. "What the fuck am I doing here?"

Tim doesn't bother answering. Instead, he walks to the bar behind his desk and pours two glasses of something that I hope isn't water. He returns with two crystal tumblers of bourbon that look to be a doubles, if not triples. He hands one to me and sits in a wing chair facing me. I take a healthy pull and revel as the bourbon burns its way down.

"Bless you."

"I figure you earned it after that meeting."

"Is it possible to survive this place without alcohol?"

"If it is, I wouldn't know," he answers.

"You never struck me as the drinking type."

"I try not to start before noon. By the time I have my first, you're usually too drunk to notice."

"It's that obvious?"

He laughs. "There are alcoholics and then there's you."

"Momma always said, if you're going to do something, do it well," I say, raising the glass in a toast.

"You mind if I ask you a question, Sean?"

"Shoot."

"You seem profoundly unhappy. Are you okay?"

I don't know how to respond. The answer, by any objective measure, is a resounding 'no,' but I can't see how responding truthfully will get me anywhere. Tim is a decent guy and all – notwithstanding the dead fish handshake and the complete lack of interpersonal skills – but he's not high on what you'd call the warm and fuzzies. Not that I'm looking for emotional support, mind you, least of all from a silver-haired automaton like Tim. But I'm not sure where this conversation would go or how it can help me.

To buy some time, I try taking another swig of my drink, relishing the numbness as it seeps through my veins, but Tim sees through my ploy immediately.

"I know I'm probably the last guy you'd want to talk to about this."

"You're forgetting about Williams."

"Yeah," Tim says with a laugh, "though if it makes you feel any better, he's too busy schtupping one of his young assistants to care."

"It doesn't."

"Figured."

We both take a sip and ponder our drinks.

"You never answered my question," he says finally.

"I was hoping you wouldn't notice."

"I don't have any young assistants to distract me," he answered with a smile.

I pause a moment to consider whether to tell the truth or just gloss over everything. Fuck it. He asked.

"No, Tim, I'm not okay. I'm about as far away from okay as one man can be. I've got a wife who loathes me, a mistress who's using me and a dick that can't seem to please either of them. I've got two daughters who don't respect me, let alone love me, and a building full of co-workers who don't value me. My wife spends money like a Kardashian only without the multimillion-dollar income, so I don't have two nickels to rub together. In fact, I've got so much debt my children's children will be born in hock and I'm pretty sure my financial advisor has a problem with the ponies. My car is totaled, my nose is broken and I just got rail-roaded into trying to convince two women to accept an insultingly small bribe to keep quiet about how we killed their husbands through colossal incompetence. Oh, and did I mention that this unenviable task falls to me because the top executives at the company are too chickenshit to do it themselves?"

"Is that all?"

"I don't have a dog."

He looks surprised. "Would it help if you did?"

"Fuck no. It would probably just shit in my shoes."

He laughs. "And you don't think you're being just a little melodramatic?"

"Not by a long shot, Tim. And that's just my personal life. To top it all off, this company is going down the shitter and no one seems to give a fuck."

"That's a bit much," he says, an edge creeping into his voice.

"No, it's not. The *Times* is going to come down on this place, Tim. And when it does, countless government investigations will follow. We will be Public Enemy Number One and there won't be a damn soul coming to our rescue. We'll be lucky if Congress doesn't pass a law slashing our Medicare rates to nothing." I pause to sip my drink. "Don't Williams and the rest of them understand that all that good press we got this week is illusory? Once the facts come out, we're toast."

"They think you can make it go away."

"Are they insane?"

"They prefer optimistic."

"Okay, let's say they're right. Let's say, against all evidence to the contrary, I'm able to waive my magic pixie dust and make it all disappear. What then? Is Williams going to change anything? Is he going to invest back in the business and improve things out in the field, or is he going to keep lining the pockets of stockholders and the senior execs to the detriment of patients?"

Tim's silence is all the confirmation I need.

"Nothing will change, Tim. Not a goddamned thing. It doesn't matter what anyone says – not you and certainly not me. I think the only way people around here start paying attention is if someone slaps cuffs on them and says, 'You have the right to remain silent.'"

We are both quiet for a moment as we let this sink in. I don't think either of us is surprised this is where the conversation has led, but that doesn't make it any easier to hear.

"I don't know how you do it, Tim," I say finally.

"Do what?"

"Live with this place. You're surrounded by refuse. Absolute garbage. How do you put up with it?"

He ponders his drink for a moment then looks me square in the eye. "I do my job. I uphold my fiduciary duty to the board to the best of my ability. And, if I'm lucky, I make it easier for our caregivers to do better by our patients along the way."

"And if you can't?"

"If I can't what?"

"If you can't help improve patient care. If you can't uphold your fiduciary duty because your boss gets in the way. Then what?"

"Then I suppose I'll have to make a decision. But so far, it hasn't reached that point."

"So you're okay with everything that goes on here?"

"No, Sean, I'm not. But I do everything in my power to make it better. And if there comes a day when that's no longer possible, then I guess I'll have two choices."

"And what would those be?" I ask, knowing I won't like the answer.

"I'll either do something about it," he says, holding my gaze intently, "or I'll disappear down a bottle."

I finish the rest of my drink, angry at myself for asking. I *knew* I wasn't going to like the answer.

I get up to leave but before I get to the door, Tim calls after me. "Randall Simon will brief you on tomorrow's meeting with the widows."

"Simon? I thought he was fired after Monday's debacle."

"If I fired everyone Williams demanded, I'd be half of a two-man company."

"You have to admit. Simon did shit the bed something awful in that meeting."

"It was pathetic," Tim agrees. "But no worse than you showing up to work drunk every day – if you show up at all."

"Fair point." Damn if Tim doesn't know my comings and goings better than I thought. I turn to leave then think better of it. "Why Simon?" I ask.

"What do you mean?"

"I get why Williams doesn't want any part of this meeting. He doesn't want his fingerprints on it in case it goes bad. Always better to have a scapegoat handy."

"You've thought this all out."

"Of course. I'm expendable, which is why Carefest was dropped in my lap."

"So what's the problem?"

"I still don't get why you're sending an underling tomorrow. I thought this kind of high profile settlement negotiation would be right up your alley."

"Same reason Williams wants you there instead of him. Simon is expendable and I get to keep my hands clean." I look carefully at Tim, who stares back impassively. "I said I was clean, Sean. I never said I was a saint."

"You're a complicated man, boss."

"More than you'll ever know."

I think for a moment. "You know we're going to end up apologizing, right Tim?"

"Yeah," he says wearily. "I know."

"It should be tomorrow. We should look the widows right in the eye and say we're sorry."

"That's not going to happen."

"And Williams should be the one to do it. Show a little humility, some empathy for the people his company has hurt."

"That's *definitely* not going to happen."

"Because it doesn't jive with our boss' galactically outsized ego?"

"That, and an apology would be an admission of guilt, which our insurance carrier can't condone."

"Just wait until this plays itself out in the papers and we end up settling for fifty times what we could tomorrow. Then we'll see what they can and cannot condone. An apology is going to come sooner or later, Tim. It's just a question of whether it's voluntary or forced."

"What you and I want has very little to do with reality."

"A lesson I learn every fucking day." I turn to leave. I'm almost to the door when he calls after me again.

"Hey, Sean?"

"Yeah?"

"Try a little concealer for the nose. You don't want to scare the poor widows to death before you browbeat them into submission."

I shake my head and walk out the door, the only sound behind me the clinking of ice cubes as Tim finishes his drink. I have no idea if he's joking.

21

The rest of the morning is a blur. I do a flurry of follow-up calls with reporters across the country too lazy or stupid to find to their own stories. I spout off some ridiculous pabulum about the company, which satisfies their needs. They now can slap their name on a largely regurgitated puff piece and present it as something new and different to their editors.

This charade is the blessing and the curse of modern American journalism – any story generating a smidge of eye traffic will beget dozens of follow-up pieces, each hoping to yield even a fraction of the original story's interest. It is a phenomenon that serves us well today, as Naomi's well-coordinated press blitz has spawned a hundred more articles and television spots, each rosier and more fawning than the last. But there's a growing pit in my stomach that the same process will work to our detriment once the tide begins to turn with Marcus' article. The lemmings that fawn today will become the vultures that feast tomorrow.

My calls complete, I meet with three lackeys from marketing, who give me a rundown of CareFest. They are practically breathless as they walk me through the program, show me a diagram of the dais and coach me on what I have to do. I try to keep the eye rolls to a minimum. But while nauseating, they are thorough. The entire affair has been orchestrated down to the second. Every session is meticulously planned and every intro tightly scripted. All I need to do is show up (which is improbable) and look pretty (which is impossible). Still, if there's any silver lining to the shit pile that this event will undoubtedly be, it's that there's nothing for me to do to get ready for it. I can focus on other dumpster fires for the next day and half.

On their way out of my office, the smarmiest of the three flashes a million dollar smile and says, "Don't worry about your face. Just get there an hour before call time and we'll have our makeup artist take care of everything."

Thanks, jackass.

Just as the Three Stooges leave my office, Diane walks in with Naomi. It's unclear who is ushering in whom.

"She wouldn't wait," Diane complains.

"She rarely does," I agree.

"Tim's office called. The widows' meeting is tomorrow at nine."

"Where?"

"Executive conference room."

"Dumb fucks," Naomi interjects. She's right. Some over-eager lawyer – my money's on Randall Simon – thought they were doing the company a favor by scheduling the meeting in the conference room. They're probably thinking it will give us a home field advantage, intimidate the widows into settling. But the truth is, it will do the exact opposite. It will reinforce the idea that we are money-grubbing whores who value the trappings of power more than caring for our patients. Plus, the luxurious surroundings will put the lie to any claim that, as a healthcare company scraping by on paltry government reimbursement, we don't have the money to settle. It's a bush league move all around, and shows (once again) that we're not playing with the A-team.

"Change it," I tell Diane. "Find a neutral site, preferably a hotel conference room. Nothing too fancy – not the Four Seasons or the Ritz. Get something generically corporate. The Marriot or the Hilton."

"Catered?" she asks, scribbling down notes.

"Coffee and water, but no food. This needs to be no frills all the way. Besides, I don't want this thing dragging out any longer than necessary. Put out a big spread, and they'll think we're going all day."

"Mr. Simon's not going to like it."

"Mr. Simon can go screw."

"How big a room?"

"Eight people, max."

"Mr. Simon's office said you'll have a team of ten."

"Yeah, well Simon is a clueless douche."

"Should I tell him that?"

"Tell him it will be me and him and that's it. We're trying to make peace, not invade China. And tell him if he's got a problem with any of this, he should take it up with his boss. Tim's given me carte blanche on this."

"Really?" asks Naomi, impressed.

"No, not really. But Simon doesn't know any better, so fuck him." I turn to Diane. "What else?"

"Marcus Cannon called."

"Leave any message?"

"Only that you should call him. And that it's important. And that he'd like a statement."

"Anything else?"

"He said—" she flips a page on her notepad and starts reading, "'your bosses are going down one way or the other so call me or don't call me, I don't care.' I mean, he doesn't care. He said he doesn't care so that's why I said 'I.' Not he. It was him. Not me."

"Diane?"

"Yes?"

"Don't hurt yourself."

Naomi giggles and Diane looks wounded. I should feel bad but I couldn't help myself.

"That's it?"

"Your wife called," she snips, relishing her revenge.

"Great. Thanks."

"She wants you to call."

"She said that?"

"Well, no. But she does."

"What did she say?"

"She said—" She flips to another page of the notepad. "—'Tell that fucking deadbeat he's on his own for dinner tonight. I'm taking the girls out.' She's taking the girls out. Not me."

"Got it."

"I was quoting her."

"I understand."

"That's why I said 'I.' I meant 'she.'"

"Diane?"

"Yeah?"

"You can go."

She retreats to her desk. I can hear her plop down when she calls out. "You should call her."

"Thank you," I yell back.

"She does that intentionally," Naomi says irritably.

"Does what?"

"Every time I'm with you, she brings up your wife."

"No she doesn't."

"Yes she does. She does it to remind you that you're married."

"Believe me, I don't need a reminder."

"And to get a rise out of me."

"It seems to be working."

"She should mind her own fucking business."

I shrug. "She's old fashioned."

"She's a bitch."

"She's an old fashioned bitch."

"Let's go."

"Where?"

"Anywhere but here. I need to fuck."

"God, you're romantic."

"I'm serious."

"Well, I need a drink."

"It'll be like old times," she says. "We'll both get naked, you'll drink until you pass out and I'll leave wholly unfulfilled."

"You have to admit, I'm quite a catch."

"It's amazing no one's stolen you from me."

"Don't forget, I'm a married man."

"With Sister Diane out there, how can I?"

"Let's go," I say, slinging my computer bag over one shoulder and grabbing my jacket off the back of the door, all while surreptitiously checking my pocket for the little blue pills. "You can make a dishonest man out of me."

22

The afternoon tryst is only marginally better than Naomi's prediction. As expected, I raid the minibar and clean them out of gin. And, as expected, I pass out before I'm able to consummate any of the more flagrant varieties of infidelity (though, I do recall being able to perform some aggressively heavy petting). Waking up, it is clear that my partner in crime (moral if not legal) is less than thrilled with the results.

"Was it good for you?" I ask groggily.

"I got off, if that's what you're asking."

"So I did finish the job," I say proudly.

"Your dick was inside me," she allows as she fastens her bra, "but you were neither a conscious nor willing participant."

"Seriously?"

"A girl's got to do what a girl's got to do. I knew you'd get drunk and pass out, so I took some initiative and forced that pill down your throat."

I look at the nightstand next to me and see three empty nips of gin and the bottle of Viagra. It's becoming an all too familiar sight.

"You do know you just ticked off every element of rape, right?"

"You think there's a cop in the world that's going to believe that *I* raped *you*?"

"You make a compelling point."

"Besides, you're too much of a pussy to report it," she says, zipping up her dress. "You've got way more to lose than I do."

"You think I have something to lose?" I ask, sitting up and propping two pillows behind my head. "Name one."

"I'll name three," she replies defiantly as she ties her hair into a ponytail. "Your job, your wife and your kids."

I burst out laughing.

"I'm not joking."

"That's what makes it so funny!"

The tired bedsprings register their disapproval as she sits down to put on her shoes. "You asked me a question and I answered. It's not my fault if you don't believe me."

"Naomi, my boss is about to fire me, my wife is about to divorce me and my kids would like to disown me."

"You're full of shit. Williams isn't going to fire you. He needs you. You're the only one who can clean up his mess."

"That's not true. You can do it. Anyone with half a brain can do it."

"Yeah, well he doesn't know that. No one at this place has the first clue about communications."

"So I'm not going to get fired because my boss is a moron. Your argument needs some work."

"And if you're wife was going to divorce you," she continues, ignoring me, "she'd have done it a long time ago. Like when you and I started doing—" she waves her hands at the dingy hotel room "—whatever it is we're doing."

"Inertia is saving my marriage? Not exactly the Norman

Rockwell ideal. Do yourself a favor and never become a therapist. You suck at it."

"And your kids?" she asks, her voice rising. "Your kids are teenagers, Sean. Do you even remember what that was like? How hard it was? Don't you think – just once – your kids might want to come home to someone they can talk to as opposed to the drunk who greets them at the door every night railing about how unfair the world is? Why don't *you* do yourself a favor, Sean, and come out of that self-absorbed bubble you've been living in. For once in your miserable existence, try to think about somebody other than you."

Neither of us speaks. I can feel the bed shake from her trembling.

"Jesus," I say finally. "Where the hell did this come from?"

She stands, grabs her bag off the dresser and then turns to look at me. Her eyes are piercing. "It's been right in front of you all along."

"Things aren't nearly as simple as you make them out to be."

"Guess what, Sean. You're wrong. About everything." She slings her bag over her shoulder and heads for the door, her ponytail swinging behind her. As she calls farewell – "See you at work, asshole" – I have a surprisingly sickening feeling that this will be our last afternoon together.

The door slams behind her and in the quiet that follows, I see the sheet propped up on my dick like a pup tent. I contemplate beating off so Naomi won't be the only one to benefit from the Viagra, but the moment passes and I begrudgingly swing my legs out of bed to take a shower. Doing anything else seems like too much work.

Twenty minutes later, I take the elevator down to the lobby. Showering drunk always throws me off. Showering drunk in the middle of the day is positively disorienting. Now, as the elevator doors open and sunlight streams in, I am completely out of sorts. My body is clean and fresh, but my head is hazy and stale.

I walk outside, skirting the crowd of people milling out front, and hand my car ticket to the bellman. Four minutes later, the Chevelle comes rumbling around the corner. The crowd's raised eyebrows turn into outright horror as the Chevelle turns into the hotel driveway and rolls up to the front door. I can't help but smile as I hand the valet a couple of bucks and climb in. It shouldn't amuse me so much to scandalize an uptight crowd of business travelers and tourists, but given the week I'm having, I'll my take my joy where I can get it.

I rev the engine and contemplate my next move. It's too early to go home but I can't bear to go back to work. I want to climb into a bottle and disappear, but even that seems a little aggressive at two o'clock in the afternoon.

"You need directions?" the valet asks, snapping me out of my reverie.

"No," I say, the outline of a plan beginning to form. "I'm good."

I'm not sure that's the right characterization of the idea bouncing around my head, but none of the alternatives sound any better.

23

I pull off the highway, the fillings in my teeth decidedly looser than when I started this trip. The novelty of 450 horsepower is beginning to wear off. I pass a series of vaguely familiar strip malls and am surprised to discover that my childhood hometown hasn't changed much at all. That's right: I'm a local. Never had the balls to stray too far from the nest and ended up settling down less than twenty miles away from the very place I swore on all things holy I'd come back to when I grew up. Now that I'm back, the only thing that comes to mind is that this doesn't look like a terrible place to end it all.

Getting my bearings, I make a right on Packard and head east for a few blocks, hoping my memory isn't failing. I needn't have worried. Waiting at the light to take a left on South Main, my turn signal blinking monotonously, the familiar neon sign puts me at ease. The Blue Front is a local institution, a liquor store conveniently located a block from the high school, the American Legion hall and the police station. Whether you're a fresh-faced student with your best days in front of you, a grizzled local with your best days behind you, or a mustachioed cop with no sense of which days are which, the Blue Front has what you need to make your dreams come true or your troubles go away.

Sometimes, I suppose it's hard to tell the two apart.

I pull into the parking lot and head in. Growing up, I would have gone straight to the beer coolers and their endless rows of the standards. But that was a long time ago. Today, I walk straight to the liquor aisle and grab two pints of Tanqueray. I pretend like the clerk's not judging me as she hands over the obligatory brown paper bag and head out to the car, the bottles clinking merrily as my shoes crunch along the gravel parking lot. I yank open the car door, the hinges squeaking in protest, and plop down on the driver's seat, only to receive a spring up the rectum for my trouble. Grimacing, I put the keys in the ignition and turn the car over, revving the massive engine two times too many for the locals. Fuck 'em. I slam the car into drive and gun it, sending gravel flying as I fishtail out of the parking lot.

I take a hard right on South Main, then pull even harder right as I realize that a couple of MexiMelts would really hit the spot (because who doesn't love cheese shot out of a caulking gun?). The tires screech as I careen into the Taco Bell parking lot. I'm doing close to thirty and I've gone no more than a hundred feet. I yank the wheel hard back to the left and slam on the brakes, coming to a noisy, reckless but otherwise perfectly executed stop in front of the Drive Thru microphone. I bark my order at the teller and floor it for the fifty-foot drive to the window. As I wait for my food, I grab one of the bottles of gin, open it hungrily and take a greedy pull, not bothering to use the brown bag as camouflage. There's something oddly comforting about brazenly drinking behind the wheel of the Chevelle, as if law breaking is precisely what the car was built for. And if I know Mac like I think I know Mac, this isn't close to the first law that's been broken in this thing.

Two minutes later, after throwing some loose change at the

pimply-faced teller and grabbing the plastic bag of cheesy nirvana in return, I'm cruising the streets of my childhood with a MexiMelt in one hand and gin in the other. The steering wheel I leave to my knee. Half a mile later, I spy Langston Hughes Elementary, my old stomping grounds. With two more Mexi-Melts and two crunchy Taco Supremes to go, I'm in no position to stop eating, so I decide to ease the car to the curb and take in the familiar surroundings as I take my time enjoying the rest of my midday meal.

School is just getting out as I tuck into the last taco (always end with a crunch. You'll thank me later), and I watch the kids, boisterous and giddy with freedom, bound out of school and into the waiting buses. Even from across the street, I can hear their squeals and shouts. Closing my eyes as I take another slug of gin, it sounds like a passel of pigs battling for the best place at the trough. Opening my eyes, I watch the never-ending stream of kids pile into buses and find myself growing nostalgic. I don't know why, mind you. I hated this place when I was a kid. The teachers were tyrants and the students were even worse. One kid – Forrest Shipley – took it upon himself to make every day my worst day. From the time I got on the bus at 8:33 in the morning to the time I stepped off at 3:22 in the afternoon, he would make fun of my clothes, knock my books out of my hand, or grab my *Welcome Back, Kotter* lunchbox and throw it to his gang of nitwits – anything to inject a dose of misery into my otherwise wretched existence.

Truth be told, I don't blame Forrest. I really don't. I blame his parents. I mean, who the hell names their child Forrest Shipley? You're setting the poor kid up for a life of torment and ridicule. It doesn't take a psychologist to figure out that even a moderately well-honed defense mechanism would turn this kid into a bully. He found the weakest kid he could and pounced. It was a classic case of kill or be killed.

Not that this realization made my third grade experience any easier, of course. Every day, I begged my parents to let me skip school. I got down on my knees and begged them like a dog. Every. Single. Day. But every morning, my mom would coax me off my knees and usher me to the table as she fixed me breakfast. And every day, after placing a plate of waffles in front of me and drenching them with syrup as I wiped my eyes and sniffled, she would tell me to brighten up. "Today, will be the very best day," she would say. "Just you wait and see." But I didn't want to wait and see. I wanted to go back to bed and sleep until I was eighteen. But Mom never let me. Instead, she'd send me out to bus stop with a big sloppy kiss and a pat on the ass. I could never make her understand the torment I was going through. I mean, how does an eight-year-old convince their mom that life is nothing more than a shitstorm of disappointment, despondence, bullying and betrayal?

And yet, as I sit here watching the buses depart, the kids making blowfish faces in the window as they pass my car, I find myself wanting to switch places with them. It's like I'm pining for a yesteryear that never was. Maybe that's all nostalgia is. Yearning to trade a future that never will be for a past that never was.

I start to take another healthy pull on my gin bottle and discover it's empty. No problem. That's why I bought two. I toss the empty bottle on the passenger floorboard and reach for the other one. As I twist open the cap and bring the bottle to my lips, I'm startled by a rap on the window. Gin drips down my chin and onto my shirt as I roll down the window. It's an old school hand crank, so by the time the window is open, I'm winded.

It's a crossing guard. In full crossing guard regalia, complete with neon yellow vest, ridiculous crossing guard hat and pretentious crossing guard white gloves. And, judging by the hands on her substantial hips, the thrust of her even more substantial chest and the furrowed brow beneath the mountain of gray curls, she means business.

"Sir, you can't be here."

I belch.

"Sir," she tries again, her neon yellow vest now leaning closer into the open window. Bad idea. This car smells like gin, tacos and ass. Not necessarily in that order.

"This is a public street," I protest. "People are allowed to park here."

"People are," she allows, her indignation rising, "but not drunks."

I wipe gin off my chin with my sleeve. "What do you mean?"

"I mean you're drinking. A lot, by the smell of it."

"So?" Half spoken, half burped. That hurt. The MexiMelts are threatening to make a reappearance.

"So," she says, her voice rising as she adjusts her hat like she's the new sheriff in town, "you're breaking the law. It's illegal to drink while operating a motor vehicle."

"I'm not drinking while operating a motor vehicle," I correct her. "I'm drinking while parked in a motor vehicle. Critical difference." I wink at her and take another healthy sip.

"Not to the local police." She makes a move to her waist, where I see a walkie-talkie in its holster.

"Does that thing still work?" I marvel.

"Don't test me," she warns.

"Or what?"

"Or we'll see what the cops think of a middle-aged drunk parked outside a school leering at children."

"I wasn't leering," I answer meekly.

"Oh really? What would you call it?"

"Watching."

"Lasciviously."

"There wasn't anything lasciv—"

Who am I kidding? I can't say that word at this point. I'll sound even drunker than I am. And I'm pretty drunk.

"—inappropriate about it. I was just … admiring their optimism."

She leans back and sighs. I'm even more pathetic than she could have imagined when she knocked on my window.

"Listen, buddy," she says softly. "I don't know what's going on here. And truth is, I don't want to know. But you can't be parked outside of a school drinking alcohol. A police officer comes here and you're going to spend the night in jail. Do you understand what I'm saying?"

"Yeah," I sigh. "I do." I screw the cap back on the pint and tuck it between my legs. I reach for the shifter and my stomach registers its disapproval with the MexiMelts, the gin – the general goings on, really. I take a moment to steady myself and calm my bowels.

"You all right?"

"Never better." As if to prove the point, I throw out a hiccurp, the simultaneous hiccup and burp. It hurts like hell. Never one to miss a party, my stomach does another flip. I'd fart, but I'm pretty sure I'd shit myself. Every orifice of my body is in revolt.

"Do yourself a favor and don't come back."

"Don't worry," I say, my breathing suddenly shallow. "You'll never see me again."

I'm sweating as I make the U-turn and quit the scene. I don't even think. The car seems to drive itself down Maple and left onto Buchanan. Before I know what's happening, I take another left on Webster and ease into the driveway at number 7702. The car door squeaks loudly and I stumble out, careful not to stand too upright lest I upset my bowels. I lurch past the elm tree that still shades driveway basketball hoop and head around the garage to the back porch. The key is under the red flowerpot, right where I left it, though I don't remember the geraniums looking so wan the last time I was here. Perhaps watering them more than once a year would have made a difference.

I pull hard and the screen door flies open, slamming loudly into clapboard that is several years overdue for a new paint job. Looks like the door spring could use some work, too. Still sweating, I wipe my brow and fumble with the key, willing it into the deadbolt. Finally, the lock gives way and I wrench the door open, sending a plume of dust into my nostrils. I cough uncontrollably as I cross the threshold, liberating more plumes of dust with each heavy footfall. By the time I reach the stairs, I'm in a full-blown paroxysm, hacking up all measure of fluids. Halfway up, my bowels join the fray, clenching up and sending me doubled over in pain. I grab the railing tight and wonder if I should press on or just give in and shit myself on the stairs. I take a moment to let the worst of the cramp pass and decide to soldier on. The contractions are quickening and I know I don't have long, so I shuffle quickly up the last three steps. With a last burst of energy, I cross the hall and duck though the second door on the left. Sensing I'm close, my bowels begin to give way. *Jesus, no*, I pray as I fumble with my belt. I claw furiously at my pants button, finally ripping it off so I can start going at the zipper. I kick the seat cover open – too hard, as it turns out, as bounces off the tank and slams back down.

"FUCK!"

I pull my pants down with one hand and awkwardly try to put the cover back up with the other. Finally, I slam the seat cover against the tank and, with one pant leg above the knee and one below the other, I plop down, unleashing an unholy mixture of shit, piss, liquid cheese and regret. The pain subsides momentarily and I notice the tears that are streaming down my face. I grasp the towel bar to my left and try to get my breathing under control. I'm close to feeling human when another wave hits. Every muscle contracts and I once again destroy the back of the bowl. I give myself a courtesy flush – and then another – and wait ten minutes to make sure the purge is over. My legs numb and my shirt drenched in sweat, I resolve that the next time I go to Taco Bell, I'm going to buy a Burrito Supreme, walk into their bathroom and dump it in the toilet.

I'm tired of being the middleman.

I clean up and flush twice more for good measure, careful to jiggle the handle so the toilet doesn't run all night. Old habits die hard, I guess. Too cheap to call a plumber, my dad insisted on installing the toilet himself, saving himself a couple of hundred bucks but costing me countless sleepless nights growing up listening to clattering pipes. I still think of this as the new bathroom, but that renovation must have been thirty years, Mom's death and Dad's Alzheimer's ago.

I wash up in the sink, splashing my face with water and taking a good, long look in the mirror. Big mistake. I look like shit. I've sweat through my dress shirt and undershirt so it's now possible if you look closely (though I would strongly advise against it) to see the outlines of my tits (they're everything you'd hope for — soft, supple with just the right amount of girth. I swear to God, if I was twenty years younger and forty pounds lighter, I'd take a run at me.). The yellow pit stains are even more pronounced than usual and, though I didn't think it possible, my nose has become even more repulsive than it was this morning. Mottled with burst capillaries the size of IEDs, it looks less like a body part and more like the road to Kabul. My eyes have shrunken even further into their sockets and what hair I have is plastered to my overheated red pate. My entire skull looks like an art student's color study gone horribly wrong. Wild shades of crimson, fuscia and eggplant blend in and out of each other in seemingly haphazard fashion, creating a tapestry of horror that should adorn no face, human or otherwise.

Assuming I make it that long, the widows at tomorrow's meeting are going to shit their pants.

To top it all off, I smell like ass. And I don't think that's just the toilet talking. Gin-infused sweat, fueled by what is now a thirty-eight day bender, oozes from every pore. And, while I'm not proud of it, I believe my body has just exceeded the outer limits of my extra strength deodorant's capabilities.

I make an executive decision to shower. It may not solve all of my issues – I'm likely to secrete gin until the end of days – but it can't hurt. Besides, if recent memory is any guide, failure to thoroughly cleanse my nether regions after the damage I just inflicted on the toilet will lead a flaming case of swamp-ass. I don't see any soap, but after rummaging through the linen closet, I find a towel that isn't completely moth-infested and a travel size container of Johnson's baby shampoo whose expiration date is at least in this century. Mom must have purchased it in the vain hope that one of her offspring would sire grandkids. I hope she wasn't holding her breath. On second thought, maybe she should have. Then she might have died before the Parkinson's got her.

It's only after I strip down and jump in the shower that I wonder what to do with my clothes. The last thing I want to do is get clean (or as clean as a travel size bottle of Johnson's shampoo can get me) and step back into clothes so rancid they should have their own slab reserved for them at the county morgue. I ponder whether the shower was the right call for a second until I realize just how glorious the piping hot water feels. This is my third shower of the day – second drunk – and each one just keeps getting better. If this keeps up, I'm going to keep drinking gin and take a shower every hour on the hour until I pass out. Or maybe I'll just bring a bottle of gin and a lawn chair into the shower at home.

Fuck me, that's it. I'm a genius.

I take my sweet time digging into my cracks and crevices, careful to give them a nice hot soak. Only when my extremities resemble dried prunes do I reluctantly turn off the water. I grab the towel and dry off, forgetting for an excruciating moment that my frugal mom was never a fan of fabric softener. The towel is closer to sandpaper than cotton at this point, and each pass across my skin is less an exercise in exfoliation than sado-masochism. I forego the towel and decide to air dry as I wander naked through the house in search of clean clothes.

It's been a long time since I've been in this house looking for anything other than a hidden liquor bottle or a respite from the real world (and yes, I'm aware those are often the same thing). My old man used to hide his booze from my mom, which was as comic in its undertaking as it was futile in its execution. Mom was on to him from the jump and invariably found the flask of bourbon or pint of vodka in some dark corner of the house soon after Dad had snuck it there. At first a source of tension, if not outright hostility, over time it became a game between them, an acknowledgement that marriage, like life, was a struggle and they were in it together until the end. Unfortunately, Mom's end came far sooner than Dad's. After she died and the Alzheimer's started its pernicious assault on Dad's mind, he nonetheless kept playing the game, though the combination of his forgetfulness and Mom's absence dulled his skills. On my rare visits home, I would find bottles stuffed between the couch cushions or behind the still unread complete works of Shakespeare. When the house became too much for my dad and he finally moved into a home, I must have found twenty bottles lying around in varying states of camouflage. For an alcoholic following in the footsteps of my old man, it was like receiving a gift from beyond the grave. Okay, technically he's still alive, but as anyone with a loved one suffering from dementia can attest, the person in the nursing home stopped being my dad a long time ago.

Caring for Dad alone has been a kick in the balls. I've reached out to Kevin for help but, not surprisingly, he doesn't take my calls. I try to be gracious and chalk it up to the fact that it's tough to help an ailing parent from across the country. But it's hard not to think he's sitting in his big-ass house in Seattle laughing at the irony of me caring for someone to whom I should have no legal obligation. That vindictive fucker is definitely getting the last laugh in our little morality play.

Without thinking, I open the first door I see, which — while good for nostalgia — is lousy for remedying my current state of nakedness. Crossing the threshold, I'm hit with a wave of mothballs and pre-pubescent desperation. I don't look to my left, but I know the black Porsche 911 poster is still there. And I definitely don't look to my right, not because I don't want to see Heather Thomas tugging on her pink bikini, but because of how much I want to. I'll spare you the details, but it certainly wouldn't be the first time where that bikini was the only thing either of us was wearing. Not by a long shot.

Instead, I can't stop looking at the faded Boston Bruins bedspread. I reach out my hand, then pause, worried that if I touch it, it will crumble into dust. I remember begging my parents to get one for my twelfth birthday. There was nothing on earth more important that this godforsaken bedspread, a point I believe I made clear in several late night sob sessions when I feared my pleas were falling on deaf ears. But love for their eldest son (and the fervent hope that capitulation would bring my tantrums to an end) won out and the bedspread quickly became my most prized possession. No matter how bad the day – no matter how many Forrest Shipleys there were – I could come home, wrap myself in the black and gold spoked-B and find peace. So I guess I shouldn't be surprised that now, as tears run inexplicably down my face, I pull the covers back on the still made bed, fold my naked body into the creaking twin bed and wrap myself in sheets so soft, it still feels like lying on a cloud. I inhale deeply, and sure enough, my nostrils are filled with the soothing scent of childhood wonder. I breathe deeply once more and feel myself slipping back to a place I didn't know still existed.

Home.

24

For the few weeks after Jenny propositioned me, I did my level best to avoid her, no mean feat given that I sat behind her in Eastern Philosophy and she still came over to my house every afternoon. I solved the former by keeping my eyes as far away from her ass as possible and actually started paying attention to Ms. Fiedler's lectures. Mind you, since the weather had finally turned warm, it took Herculean concentration not to stare at the ridiculously tight shorts Jenny had started to wear (okay, maybe I snuck a peek from time to time but that was just in the interest of keeping tabs on the decline in standards of American youth. Honestly, her attire was nothing short of scandalous.).

Avoiding her at home was a little more challenging. Lacrosse practice helped, but Kevin was on the team, too, so Jenny would just meet us at home after practice. Usually, I begged off with excuses of phantom study groups at the library or group projects at a friend's house, but they both started to get suspicious. It was a month before graduation so my newfound studiousness was hard to justify, especially since I hadn't studied as much in my first seventeen years combined as I had in few months they had been dating. So I mixed things up and started to go for runs. Lots and lots of runs. I ran so much the lacrosse coach started to wonder if I was cheating on him with the track team. I practically could have run a marathon without breaking a sweat. The only problem with all of that exercise is that I was in such good shape, I looked even more attractive than usual. It was a vicious – yet rewarding – cycle: the more I avoided Jenny, the better I looked. As April turned to May, things got so bad that every time she saw me, she practically devoured me with her eyes.

I was downright irresistible.

Unfortunately, Kevin wasn't doing quite as well. As I was to find out later, Kevin wasn't fooling around with Jenny because he didn't want to; they weren't messing around because he didn't know how to. He had never even kissed a girl and now that one of the hottest girls in school was throwing herself at him, he didn't have the first clue how to respond. It only got worse when Jenny took off her shirt. Confronted with one of the most beautiful and arousing sights he had ever known, Kevin's brain overloaded. It shut down, opting for trig problems instead of a half naked girl. The irony, of course, was that if he just caved and given in to his carnal fantasies, everyone's problems would have been solved. Jenny's itch to hook up with him would be scratched, Kevin's cherry would be popped, and I could finally stop training like I was trying to take down the Ethiopians at the New York City marathon.

No surprise, the stress was taking its toll on Kevin. Walking in the halls between classes, they looked less like a couple and more like a terrorist and her hostage. Jenny scowled fiercely while Kevin's eyes darted back and forth, looking for an excuse to run as far away from her as possible. I wasn't the only one who noticed. This being high school, it wasn't long before people started taking odds on their demise as a couple. Oddsmakers set the over/under on them breaking up by the end of the month. Smart money had the under.

To add to the misery, prom was around the corner. Because nothing says sex as a coping mechanism for unmet expectations quite like prom, every junior and senior was even more of a bundle of nerves than usual. I'm sure prom started out as a well-intentioned opportunity for kids to dress up, get drunk and blow off some steam, but since then, the mere thought of it turns even the most well-adjusted kid into a teeming pot of hormones, excitement, jealousy, rage, and nausea. It's no wonder murder, suicide and castration rates skyrocket every spring.

It's true. You can look it up.

True to form, I planned to avoid the entire enterprise by hanging out with friends – just a few buddies, a keg and the entire catalog of Patrick Swayze movies (again, people, it's important to remember this was the 90s. Try not to judge.).

The Tuesday before prom, Kevin and I were walking off the practice field when one of my buddies drove by, leaned out the window and yelled something to the effect of "SWAYZE RULES!" just before swerving wildly to avoid hitting a pedestrian (I'm as libertarian as libertarian can be, but there's a reason serious consideration should be paid to raising the driving age to 18: high school boys are morons). I laughed and yelled something back (most likely, "Drive your car, shit brick!"), when Kevin turned to me, morose.

"You're really not going to prom?"

"When *Red Dawn* and *Road House* are on the docket? Not a chance."

"Yeah, but it's your senior year. Aren't you worried about, you know...?"

"No, what?"

"Missing out."

"On what?" I laughed. "Getting dressed up in an uncomfortable tux that a hundred other guys have worn and probably thrown up on? Or shelling out a boatload of cash on a limo and a stuffy dinner that I'm probably going to hate anyway? No, I know. You mean missing out on seeing a bunch of people I don't care about embarrass themselves on the dance floor while trying to convince each other they're having the time of their lives, right?"

He looked sullen as we crossed the parking lot towards the locker room.

"I just thought we could, I don't know, go together."

I stopped and put my hand on his shoulder. "Kevin, I don't know what to say. I didn't know you felt that way about me."

"Shut up," he said with a wan smile, batting my hand away.

"I'm touched, Kevin, really. It's just that I've never really thought of you as anything more than a brother. Besides – and please don't take this the wrong way – what you're suggesting is illegal in most states."

"Fuck you." He was almost laughing as we started walking back towards the locker room.

"Not in Alabama, of course. Or Mississippi. Probably not in Louisiana, Georgia, Kentucky or Arkansas, either. Pretty much the entire SEC. I'd have to do a little research."

"Forget I asked."

"Kevin, believe me. You'll have way more fun without me. You and Jenny should just relax and have a great time."

"I just wish I could."

"Could what?"

"Relax."

"What are you talking about? You can relax."

"Around you, maybe. But not with her."

"Kevin, what's going on?"

"Jenny's pissed."

"At what?"

"At me."

"What did you do?"

"It's more like, what didn't I do?"

Here we go. When, exactly, did I become relationship counselor for these two? It was exhausting. And more than a little uncomfortable, if you don't mind me saying.

"What do you mean?"

He sighed heavily and pulled me aside as the rest of the team filed into the locker room. No surprise, this wasn't exactly a conversation he wanted to share with the rest of the team. He dropped his stick and pads on the ground and looked at me gravely.

"Jenny and I haven't, uh, done much."

I knew what he was talking about but I couldn't resist twisting in the knife a little. "What are you talking about? You go out all the time? You guys have done a ton together."

"We do things with each other," he whispered, looking around to make sure no one could hear. "We just don't do things *to* each other."

"Oh. I see."

"It's not that she's not into it," he whispered quickly. "She's into it. She's *really* into it. It's just that..."

"You're not into it."

"Right. No. I mean, I don't know."

"Kevin, it's okay."

"Really?"

"Of course. Lots of people are gay. It's nothing to be ashamed of."

"I'm not gay!" he yelled, much louder than he intended. Two people across the parking lot looked over. He lowered his voice. "Of course it's okay if I'm gay. It's just that I'm not."

"You're not."

"No! You know that."

"There was that time you dressed up in Mom's clothes and called yourself a princess."

"I was four!"

"Studies show even at that early age, children have a strong sense of their sexual orientation."

"I knew I shouldn't have brought this up with you," he fumed, picking up his pads and stick. As he started to walk to the locker room, I grabbed his shoulder and turned him back towards me.

"Kevin—" I said, trying to contain my laughter.

"Fuck you."

"I'm sorry." No laughter this time. Just a big smile. And maybe a snicker or two.

"Fuck you."

"Are you gonna say anything other than 'fuck you?'"

"Fuck you."

"I'll put that down as a hard no."

He stared at me and his eyes flashed between anger, fear and confusion. He was reaching out to me for help and all I could do was joke around. I felt awful. I dropped my gear and apologized.

"I'm an asshole. I can see how hard this must be for you and I'm sorry. I shouldn't have acted that way." He said nothing so I plowed ahead. "Look, it's no big deal if you guys haven't fooled around. I know most guys in this school brag about how much they've done or how far they've gotten with a girl, but they're all assholes. The only thing that's important is that you guys like each other."

"But that's just it," he said sadly. "To her, fooling around *is* important."

"What about you?"

"If it's important to her, it's important to me." That was the line that made my heart break. Most guys wouldn't talk like this.

They wanted to hook up not because it was what the girl wanted, but because it was what they wanted – or what they assumed they were supposed to want. Confused and scared as Kevin was, he wasn't like that. He was only focused on doing whatever he could to make her happy. He was a sweetheart in a world of asshats.

"It's not like I don't want to," he was saying. "It's just that I get so damn nervous when I'm with her that I can't seem to do anything. I just freeze up."

"Have you told her any of this?"

"I've tried a few times."

"That's good. What did you say?"

"Usually, I tell her I need to do homework."

"I'd say your delivery needs some work."

He dropped his gear and grabbed his hair with both hands like he wanted to rip out every strand. "I'm such an idiot!"

"You're not an idiot, Kevin. You're just nervous."

"I'm a pussy!"

"You're not a pussy."

He looked at me, his eyes watering.

"You're not a pussy, Kevin."

He held my gaze, a single tear sliding down his cheek.

I reconsidered. "On the lacrosse field, maybe. But not about this."

He shook his head like he was considering hitting me, but the smile spreading across his face betrayed him. "You're an asshole."

"Of course I am. It's my defining characteristic."

"How do you do it?"

"Be an asshole? It's easy."

"No," he said, laughing and crying at the same time. "Be with girls. The way you talk to them, hang out with them ... you make it look simple."

I shrug. "I dunno. I guess I just try to put them at ease. If they're relaxed, then I can relax. There's no magic to it."

He rubbed his eyes with the heels of his hands. Six foot four and yet he looked like a little kid.

"It sure looks like magic from where I sit."

"Just be yourself, Kevin, and you'll be fine. And if you do that and a girls still doesn't want to be with you, then fuck her."

"Except that not fucking her is precisely the problem."

We both laughed and it struck me how little we can know someone even when we live under the same roof with them.

"Think of it this way. If I can do it, you can do it. We've both got the same DNA, right?"

In retrospect, I should have paid closer attention to the strange look that flashed across his face right before we grabbed our sticks and pads. Maybe then I would have paid closer attention to what was to come and not made a complete mess of everything. As it was, we both headed to the locker room, smiling and happy, brothers for at least a few moments more.

25

There's a certain elegance to every one of Patrick Swayze's performances. In *Red Dawn*, his Jed is the reluctant but able warrior. In *Point Break,* he makes Bodhi a poet. But in *Road House*, he puts it all together to transform Dalton into a warrior poet. Give me a bouncer getting stitched up in an E.R. who tells the gorgeous blonde doctor that "pain don't hurt," and I'm hooked. Of course, ply me with twenty beers and three keg stands, and I'll probably fall in love with any movie that comes on. ßHence the beauty of Swayze-fest.

Prom night had arrived and, true to my word, I was in the basement of my buddy Steve's house with the rest of my delinquent friends basking in the glow of Sam Elliott's arrival to the Double Deuce, waiting for him and Dalton to vanquish the evil Brad Wesley and his band of henchmen. A shirtless Dalton was just about to battle Jimmy, Wesley's chief heavy and designated martial arts guru, in one of the all-time great cheesy 80s fight scenes when Steve came stumbling into the basement.

"Sean, dude. You gotta come upstairs."

"Fuck that. Swayze's about to go off."

"I'm serious. You gotta come. Now."

Of all the times to be interrupted, this had to be the worst. I had waded through four Swayze movies to get to this point and now I was about to miss it. It was the cinematic equivalent of blue balls.

I grudgingly struggled out of the couch and stepped over two of my friends who were snoring on the floor, oblivious to the tension building onscreen. I followed Steve upstairs but before I could give him my best "what the fuck?" look, he pointed to the kitchen table. Sitting at the head of the table, still in her black prom dress, was Jenny. We locked eyes and she stood up, her blonde hair falling to her shoulders, setting off the sleek black dress that hugged her hips and fell all the way to the floor.

Oh fuck. Fuckity, fuck, fuck, fuck.

I looked at Steve, silently pleading for help, but he shook his head and took his leave, but not before hesitating at the top of the stairs, unsure whether it would be better to watch Dalton going medieval on Jimmy's ass or the travesty that was about to unfold in his own kitchen. In the end, he opted for Swayze. Good choice. Too bad I had no such option.

I took a deep breath and tried to think of something to say.

"Hey." Strong choice, I know.

"Hey," she answered softly.

"Didn't expect to see you tonight."

"I didn't expect to be here."

"You're a little over-dressed for Swayze-fest."

She smiled nervously and smoothed her dress. "I thought I'd class the place up a bit."

"How was prom?"

"It was okay. The band was pretty good."

"Jenny?"

"Yeah?"

"What are you doing here?"

"I came to see you."

"That's funny, 'cause I'm pretty sure you're supposed to be at prom with my brother."

"He's at your house, asleep."

"Asleep?"

"Passed out, is more like it."

"You're kidding."

"I think he was a little nervous so he had a few drinks to calm his nerves."

"A few? He's six-four. How many drinks did he have?"

"More like eight."

"Eight?"

"Okay, ten."

Kevin wasn't a big drinker, so ten drinks would have meant that he was falling all over himself. He was lucky he wasn't caught by the administration. He would have been suspended for a week.

"How the hell did he not get in trouble?"

"A few of us got him into the limo and took him home."

"That was nice of you."

She shrugged. "It was the least I could do. Besides, I didn't really want to be there anymore."

"Why not?"

She bit her lip and pulled her best sultry look. It didn't suit her. At the risk of too many dated references, she needed a little less Melrose Place and a little more 90210. That said, it was certainly enough to get the blood racing.

"Because I wanted to be with you," she whispered, taking a step towards me.

"You're with Kevin."

She took another step closer. "I don't have to be."

She took two more steps until our chests were practically touching. I looked down and saw she wasn't wearing a bra. My breath quickened and my stomach fluttered.

"But you are."

"Not tonight."

She leaned forward and kissed me, taking my breath as her lips pressed softly onto mine. She slid her hands around my hips and I found myself answering in kind, pulling her towards me so I could feel her nipples pressed against my chest. She opened her lips and her tongue danced with mine. I wanted to devour her. I pulled her closer still, pressing my hips into hers, the curves of our bodies fitting just right. And then, as quickly as I had forgotten myself, I remembered who we were and why she was here. I pushed her away gently. The sweetness of her lips lingered on mine.

"Jenny," I whispered hoarsely, "we can't."

She took a step back and slid the thin straps of her dress over her shoulders, letting the gown drop to the floor. Wearing nothing more than a black thong, she stared at me brazenly. I struggled to find my breath even as my heart pounded. She was perfect –absolutely perfect – as she stepped towards me and kissed me, harder and deeper than before. I was lost, completely hers to do with whatever she pleased. As she pressed her body into mine and slid her hands down my pants, I thanked a god I didn't believe in that Steve's parents were out of town. Then I led her upstairs to the first empty bedroom I could find and let her have her way with me.

26

Here's how it happens.

You're at lacrosse practice the following Thursday. You're going through the motions during warm-up, your mind mercifully blank as it focuses solely on catching the ball in your stick, cradling it and sending it back to your warm-up partner. You don't think about anything else, least of all the fact that your partner is the same guy whose girlfriend you fucked five days earlier. There's raucous laughter to your right and you think it's the product of the usual high school banter, boys giving shit to other boys. You look over and see two of your teammates point first at you, then your warm-up partner and then break into hysterical laughter. You hear words like 'skank' and 'slut' followed by even more laughter. You look at your warm-up partner, whose face, seconds ago filled with the joy of playing a sport he loves, has grown ashen. He takes a few steps towards your teammates, the ball falling out of his stick as his hands drop to his slide. Before you can call to him, urging him to come back and continue warming up, you hear him ask your teammates what's so funny. You try again to yell his name but find you can't make a sound. You can't breathe. You can't move. You can't do a thing except listen to the words you know are coming but can't bear to hear.

"We think it's great you and Sean are so close you decided to become Eskimo brothers," says a kid you thought was your friend.

"What do you mean?" asks your warm-up partner. You want to call him something more than that, but you know you can't. You've lost the right to call him your brother.

"Sean," another teammate says. "He fucked your girl."

He's turned away from you, but you know there's no color in your warm-up partner's face. He's trying not to believe it, but deep in his heart he knows it's true. He knows you fucked him over, betrayed him with his first love. He knows your soul is black and your heart is stone. He's always known. And so have you.

He turns and you see his face. It's just as you imagined. His eyes, lifeless pools of blackness, have recessed into his skull, and his cheeks are devoid of all color. His lips are pressed together, forming an angry gash across his face. He stares at you for what must be a second but what seems an eternity, then turns and walks off the field.

You look down at the ground, hoping no one can see the tears streaming down your face.

27

I didn't go home until much later that night. When I slinked in through the front door, dinner had long since been cleaned up, which was just as well since there was no way I could have kept food down. Not that I deserved to eat. The house was quiet but I knew everyone was home. I could feel their presence. There was a heaviness in the air that was impossible to escape.

I dropped my backpack and lacrosse gear in the foyer and walked through the kitchen towards the back of the house. As I approached the family room, I took a deep breath. It was time. I turned the corner and saw them waiting for me. My father was sitting in his favorite chair, staring at me even as the Sox game flickered silently on the television. My mother sat on the love seat, her eyes cast downward. Across the room, Kevin slumped on the sofa, head back and eyes closed, with one of my grandmother's embroidered pillows on his lap.

"Hey," I said.

No one moved. No one made a sound. They had said all they were going to say to each other.

I thought of sitting on the love seat next to my mother but

thought better of it. I didn't want to presume I was welcome here, so I stayed where I was, sliding down to the floor with my back against the doorframe. I closed my eyes and waited. I needn't have bothered.

"Don't you think you should say something?" My father's eyes bored into me.

"I've been trying to think of what to say all week," I said quietly, my eyes on the floor, "but I can't come up with the words to express how sorry I am."

"Well, why don't you try?"

I took a breath and looked across the room. "Kevin, I am so—"

"GET OFF THE GODDAMN FLOOR!"

I looked at my dad, his face was flushed and his eyes were on fire. I had screwed Kevin's girlfriend, but by the veins bulging out of my father's neck, you would have thought I had had sex with my own mother on the living room floor. I scrambled to my feet and took a step towards Kevin.

"Kevin, I don't know what to say except I'm sorry," I said the words pouring out of me. "I know that doesn't make things right, not by a long shot, but you have to know that I am. I don't know what I was thinking. I mean, I was really drunk—"

"So that makes everything okay."

"No, Dad, of course it doesn't. But then she came over and—"

"So now it's her fault! Jesus, Sean, isn't anything ever your fault?"

"Pete, please. That's not what he said."

"DON'T YOU DARE TAKE HIS SIDE ON THIS!" he thundered at my Mom. "You, of all people, have no right! No goddamned right!"

Wounded, my mom grew quiet, her lips trembling. I began to wonder what I had walked into.

"It's no one's fault but mine," I said softly. "That's what makes this so hard. Kevin, I didn't mean to hurt you. I really didn't. I did an incredibly selfish thing and there's not a second that goes by that I don't wish I could go back and change everything."

"Was she everything you'd hoped?" Kevin asked without opening his eyes.

How the hell should have answered that? *She's the fuck of the century, Kevin. She has a body that doesn't quit and is an absolute freak in the sheets. She made me see God.* Yeah, I didn't see that going over well, either.

"I honestly don't remember."

He lifted his head and looked at me, his eyes glinting wickedly. "You fucked my girlfriend – the girl you've lusted over for years – and you don't remember? How's that for irony?"

I kept my mouth shut. There was nothing I could say that would make things better.

"That's it?" Kevin said, sitting up. "No witty retort? No biting social commentary? Is the mighty Sean Reilly finally at a loss for words?"

"What else can I say?" I asked quietly.

"Are you kidding?" He stood up, taking one large step so he towered over me. "Are you out of your fucking mind? How about, 'Sorry for turning you into a laughing stock, Kevin? Sorry for turning your into the biggest joke Wilson High has ever seen?' How about, 'Sorry for not having the balls to admit what I did to your face? Sorry for making things worse by playing along with that cunt Jenny as if nothing had happened?' And while you're at it, Sean, how about 'Sorry for being the worst fucking brother and the saddest excuse for a human being that anyone has ever seen?'"

"I am sorry," I whispered. "I'm sorry for all of that."

"REALLY?" he screamed, leaning in close and covering my face with spittle. "HOW ABOUT BEING SORRY FOR FUCKING THE ONLY GIRL I'VE EVER LOVED?"

My throat tightened and my eyes welled up.

"I'm sorry," I sobbed. "I really am."

"DON'T CRY, YOU COCKSUCKER!" he screeched. "DON'T YOU FUCKING DARE!"

I saw him rear back and cock his fist, but I didn't move. I just watched as his arm came forward and he shifted his weight to get everything he could into the punch. I made no effort to avoid his fist as it made contact with my chin, snapping my head back and sending me down like a sack of bricks. I lay on the ground, my head exploding in pain, waiting for more.

"GET UP!"

Mom stood up. "Kevin—"

"SHUT UP!" my father yelled, not letting her finish.

I struggled to my feet, my head throbbing and my legs buckling. I tried to apologize again but it was difficult to form words with so much blood in my mouth. No matter. Kevin quickly smashed his other fist into my stomach, pushing all of the air out of my lungs and sending me crashing to the floor once more. I gasped for air.

"Kevin." Mom's voice was quiet but firm.

"GET UP!"

"Kevin, that's enough."

"GET UP, YOU FUCKING PUSSY!"

"You've made your point, Kevin. You've hurt him as much as he's hurt you."

I looked up and saw Kevin whip around to face our mother, his eyes wild.

"HE'S NOT EVEN CLOSE TO FEELING WHAT I FEEL!"

"I know, son. I know. But beating him to a pulp won't solve anything. Believe me, you'll only feel worse when you're done."

Dad stood up and put his hand on Kevin's shoulder. "Your mother is right," he said, sounding reluctant. Not that I cared. At that point, I'd take any and all allies, reluctant or not. "Leave Sean alone."

"I want this asshole to understand what he's done to me," he seethed.

I struggled to my feet once more. I steadied myself as a wave of nausea washed over me. Every part of me hurt.

"I know you don't believe me," I croaked, "but I know what I've done. And I'm sure I'll never be able to tell you how sorry I am."

"Fuck you." There was pure enmity in his eyes.

I nodded. "You've got every reason to hate me, Kevin. I'm an asshole, just like you said. But I'm also your brother and I'm standing here begging for your forgiveness."

"You were barely my brother before this. You're definitely not my brother now."

"I know why you say that. I did something a brother should never do."

His face contorted into a malevolent smile. "You have no idea what I'm talking about."

"Of course I do," I replied with a nod, blood dripping down my chin and on to the carpet. "We're so different sometimes it seems like we're not brothers. And what I did makes it that much worse. But I swear to you, Kevin, that I'll do anything I can to—"

"You know why we're so different?" His voice was eerily calm.

My mother gasped. "Kevin, please."

"No, Mom. It's time. It's time for Sean to know where he came from."

"Kevin..." Mom sat back down awkwardly, sobbing.

"She was always there to protect you," Kevin said, ignoring her. "But not now. Not any longer."

"Kevin," Dad interjected, "think about what you're doing."

"I know EXACTLY what I'm doing," Kevin snapped. "I'm doing what you should have done a long time ago."

"What is going on?" My voice was small, barely a whimper. I turned to my father, who had the resigned look of someone who sees a car crash coming before it happens. "Dad?"

"He's not your dad."

"Dad?" My voice was hoarse.

"I said, he's not your dad."

The room spun and the roar of blood echoed through my head. I was unmoored. Stumbling backwards, my arms flailed, searching for something to brace myself against. I bumped against the wall and slid back down to the floor.

"Mom fucked a client and you popped out nine months later." Mom gasped but Kevin couldn't be stopped. "No surprise, the deadbeat didn't want anything to do. Dad didn't either, but he's too good a person to put you and Mom on the street."

"Kevin," Dad begged, his voice hoarse, "please."

My father – if that's what I should have even called him; I didn't know anymore – wobbled backward, as if Kevin's words themselves were too much to bear. I knew how he felt.

Kevin ignored him. "So Dad – *my* dad – said she could raise you here."

"How did you...?" I couldn't finish. I put my hands to my ears, not wanting to hear anything more but knowing I would listen all the same.

"I overheard Mom and Dad talking one night when we were kids. It wasn't hard to figure out. You've never been like me or Dad. You've always looked and acted differently."

I looked at my father, tears streaming down both of our faces. "Dad?" I whispered.

"You don't get to call him that, anymore," Kevin said, his voice cold.

"Mom?"

"Don't you get it?" Kevin asked, ignoring me. "We don't want you here. We never did. You don't belong."

"That's enough."

"You're as big a whore as Mom."

"I said that's ENOUGH!" My father slammed his palm on the sideboard next to his favorite chair, the sound like a gunshot. An ashtray skittered off the top and exploded on the wood floor, crystal shards caroming across the floor.

I struggled to my feet. Dad looked at me plaintively while Mom sobbed into her hands. We were no longer a family. We were as broken and shattered as the ashtray. I looked at Kevin. His eyes were blank, his face impassive. I clenched my fists and found my voice.

"Call our mother a whore again and I will end you."

I turned and walked towards the stairs. When I reached the railing, I turned.

"I'll move out right after graduation. You won't ever have to deal with me again." I climbed the first riser, wincing with each step.

"Was it worth it?" he spat.

"No," I croaked, pausing to wipe the blood from my mouth before resuming my climb up the stairs. "Not even close."

28

When I open my eyes, it's dark. Naked and alone in a twin bed. It's my teens and twenties all over again. Only I'm forty-two, drunk and lying in a kid's bed.

I shake my head clear of the memory of Kevin, Jenny and Patrick Swayze, but it's still fuzzy. I look to my left. The clock radio on my bedside table says 8:24, but that's suspect. I'm guessing the last time those numbers changed was sometime in the back half of the Carter Administration. I trudge back to the bathroom where my filthy clothes lay in a heap on the floor and rummage through the pockets in search of my phone.

Naturally, it's dead.

Cursing, I paw around the vanity where I find my wallet, keys, Burt's Bees and Lactaid (because of course I'm lactose intolerant. I'm sure a gluten sensitivity is right around the corner), but no watch. Dammit. I stomp furiously on my clothes, convincing myself that this is an effective pat down technique and not the tantrum of a spoiled three year-old that it appears. Still, no watch. Exasperated, I let out a long, barbaric scream and try not to look at the pasty, pathetic man staring back at me in the mirror. Finally, next to the toothbrush holder that is covered with decades of soap scum, toothpaste and dust (to say nothing of the toothbrush in it. I'm not sure which is greener – it's Incredible Hulk handle or its moldy bristles), I see my watch, which brings both good news and bad: the antediluvian clock radio still works. On the downside, it's nearly eight-thirty at night and I'm nowhere close to home.

Alex is going to be pissed.

Swearing once more, I gather up my clothes and personal effects and lumber down the hall to my parents' room. Praying for a miracle, I cross their moldy carpet and throw open the closet to look for something I can wear. But once again, every sense is overwhelmed by smell. It has been at least a decade since this closet has been opened and the combination of an oxygen starved environment and my mom's prolific use of mothballs has resulted in a highly concentrated brew of camphor, mold and sadness. Decades in the making, it has been lying in wait, aching for some poor bastard to come along and release it so that it can wreak its havoc upon the world.

The toxic cloud sends me backwards, knocking me on my ass and sending my clothes flying. My eyes burn as I hack up intestinal lining. Gasping for air, it dawns on me that sealing myself in my parents' closet would have solved my dilemma of how to kill myself at the end of the week. I thought the car crash thing was foolproof, only to be foiled by airbags. Since then, I've been toying around with everything from death by gunshot, hanging, jumping to slitting my wrists. But every option seems either too gory, too public or (let's face it) too ballsy. I'm still casting about for the Goldilocks method, one that's clean, effective and doesn't require too much in the way of courage. On my part, that is. I want something that even a complete pussy like me could pull off and doesn't inconvenience anyone else too much.

Lying bare-assed on my parents' moldy carpet, I realize that my Goldilocks solution may have just passed me by. Twenty seconds in that closet and I would have been a goner. Instead, all I have to show for my efforts is a mold infection in the anal cavity.

I clamber to my feet, stagger to the closet and grab the two hangers closest at hand. I'm relieved to discover that I'm holding tan Dickie's and a red sweatshirt. With my dad's taste in clothes, it could have been far worse. I think about grabbing a pair of his shoes, but that's a total loss – in addition to being five inches shorter than me, my dad has notoriously small feet. It's a wonder he hasn't blown over in a stiff breeze. Luckily, I see a pair of lime green flip-flops that might do the trick. For a second, I ponder rifling through Dad's dresser for some underwear, but that's a little too Oedipal even for my taste. Pulling on the Dickie's, which were never known for their soft touch, I fear the executive decision to freeball it may prove unwise. Already rubbed raw by the starched towel, I cringe at the chafing my nether regions will soon suffer. But it's too late to find another pair, so I pull the sweatshirt over my head, squeeze into the flip-flops and head for the door.

On my way out, I catch a glimpse of myself in the mirror above my mom's dresser. It's even worse than I thought. The pants barely make it to my calves, so they are more culottes than trousers. Compounding matters, they're baggy as hell in the ass, skin tight in the thighs and flared out below the knee, leaving me to wonder whether it's my dad who has the most curiously proportioned lower body in history or me (either he's a hobbit or I'm a troll. Neither option is particularly appealing.). And while the sweatshirt fits – more or less – it's not one I would have bought given the opportunity. Don't get me wrong – I'm as ironically enthusiastic as anyone about an ugly Christmas sweater. But a bright red sweatshirt emblazoned with "JINGLE MY BALLS" wouldn't be my first choice, that's all.

At least the flip-flops round it out nicely. I look like a woman in the middle of a gender transition gone horribly, horribly wrong.

I get in the car and drop the hammer on every one of the Chevelle's 450 horses. Peeling out of the driveway and down my parents' cul-de-sac, I fish around my computer bag hoping that, against all odds, I remembered to grab my car charger after totaling my Infiniti. Miraculously, my fingers find the familiar coiled wire and I plug the jack into the Chevelle's old school lighter. My knee guiding the steering wheel as I hit sixty, I plug the phone and wait for the Apple icon to come to life. I don't know if it's grogginess from the booze and the nap, or a misplaced sense of guilt brought on by too many CCD classes as a kid, but it seems very important to me that I call Alex and explain that I'm on my way. I'm sure I'd be better off just heading home and taking the brunt of her ire in one concentrated dose, but I've never been accused of being the smartest guy in the world.

But instead of the Apple icon of life, my phone gives me the red empty battery icon of death, so I turn my attention back to the road and wait. I run through the day in my head and try to take stock. I started off by pissing myself and the day went downhill from there. Alex and I went ten rounds over finances; I got into a shouting match with my CEO and was rewarded by being tapped to give a non-apology apology to the widows of two patients we killed; I fucked my subordinate (poorly); I had Taco Bell and gin for dinner; I almost got arrested by a rent-a-cop; and I shat myself. Oh, and I voluntarily dressed up as a mentally challenged transvestite.

All in all, a solid day's work.

I try to laugh but it gets caught up in a sob and the resulting convulsion sends a snot bubble shooting out of my nose all over the windshield. Christ almighty, I'm a fucking mess. I can't even mope properly. I reach over to the glove compartment in search of something to clean off the windshield, but instead of napkins or tissues, all I see is a bank receipt and a wad of greasy old Wendy's wrappers. And judging by the smell that follows, they've been in there for almost as long as my daughter, Jules, has been alive.

Keeping one eye on the road, I keep searching, patting my hand deeper into the compartment. My fingers move quickly across what feels like a used condom and a dead cockroach until they reach something much harder, much colder and far more ominous. Their touch becomes lighter until I'm certain about what they have found. I wrap my fingers around what feels like a handle and then withdraw it from the glove compartment so I can see what it is.

A gun. A .38 Special, to be precise. A snubnose revolver favored by run of the mill street thugs. Definitely not what one would expect a 40-something public relations exec to be holding during the Wednesday evening commute. If I were the type of person who subscribes to conspiracy theories (and I am), I'd consider this a fairly strong sign someone up is trying awfully hard to push me to one side of the "Should I or Shouldn't I?" fence. Apparently, even the man upstairs thinks I should off myself.

And here I thought God wasn't real.

But even though He wants me dead, I have to give the man upstairs props. At least He wants me to be a man about it. Only at the end, just as I pull the trigger, will He give me the strength to stop being scared and have the balls to do something grand. A lot of good it will do, mind you, what with me lying on the ground and bleeding out through a gaping head wound. But if that's what He wants, who am I to tell Him no? I had no idea God is such a sick son of a bitch. I have to say, I kind of admire that about Him.

Now, admittedly, there is the possibility that something far simpler is going on. Rather than acting at the behest of some all-powerful deity, Mac may have been simply trying to foist criminal evidence onto an unsuspecting rube. And why not me, the rubiest of rubes? It certainly makes sense and doesn't require belief in God, let alone the notion that said God would bother taking an interest in little old me. Occam's razor, and all that. But that takes all the romance out of things, don't you think? I'll stick to the theory that God is real, He's vengeful and spiteful, and He's choosing to visit that vengeance and spite upon yours truly, thank you very much.

You want to do it the other way? Write your own goddamned book.

Speeding down the highway in a hot Chevelle, the steering wheel in one hand and the gun in the other, I realize I finally have the means to end it all. All I have to do is pull a trigger. That's not so hard, right? One twitch of the index finger and it's done. Sure, I'll be nervous. My palms will be sweaty, my hands will be shaking and I may even piss myself. But I can pull it off, right?

Who am I kidding? I'll probably miss me and kill some innocent bystander. One minute little old Mrs. Ladd will be sitting at her window across the street knitting a blanket for her new granddaughter, and the next she'll be dead on the floor because my sweaty-ass palm couldn't hold the gun straight. I'll end up serving thirty years upstate sharing a cell with a six-foot-six skinhead who goes by the name of Martha.

Before I can think of checking to see if the safety is on, I toss the gun on the passenger seat. Only after it lands without going off do I curse myself for being such a dumbfuck. Thirty seconds ago, I was a man with a plan. Now I'm back to being a clueless shitbird with only the vaguest notion of desperation. I've said all week I want to end it all, and now that I finally have the means,

I'm too much of a coward to pull the literal and figurative trigger.

I hear a chime and look over to see that the red empty battery icon of death has given way to a fully functioning iPhone. With life, however, comes complications, or – at least in the iPhone's case – messages. A lot of them, in both text and voice form. Jesus Christ, the annoying number on the Message icon can hardly keep up. The phone has only been dead for a couple of hours, and I've already got 43 messages and 17 voice-mails. Who the hell needs to get a hold of me so badly? With one eye on the phone and one eye on the road (yes, I'm aware that driving and texting is illegal, but I'm drunk, driving a stolen car with a gun on the passenger seat. I'm fairly certain I'm well beyond throwing caution to the wind), I scroll through the texts and see that nearly all of them are from Alex. Most are garden variety spousal communications, full of vitriol and contempt:

WHERE THE FUCK R U

R U COMING HOME OR R U TOO
BUSY FUCKING YOUR SECRETARY?

Secretary? Yikes. Thanks but no thanks. Props to her for guessing it was intra-office, though. Guess I'm not as discreet as I had hoped.

She goes on:

WE WENT TO DINNER
WITHOUT U. HOPE U AND
UR CUNT GIRLFRIEND
HAD FUN

I HOPE UR FACEDOWN

IN A DITCH AND DON'T
EVER WAKE UP

Classy broad, my wife. But just as I'm about to give up and ignore the rest of her texts, they take a surprisingly tender turn:

R U OK OR JUST BEING
A PRICK?

Well, tender for her anyway. She goes on:

THIS IS THE WINE TALKING
BUT I DON'T ACTUALLY HOPE
U R DEAD. JUST MAIMED
AND BLEEDING PROFUSTLY

I assume she means 'profusely.' She did say wine was involved.

And then there's this one:

I KNOW I'VE BEEN A BITCH.
BUT WE NEED TO TALK.
PLS COME HOME

Contrition? Courtesy? Who is this woman? She wraps it up with this pièce de la resistance:

IF U R NOT DEAD, I'M
GONNA KILL U RIGHT
AFTER I PISS MYSELF.
MIND THE PEE SPOT

This text has something for everyone: the threat of

retribution from a woman scorned, the matter-of-fact acknowl-edgement of drunken boorishness to come and the adorable concern of a woman who knows she's inconvenienced her spouse by pissing the bed. Strong work all around.

Alas, none of the other messages offer nearly the same roller coaster of emotions. Marcus left two texts and three voicemails urging me to call him back at my earliest available convenience (which I'm pretty sure was meant to be ironic); Mr. Williams and Tim both left rather loud exhortations to call back "immedi-ately, Goddammit!" (not at all ironic); and several members of the Infirmus legal team checked in to remind me once again when and where the Widows' Summit is taking place tomorrow (just plain moronic). On the upside, I am pleased to see the minions have given the big meeting a name. And it's not the antiseptic moniker I would have expected either, such as "The Mediation" or "Status Meeting." It's a fairly honest assessment of what's going to transpire. Good for them.

The rest of the messages are a hodgepodge of unsolicited solicitations, unrelated (and decidedly non-emergent) work issues and automatically generated HR notifications that I stopped paying attention to years ago. I'm about to throw the phone on the passenger seat next to the gun when I see that the most recent voicemail is from Jules. I know I shouldn't, but I put the phone on speaker and let her rip.

Hey, Dad, it's Julia.

Already, I'm a puddle. I constantly bemoan the fact that she's growing up so quickly but when I hear her voice on the phone, she still sounds like a four-year-old, high pitched and full of wonder.

I know you're probably working late and you're really busy and all, but I just wanted to remind you about my dance recital tomorrow night. It's no big deal if you can't make it, but if you're around and want to go, that would be cool.

I've done everything I can to fuck up my relationship with my kids. I'm rarely at home and when I'm there physically, I damn sure ain't there mentally. I regularly forget to pick them up at school, and on the off chance I do remember, I've usually had so many drinks that I shouldn't be driving anyone, least of all the two people I'm supposed to care about more than anyone else on the planet. I never seem to know what to say to them and when I do open my mouth, I either piss them off, embarrass them or both.

But every so often, something happens that gives me a glimmer of hope. Like now. Julia knows full well I've forgotten about her recital but she's not mad. She knows I'm an idiot who needs constant handholding. So she leaves the nicest, cutest, most adorable voicemail to remind me. And it kills me. It cuts straight through into what little remains of my soul. Driving down the highway, going way too fast for a man who is I don't know how many cocktails deep, I'm a mess. I've got tears streaming down my cheeks and snot pouring out of my nose.

So, yeah. Tomorrow night, seven-thirty at the high school auditorium. You heard right – the high school. We have officially hit the big time. Be there or be square, Daddy-O.

Not sure where she pulled that turn of phrase from, but in her little voice, she could say anything and I'd be Jell-O.

Oh, I almost forgot the best part. Mom even said she could drive everyone in the Audi—

I let loose another sob/chortle and douse the windshield once more with a globule of snot. I can't believe it. Julia has done the impossible. In the middle of the worst day of the worst week of the worst life I wouldn't wish on my worst enemy, she's given me a reason to smile. Her sweet voice is a sign that maybe life isn't the steaming pile of manure that it seems. Her joke, playing on our conversation this morning – my God, was it really just this morning? – has to be a signal that everything isn't quite as irretrievably fucked as I had always thought.

And then this happens.

> *Alex*: Julia, who are you talking to?
> *Julia*: I'm leaving a message for Dad.
> *Alex*: You tell that cocktard he can find his OWN
>   FUCKING RIDE!
> (a beat)
> *Julia*: So, yeah. Gotta go. See you tomorrow.
>   Or not.

So much for that hope thing.

I consider trying to marry up the voicemail time stamp with Alex's texts to glean which one of her mood swings had her by the tits when she bogarted Julia's voicemail, but that seems like a lot of work. I can't see straight as it is and the thought of toggling back and forth between apps while navigating the road seems well beyond my mental capacity (important side note here: Apple, for the love of Christ, get off your ass and give us split-screen technology already. The whole one app at a time thing is bullshit. Thank you. Today's TechMinute has been brought to you by Samsung).

I look up and see my exit looming in the distance. I ease the car on to the exit ramp and feel the automatic transmission downshift as it moves from the four-lane interstate to double lane country road. My avoidance target shifts as well from cop to deer. The moonless night, coupled with the Governor's recent decision to help resolve the state's cash crunch by removing superfluous streetlights doesn't make things easier. It's so dark I won't see a deer until I've driven straight through it, which leads to only one logical conclusion.

I speed up. If I can't pull the trigger myself, I'll see if a deer can do it for me. Suicide by nature, I always say. That and a stolen Chevelle.

Feeling cocky, I up the degree of difficulty by calling Marcus. The phone rings a few times more than I would have expected and, just as I start to feel guilty about calling so late, he answers.

"Sean."

"Marcus."

"Trying to avoid me?"

"Playing hard to get. There's a difference."

"How so?"

"Avoiding you does me no good. You'll only get pissed off. But I play hard to get, you're bound to like me more and more."

"Where did you learn to do your job, a John Hughes movie?"

"*Sixteen Candles* is like the Bible to my generation."

"It's an ancient relic to mine."

"You cut me deep, Marcus."

"And you do know black people don't watch that whitebread crap, right?"

"Please. John Hughes' shit is universal."

"Yeah, well, your theory still blows."

"How so?"

"Avoid me. Play hard to get. Either way, you get fucked. That may be good in rom coms, but not in real life."

"Huh."

"Huh what?"

"I'm beginning to think Molly Ringwald may not have all the answers."

Marcus chuckles. "It'll be a shame to see you go down, Sean. I still have no idea if you're any good at your job, but I have to admit, you're different. And in today's world, different is definitely good."

"See? I play hard to get and you're practically proposing."

He laughs again and this time, I can't help joining him.

"I want to see if Infirmus or Vern Williams have any comment," he says finally.

"Everyone at Infirmus, from Mr. Williams on down, wishes Marcus Cannon and Sean Reilly a long, loving and healthy life together."

"Are you drunk?"

"No," I lie. "Why? What have you heard?"

"I'm about to destroy your company and all you want to do is crack wise."

"I thought we were having a few laughs," I say, turning on to an even darker single lane road. When Alex demanded to move further out from the city ten years ago, I assented partly because it's always easier to say yes to that woman than pick a fight (which, now that I think about it, may explain our current financial woes), but also because I love it out here. But there is a challenge to living in the sticks: it is damn hard to drive drunk when you can't see shit.

"We were," Marcus is saying, "and if that's all you want to do, that's fine with me. But I thought I'd give you a chance to give me your side of the story before I nail your collective asses to the wall."

"Sounds to me like you've pretty much settled on your angle with or without a comment from us."

"That's one way to play it." I can practically hear him shrug.

"Listen, Marcus, I'll get you a comment but you've got to give me more time. At least until tomorrow afternoon."

"Why should I? What happens tomorrow?"

"Please. You're more plugged into this company than I am."

"Fine. You've got the Widows' Summit at nine."

"Bad news travels fast, I see."

"You really think you're going to resolve anything at that meeting?"

"I'm a miracle worker, Marcus. Don't you know that by now?"

"I saw your interview on local news. Some miracle. Looked more like dumb luck to me."

"Call it what you will, I'm a force to be reckoned with."

"That sound you hear is me quaking in my boots."

"That's more like it."

"I'll give you until the close of business tomorrow. After that, I'm running the story, quote or no quote."

"Fair enough."

He pauses.

"Sean, can I ask you something?"

"Isn't that the basis of our relationship?" I ease to a stop at a flashing yellow light and take a right on Kirby Lane. Almost home.

"You seem like a decent guy. Why do you work for these pricks?

"What do you mean?"

"The people running Infirmus. They're bad people. I mean, really bad. Doesn't it ever get to you, defending these slimeballs day after day?"

"They're not monsters, Marcus. Remember, we take care of people for a living."

"Come on, Sean. You don't believe that any more than I do.

Providing medical care is a front. Infirmus is nothing more than a money laundering scheme."

"Print that and you've bought yourself a libel suit."

"There's not a jury in the world that would convict me."

"Doesn't matter. Williams will litigate you into the poorhouse before you even get to a jury."

"Still, there's no other way to describe Infirmus."

"How about one of the largest healthcare companies in America, one that provides high quality care in your neighborhood, and every neighborhood across the country?"

I could hear him gag over the phone. "Spare me the bullshit, Sean."

"What did you expect? You're talking to a flak. Of course you're going to get talking points in return."

"You're not a flak."

"I run corporate communications," I correct him as I make the last sweeping turn before my driveway.

"That's your employer's problem."

"Hey—"

"You may run comms, Sean, but you're not a flak. Not by a long shot. You proved that the first time we spoke."

"What do you mean?"

"For starters, you say shit no P.R. man in his right mind would."

"Like what?"

"Like telling me – *on the record* – that I was full of shit right after you said the government's rating system is not to be trusted. A *Times* reporter looking to bust your company calls you for a quote and you immediately go DEFCON 1. That's some gangster shit, man. Most corporate P.R. guys would butter me up with flattery and then weave in some garbage about all the great work Infirmus does in the community. But not you. You come out guns blazing, consequences be damned. You may be a lot of things, Sean, but a flak ain't one of them."

"What's your point?" I ask wearily as I pull into my driveway. I wait for the garage door to finish its silent ascent and then ease the car into the garage, where the echo of the Chevelle's lumbering engine threatens to loosen my fillings. I turn off the engine so I can hear Marcus' response, though I'm not sure I want to.

"My point is I still can't tell if you're in over your head or you just don't give a shit. But either way, you seem like a nice guy who doesn't deserve what's coming to Williams and the rest of his goons."

"For what?" Now I *know* I don't want to hear the answer, but I can't help myself.

"For treating Infirmus like their own piggybank. For defrauding their stockholders, the government and every major commercial insurer. And for putting patients at risk by delivering substandard care.

"This is a witch hunt," I answer, even though my heart's not in it. "You're alleging some sort of grand conspiracy without being able to offer a shred of evidence to support it. You need to be careful, Marcus."

"No, you're the one who needs to be careful. I've got sources, documents, phone records and email transcripts. I've even got copies of a text conversation that shows that Williams was involved in every aspect of the fraud and deception, no matter how minute. Your company is dirty, Sean, and everyone is going to read about it on Sunday."

My head is spinning and I'm not sure if it's what Marcus it telling me or the gin. I get out of the car and take two woozy steps before slamming the car door shut.

"You still there, Sean?"

"Yeah." I put one arm on the roof of the car and rest my head on it. "I'm here."

"I'm sorry to be the guy to tell you all this, but someone has to. You guys are the darlings of Wall Street because you post record profits, but those profits are a sham. Or, at the very least, they come at the expense of the health of the patients you purport to serve. Everyone knows there are two ways of boosting profits – slashing costs and inflating revenues. You guys have figured out a way to do both in ways that puts patients' lives at risk."

"Bullshit."

"Are you serious?"

"You heard me," I answer with a conviction I don't really feel. "You make these accusations but you don't have anything to back it up."

"Look at your phone."

"What?"

"I just texted you something. Go ahead and look at it. I'll wait."

I take the phone from my ear and check my texts. Sure enough, there is one from Marcus – no words, just an attachment. I open it up.

"I can't read this. The print is tiny."

"Do you even know how to work your phone? Enlarge the text, dummy."

I enlarge the document but as soon as I do, I wish I hadn't. It is a memo from a regional director at Infirmus to a field manager ordering her to cut expenses. The memo notes the objections of field staff but overrules their concerns, concluding with this gem:

Any and all personnel who fail to implement these measures,

regardless of their impact on operations and patient outcomes, will
face discipline, including, without limitation, termination.

As if that's not enough, the author cc'd the CFO, which means headquarters was aware, if not complicit, in the order.

I don't say a word. I don't have to.

"See what I mean, Sean? You dumb fucks ordered people *in writing* to cut costs or be fired, patient outcomes be damned. I've got dozens more documents just like this one. I've also got current and former Infirmus quality managers telling me everything *on the record*. You rewarded staff financially for slashing costs irrespective of the impact on patient care. You furloughed experienced caregivers because they were more expensive than inexperienced ones. You even staffed clinics and hospitals below recommended levels. No surprise, at least a dozen patients have died under your care in the last seven years. And those are just the ones that people are willing to discuss on the record. I've heard whispers of dozens more."

I turn around and slide down the side of the car until I slump on to the greasy floor.

"Still with me?"

"Unfortunately."

"Good. Because I'm not talking about corporate malfeasance or breach of some kind of fiduciary duty. I'm talking about criminal activity. The company *knew* it was providing substandard care that could reasonably lead to patient harm or even death. I'm no lawyer, but that doesn't sound very good. In fact, it sounds a hell of a lot like murder, or negligent homicide at the very least."

He pauses for effect but I don't say a word. What could I possibly say?

"You still think this is a witch hunt?"

"This is all going in the story?"

"All of it and more. Hell, I've even got documentation showing high-level execs having affairs and paying off their mistresses with corporate funds. At any other company, that would be the lead but with you guys, it barely merits a footnote. I've got to hand it to you, Sean. You guys have taken Medicare fraud to a whole other level."

If Marcus can prove even half of what he's said, this is criminal behavior the likes of which American healthcare has ever seen and there's not a thing I can say or do to refute it.

"Your boys are going to jail, Sean," he says, reading my mind. "And if you're not careful, you are, too."

"So now you're judge and jury?" I ask, trying to muster indignation that I no longer feel, and haven't felt for a long time.

"Goddamn right. This is unlike anything I've ever seen, and I haven't even gotten to the revenue side of the equation. You made Enron look like child's play."

"We're innovative," I say in a lame attempt at a joke.

"Arrogant as fuck is more like it. You didn't like government reimbursement, so you pushed patients on to commercial insurance plans that paid you higher rates. If a patient didn't want that plan, you ignored them. And if they couldn't afford it, you paid it for them. Not you directly, mind you. That would be too overtly illegal, even for you guys. So instead, you set up a whole *network* of charities to pay the insurance premiums on patients' behalf."

"Dialysis Support Network." I'm no longer challenging him. Now I'm just helping him along.

"Dialysis Support Network, Cancer Support Network, Addiction Support Network – the list goes on. It's a fucking alphabet soup of graft. You guys came up with one for every disease, each one of them the same shell game. First, Infirmus funnels money to the charities in the form of donations. Then, the charities pay the insurance companies in the form of patient premiums. Finally, the insurance companies send the money back to you in the form of astronomically high reimbursement rates. Only, joke's on the insurance companies because the amount they're paying you is ten times what they received in premiums."

"All pursuant to contracts negotiated in good faith..." I say quietly.

"Tell you what, Sean," he snaps. "You do me the courtesy of sparing me your bullshit talking points, and I'll do you the favor of treating this entire conversation as off the record. Sound good?"

"Yeah," I mumble, thoroughly beaten.

"Good. Because there's no getting around the fundamental depravity of this scheme." He pauses. "You know what? Scratch that. Calling it a 'scheme' doesn't do justice to what you, Williams and the crew put together."

"Don't lump me into this," I say weakly.

"Why not? You're central to the entire operation. You're the mouthpiece, making sure no one outside the company looks under the hood."

"Clearly, I've done a bang-up job," I say, the sarcasm doing little to mask my misery.

Marcus goes on, cataloging Infirmus' misuse of Medicare dollars, which no doubt will lead to a whistleblower suit, assuming the feds don't jump in first with an indictment of their own. Every component of the company's operations is geared to maximize profits, even at the expense of patient care. Once the legal and compliance teams create the charities, clinical staff is trained to steer patients to insurance plans that pay the highest reimbursement rates. Social workers are even taught how to look out for particularly vulnerable patients – the older, sicker or poorer the patient, the better. Not wanting to question the people who are quite literally keeping them alive, patients go along with whatever staff tells them to do. It's practically foolproof.

What the patients don't know, however, is that their new coverage is usually temporary, just long enough to pay for the treatment episode. Once the treatment regimen is over – the surgery is complete, the chemotherapy has run its course, or the patient has been discharged from the hospital – the charitable assistance ends, health insurance gets canceled and the patient is on her own.

I've always known that Williams and Tim brought me into this mess because I was the perfect patsy. They made me the face of the company so they could offer me up as a sacrificial lamb when the feds came calling. But until this moment – until I hear Marcus lay everything out – I had never truly appreciated the enormity of the shitstorm facing me.

I'm guilty of a lot of things. I'm an incompetent worker, a terrible father and an even worse husband. But as bad as I have acted in nearly all aspects of my life, never did I think any of those transgressions rose to the level of criminal culpability.

"I'm going to be sick," I moan.

"Well, get a bucket, pal, because it's about to get worse."

"What?"

"I haven't even told you the best part." His use of adjectives needs work.

"There's more?" I ask incredulously.

"Would you believe Infirmus staff has been trolling safety net hospitals in certain states to move your undocumented dialysis patients into Infirmus clinics? What am I saying?" he says gleefully, answering his own question. "Of course you'd believe it. You guys have no shame!"

"Which states?"

"You only target those states that offer plans that allow undocumented workers – i.e. those with no social security numbers – to enroll. You then move these patients by the hundreds into commercial plans to pad your bottom line."

"How much?"

"Best I can tell, your company pocketed almost 50 million dollars last year in just three states."

"So you're saying the company makes money by moving illegal aliens—"

"Now, now, Sean. The correct term is 'undocumented workers.'"

"—on to commercial insurance plans with help from this network of charities?"

"That's right."

"With the benefit being that Infirmus gets paid much higher reimbursement rates than we otherwise would receive."

"Exactly. It's particularly lucrative in dialysis. Apparently, illegal aliens aren't the healthiest folks in the world and tend to suffer from kidney failure at a disproportionately high rate."

"We ran a campaign several years ago touting our work caring for these people," I say ruefully.

"I know, I saw it. Were you behind that?"

"Yeah," I acknowledge morosely.

"It was slick," Marcus says, relishing my anguish. "Remind me again … what was that tagline?"

I take a deep breath and get it over with. "'Because there's nothing illegal about high quality care.'"

He bursts out laughing. "No irony there."

"Fuck you."

"You want to be angry at someone, be angry at your bosses. They're the ones who turned a public health crisis into a profit-making machine."

"They always say we're ready to help no matter where the need arises."

"With profits like yours, it's no wonder. I'm telling you, I don't know how you stomach that place. I'd need heavy sedation just to get to sleep at night."

"Why do you think I'm a functioning alcoholic?"

"You sure you're functioning?"

"My wife doesn't think so."

He laughs again. He's enjoying this immensely. I'm not feeling quite as mirthful.

"Sean, this is going to get ugly."

"I know."

"I mean, real ugly. Do you have any idea how this will go over in the current political climate?"

"We'll get tarred and feathered."

"And that's if you get off easy. But that's not the best part."

"I thought you just told me the best part."

"For you guys, sure. But not for me."

"Okay," I groan, "what's the best part for you?"

He's practically giggling. "Some of the plans you bilked for higher reimbursement rates? They're government-run plans. And do you know what that means?"

"Yeah," I sigh.

"Are you sure?" he asks, now overtly chortling.

"It means you get the Pulitzer and I get ten to twenty in minimum security prison."

29

I t doesn't take a psychiatrist to figure out what came after I slept with Jenny. Our family broke apart, the strands of love between us not nearly strong enough to withstand Kevin's bombshell, sending each of us careening on our own axis. Mom and Dad nominally remained a couple, but something between them broke that night. For the next fifteen years, their marriage existed only as a product of routine, with each "How was your day?" answered with an equally perfunctory "Fine, how was yours?" Only when Mom got sick did the emotional gap start to close. Rather than resenting having to bathe and feed her at the end, he came to treasure it as if he suddenly remembered why she was the only woman he had ever loved.

Kevin and I made our separation more permanent by layering physical distance on top of the emotional one. We each picked a different school as far away from each other and our parents as possible, but with markedly different results. True to my word during my dramatic departure the night Kevin shattered my world, I shunned my family's help, getting only as far as my meager funds and a bone crushing financial aid package would take me, which turned out to a small liberal arts school in Ohio, thus spiting no one in the end but myself. Kevin, though, had no such qualms. He took his Dean's List grades and Division I athleticism all the way to Stanford, thereby getting a much better education than me and exacting financial revenge on Mom in the process. Of course, Dad got caught in the crossfire, but you can't really blame Kevin for that. He wasn't exactly thinking clearly at the time. None of us were.

Kevin ended up finding a lovely girl, marrying her and raising three gorgeous kids (if his Christmas card propaganda is to be believed), all while founding some tech-start up that's made him a millionaire many times over. He became everything the rest of us Reillys never were and likely never will be: emotionally stable, socially well-adjusted and financially prosperous.

I, on the other hand, while not sharing nearly as many genes with our parents as Kevin, ended up far more like them than he would. Not to brag, but I turned into just as big a philanderer as Mom and an even more prolific alcoholic than Dad. And yes, I still refer to Pete Reilly as 'Dad.' He may not be a blood relative, but he's the only father I've ever known.

Kevin, if you're reading this, suck on that.

I suppose the poetic thing to do would have been to marry Jenny and turn her into a constant reminder of Kevin's greatest failing. I could have even sent annual reminders just to make sure he never forgot. Hey, if he's going to send Christmas cards rubbing his Stepford family and enormous mansion in my face, the least I could do is shove airbrushed portraits of me and his prom date right back in his. Merry Christmas, asshole.

Poetic, but not realistic. Two days after Kevin went Jerry Springer on my ass, Jenny told me she could never be with me, claiming that being alone with me brought her too much sadness. If that's not a blow to an eighteen-year-old boy's sexual ego, I don't know what is. Can't say I blamed her, though. There was nowhere to go but down after that torrid night together. And, as long as we're being honest, she lost all allure to me once we hooked up – thrill of the chase, and all that.

Perhaps just to prove to myself how over her I really was, I decided to marry the first girl I slept with in college. Shrewd, I know, albeit a little shortsighted. But that's me, quick to make a dramatic gesture in retaliation for any slight, real or perceived. I once saw a therapist who said I have an overdeveloped sense of vengeance, spiting others only to torment myself instead.

No shit. But then, I think she had just watched too much *Princess Bride*.

So, yes. Alex and I met in college. I was in the basement of some fraternity, drinking warm beer and trying to ignore the overpowering stench of urine with a few buddies whose names escape me now. A very attractive undergrad – a freshman by the look of her – was fending off the advances of a drunken troglodyte who was trying to convince her to find a room upstairs so he could – and I quote – "make her dreams come true." This being several decades in advent of the #MeToo movement, this kind of behavior was what passed for romance at the time. The young woman had the good form to gently parry this asshole's advances without offending him (not that he would have noticed; he was so drunk, I doubt he would have remembered anything the next morning), but she was clearly looking for a way out. Seeing her predicament, I splashed a few drops of beer on my face, handed my cup to my "buddy" and ran over to her, out of breath.

"Hey, honey," I panted, planting a kiss on her cheek. "Sorry I'm late."

Without hesitating, she returned the kiss and flashed a smile that knocked me backward. Her dirty blond hair was pulled back into a ponytail and threaded through the snapback of her tattered

Minnesota Twins baseball hat. And even though she had the hat pulled down low, it couldn't hide her pale blue eyes, which glittered in the dim basement. Smiling with the ease of someone who's always in on the joke, she then took a step back, put both hands on her hips and raised her eyebrows at me suggestively.

"Where the hell have you been?"

"Running all over campus, looking for you."

"I've been here all night talking to..." She turned to the troglodyte expectantly, but he just stared back slack jawed, struggling to keep up. "This lovely gentleman," she finished for him.

"Thanks a ton," I said to him, thrusting my hand out to him. "I'm Sean."

He took my hand and shook it slowly, his mouth still agape. "Dutch," he grunted. Because, of course, that was his name.

"Great to meet you, Dutch. Listen, at the risk of being rude, I'm exhausted from looking for this little minx—" She smiled coyly and gave an aw-shucks shrug. Then, sliding her arm around my waist, she nuzzled close and sent my blood pressure up thirty points. "—so I think we're going to call it a night. Thanks for putting up with her, though. I really appreciate it."

We bounded up the stairs, leaving Dutch to wonder how a skinny runt just absconded with his sure-fire conquest. We laughed our way out of the fraternity house and on to the front lawn.

"Thanks," she said. "You're pretty good at the knight in shining armor thing."

"I do what I can. But it's not that hard when the Neanderthal is so drunk he can't form complete sentences."

"Don't be so hard on him. He had 'Suck me now' down pat."

"Classy."

"He should be. He's the house president."

I groaned. "Allow me to apologize on behalf of all men."

"You're really going to take on that kind of responsibility? That's a lot of rape, genocide and buffoonery to fess up to."

"Buffoonery?"

"Yeah. You're signing up for everything from the annoying jackass whistling at women on the street to psychopath mass murderers. It's the full spectrum of depravity."

"Where does Dutch land in that spectrum?"

"The annoying but ultimately harmless harasser. Though he did strike me as having the potential for growth."

"Into?"

"Full blown rapist. Actually, now that I think of it, I wouldn't be surprised if he had a few roofies in his pocket."

"So I'm a hero."

"I wouldn't go that far, sport," she said, slapping me playfully on the chest. "But you certainly did me a solid, that much I grant you."

This girl was smart, funny and full of sass. I was all kinds of smitten.

"I'm Sean," I offered.

"You gave him your real name?" she guffawed. "You're braver than I thought."

I shook my head. "Just dumber."

"Cute and dumb. Just the way I like 'em."

We held each other's gaze for a long moment as I tried not to blush. I failed miserably.

She took a step forward and gave me a long, soft kiss. Pulling back, she brought her mouth to my ear and whispered. "I'm Alex."

"Nice to meet you," I said hoarsely, the taste of her still lingering on my lips.

She took a step back, stuffed her hands in her jeans pockets and bounced on the balls of her feet, her eyes dancing. "What now?"

"Whaddya mean?"

"We're not really calling it a night, are we? I mean, we just met."

"What did you have in mind?"

She offered me the crook of her arm and I took it, completely unsure as to where she was taking me and not caring in the least.

30

I am alone. Somewhere in the house, the girls are puttering about, perhaps lying on their beds, faces buried in their phones as they escape the real world in favor of its digital counterpart. Alex is probably passed out or cursing me silently as she slams glass after glass of merlot. They hate me. What's worse, I hate me. I hate the man I've let myself become. I can rail all I want against people who have wronged me – and there are plenty – but in the end, I have no one to blame for what's become of me but me. It's my life. I've just chosen not to live it.

Which is why I am sitting in the quiet dark of my study.

Alone, a glass of bourbon in one hand and a gun in the other. I take a sip out of one and curiously eye the other. The revolver gleams in the moonlight peeking through the window and the trees beyond. I turn it over in my hand, my fingers brushing across the burn marks on the muzzle and scratches on the trigger guard. It is well used though not, I suspect, always used well.

I take another sip and place the tumbler on my desk, giving full attention to the gun. I kick off my dad's flip flops, stand and point the gun at the window, taking aim at the reflection looking back at me. My index finger slides to the trigger and I wonder if I have the guts to pull it.

Do it.

I bend my arm and put the barrel to my temple. Nodding softly, a tear rolls down my cheek as I stifle a sob.

It's time.

My breathing grows shallow as I cock the hammer. My trigger finger tenses and the gun wobbles slightly.

No one will miss you, Sean. No one will care.

I try to hold the gun steady, willing my finger to move.

PULL THE GODDAMN TRIGGER YOU PUSSY! PULL THE FUCKING TRIGGER!

I can't. I look at my reflection, tears streaming down its face, and I hate what I see. I cannot imagine another second as the weak and pathetic man who stares back at me, yet I cannot muster the courage to do anything about it.

I feel empty, a bottomless pit of despair.

Disconsolate, I flop back in my chair and drop the gun on my desk, opting instead for my weapon of choice: alcohol and the long road to oblivion. I empty the glass in a single swallow and reach for the bottle to refill it.

"Sean?"

My only response is the clink of ice cubes as I take a long, slow sip of Blanton's and savor the burn as the bourbon slides down my throat.

"Sean, are you in here?"

I don't bother answering because I have nothing to say. My life is over. I just haven't figured out how to end it yet. I close my eyes, take another long sip and hope she goes away. I hope everything goes away.

She doesn't. Instead, she turns on a lamp and bathes my study in warm, yellow light.

She gasps at the sight of me. "Jesus Christ."

"Alas, no," I croak. "Just me."

"You look—" She pauses to consider, perhaps trying to formulate a tactful descriptor. "—really fucking awful."

"You should talk. I thought you'd be passed out by now."

"I drank some coffee."

"How'd that treat you?"

"Good enough to make me think about having one of those," she says, nodding to my drink.

"Help yourself."

"I'll pass for now." She waits a beat. "You really do look like shit."

"Try not to sugarcoat it."

"Have you looked in a mirror?"

"I'm trying to avoid them."

"Probably a good idea. You could scare the habit right off a nun."

"Curious image, but okay."

"Seriously, Sean. You look like something out of the *Walking Dead*."

"You do remember I was in a car accident two days ago, right?"

"Yeah, but I didn't realize it was your face that took the brunt of the impact."

I have nothing to gain by saying anything so I take another healthy sip instead. At this rate, that bottle won't last to midnight.

"Whose clothes are those?"

"My dad's."

"Your dad's? Oh, Jesus. Don't tell me you were at your old house."

"I just wanted to check in, make sure the house is still standing," I say defensively.

"Let me guess – you were feeling blue so you ran home to

the only place you were really loved, the place where Mommy and Daddy made everything alright?"

"You don't have the first clue what you're talking about, you know that?"

"Enlighten me."

"I needed to sort through some things."

"Like how you're such a pussy?"

"Is there a point to all of this, or do you just get off being a cunt?"

She changes tack. "Are you coming to bed or are you going to drink alone in the dark all night?"

"You make it sound like a bad thing."

"You know, when some people are faced with challenges, they don't feel sorry for themselves and drink themselves into oblivion. They get up off their asses and do something about it."

"Some people? Like who – you?"

"As a matter of fact, yes. People like me."

"Don't make me laugh."

"I go to work every day, Sean. I'm out there doing my best to make money. Every fucking day."

"Yeah, and you spend all the money you make eight times over. Every fucking day."

She has no retort so I declare myself the decisive winner of round one and finish the glass to celebrate.

Alex opens round two. "You're a pathetic drunk, you know that?"

I eye her steadily as I fill the glass to the brim. "And a proud one at that."

She considers a response and then thinks better of it. Sighing, she grabs an empty glass from the sideboard and pours herself a bourbon before plopping into the leather chair facing me. "It's the only thing you've ever stuck with, I'll give you that."

"I stuck with you and the girls," I answer quietly, trying to meet her halfway.

She snorts in response. "Please don't tell me you're going to make that argument with a straight face."

"What? I'm here aren't I?"

"Physically, maybe, not that that's any great shakes."

"What are you talking about?" I press, knowing I should shut my mouth.

"You really want to have this conversation?"

"No, but we're doing it anyway, apparently."

"Admit it," she snaps, ignoring me. "You've been fucking around."

I don't hesitate. "Yes."

"I knew it!" she yells, then eyes me curiously. I don't think she expected me to concede defeat so quickly, marital infidelities being the least of my issues at this point. "Who is it?"

"Does it matter?"

Stumped again, she settles for an old standby. "You're a fucking pig."

"That's big out of you."

"What's that supposed to mean?"

"So that life coach of yours isn't doubling as your fuck buddy?"

"What the hell was I supposed to do?" she seethes. "I needed companionship."

"Is that what they're calling it these days?"

"You haven't looked at me with any love in your eyes in years. Do you know what that feels like? And don't even get me started on the girls," she says harshly. "You've been an absentee father so long they're practically orphans."

"It's tough to be a father to someone when their mother is always telling them what a deadbeat I am."

"Don't blame me for your inadequacies as a parent."

"You poisoned my relationship with them beyond any hope of repair."

"Explaining why you overslept or missed another game or bagged another recital is hardly 'poisoning a relationship.' It's called doing play-by-play of an alcoholic's life."

"Well," I stammer, struggling for a decent counter-punch, "you didn't have to do it with such vigor."

Whiffed on that one. She's drawn even on points.

We both retreat to our corners and sip our drinks for emotional nourishment. I look at Alex and try to remember the woman I fell in love with. It seems like a lifetime ago. The changes are more than just physical. Yes, she has a few more wrinkles around her eyes and her body isn't as toned as it used to be, but Alex remains stunning. There is a severity to her now, though, a hard edge that is unmistakable in her demeanor. It's not just with me; it's as if she has a score to settle with the world. But there are times, moments that have become all too fleeting, when she drops her façade and seems closer to the daring, open and honest woman I met in college than the cold, hard woman who sits across from me. Feeling me watch her, she looks up and holds my gaze, the vitriol I saw a moment ago dissolving.

"We're a long way from the fraternity house."

I smile. "What do you think Dutch is up to?"

"Doing ten to life upstate?"

"Nah. He's probably CEO of an investment bank."

She nods. "Married with three kids, and chairman of the board of his local United Way."

"With a hussy on the side."

"Who he cheats on."

"A side piece to the side piece? What an asshole."

"Our Dutch can't be tied down."

I smile and take a sip of my drink. I try to remember the last time Alex and I joked around at someone else's expense. I don't have that long a memory.

And then she returns to form.

"Does your side piece know you can't get it up?"

"Everything seems to be in good working order when I'm with her," I lie.

"So she's a blackout drunk like you?"

I burst out laughing. She's a bitter, spiteful shrew, but she still makes me laugh.

"You'd like her," I say, sipping my drink. "She hates me almost as much as you do."

We are quiet once more and I notice her staring at my desk.

"Is that a gun?"

I nod.

"You mind telling me where you got it?"

"You wouldn't believe it if I told you."

"Try me."

"Let's see," I say, trying to piece together the best way of describing my surreal week. "Turns out I totaled my car in the accident so I went to the scrapyard where it was towed and worked out a deal."

"So that explains the monstrosity in the garage."

"Bite your tongue. That's a Chevelle SS. She's a classic."

"A classic piece of shit."

"You have no soul."

"And you have no dick."

"I thought we covered that. I have a dick. It just doesn't work anymore."

It's her turn to laugh. "So that's how you got the car. It doesn't explain the gun."

"The gun was in the car."

"I beg your pardon?"

"In the glove compartment. I was looking for a napkin and found the gun."

"Why was it in the car?"

"I guess Mac must have put it there."

"Mac?"

"The owner."

"Of the car?"

"Of the scrapyard. And the car, now that you mention it."

"And he just gave it to you?"

"No, I traded him my car for it. I already told you that."

"You traded your car for his car. Not the gun."

"We've really got to work on misplaced pronouns."

"So how did you get the gun?"

"We've been through this. It was in the glove compartment."

"Yes, but why? Why did Mac give you the gun?"

"I don't know. Maybe he forgot it was in there."

She shoots me withering look. It makes me want to crawl under the chair and shit myself. Instead, I just drink more bourbon.

"Don't you think it's odd for someone to just misplace their gun? That seems like something you'd want to hold on to."

"Unless they didn't want to hold on to it."

"Exactly," she says. That may be the first thing we've agreed on in months.

"Your point being?"

"He wanted you to have it. Why?"

"Maybe for my protection. The junkyard was in a pretty tough neighborhood."

"You're shitting me, right?"

"Little bit," I acknowledge.

"So Mac gave you a car and a gun, all for a song, and now your fingerprints are all over them. What are the odds the cops come calling?"

I shrug. "That's the least of my problems right now."

"What do you mean?"

"You don't want to know."

"Our finances?"

"You mean the fact that we have no finances?"

"Right," she says with a dark laugh. "Is that why you're here in the dark feeling sorry for yourself?"

"No. I mean, yes, that's part of it, but..." I trail off, searching for the words to describe the cavern of despair I'm facing. "It's everything. It's my dead-end job. It's my asshole bosses. It's my inability to find joy in absolutely anything. It's how my daughters hate me and my wife loathes me. It's our finances, our family and the fact that I'm almost certainly going away on an extended forced vacation."

"Where?"

"Wherever the closest medium security facility is."

"Prison?" she asks, dumbfounded.

"Prison," I agree.

"What for?"

"Fraud, murder, stock manipulation – a whole host of things."

"Murder?" Her face has lost all color. I've got her attention.

"Relax. I didn't do it."

"Says you." Gotta hand it to her. She's still got it. "When?"

"When what?"

"When are you going to prison?"

"After the trial, I suppose. Assuming we even get that far. I don't know how it works, but I have to think shit's gonna start happening soon."

"Is that why you have the gun?"

"What? No! I told you. That's Mac's gun."

"What are you two tied up in?"

"Listen, I don't know Mac. At least, I didn't before yesterday. I totaled my car, then traded it for Mac's car and he gave me the gun, almost certainly to frame me for a crime he committed."

"And that's why you're going to jail."

"No. I mean, I might go to jail for whatever he's framing me for, but that's not the real reason."

"You mean you've committed another murder?" She's totally lost.

"No," I answer, trying unsuccessfully to stifle a laugh at the absurdity of this conversation. "I haven't. But I'll probably go down for it."

"You're being framed for *two* murders?"

"More than two."

"Sean," she says darkly, putting her drink on the table next to her and adopting the stern tone of a parent talking to a delinquent child, "what the fuck is going on?"

"Work."

"You're a P.R. flak. How could you possibly be caught up in anything so nefarious?" Professing my innocence while simultaneously deriding my profession. She's a peach, my wife.

I take a deep breath and explain my week with Williams and Tim. I tell her about the widows meeting tomorrow and my many conversations with Marcus. I sketch out the story that the *Times* will publish on Sunday and what that will ultimately lead to – the investigations, the arrests and the prison time.

"But you didn't do any of it," she says when I finish. For once, she seems to be genuinely on my side.

"Nope, not knowingly. But I'm not sure that matters. If I understand this right, it's all going to come down to what I should have known."

"And what should you have known?"

"That my bosses are crooks, the company is a house of cards and we've been killing people through shoddy care. It's all there.

It has been for years. I've just been too dumb and too disinterested to notice. Or care."

"And that's enough to send you to jail?"

"I don't know," I say with a shrug. "But I'm pretty sure Williams and Tim are cooking up documents right now making it look like it is. In fact, they'll probably make it look like I was one of the masterminds of the whole scheme and they were duped like everyone else."

"You think that will work?" she asks dubiously.

"Who knows?" I answer, taking a big sip. "But they'll have a gaggle of lawyers on their side. And I—"

"Will have a public defender," she finishes for me.

"You thought I was an absentee father before? Just wait until the SEC and FBI get through with me."

"Jesus Christ."

"I'll drink to that."

We raise our glasses dejectedly and finish our drinks. We are quiet for another moment until Alex nods towards the gun.

"Is it loaded?"

"I don't think so. Besides, the safety is on. It's harmless. Look."

I stand and walk to the desk. Placing my glass down, I pick up the gun and weigh its heft. Then, I turn, take aim at the spathiphyllum across the room and pull the trigger. A flash erupts from the muzzle and the resulting noise is deafening. My arm flies back from the recoil, and I nearly punch myself in the head. Alex shrieks and we look at each other in horror.

"You killed the plant!"

I look over at the peace lily and see smoke wafting up from the shattered flowerpot. Dirt is everywhere as the plant lies on the floor, its once perky white flowers now listing sadly. The smell of cordite is overpowering.

"Holy shit," I whisper.

"What are we going to do?" she asks, her voice quiet but urgent.

"Buy another plant?" I suggest.

She shakes her head in disgust. Too bad. I actually thought that was kind of funny.

"You're not thinking of using that on..." Her voice trails off.

"More than just the plant?"

She nods.

"Whatever would give you that idea?" I ask facetiously.

"Oh, I don't know – the fact that I found you alone, shitfaced in the dark, facing a lifetime behind bars."

"After being framed by my boss."

"And some meth dealer at the junkyard."

"Don't forget surrounded by a family who hates me."

"We don't *hate* you—"

"While drowning in debt."

"Okay, *that* we hate you for."

"With a scapegoating wife."

"Who's drop dead gorgeous."

"And delusional."

We pause, knowing we could do this for hours, only to end it when one of us gets bloody. And I think we both know that person would be me.

"Is this the beginning of the end?" she asks finally.

"More like the end of the end."

"For us or for you?"

I see her eyes move from my face to my hand, which rests by my side, still clutching the gun, and back again. I hold her gaze and while her eyes show no love for me, I see at least a glimmer of concern; she definitely doesn't love me, but I don't think she wants me to die. At least, not here anyway. That would leave a tremendous mess to clean up.

"For us," I answer. "Who gives a fuck what happens to me?"

"I do."

I frown.

"I do," she protests, then catches herself. "I mean, it would be good for the girls not to have a convicted felon for a father."

"Or a suicide victim."

"That they could probably get their heads around."

I laugh even though I can't tell if she is joking. I raise my hand, bringing the gun close to my face. I hear her inhale sharply and look up.

"What's wrong? You tell me to kill myself every other day."

"I don't mean it," she says weakly.

"Bullshit. You've never been more persuasive."

I look at the gun, urging myself to find the will but knowing I'll come up short. I shake my head sadly and extend the grip of the gun to her.

"Take it."

"You sure?"

"No, but you know me. I'm too much of a pussy to use it anyway."

She exhales and takes the gun from me.

"I'd say everything is going to be okay," she says, a sad smile playing across her face.

"Except it's not," I finish for her.

She holds the gun awkwardly in both hands. "Are you going to be okay tonight?"

"No," I answer matter of factly. "But that's no different than any other night."

She considers this. "You know, I really did love you once."

"Me, too. But those times are long gone."

"Yeah," she agrees softly, "I guess they are." She turns to walk out the door. As she is about to leave, she stops to look back at me. "But that doesn't mean I hate you."

"Sure you do."

She smiles sadly. "Yeah, maybe. But I still don't think you should do anything stupid."

"I think we both know that ship sailed a long, long time ago."

One last sad smirk and she's gone.

I look at the bottle and see there's only an inch of bourbon left. I chug it, pleased that the burn has given way to a comforting warmth. I might as well be drinking Earl Grey. Holding the empty bottle to the light, I think I've finally graduated to full-blown degenerate drunk status. I drop the bottle on the floor and lean back against the chair, closing my eyes and laughing silently. Only a moron like me would kill himself in a way that takes years instead of seconds. My cowardice knows no bounds.

I sit for hours, drifting in and out of lucidity as I try to make sense of everything my life has become and everything it hasn't. I try to chart a way through the morass but no clear path emerges. There are too many obstacles to navigate and my muddled and fuzzy mind can't make sense of it all. No matter how many times I turn the problem over in my head, the only answer that makes sense is my demise. I can't think of anyone – not one fucking person – who would be better off if I live.

Not even myself.

I stagger to my feet and nearly trip on the empty bottle, my first unsteady step sending it scurrying across the floor. It hits the far wall with a crash, exploding into a swirl of misshapen shards that catch the light – twisting it and shaping it into a brilliant kaleidoscope of color – and disappear a moment later, leaving me to wonder if it was real. That's me, I think, swaying wildly. A flash of light then nothing, scattered pieces of refuse the only remnant of my existence. This is how I am destined to depart.

Not with a bang but a whimper. Me and Mistah Kurtz.

I steady myself on the desk and let out a pained howl. I am

so scared, so appallingly frightened, but I don't see any other way. I am nothing. I deserve to be nothing. My entire body shakes as I wail, tears streaming down my face as I think of Alex and Claire and Julia. Mom and Dad and Kevin. Everything and everyone I once loved flashes in my head as I say goodbye one last time. They'll be better off without me, I tell myself. They always will.

The sobbing subsides and my breathing steadies so I let go of the desk and lurch toward the door. My stomach, sour after the punishment I have leveled on it today, registers its disapproval with each lumbering step. I careen down the hall past my girls' bedrooms, trying not to wake them but failing miserably as I bounce from one wall to the other, knocking pictures off the wall as I go. One of them, I see, is our wedding portrait. Even in this state, I can't help but laugh at the symbolism. I think I hear one of the girls asking sleepily what's going on, so I blurt out a barely intelligible, "I'M FINE!" following by a loud belch to assuage their concerns. Swerving into the bathroom, I have a fleeting thought that I may be making things worse.

I rummage through the vanity drawers, grabbing bottles at random, struggling to read the labels and then tossing them over my shoulder when I realize they are not what I'm looking for. Tearing through one drawer then another, I turn the bathroom into a war zone, littering the floor with medicine bottles and gauze pads and filling the air with anguished cries and epithets.

"What the fuck?"

I look up and see Alex looking at me with wild eyes and even wilder hair.

I stand up and woozily survey the carnage. I turn back to her and shout the same assuring words I gave to the girls.

"I'M FINE!"

She shakes her head and turns to trudge wearily back to bed. She seems unconvinced.

I, however, am undeterred. I return to my search until it hits me. The medicine cabinet. I jump up and whip open the cabinet door, knocking bottle after bottle off the shelves until I find the one I want. I slam the door shut and catch a glimpse of my grotesque face in the mirror before heading out. Alex was right. I could wake a corpse with this face. Good thing the widows won't have to see it tomorrow.

I decide to spare Claire and Julia any more noise, so I take the back stairs to the kitchen, grabbing a can of IPA from the fridge as a reward for my courtesy. I find my way back to the study but, forgetting about the broken bourbon bottle, I walk through a minefield of broken glass. Swearing loudly, I take four excruciating steps in stocking feet and drop unceremoniously into the desk chair. Gingerly, I peel off my socks and check the soles of my feet to find rivulets of blood oozing past half a dozen shards of glass. Any question of where the gods stand on me taking my life have been put to rest.

You want me dead? Fine, fuck you, too.

I open the beer and take a monstrous sip – too big, in fact, as my mouth is quickly over capacity, sending beer pouring down my chin. I put the can down with a thunderous belch, which my stomach – now in a state of open revolt – views as the perfect opportunity to send what I contend is an unreasonably large dose of bile northward. Clamping my mouth shut to avoid hurling all over the study (I may be on the verge of killing myself, but that doesn't mean I have to be a slob about it), I swallow hard and then take another swig of beer to wash away the taste of gastric acid, MexiMelts and self-loathing. My stomach, naturally interpreting this as a sign of escalation, responds in kind, sending still more bile upward, thereby sending me down the worst kind of shame spiral: Swig, boot, swallow, repeat.

This goes on for longer than I care to admit until, finally capitulating, I collapse in front of the trash can and let my stomach purge itself of the contents of most of my liquor cabinet. If the smell is any indication, my insides are already dead, so I try to get on with the business of bringing the rest of my body there along with it. I find the bottle I stole from the medicine cabinet and, with bleary and bloodshot eyes, try to make out the label once more.

Ambien.

I shake the bottle and am rewarded with the satisfying rattle of dozens of little white pills. Unfortunately, opening the bottle proves too much for my current state. As much as I twist, turn, grasp, grunt and scream, the goddamn bottle refuses to yield. Bathed in sweat, I slump against the side of the desk and catch my breath. I can't believe it. Thwarted by a fucking child safety cap.

Fuck that. Fuck this bottle, Fuck the do-gooder engineers who made it and fuck anyone who thinks they're going to get between me and sweet oblivion.

I push myself up, swaying wildly as I get to my feet. I steady myself against the desk once more and catch my last reflection in the window. Tears pour down my cheeks, snot streams from my nose and a string of vomit swings like a pendulum from my chin. With a loud sniff, I wipe my face with the back of my sleeve and look around the room for something to help.

I try stabbing, cutting and whacking the bottle with scissors, a letter opener and even a stapler, but the bottle still refuses to yield. I'm on the verge of giving up when I catch a glimpse of moonlight reflecting back at me from the far corner of the room. I stumble over to investigate and, after clambering over a stack

of extra printer paper and pushing aside a box of obsolete Black-
berry and Nokia power cords, a smile creeps across my face.

Leaning against the wall next to the filing cabinet, is a sword.
And not just any sword. A katana. A gently curved 28-inch
single-edged blade with two-handed hilt used by the samurai
before that particular vocation fell out of favor. Five years ago, as
part of its first foray into international markets, Infirmus tried to
acquire a small chain of Japanese hospitals. Williams, drunk
with adoration from Wall Street, began to share its opinion that
his shit didn't stink and thought he could do internationally
what he had done in the U.S. Spurred on by investment bankers
who never met an acquisition that wasn't worth pursuing, he
flew a bunch of us over to Tokyo to negotiate and close the deal.
I'm still not sure how I got invited. Presumably there to craft a
public announcement, I spent most of my time conducting what
I believe remains the definitive review of Tokyo sake bars and
massage parlors.

Unsurprisingly, the deal was atrocious. The Japanese
company, rife with accounting errors and built on a foundation
of lies only slightly less audacious than what we ended up
building in the U.S. several years later, was a house of cards.
Once the fraud came to light a year later, the company was
forced to write off the entire deal for next to nothing. It was the
one significant blemish on Williams' otherwise sterling record.

You know, until now.

None of this was known at the time, of course – at least, not
to those of us on the American side of the table. Instead,
convinced of our own brilliance in taking the first step towards
the creation of an international healthcare behemoth, we were
flush with excitement. And why not? With the Street's favorable
response, we had earned the right to blow off some steam. So it
was no surprise that, in the afterglow of the deal's announcement, both management teams went to a lavish celebratory

closing dinner. The night was a blur, with countless toasts to our good fortune and the continued success of our combined enterprise. Each speech was met with a deafening chorus of "SAKE BOMB!!" from the once staid but now frenzied executives.

The highlight, though, was when Mr. Akiyama, chief executive of our new Japanese subsidiary, rose to speak. The entire table came to a fevered hush as he ushered in two beautiful young women dressed in traditional kimonos pushing a cart draped with a Japanese flag. In halting English, he spoke to us of duty, honor and humility, telling us, with his voice breaking dramatically, that this was the proudest moment of his life. A discreet nod signaled the women to lift the flag, revealing a dozen gleaming katanas. Taking one of the swords, he turned to Williams, bowed deeply and presented it to his American counterpart, a gesture he repeated with each of us around the table. It was a deeply moving experience, not the least because it meant the next three hours was a bacchanalia of sake, screaming and swordplay. It was a wonder we got out of there alive.

Needless to say, the swords were a big hit, though they did cause a kerfuffle at the Narita airport when a bunch of hung over American healthcare executives tried to stuff an army's worth of folded steel into the overhead compartments. Apparently, that shit don't fly in the friendly skies. Alex was similarly unimpressed when I poured myself out of the cab and stumbled up the walk into our house, a garment bag on one shoulder and a sheathed sword on the other. She forbid me from displaying the weapon and banished it to my study, though the deep recesses of the attic were her preferred destination for it.

Now, five years later, standing here in the early morning quiet, drunk to the point of collapse and morose to the point of surrender, I reach out and grasp the sword's hilt. In stark contrast to the clunky and crude revolver, the katana is surprisingly light and elegant. I grasp it with two hands and move it slowly in front of me, mesmerized by the moonlight glistening off the blade.

It is perfect.

I walk back to the desk and place the bottle of pills upon it. I take one step back and steady myself, taking a wide stance before raising the sword above my head. With a deep breath, I close my eyes and bring the blade down with every fiber of strength I can muster. I hear something ricochet off the book-shelf to my left just as the sword embeds itself in the desk with a mighty thump. Opening my eyes slowly, I see the blade has sunk nearly an inch into the reclaimed wood but the pill bottle has disappeared. I let go of the sword and decide to go in search of the bottle and what I imagine are dozens of pills scattered across the room, freed by my mighty swing.

And that's when I see the bottle, lying innocuously on the floor a foot to my right, not a scratch on it.

Mother of pearl.

Cursing, I grab the bottle and place it back on the desk. I take another deep breath followed by an even mightier swing and bury the blade even deeper in the desktop. But once again, the bottle receives only a glancing blow, shooting out from beneath blade and skidding across the room. I make five more attempts, each with increasing vigor, but all I have to show for my efforts are five more gashes in a once priceless desk and steadily larger pit stains on my dad's sweatshirt.

I start to sob. This can't be happening. And yet, how else did I expect it to go? I've been a failure all my life, so why wouldn't I also be a failure in ending it? Not knowing what else to do, I trudge across the room to fetch the bottle, its indestructibility mocking me as I place it on the desk once more. Raising the blade above my head, I realize my heart's not in it anymore. I find myself wondering if this is what Sisyphus felt like. Did he keep pushing the stone not because he wanted to get to the top of the hill, but because he had nothing better to do?

I'm not even looking at the bottle when the blade comes down weakly, which is why what comes next is so surprising. The blade hits its target and the bottle slices in two, sending pills skittering in all directions. I'm so surprised, it takes me a moment to realize what happened. Then, with an excitement I didn't think I could muster any longer, I drop the sword and crawl around the room in search of Ambien. Undoubtedly the most macabre treasure hunt I've ever been a part of, it is a success; after five minutes of stabbing myself in the knees and palms with shards of glass, I have enough pills to do the job, even if some of them are now red with blood.

Flush with confidence, I walk back to the desk and take a big swig of warm beer with impunity – my stomach having already emptied itself of ammunition for another counter-attack – and start gobbling up pills. I suck them up like a fucking Hoover vacuum, pausing only to take a swig of beer every ten or twenty pills to wash them down. My hands finally empty, I slump down on the floor, suddenly exhausted again, and wait for the pills to do their job.

Between the gin, the bourbon, the Ambien and the drudgery of life, I'm tired. Unrelentingly exhausted. I want to sleep and never wake up. Closing my eyes and shifting my weight to get comfortable, I sigh contentedly, ready at last to surrender myself to oblivion.

THURSDAY

31

I t probably comes as no surprise that the Almighty and I
have a complicated relationship. We've had our share of
conversations, though these have mostly been one-sided
affairs in which I pleaded for His intervention (usually in the
form of passing grade, a negative pregnancy test or an early end
to a particularly egregious hangover) while He remained
conspicuously silent. It was enough to make me think He
resented my entreaties. As a kid who was dragged to church
every Sunday, this started to grate on me. I mean, if I was forced
to get dressed up and go to a friend's house every Sunday, the
least he could do is throw something my direction when I went
all hallowed be His name on His ass. I would have liked something in return, especially seeing as I was expected to feast on
his body and blood on a weekly basis.

I'm not suggesting I wanted to go Old Testament and have an
honest to God back and forth with Him like David or Noah. In
the first place, I was in no position to build an ark or combat
pestilence or deliver an entire people from a monarch with a
God complex to safety. I was twelve, for Christ's sake. All I'm

saying is that it would have been cool to get a sign like the ones I learned about in Sunday school. Nothing big or obtrusive – maybe a burning bush or a quick visit from a seraph or two. That's all.

But as I got older, I began to understand the folly of such hopes. I don't want to start a theological debate here, but I think we can all agree that there is significant difference of opinion as to His existence. Second, assuming He does exist, I doubt very seriously He gives a rat's ass about me, or any other individual for that matter. With 7.5 billion people on this planet – and who knows how many hundreds of billion more plants, animals and insects – the sheer numbers are against it. It's really just a matter of statistics. He's got too many other things on His mind. Now, if we're talking genocide on a mass scale – something like the Holocaust or the Hutus vs. the Tutsis – then maybe that's different. Maybe His interest gets piqued. But even then, I think we can all agree that His record ain't the greatest on this front either.

And then there's question of what would have happened if He did decide to reach out for some reason. Can you imagine what a bunch of twelve and thirteen-year-olds would have done to me if, all of a sudden, I started conversing with a burning bush on the way to school? Or if an archangel paid me a visit during recess? They would have crucified me. For real, I mean, with the cross, and nails and everything. And, don't forget this was back in the day, well before counseling and mindfulness and all the other hand-holding crap that kids get in school today took hold. You think Mr. Powell would have stepped in to save me during homeroom? You're out of your mind. He would have channeled his inner Pontius Pilate and found an excuse to go to the can to wash his hands, or maybe run out back for a smoke.

The point is, me and God don't have the best relationship.

I'm not saying it's bad, necessarily. I'm just saying we have come to an understanding that we'd both be better off if neither of us bothered the other all that much, which is to say not at all.

Given that God and I haven't seen eye to eye on too many things and given that I just took my own life, which, as I understand it, is frowned upon by virtually all of Christendom, a unanimity that is, ecumenically speaking, quite rare these days – given all of this, I did not hold high hopes of being welcomed into His kingdom (let alone His arms) once I departed my Earthly vessel. So you can appreciate my surprise at my current circumstances. I never expected to being surrounded by bright light and hearing His name being invoked repeatedly. Admittedly, I've been down this road before, as recently as Monday when I thought my reward following the car crash was entry into His home in the clouds, only to discover that the only cloud I'd be touching was an airbag and the only reward I would receive was a disfigured face.

But I'm a sucker for punishment. Plus, this feels markedly different. In the first place, I feel squishy and warm, and not in a bad way. It is as if I'm enveloped in the comforting amniotic sac of my rebirth. And second, it's not my own voice I hear invoking the name of the Almighty; it's that of a delicate flower. The fear and disdain of my Earthly bound life is gone, replaced with angelic murmurings of love and concern.

I sigh contentedly, though, if we're being totally honest, that deep breath does reveal one incongruence I could do without: the smell. I had no idea God would put up with the kind of filth that is wafting into in my nostrils. It is at once funky, fetid and sour. It smells like a wet dog ate a dead rat, puked it up and wallowed around in the vomit before expiring himself. In fact, it may be the worst and most intense odor I have ever experienced. But, if this is the price of admission to life ever after, then I guess I can stomach it.

(But, wow, is it rancid).

Thankfully, the rapturous voice continues its melodic chant. Its repeated invocation of the Almighty gives me comfort and makes me think that, finally, everything will be better. With one last deep (and just as rancid) breath, I take a chance and open my eyes.

Which is precisely when everything goes to shit.

I'm not in heaven; I'm in my study. I'm not bathed in a celestial amniotic sac; I'm lying in a pool of my own vomit. And there's no angel chanting rhythmically to God; there's only an ashen-faced Claire, kneeling in front of me, rocking back and forth as she repeatedly whispers in a panic-stricken voice, "Oh God. Oh God..."

She should save her breath. There is no fucking God.

I try to pick my head up, which is a mistake. The pain is unbearable. To calm Claire, I resort to a groan, which, while impersonal, is the best I can muster. Trouble is, once she sees that I am alive, her volume increases exponentially.

"Oh God! Oh God!" She really needs to find another mantra. "You're alive!"

"Barely," I croak. My tongue feels like it's been dipped in plaster.

"Oh God! Oh God! Oh—"

"Claire, we need to get past that."

"Sorry. I mean, I needed to use the printer and then I saw you."

"In all my glory."

"I thought you were dead."

"So did I."

"What happened?"

Well, Claire, your old man decided to off himself. But, as with every other phase of his life, it has ended in unmitigated failure.

"Drank too much."

"But what about…"

She trails off. I look at her face but she isn't looking at me. She's looking at the floor. I turn my head to follow her gaze and feel bile and booze ooze out of the carpet under my head. There are dozens of little white pills sprinkled across the floor, like Jimmies on a vomit sundae.

"Did you…?" She can't finish the question, which is just as well because I can't answer it.

"I drank too much, Claire. And when you're drunk, you do some stupid shit."

She looks up and stares right through me. A single tear rolls slowly down her cheek. We hold each other's gaze for at least a minute, a thousand words exchanged between us but not one of them spoken. When I am too ashamed to face her anymore, I look away, defeated. She gets up and walks to the door. As she's about to leave, she turns and looks at her father once more, a broken man lying in a puddle of his own filth.

"Dad, you stink."

Before I can ask if she means the choices I've made or the way I smell, she's gone. She doesn't have to answer. I already know.

She means both.

I spend the next hour cleaning myself and as much of the study as I can. I douse the carpet with cleaner and scrub it until my knuckles are raw, but to no avail. The acrid stench is still as powerful as ever. I bomb the carpet with deodorizer and fill every outlet with plug-in air fresheners, but even that doesn't make a dent. Now, the room smells like vomit and roses – not exactly the scent Glade was going for. Humbled by the strength of my own stomach acid, I quit the field and declare defeat. Short of the EPA moving in and declaring it a Superfund site, the study is a total loss.

I peel Dad's clothes off me, double bag them and throw them

in the trash barrel in the garage, taking care to make sure the lid is secured tight, lest the paint peel off the walls from the smell. Thankfully, the girls have left for school, so I traipse naked upstairs with impunity to my bathroom where I shower, using every potion and gel in Alex's arsenal to wash away the stink. Twenty minutes later, smelling of lavender, chamomile and sandalwood with only an occasional whiff of gastric acid, I cut the water, taking care not to wrench the brand new shower handle off its moorings. After drying off and dressing in my own clothes, I trudge back downstairs to rummage for food. With the kids gone and Alex skulking about somewhere (probably in her closet, paralyzed with indecision over which of thirteen pairs of Manolo Blahniks to wear), I sit at the island in merciful silence, pondering my options over a bowl of granola.

It's not even eight o'clock so there's more than enough time to make the Widows' Summit – assuming I still give a shit. Or, I could blow off the rest of the day and enjoy myself. I try to think of what stay-at-home moms and dads do when everyone else is at work – spa days, liquid lunches, afternoon matinees – and realize with a start that there's not one thing I enjoy doing. And even if there was, I can't afford it.

I turn back to my granola, which has turned out to be a horrible breakfast choice. In the first place, it's the loudest cereal known to man. Every bite is like a jackhammer to my skull, every crunch a punch to my frontal lobe. I'm not even halfway done and already my eyeballs ache. Second – and this is no disrespect to the good people at Quaker Oats – granola is dry. I mean, really dry. Like licking the Sahara dry. I'm chasing each bite with what seems like a gallon of orange juice and still there's not an ounce of moisture in my mouth. Jesus, I can't even pick a breakfast food properly.

Which brings me to my next idea. Maybe I should just man up and finish the job I started last night. I should go upstairs, march into my bedroom and get the gun out of the shoebox under Alex's side of the bed where she keeps all of the things she doesn't want me to find, like her IUD, spare cash and love letters from Robbie Mueller, the head of our neighborhood association.

On cue, I hear the click of Alex's heels marching purposefully behind me, stopping only when they're right behind my chair. I don't turn around because I don't need to. Her disdain is palpable. I table the gun idea. For now.

"So much for not doing anything stupid."

"Whaf fat fuppose foo mean?" I ask, my mouth full of granola. Jesus, some saliva would help. I figure I can't get any lower in Alex's eyes so I take a huge swig of orange juice directly from the jug.

"Do you remember what we talked about last night? Or did you black out again?"

"I remember," I say, not wanting to admit that the details of our conversation – let alone that we had the conversation at all – are fuzzy.

"So?"

"So, what?"

"So," she sighs, "wouldn't you consider downing an entire bottle of sleeping pills stupid?"

"Not if you're hoping never to wake up."

"Jesus, Sean. How fucking selfish can you be?"

"Are you kidding me?" I ask, turning to face her. "This coming from the woman who never met a dollar she wouldn't spend on herself?"

"Do you have any idea what you've done to Claire?" she persists, ignoring my retort. "To both girls?"

"They're fine."

"Your daughter finds her father face down in a pool of vomit and sleeping pills and you think she's *fine*?"

"I wasn't face down."

"FUCK YOU, SEAN!" She pushes me in the chest with both arms, slamming me backwards into the island countertop. Mother of pearl, that's going to leave a nasty bruise. Right around L1/L2, if my high school bio class serves me correctly. Wild-eyed, she stares at me, daring me to say something. I take the pussy's way out and keep my trap shut. "You can hate me all you want," she says, her voice breaking, "but don't hate your daughters."

"I don't hate them," I say quietly.

"Then show them something more than the contempt you feel for everyone else."

"What about the contempt they have for me? While we're at it, what about the contempt you have for me?"

"This isn't about us, Sean. It's about you. You hate your life? Fine. Change it. Get a new job. Get a new wife, for all I care. But don't take the coward's way out."

"You don't think it takes guts to do what I did?"

"Not one little bit," she seethes. "You're a fucking coward, Sean. You always have been."

"So this is all my fault?"

"What do you want? To blame someone else for your shitty life?"

"Just like you to try and wriggle your way out of any responsibility for the shit we're in."

"Oh, no! Don't you dare do that, you son of a bitch. I'll take my share of the blame for our wrecked marriage but that's not what this is about."

"That's entirely what this is about!"

"No it isn't! This is about you and your desire to wallow in misery."

I'm incredulous. "You think I like being miserable?"

"You don't just like it. You thrive on it. It fuels your enmity."

"You're out of your fucking mind." I turn away from her and grip the counter, clenching my teeth as my breathing grows shallow. My heart pounds. My whole body shakes. I lash out with my hand and send the cereal bowl and orange juice flying off the counter, the bowl shattering as its flight is cut short by the far wall. The jug cartwheels off the counter and on to the floor, sending orange juice pinwheeling across every surface. First the study and now the kitchen, I'm a one man wrecking crew.

I turn towards Alex, my eyes narrowed in anger. "I've got nothing!" I spit at her. "I am nothing! My whole life, I've convinced myself that I'll be nothing like my parents. I'll be a loyal husband, a wonderful father and a great big success. Guess what? I'm none of that!"

"News flash, asshole. The whole world tries to run from their parents only to end up being exactly like them in the end."

"Not Kevin. The guy who went to such lengths to show how worthless I was because I was the bastard son, he's the one who ends up being rich beyond anyone's dreams."

"Is it really all about money with you?"

"No!" I yell, trying to hide the fact that, yes, I really am that shallow. "But it would certainly help!"

She shakes her head in disgust. "There are other ways of measuring worth, you know."

"Yeah, but as you're so fond of pointing out, I don't exactly score well in those categories, either. I'm a fucking failure, Alex. And if you still need convincing, name one person who would miss me if I was gone."

"Your dad."

I laugh. "As far as he knows, I'm Mary Queen of Scots."

"She was beheaded, you know."

"Heavy is the head that wears the crown."

"He knows who you are," she says, a hint of sympathy

creeping into her voice. "And while you're caring for him like a good son, your brother is nowhere to be seen."

"He's too busy making piles of money."

She rolls her eyes. "Okay, how about your daughters, you dumb fuck?" So much for sympathy.

"Please. They'll be way better off without me."

"Yeah, 'cause studies show kids of parents who commit suicide are so well adjusted."

"So I should stick around just so they can stay out of therapy?"

"No! You should stick around because they love you."

"They don't love me! No one does!"

"Jesus fucking Christ, Sean, get over yourself! They're teenagers. They're sullen and rotten and self-absorbed. But doesn't mean they don't love you."

"They should try showing it once in awhile."

"It's hard showing something to someone who's drunk all the time."

"So it's my fault again."

She shakes her head sadly, her eyes suddenly brimming with tears. All of the air seems to have gone out of her. "This isn't about whose fault any of this is," she says quietly. "This isn't about the girls or me or anyone else. It's only about you. It always has been."

She takes a deep breath and smoothes front of her suit. She wipes her eyes dry and I realize that the lines around them have deepened. We have both grown so much older in sixteen years of marriage though, clearly, not much wiser. She looks at me sadly.

"I can't fix whatever's broken inside of you, Sean. No one can. But it's not because we don't want to. It's because you won't let us."

"That's not true," I whisper.

"Yeah, it is. And I'll tell you something else. The only person who hates you, Sean, is you."

She slams the door behind her and I am alone once again, the only sound the incessant drip of orange juice from every surface of the kitchen.

32

"Pleased to meet you, Mr. Reilly."

I stare at the outstretched hand and wonder what I'm supposed to do with it. Ninety minutes earlier, I decided to leave Mac's gun exactly where it was and do something else to occupy my time. How meeting the widows of two people my company murdered is an improvement over climbing back into bed and being alone with my thoughts is a question I've decided to table for the time being. In the interim, I'm wracking my brains to figure out who is offering to shake my hand. She just introduced herself, but I'll be damned if I was listening.

"Mr. Reilly?"

My eyes move from a gray, wrinkled hand to a kind, wrinkled face. Even the eyes smile at me. I take the hand and scramble to find my voice.

"Pleased to meet you as well. Sorry, I ... uh, I think I was somewhere else just now."

"I'm sure we'd all like to be somewhere else," she says, still smiling even as sadness creeps into her eyes.

"You're absolutely right, Mrs...?"

"Wheeler."

"Wheeler?" I ask, surprised. "I thought Mr. Wheeler was thirty-two years old."

"He was."

"Well, excuse me for saying so, Mrs. Wheeler, but you're a little older than I expected."

"That's okay," she says sweetly. "You look a whole lot shittier than I expected."

Son of a gun. The old lady has a potty mouth. "Er, yes," I stammer. "I suppose I am."

"The man you killed, Keith Wheeler. He was my son. I'm his mother."

"And *I'm* his wife," says a frigid woman in her early thirties on the others side of the table. Her frosted hair only adds to the effect. This woman could keep ice from melting in the Mojave. She makes no effort to shake my hand.

"I guess that makes me an asshole," I say. "I'm very sorry to you both. You'll find me being an idiot is part of my charm."

"Maybe if you had any," she says coolly. I'm beginning to rethink leaving Mac's gun at home.

Introductions are made and I meet the other people scattered around the table. Whereas Widow Wheeler is an icy bundle of hate, Michelle Swanson, the widow of the dialysis patient we killed by mistaking him for one of our own, seems like the kind of person you'd like to wrap up in a hug and let her warmth envelop you. Her eyes aren't so much sad as weary, tired of being in rooms like this, surrounded by stale coffee, wood veneers and even faker people.

You know, lawyers.

I dutifully shake the lawyers' hands – three for the Wheelers, two for Mrs. Swanson and one sad sack named Skip Jenkins for the doctor who cut off Mr. Wheeler's leg – and accept their business cards, even though everyone in the room knows I'm throwing them into the first trash can I see after the meeting. They, in turn, do their best not to recoil at my appearance but fail miserably. A couple wince, one gasps audibly, but my favorite is the senior member of the Ice Queen's team, a bespectacled silver haired partner from Fallon, Vaughn and Puffinstuff (I'm pretty sure I have that right. I'm not good with names) who has his back to me when I first walk in. As I reach out my hand and say hello, he turns, takes one look at my face and exclaims, "Judas Priest! What happened to you?"

It's hard to blame him. I look like I crawled out from under a bridge.

Coming to my rescue is the venerable Randall J. Simon, Esq. His wounds seemingly healed from the thrashing he took from Mr. Williams earlier in the week, he takes command and asks everyone to sit. We squeeze around the Marriott's conference table and the effect is exactly what I had hoped. There is no vast expanse of mahogany separating the widows and us; instead, we sit shoulder to shoulder, a unified group seeking a common solution. Will it work? Hell if I know, but the optics sure are nice.

Simon starts to walk through the usual legal pabulum (all communications this morning should be considered settlement negotiations for the purposes of Federal Rule of Evidence 408 and are therefore inadmissible in any proceeding relating to the issues discussed herein ... blah, blah, freaking blah. Honestly, if I was a lawyer, I'd shoot myself in the face – you know, assuming I had the balls to do it, which last night definitively proved I do not.). I catch one of the Ice Queen's lawyers stifling a yawn and decide to spice things up a bit.

"We all know why we are here," I say, earning a silent rebuke from Randall Simon. "Each of your loved ones lost their lives while in our care."

"You killed them," Mrs. Wheeler the Younger snaps.

"We killed them," I agree somberly.

"Causation has not been established or conceded," Simon interjects, kicking me under the table. Mother of pearl, that hurt. Son of a bitch must have played D-1 soccer.

"Duly noted," Ice Queen's senior lawyer says with a yawn. In sixty seconds, Mr. Puffinstuff has gone from horrified at my appearance to bored beyond belief.

"We killed them," I say again, receiving another kick from Simon for my efforts. I turn to him before the bastard breaks my shin. "Listen, Randall, you already made the point that the discussions here today are privileged. And it's no secret that if these cases go to court, the plaintiffs are going to argue that we caused the deaths of their loved ones. This is hardly a state secret. So how about you stop kicking me under the table and we get on with it?"

Simon glares at me, his face nearly as red as my eyeballs. He sputters for a second but otherwise appears incapable of formulating coherent speech, so I press on.

"Let me do everyone the courtesy of speaking plainly. What happened to each of you is horrible. You trusted us to care for your family members and we failed you. That's a loss that can never be filled and for that, I can only say I'm sorry. But the truth is, there's nothing I can say and – contrary to what your lawyers may tell you – no amount of money we can give you that will make you feel any better. Oh, there's retribution," I say with a pointed look in the Ice Queen's direction, "but even that will fall short in the end. It doesn't matter how much money you get out of us, it's not going to hurt us. We're just too big."

I stop, checking on Simon to make sure he hasn't had a coronary. He's holding the edge of the table so tightly his hands are shaking, but otherwise seems fine. Jenkins, the doctor's lawyer, just seems happy to be here. Sitting in his stained chair with his stained striped tie threaded through a stained shirt collar that is two sizes too big, he is content to watch the back and forth without any interference from him. The widows' lawyers, meanwhile, don't know what to do. No one has ever dared speak like this at a settlement hearing. Stupefied, they're excited to see where this is headed.

"It's not your money I'm after," Mrs. Swanson says quietly.

Mrs. Wheeler the Younger pounces. "Speak for yourself."

"What do you hope to get?" I ask Mrs. Swanson, ignoring the Wheelers entirely for the moment.

"An apology."

"You have it."

"Not from you."

"I had a sneaking suspicion that would be the case," I say with a sympathetic smile.

"I want a formal apology from the company. And not just some statement sent to the press in the dead of night. I want your CEO to look me in the eye on TV with the whole world watching as he says how sorry he is for killing my husband."

"She can have the apology," the Ice Queen interjects. "I'll take twenty million dollars." Her lawyers nod eagerly in agreement.

"Oh, I'll take that too," Mrs. Swanson says, smiling for the first time, though there is no joy in her eyes.

"I understand you're hurt and angry," I say, shaking my head. "Frankly, I don't understand how either of you is able to get up each morning and go on."

"What choice do we have?" Mrs. Swanson shoots back. "To kill ourselves? That's the coward's way out." I try not to hide my shame as she continues. "I have people who depend on me. What happens to them if I abandon them? Because that's what taking your own life is – abandoning the people you love just because you're not strong enough to deal your own problems. There's nothing strong or romantic about that."

"There were plenty of times I wanted to end it all,"

Widow Wheeler chimes in. My face flushes as her pale blue eyes bore into me. I am so much weaker than these two women and everyone in the room knows it. "But that would have meant that your boss would win. He took everything from me. *Everything*. And I bet he didn't even bat an eye. My husband is just a statistic to him – a cost of doing business. Well, not any longer." She sits back, her eyes boring into me, daring me to challenge her. "I'm going to make him pay."

"Mrs. Swanson, Mrs. Wheeler," I say slowly, taking care to look each of them in the eye, "I'm about to admit some things I shouldn't—"

"Then don't," Simon interrupts nervously.

I wave him away. "—but there are things you should know about this company."

"Sean—" Simon tries again, but I ignore him.

"First, we will fight these lawsuits with a fervor that you simply can't match. We've got dozens of firms on retainer ready to battle you to the end of days if that's what it takes."

"We're ready for a fight," Mrs. Wheeler says icily.

"I don't doubt it, Mrs. Wheeler. But that doesn't mean you can win. You may think you can, but you can't."

"And why not? You killed my husband by cutting off his healthy leg."

"And you killed mine because you thought he was someone else," Mrs. Swanson chimes in. The two women, so different in demeanor are now squarely working on the same side. If we do nothing else, Infirmus brings people together.

"That's textbook malpractice," opines Puffinstuff in his deep baritone.

"It doesn't matter," I sigh. "You may have the facts on your side, but we've got something better: time. We'll drag this out so long, your children's children will be gone before this case is resolved. Mrs. Wheeler, you won't see a dime. And Mrs. Swanson, you'll never get that apology."

"You're not telling us anything we don't know," intones Puffinstuff haughtily. I don't even bother hiding my eye roll. Another stuffed shirt proving how smart he is. "But we are prepared to weather the storm, for as long as it takes."

"I know *you* are," I sigh. "You're thrilled to keep churning out the bills. But is your client?" I look at Mrs. Wheeler and see the first cracks in the steely veneer as she stares mutely at the table. I turn to Mrs. Swanson who similarly averts my eyes. "Are you?" Her silence is enough.

I pause, ostensibly to let our adversaries stew in their discomfort. But as I see Simon looking at me admiringly, I know I'm at a dangerous crossroads. Ordinarily, this would be the point where I'd make the hard sell for a settlement. I've flattered the opposition, ingratiated myself as an apparent honest broker and forced them to confront the real likelihood of defeat. In Simon's eyes, the summit has gone better than anyone could have hoped. I've got the opposition plumped, primed and prepped. All that's left as a good corporate soldier is for me to jam a lowball settlement offer down their throats.

But if I'm anything, a good corporate soldier isn't one of them. Not anymore.

"Randall," I say, turning to face my colleague, "can I call you Randy?"

"No."

"Okay, Randall it is." I lean towards him, my shift in tone throwing him off balance. "Randall, you need to leave."

He stares back at me, dumbfounded.

"I mean it. It's time for you to go."

"Sean," he whispers urgently, "what are you doing?"

"Something I should have done a long time ago. And something you can't be a part of."

"Can I talk to you in the hall?"

"No, you can't. I'm not leaving, but you have to."

He throws a panicked look at the others in the room, but he's met only with confused but expectant stares. "Sean—" he pleads. His whisper has gone up an octave. "You can't do this!"

There was a time, not so long ago, when I would have agreed with him. I couldn't do a lot of things. I couldn't stand up for myself. I couldn't give a rat's ass about others, and I sure as shit couldn't be bothered to help anyone else. That's an awful way to live. And lonely. But as I sit here in this room, faced with pathos and loss that I can't even fathom, I realize that I don't have to live like that anymore. At least, not right now. I don't know what it is about these two widows, but something inside me – something small, to be sure, but something nonetheless – wants to live, at least for a little while. It wants to live and see if there is something I can do to help someone other than myself.

I could chalk this up to some newfound bravery brought on by a life-changing epiphany, but I think we all know that's a stretch. Suffice it to say that waking up in a pool of one's own vomit after unsuccessfully trying to end one's life is cause for self-examination. And the conclusion I've reached is this: I really suck at suicide, so much so that I probably ought to put it on the back burner as a strategy, at least for the moment. I'm not saying I'm completely taking it off the table. I'm just saying that – for today, anyway – it's time to try something different.

"Randall," I say finally, "we don't know each other very well but I'm asking you to trust me. I'm about to get brutally honest with these people and I'll likely say some things that you won't want to be a part of. Now, you can either be complicit in what's about to happen, or you can get up out of that chair, leave the room and be able to declare to your higher-ups that you had nothing to do with any of it."

"I could stop you," he offers meekly.

"No, you couldn't. You could try, but no one back at head-quarters would believe you. Mostly because I would tell them that you were in on it from the beginning." I pause and look at him wistfully. "You're a young man, Randall. You have your whole career ahead of you. Don't throw it away defending assholes like the people who run this company. They'd sell you out the minute they concluded it would make them a few nickels."

"No, they wouldn't." His voice is so quiet, I almost wonder whether he said anything at all.

"Of course they would. In fact, they already have. Why do you think you're here? These are high profile cases, with tens of millions of dollars at risk, yet the company only sends a junior attorney and an over the hill P.R. hack to deal with them. Does that make any sense?"

"No," he whispers.

"Face it, Randall. The only reason we're here is to protect our bosses. If we're successful and broker a settlement, the bigwigs will swoop in and take credit for it. But if we fail – and that's always been the most likely scenario – they'll point to the two of us and blame us for everything. You and I are sacrificial lambs, sent by higher ups to the slaughter. Do yourself a favor, Randall. Get out of here and save your soul. And while you're at it, find yourself a new career."

He cocks his head at me like a puppy, uncertain about what he's being asked to do. Slowly, he pushes his chair back and gets to his feet. He coughs, smoothes his tie and buttons his jacket, an absurd yet endearing display of a drowning man struggling to find his dignity. He clears his throat once more and looks at me unsteadily, his bottom lip trembling. Finally, with a curt nod, he turns and leaves, the only sound the pneumatic hiss of the door closing softly behind him.

The widows eye me curiously, neither wanting to break the

spell of what they just witnessed. The lawyers at the table are likewise captivated, wondering what the crazy, disfigured man from Infirmus is going to do next. Only Jenkins, the doctor's lawyer, is dispassionate, too busy scraping the remnants of breakfast off his tie to care.

I inhale deeply, wondering how I got from a pool of vomit to a poorly lit Marriott conference room (someone would say they're the same thing – Hay-o!) in the span of two hours, and start talking.

"This case isn't about money or an apology," I begin. "Those are just the byproducts. This case is really about shame. You need to publicly shame Infirmus and its management to such a degree that they have no choice but to pay you gobs of money and tell you how sorry they are."

"You're talking about a P.R. campaign," says Puffinstuff dismissively. "We've already got a firm engaged to sway the court of public opinion."

"And we've both talked to *the Times*," adds Mrs. Wheeler.

"That's good," I acknowledge. "But Marcus Cannon is just the tip of the iceberg. He's going to write a think piece about the misaligned incentives of the American healthcare system, using Infirmus as Exhibit A. But by framing your husbands as the casualties of that flawed system, Marcus is going to let Infirmus off the hook. He doesn't think he is, but that's what will happen. Picture it: Vern Williams, Infirmus' CEO, looking humble and contrite as he sits down with *60 Minutes* a week after the story comes out to issue a bland *mea culpa* for the tragic events that led to your husbands' death. He won't fess up to killing them, mind you. Instead, he'll ascribe their unfortunate fate to the over-regulated, under-funded American healthcare system. He'll turn the whole mess to his advantage, issuing a call to arms and pledging to set up a foundation to explore ways to reform the system. In a single interview, he'll transform himself from villain to white knight, imploring all well-meaning Americans to join him in this noble cause to ensure that great men like Douglas Swanson and Keith Wheeler did not die in vain."

"How can you be so certain?" Mrs. Swanson asks.

"Because it's exactly what I would do."

"What a crock of shit," mutters the elder Mrs. Wheeler.

"Indeed. The foulest smelling crock there ever there was. There will be hearings and town halls and lots and lots of naval gazing. Patients will tell their stories, experts will opine and politicians will dither. And in the end, nothing will get done. Infirmus and the other major providers will come together under the guise of an innocuously named coalition – something like 'Americans for Better Care' – and spend a few million dollars on TV ads to make everyone feel better about the crappy care they're doling out. We'll hold hands as a nation, congratulating ourselves for protecting the least among us while perpetuating a system that enriches only the wealthiest among us. Not a goddamned thing will improve, except of course the Infirmus stock price, which will skyrocket at the news that the status quo is here to stay. Because *that's* what this is about. It's the first commandment of American healthcare: honor thy father and mother, so long as you honor your stockholders first."

"So we can't win in the courtroom and we can't win in the press," says an exasperated Mrs. Swanson. "You're saying this is a lost cause?"

"Not at all. In fact, it's the best cause of all: a hopeless one."

"Beg your pardon?"

"What do all Americans love?"

"Puppies," offers a junior lawyer across the table.

"Chocolate," says another.

"Porn," tries a third.

"An underdog," I correct. "We freaking love underdogs. Hell,

the entire Hollywood machine is built on making movies celebrating the underdog."

"And the Kardashians," says the junior lawyer with a chocolate fetish. I make a mental note to disinvite the lawyers next
time.

"Think of it. David versus Goliath, the '80 Olympic hockey
team, any movie with Anna Kendrick – everyone feels good
cheering for the underdog."

"We're already taking Infirmus to court," Mrs. Swanson says.

"Which is all well and good. But it doesn't really provide a
forum to get people excited or engaged."

"We've referred our case to the local prosecutors," offers one
of Mrs. Wheeler's junior attorneys. "They seem inclined to bring
a case."

"That reminds me," I say, turning to Jenkins, the attorney for
the doctor who hacked off Mr. Wheeler's healthy leg. "Your
client should plead guilty." He opens his mouth to say something, then thinks better of it and slumps back in silence. "A
criminal case is good," I continue. "It will gin up some publicity
and start to get the public on your side. But it will take time. You
need to do something now."

"Which is why we hired a P.R. agency," Puffinstuff says irritably. "They'll generate a grass roots campaign as soon as we file
suit."

"Facebook ads and letters to the editor aren't going to cut it.
The only way to really capture people's attention is to create a
confrontation, ideally on Infirmus' own turf."

"You mean like a sit-in?" asks the elder Mrs. Wheeler.

"Something a little more this century," I say with a smile.
Turning to Mrs. Swanson, I ask, "You want face to face? How
about hijacking their corporate lovefest tomorrow?"

And then I see something from her I thought I'd never see. A
genuine, honest to God smile, eyes and all.

33

An hour later, I stride out of the elevator on the tenth floor feeling like a man with a newfound purpose. Call me a sap, but something the widows said struck a chord with me. They called suicide the coward's way out, which is exactly the way Alex characterized it this morning. But when Alex said it, I discounted it immediately. We're a couple with too much time in. At this point, we're honor bound to discount whatever comes out of the other's mouth – assuming, that is, we're even listening. She could be giving me permission to bang the entire secretarial pool and I'd have no idea.

No, I needed two strangers to say it, to slap me in the face with it. Listening to the widows, I realized two things. First, I really hate Infirmus. I hate what it's done to me and I hate what it's done – and continues to do – to people like these two women. And while none of that is any surprise, what I've decided to do with that hate is. I'm taking a page from the widows' playbook and going on the offensive. It may be foolhardy, but it's got everything to do with my second realization: I can't abandon my girls. They may not like me, but that doesn't absolve me of my responsibility to be there for them as a father. And, just like Mrs. Wheeler and Mrs. Swanson, I can't let bastards like Williams win. They want to take everything away from me to cover up their misdeeds? Fine, but I'm not going down without a fight.

Sure, the odds are against me. I'm not exactly what anyone would call a fighter. And yes, I can hear what you're thinking: it's borderline insanity to think the widows and I have the resources to take on a Fortune 100 company and win. But you only say that because you don't really know me (you know, ignoring everything that happened this week. Fuck you and the fact you've been paying attention. I didn't ask you to read this book). I'm Polish, motherfucker. Okay, Polish-Irish if you want to be precise. But that just means I come from a long line of people prone to foolishly romantic military campaigns that cost millions of lives and gain nothing in the end. In fact, I'm genetically predisposed to them.

The way I figure it, the widows and me have courage on our side. Williams and the rest of Infirmus are Nazi Germany and we're Poland (and yes, I'm well aware that comparisons to Nazi Germany aren't exactly smiled upon these days. For the record, I'm referring not to Nazis' morally abhorrent racist and anti-Semitic attitudes, but to their military superiority over the Poles. Although, now that I think about it, neither Williams nor any of the other execs have been all that welcoming to people with anything other than the lightest of skin tones. Fuck it. They're Nazis. I stand by the comparison.). Sure, Poland versus Germany didn't work out all that well for the good guys, but you have to give Poland style points. We Polacks have taken a lot of shit over the years and, while you can question our intelligence for advancing on a fully mechanized army with nothing more than horses and a few popguns, you certainly cannot question our courage. Dumb we may be, but dumb and cowardly we are not.

Besides, if there's one other thing last night's foray into self-destruction revealed to me, it's that I've got nothing. Less than nothing, if you believe the accountants. And while I used to believe that kind of nothing meant everything, I'm beginning to see things differently. The two widows had everything and they lost it. No wonder they're looking for retribution. But me? It's been a long time since I had anything close to what they had. And while it sounds pathetic, finding out you have nothing left to lose feels pretty damn good.

And that's probably as close as I'll ever get to bravery.

Full of piss and vinegar, I turn the corner and see Diane. Even her sourpuss can't get me down. I stride confidently towards her, ready to parry whatever snide comment she unleashes, but then she does something that throws me off stride. Unfazed by my appearance – doesn't everyone come to work looking like they just went ten rounds with Tyson? – she simply nods toward my office and smiles.

"There's someone here to see you."

I stop short and see a bored uniformed cop picking his nose while two detectives pick through the papers on my desk.

That doesn't augur well for the offensive.

I take a deep breath to steady myself and walk in.

"Can I help you?"

The startled cop by the door takes his finger out of his nose and fails miserably in trying to surreptitiously wipe it on his pant leg. The two detectives – both mustachioed, of course – stop rifling through my effects long enough to look up. The short one recoils at my appearance while the taller one smiles easily.

"Mr. Reilly?"

I nod.

"You look like you've had a hard week."

"No different than any other," I say.

"Really? Then you must live one hell of a life."

"It's a shit sandwich no matter which way you look at it."

"It's about to get worse."

"I doubt it," I answer, not sure yet whether the bravado is false or not.

"What kind of car do you drive, Mr. Reilly?" the smaller one interjects, having recovered from his initial revulsion.

"That depends."

"Depends? On what?"

"On who the hell you are."

The smaller one looks at me menacingly while the tall one flashes another smile. I'm beginning to detect a schtick.

"I'm Detective Fogel," says the tall one, "and this is Detective Ramirez. Behind you is Officer Bieber."

"Bieber? You're shitting me."

"I shit you not," says Fogel, handing me a business card, which I slide into my pocket without thinking.

"My condolences," I turn and say to Bieber, who gives me a wan smile. This is not the first time these three have given this performance. I turn and face the detectives so Bieber can go back to picking his nose.

"The car?" Ramirez reminds me.

"An Infiniti. Until Monday, anyway."

"What happened Monday?"

"I got in a car crash."

"Thus the face," says Fogel. A statement, not a question.

"No," I correct him. "At least, not all of it."

"What happened Monday?" asks the small one.

"Like I said, I got in an accident."

"Where?"

"On the highway driving home," I lie.

"Was anyone hurt?"

"This hurt," I answer, waving at my face. "A lot."

"Anyone else?"

"No, though I'm pretty sure that asshole deer will be filing an injury claim soon."

"You hit a deer?" asks Ramirez.

"No, I missed him. But he had a litigious look about him as I spun by. I wouldn't be surprised if he files a bogus claim for whiplash or some such thing."

"Whiplash?"

I look at Fogel. "Is he for real?"

"He's very thorough."

I look back at Ramirez, who continues to eye me expectantly.

I take a deep breath, trying to remain in control. "It was dark. I didn't see the deer until the last minute. I swerved to avoid him and ran into a bridge abutment. The whiplash thing was a joke."

"Not a very good one," offers Ramirez.

"Like I said, it's been a shitty week."

"Do you own a gun, Mr. Reilly?" Fogel asks, shifting gears abruptly.

"No."

"You don't?" confirms Ramirez, ever the stickler.

"No."

"Why not?"

"I'm not a big fan of them."

"You some kind of liberal pussy?"

I look at Fogel, trying to discern if his partner is for real. He merely shrugs in response.

"Yeah, I'm a complete pussy. I hate guns and love the environment. I wish I could start each day by hugging a seal. I voted for Obama and I think the world would be a better place if we could all just get along. Oh, and I suck a lot of cock."

Ramirez doesn't laugh. Doesn't smirk, doesn't even laugh. Instead, he waits a moment then asks again. "So, if we searched your house, we wouldn't find a gun?"

"Why would you search my house?" I respond but don't answer.

"I'm asking the questions."

"Not very well."

Fogel laughs. He can't help himself.

"You mind if we look at your car, Mr. Reilly?" No smiling for Ramirez. He's going to conduct this interview whether we like it or not.

"That depends."

"On what?"

"On whether it's still a car."

"You mind explaining yourself?"

"For the third time, I was in an accident. I was driving Monday night and before I knew what was happening, a deer ran in front of my car. Being the animal lover I am, I swerved to avoid it and the next thing I know, I'm plowing head first into a bridge abutment. When I came to, a bunch of Bieber's buddies were taking my statement and calling a tow truck to haul off what remained of my car."

"Where did they take the car?"

Something in his tone makes my hair stand on end. "I don't know," I lie. "Some place across town."

"Any idea what the name is?" Ramirez asks.

"Moe's, Mike's, Mick's ... I don't know."

"Mac's?" Fogel offers.

"That might be it," I say, offering what I hope is a convincing shrug. "Like I said, I don't really know."

"Have you seen the car since the accident?" Ramirez asks. The way in which both he and Fogel look at me is unnerving. Clearly, they know the car is at Mac's, and from Ramirez's tone, it sounds like they know I went there to see it. Obviously, Mac has sent them my way. If I want to stay out of jail – at least for today – it's time to give these guys something.

"Yeah, I went to see it on Tuesday."

Fogel's eyebrows shoot up. "You did?"

"Yeah, I thought it might still be drivable. Unfortunately, it's totaled so I'm shit out of luck. Again."

"How did you get to Mac's?" Ramirez betrays no emotion with his non sequitur.

"Lyft."

"And how did you get home?" Ah, now I see where he's headed.

"I drove."

Fogel's eyebrows do another dance. "Really?"

"What car?" Ramirez asks before I can answer.

"I went to the lot to see if my car was there. The guy who owns the place – Moe or Mike or Mick—"

"Mac," they correct me in unison.

"Right, Mac. Anyway, he shows me my car, explains that it's totaled and then we made a deal."

"A deal," says Fogel. Another statement, not a question.

"That's right," I answer, "a deal." It's time to come clean. At least, as clean as I'm willing to get. "He offered to buy my car for scrap in exchange for a junker he had on the lot."

"What kind of junker?"

"An SS."

"Like a Nazi?" asks Fogel. I smile at his joke. Pretty good one, actually.

"More like a Chevelle. You know, muscle car?"

"What year?"

"Early 70s," I shrug.

"Pretty nice."

"Would be if it were in decent shape. But it's beat to hell."

Ramirez is dubious. "Sounds like a pretty sweet deal. Mac gets a pile of scrap and you drive off the lot with a 1970 Chevelle SS."

"Guess so." I offer another shrug, disappointed but not surprised they know the exact year of the car. Clearly, it's been on their radar for some time. "I was just happy the thing worked."

"Any idea why Mac would be so generous?"

"You'd have to ask him."

"We already have," Fogel confirms.

"Guess you're ahead of the curve, then."

"You're not interested in what he had to say?" Fogel dares me to ask.

"Not really. I assume he thought he could sell my car off for parts. He's the expert, right?"

"About a lot of things," says Fogel ominously.

"Before," interjects Ramirez, "when I asked if I could see your car, why did you assume I meant the Infiniti?"

"Because that's my car, or at least it was."

"And the Chevelle?"

"That's Mike's."

"Mac's." Once more in unison.

"Right. Mac's. That's what I meant."

Ramirez is impatient. "Except it's not Mac's. It's yours now. Because, let me see here—" He checks his notes. "You two made 'a deal.'" He looks up at me. "Do I have that right?"

"I guess so. The Chevelle is mine and the Infiniti is Mick's."

"Mac's." They're getting pretty good at this even though they look annoyed as hell. Fuck 'em. At least I'm having fun.

"So can we?"

"Can you what?"

"See your car. The Chevelle."

"Why?"

"We're the curious sort," says Fogel.

"What are you curious about?"

"Lots of things," he says. "Bad guys, mostly."

"And I'm a bad guy?"

"Not sure yet. But it seems to be trending that way."

"Hold up. I run communications for a healthcare company. I had a car accident on Monday. How does that add up to me being a bad guy?"

"Sometimes, people are more than what they say they are."

I burst out laughing.

"What's so funny?"

"Most people would say I am decidedly less than I say I am."

Fogel considers this. "Tell me, how does a P.R. guy get a face like that?"

"The car accident, remember?"

"You said that only accounted for some of what's going on with your mug. 'Scuse me for saying, but you look like shit. As long as we're being honest—"

"Is that what we're doing here?"

"It's what we're doing, Mr. Reilly. How about you?"

Fogel waits but I don't answer. Nothing good can come from answering that question.

Bemused, he continues. "Now, where was I?"

"You were being honest."

"Right. It kind of looks like you got tuned up."

"Yeah," Ramirez agrees. "You look a lot like what happens when one bad guy crosses another bad guy."

"Guys, you seem anxious to color me as some master criminal so let save you the effort. I'm innocent of whatever you think I'm guilty of. I haven't been involved in any shady deals and I haven't gotten crosswise with some bad guy."

"So the tune up?" Fogel waves a finger at his face.

"Sorry to disappoint. This lovely mug, as you call it, is solely the work of yours truly."

"Go a little deep in the self-loathing department?"

"You have no idea."

"You know," Ramirez says, adopting a professorial tone, "a lot of people try to harm themselves – even kill themselves – when they get in too deep with the wrong kind of people."

"I appreciate the armchair diagnosis, but you should stick to your day job."

Fogel takes on a concerned look. "You need to talk to someone?"

"Detective Fogel, I'm touched. Or—" I tilt my head, as if struck by a profound thought. "—is this you guys playing bad shrink, worse shrink?"

Fogel smiles. "Just trying to be helpful."

"I'm not a basket case," I say confidently in the biggest lie of all. "I'm just trying to get by. And sometimes, I fall a little short."

Fogel either believes me or has the decency to know when to stop. "So that's a no on the car?"

"A hard no." I smile.

Ramirez is not as easily swayed. "It'll only take a couple of hours to get a warrant. Why don't you just save us the trouble and let us take a look?"

"You know what, Detective Ramirez? A warrant sounds like an excellent idea. I'm a big believer in the Sixth Amendment, so why don't you go find a judge and convince him that I'm a threat to society. You do that, and I'll let you see my car."

Ramirez steps toward me and adopts the classic hardass cop pose. "You don't want get in the habit of pissing me off."

I can't help but laugh. "I've pissed off so many people this week, it's hard keeping them all straight."

He steps even closer and I can smell the bourbon on his

breath. I thought I saw a little anti-social alcoholic in him. Okay, more than a little.

"You know what I think, Reilly? I think you and Mac are thick as thieves. I think you two had a deal going down on Monday and something went wrong. What was it? Someone try to double cross you? Mac killed them and you drove the getaway car? Or was it the other way around?" He leans in closer, now thoroughly lathered up. Spittle lines the corners of his mouth and the sour smell of booze is overwhelming. "You don't want us looking at your house? Fine. We'll get a warrant. Call that lovely wife of yours, tell her we're coming by in a couple of hours to tear your house apart."

"You do that, Detective Ramirez, and you'll learn my wife's not all that lovely."

"Thank you for your time, Mr. Reilly," Fogel interjects, trying to lower the temperature.

"We'll be in touch." Ramirez's tone is unchanged.

"I can't wait. In the meantime," I say, nodding to the officer behind me I assume is still two knuckles deep into his nose, "why don't you take the Beebs here and get the fuck out of my office?"

Fogel nods goodbye as Ramirez walks out, Officer Bieber dutifully in tow. On their way through the door, they bump into Tim, who's built up a head of steam. Only when he sees Bieber's uniform does he stop and let them by.

"What are cops doing here?" he asks once they make it to the elevator. "And how is it possible you look lousier every time I see you?"

"It's a new skincare regimen."

"It's not working."

"No shit."

"You want to tell me what's going on?"

My face darkens. "They're on to us, Tim. They know about

everything – the drugs, the deaths, the money. We've got until tomorrow and then they're taking us all to the big house."

His eyes light up in a flash of panic and then, just as quickly, they're clear. He chuckles lightly, trying to recover.

"Sean, I'm not sure I'll ever understand your sense of humor."

"Of course not. Lawyers don't have one."

He has the good form to laugh. "Seriously, though. What was that all about?"

I wave my hand dismissively. "Nothing much. They're following up on that car accident I was in earlier this week."

"So nothing for me to worry about?"

"No, Mr. General Counsel. None of that was company business." At least, not yet.

"How was this morning?"

I look at him blankly.

"The widows...?"

"Right," I say. "The widows. Sorry. Too much going on."

"How did it go?"

"Shitty."

"'Shitty' like they're playing hardball but will eventually settle, or 'shitty' like they've got religion?"

"The latter."

"Shit."

"Exactly. We're dealing with a lot of shit here."

"You think they'll come around?"

"Let's put it this way. Unlike most of the people around here, I think they both actually loved their spouses."

"So, they're mad."

"They're going for the jugular."

"Lovely." He removes his glasses and rubs the bridge of his nose.

"It's not all bad news." He looks up, his eyebrows raised in anticipation. "Their lawyers are calling the shots."

He smiles. "So we wait them out."

I nod. "The usual game. Bury them with pleadings and tie them up in discovery."

"Their children's children won't see a penny." He's smiling so broadly, I can see his gums. He looks like a wolf. On the upside, the man's dental habits really are impeccable.

"We'll take some lumps in the press at first but it should blow over."

"What's going on with that reporter at the *Times*?"

"Marcus? He says his piece will run Sunday. He's looking for a statement from us."

"And?"

"And, we need to decide whether to give him anything."

"What do you think?"

The fact that this man is asking my opinion is comical. Either he's already made a decision, in which case he's only asking so he can tell Williams he consulted with the so-called "experts," or he's got no clue what to do and he's looking to me to decide. Either way, he's going to pin everything on me if things end up going south.

"It all depends on what we want to achieve," I say.

"We want to kill the story."

"Well, that's not going to happen. This is a Pulitzer Prize winner who smells blood. He's not going to back off just because we tell him to. In fact, we'll probably make him think there's more to the story than he already knows."

"What does he know?"

"He knows about the widows. He knows about staffing issues at clinics and he knows about DSN and the other premium support charities."

"All of which is already in the public domain."

"True, but he's going to try to connect the dots between them."

"How so?"

"We fund the charities, which fund insurance premiums, which fund higher reimbursement back to us. It's a shell game."

"So he's going to explain healthcare reimbursement? He'll be seventeen paragraphs deep before he makes his point. I can already hear his readers snoring."

"True," I respond. "But he'll also argue that we put patients' lives at risk by cutting costs to the bone."

"So that's our real risk."

"I think it could all hurt if it's written correctly, but yes, it's always more damaging when you can point to patient harm. 'Evil corporation puts profits ahead of patient care,' that sort of thing."

"So back to the question, what should we do?"

"We need to cloak ourselves in the mantle of patient care. We need to show him that the only thing we think about from the time we get up in the morning to the time we go to bed is how we can make our patients' lives better. Nothing else matters – not cost, not reimbursement, and certainly not profits."

"So we lie."

"I prefer spin."

"Whatever you call it, it's bullshit."

"Welcome to corporate communications."

"All of that's a tall order for a statement."

"Which is why we don't give him one."

He blanches. "What?"

"We don't give him a statement. He wouldn't use it anyway, at least, not in the way we would want him to."

"You've lost me. How do we tell him how important patients are if we don't give him a statement?"

"We don't tell him. We show him."

"How do we do that?"

"Gee, if only we had an event coming up that puts patient care front and center. Something where we bring patients on the stage to offer tearful testimonials about the care we provide. Something where doctors and nurses wax poetic about everything we do for patients. Some kind of well orchestrated, tightly choreographed program designed specifically to tug at heartstrings and make everyone get down on their knees and thank the Almighty for giving us a company as benevolent and compassionate as Infirmus. If only."

"CareFest." The wolf's smile is back. "Sean, I underestimated you."

I shrug. "Happens all the time."

"So we bring Marcus to CareFest and let him see how great we are. Think he'll go for it?"

"I don't know why not. He's been after me for a statement for a week. I'll explain that no statement makes sense without the broader context of what we're doing for patients more broadly. I think he'll get that."

"And if not?"

"Then we'll offer him a one-on-one interview with Mr. Williams after the program."

"We're bringing the wolf into the henhouse."

"What's wrong? Not used to letting someone else bare the fangs?"

Another wicked smile. "This goes south—"

"And it's my ass," I finish for him. "Believe me, I know the drill."

Tim leaves and I spend the next hour talking the jokers from marketing off the ledge once they hear I want a complete overhaul of the CareFest agenda. I lie, explaining that the changes come right from the top and assuring them that one night is more than enough time to get everything done. I then move to the most important part of my plan by making a call I've been avoiding all week.

"Marcus," I say enthusiastically after he picks up, "it's Sean."

"Who?"

"Sean Reilly at Infirmus."

"I'm sorry, that name doesn't ring any bells. I did know a guy at Infirmus once, but you can't possibly be him. That guy never returned any of my calls."

"Aw, you're not pouting, are you Marcus?"

"Not pouting. Complaining."

"I didn't know Pulitzer Prize winners were so sensitive."

"It's what drives us. You should see Miller over at the *Post*. She's a wreck."

"Well, I'm here now. What can I do for you?"

"Oh, now you're doing something for me? That's new."

"Really, Marcus. You should see a therapist."

"You asked for time to get a statement together and I gave it to you. Now, after days of radio silence, you call not to give me the company's side of the story, but instead to bust my balls. Do I have this right so far?"

"I've got something even better for you than a statement. Busting your balls is just an added perk."

"I'm honored."

"You should be, especially since I'm about to give you exclusive access to tomorrow's CareFest."

"What the fuck is CareFest?" He is annoyed.

"Please. Don't act like you don't know. It's only the preeminent for-profit healthcare circle jerk this side of the JP Morgan conference."

"And this interests me, how?"

"It's the annual Infirmus healthcare summit," I explain. "Docs, nurses and company execs take to the stage to explain how wonderful we are. I'm giving you exclusive access."

"Whoop-dee-fucking-do." Now he's bored and annoyed. I need to up my game.

"I'll even give you a one-on-one with Williams after the conference."

"Thanks, I'll pass. Send me a statement instead."

"The widows will be there."

Silence.

"They'll be there," he says finally. "At your conference."

"Yes."

"Along with your CEO and all of your execs."

"That's right."

"Do they know they'll be there?"

"Marcus, Marcus, do you write as poorly as you speak? Misplaced pronouns all over the place. Honestly, you must give your editors nightmares. Does who know whom will be there?"

"The execs," he answers impatiently. "Williams and the rest of them. Do they know the widows will be there?"

"Not exactly."

"What does that mean?"

"It means we're still tweaking the agenda."

"We?"

"Okay, me."

More silence.

"When is this all happening?"

"Tomorrow, bright and early."

"And you want me there."

"You'll want you here, believe me."

He sighs, taking it all in. "What kind of game are you playing, Sean?"

"Not a very good one," I admit. "But something I probably should have done a long time ago."

"This can't end well for you."

"It never could," I agree.

"Text me the details," he says finally.

"Terrific, I say about to hang up.

"Oh, and Sean?"

"Yeah?"

"I bust your balls, not the other way around."

"It's a brave new world, Marcus. I found my balls just in time to be able to bust yours."

I can hear him laughing as I hang up.

34

I n the three years I've known her, I've rarely seen Naomi sitting comfortably at her desk. For a time, I wondered if it was health related, that perhaps a bad back or a balky hip prevented her from sitting for long periods at a time. Now, though, as I stand outside her office watching her lord over her desk, slashing ad copy with a red pen, I realize that the culprit is her boundless intensity. Confining her to a chair would be like caging a leopard: cruel and inhumane.

"You free?" I ask, tentatively knocking on her door.

She looks up, blowing a stray lock of hair out of her eyes. "No. What's up?"

"Need to talk to you about tomorrow."

"What's to talk about? I ran through final changes with marketing last night. They finally stopped stepping on their dicks long enough to clean up the run of show. I think we're all set."

"There are changes."

"I know," she sighs impatiently. "We cleared them up last night."

"Yeah, there are more."

She drops her pen on the desk and puts her hands on her hips. "What did you do?"

I smile at her tone. "Was there ever a time you didn't treat me like a petulant child?"

"Was there ever a time you didn't act like one?"

"You do know you still work for me, right?"

She throws up her hands. "Why does everyone keep asking me that?"

"Because you seem not to know."

"Or maybe I just don't care."

We stare at each other a moment and then I crack first, a wide smile creeping across my face.

"What have I done to deserve such a loyal subordinate?"

"Never mind one that fucks like a champion."

"Please. If you're so good, how come I need Viagra to get it up?"

"There you go again, confusing correlation with causation."

"You ever think you just don't do it for me anymore?"

She tilts her head and seductively throws one hip to the side. She is radiant.

"You're right," I say waving my hands in defeat. "You're a goddess."

She tosses her head back and laughs. "So what are the changes?"

I explain the conversation with Tim and my brilliant idea to invite Marcus.

"That's a huge fucking mistake."

"For the company, yes. For me, hopefully not so much."

She eyes me closely. "What's going on?"

I take a deep breath and explain everything. I replay my conversations with Marcus and the meetings with Williams and

Tim. I tell her about DSN, the charities – all of it, including the widows. Especially the widows. When I'm done, I know she's rattled because she sits down heavily in her chair. I follow her cue and sit down across from her.

"I knew these fuckers were dirty," she says finally, "but not that dirty."

"This week's P.R. push has been all about trying to insulate us from Marcus."

"That I get. Doing local fluff press to insulate us from a critical *Times* piece is run of the mill P.R. But this ... this is different. If even one-tenth of what you're telling me is right, we were complicit in a criminal conspiracy."

"Not 'we.' Just me."

She looks at me closely, a mixture of pity and disgust in her eyes. "You knew about all this?" she whispers.

"Not a fucking thing. But I should have."

"How could you? It's not like you were in meetings with them."

"I'm no lawyer, but I think what matters is what a reasonable person ought to have known. And I've been here long enough and know these douchebags well enough to know they were up to no good."

"You're being too hard on yourself."

"Maybe. But that's not going to matter to a prosecutor. They're going to pick the low man on the totem pole and squeeze. I'll give you one guess who that low man is."

"All so you'll give them Williams?"

"Williams, Tim ... the lot of them."

"Will you do what they want?"

"Not in so many words."

She is indignant. "You'd go to jail to protect these assholes?"

"Not a chance," I assure her.

"So what will you do?"

"Get the truth out in the open."

"How do you plan on doing that?"

I tell her and she is rapt with attention. When I finish, I lean forward, meeting her eyes.

"This could get ugly."

"It already is," she agrees.

"Anyone who helps is going to get dirty."

She gives me a wicked smile. "I was never all that clean to begin with."

"You'll get fired."

She waves her hand dismissively. "I was done with this place a long time ago."

"I thought you were angling for my job."

"These misogynists were never going to give your job to a woman."

I consider this. "You're probably right."

"What about you?"

"What about me?"

"You're committing career suicide."

"My career was dead long ago."

She looks at me closely. "Why, Sean? Why now?"

I run my fingers through my hair. "You ever wake up and not like who you are?"

She surprises me by bursting out in laughter. "Only every morning."

"So it's not just me?"

"Why do you think I slept with you?"

"Self loathing?"

"Well, it sure wasn't your sad excuse for a cock."

"Truth be told, I've always thought it was a pity fuck."

"It was. But it wasn't you I was taking pity on."

I smile. "Tell you what. How about we do something fun for a change?"

"What did you have in mind?"

As I tell her, I begin to think this is going to be much more fun than wallowing in my own despair.

35

It is nearly five o'clock when I leave Naomi's office. Mercifully, she doesn't ask for a last fling between the sheets and I don't offer. Something has clicked between us and our days of sleeping together have ended. I'm not the least bit wistful. If anything, I'm relieved.

There are less than three hours until Julia's recital but there are still two more things I need to do before then. I head down the elevator to the garage and climb into the Chevelle. I turn the key and the engine roars, its growl intensifying as I press the gas. I fish a business card out of my pocket, then slip the car in gear. Pulling out of the garage, I dial the number on the card and hope it's not too late.

"We've been hoping you'd call," the voice says, not bothering with any pleasantries.

"What can I say, Detective Fogel? I missed you. Well, not so much you as that charming little partner of yours. How is Little Mussolini?"

"Not so great, now that you mention it."

"How's that?"

"You're on speaker. He can hear every word you say."

"Hola, amigo!"

"Nice try," Fogel says, "but I don't think that's going to make up for the Mussolini crack."

"What? Because he's Hispanic and I characterized him as Italian? I thought he'd be flattered. That's a step up."

A different and markedly angrier voice comes on. "Mother fucker—"

I hear rustling. No doubt Ramirez lurched for the phone and Fogel is fighting him off. "Is there a reason you called, Mr. Reilly?" Fogel finally asks, breathless. "Other than to flaunt your racism?" His voice sounds different. He must have taken me off speaker. Good move.

"Just checking in," I say, unable to contain a giggle. "Well, that and I want to see if I can help you out."

"Too late for that, Reilly."

"How so?"

"We're about to serve a warrant on your house."

"I wouldn't do that if I were you."

"Oh really?"

"Yes, really." Talking to these guys is like trying to debate an offensive lineman from my high school football team.

"And why not?"

"Because what you're looking for isn't at my house." That's only half true, but he doesn't need to know that.

He tries to change course. "How do you even know what we're looking for?"

Good gravy, I thought he was the smart one. I hope he can't hear me roll my eyes.

"Because you told me when you came to my office. You're looking for a car and a gun. I'm driving the car and I've stashed the gun."

I hear muffled noises. I can only assume he's put his hand

over the phone and is conferring with Ramirez. This ought to be good.

"Where are you?" First good question he's asked.

"Just out and about," I lie. "But I want to give you guys what you want."

More muffled noises.

"What if you're lying to us?"

"Then you'll know I'm thick as thieves with Mac. It'll be your dream come true. You can treat me like a black kid and kick the shit out of me."

"Don't test me," Fogel seethes. I've finally gotten a rise out of him. Took long enough.

"I'm sorry, Detective Fogel," I say soothingly, trying to mollify him. "I didn't mean to piss you off. Honestly. I'm just nervous. And when I'm nervous, I say stupid stuff. I'm not a criminal or in deep with this Mac guy. I just want to give you guys his car and the gun he left in the glove compartment."

"Why didn't you tell us all this when we spoke this morning?"

"Because I was too busy soiling myself." This may be the first honest thing I've said to him. "Think about it. Two cops come to my office and start questioning me about God knows what. Of course I got nervous."

"Tell us where you are and we'll come to you now."

"I can't. I've got somewhere I have to be. But I can meet you tomorrow. Come to my office around noon and I'll hand over everything."

"No deal."

"What do you mean 'no deal?'"

"You really expect us to let you stay on the loose?"

"I'm not going to be on the loose. I'm going to a freaking junior high dance recital."

"Skip it."

"Have you met my wife?"

He pauses, then speaks quietly. "Talked to her on the phone."

"Then you know she's batshit crazy. I miss this recital, she'll serve me my balls for dinner."

He considers this. "We can't have you going anywhere with a gun."

"I'm not bringing the gun to a school. That's a crime. Besides, I'm a pussy. Ask Ramirez. He said as much this morning."

More muffled noises. When he comes on, he sounds much more chipper. "He still thinks you're a pussy."

"Told you."

"So we'll meet you after the recital and you'll give us the car and the gun."

"Like I told you, I stashed the gun, someplace far away from here." Another lie. I'm getting pretty good at this. "It's going to take awhile for me to get it. Look, it's the end of the day and I'm sure you and Ramirez are anxious to go home and do ... whatever it is you do when you're not harassing me."

"What are you up to, Reilly?"

"Nothing, really. But if you don't believe me, have the Beebs tail me. He's got nothing better to do, except maybe pick his nose."

Fogel covers the phone again. The muffled noises are longer this time. I'm not sure they're going to go for it. When Fogel comes back on, he sounds like he just went ten rounds with my wife.

"Okay," he sighs finally, "tomorrow it is."

"Great. But there's one thing I need you to do for me."

"What is it?" he asks, a thoroughly beaten man.

I tell him. He asks the occasional pointed question but seems to listen carefully.

"You expect me to believe that crap?" he asks when I'm done.

"I'll send you a text that will explain everything."

"Fine," he says, but his heart isn't in it. "I'll see what I can do." Not exactly confidence inspiring, but it will have to do.

"I'll see you tomorrow."

"You better. Fuck us over and I'll bring down a world of hurt on your ass, you hear me?"

"Loud and clear," I assure him.

I'm about to hang up but think better of it. "Oh, and Fogel?"

"Yeah?" From his tone, it is clear I've reached the limit of his patience.

"You and Ramirez sound like an old married couple. You wouldn't happen to be hitting it, would you?"

"What if we are, Reilly? It's a brave new world."

I smile. I take back what I said earlier. I like this guy.

I hang up the phone and narrowly avoid hitting an old lady shuffling behind her walker across the nursing home parking lot. I shouldn't laugh, but I can't help it, especially not after she flips me off and yells something unintelligible. I deserve that.

Luckily, Chandice is working, so I get a huge hug as soon as I walk in the front door. She leads me down the hall to Dad's room and I ask how he's been.

"Some days good, some days bad. Same as ever."

"Is today a good or a bad day?"

She shrugs. "Bit of both."

We get to his door and she gives me another hug.

"Julius is on today, too, so just hit the call button if you need one of us."

"What would I do without you guys?"

She smiles. "Sugar, you'd be lost without me. Everyone know dat." She heads back to her desk, her laughter echoing off the cinderblock walls.

I place my hand on the doorknob and take a deep breath, playing the same little game every time I visit. First, I place odds on whether he'll recognize me. Then, I guess who he'll be that day: the innocent child, the cantankerous senior, the put-upon spouse or the forgotten father. Bonus points if he plays more than one, with the jackpot coming if he weaves in elements of each of them. I take another breath, make my silent wagers and walk in.

"Hey, Dad. How are we doing today?"

He looks up, frazzled, his eyes spinning. "Who the hell are you?" Guess that's a strong 'no' on will he remember me.

"It's me, Sean," I say gently. "Your son."

My heart breaks as I watch him struggle to sort through what is fact and what is fantasy. But as with most dementia patients, he counters quickly, dissembling to hide his confusion.

"I know that! Where the hell have you been?"

"Sorry I'm late," I shrug. "Got stuck in traffic."

I'm not late; he didn't know I was coming. Plus, traffic was non-existent. I can't stress this enough. When it comes to people battling dementia, roll with the punches. Challenge the assumptions underlying whatever reality they're living in, and you'll put them on the defensive. But play along with their delusions and there will be a lot more happiness. And far fewer tears.

"Your mother is always late." Present tense. We've got the forgotten father and the put-upon spouse; bonus points all around.

"She's a busy lady."

"Leaving me to deal with you and your brother."

"Kevin and I are eternally grateful."

"Who's Kevin?"

I sigh. It hurts to watch his brain being strangled by snippets of reality intertwined with ribbons of fantasy.

"So how's your day going, Dad?"

"Why the hell do you keep calling me 'Dad?' We've been

through this. I'm not your father. Not since that slut mom of yours cheated on me."

"What can I say? I'm a glutton for punishment."

"You and me, both. Hey, your mom isn't due home for a couple of hours still. What do you say we sneak in a drink or two?"

In case you're still keeping score, he's gone from not knowing his family to taking cheap shots at his dead wife to saying 'fuck it, let's go get drunk.' It's no wonder why I am the way I am. Score one for nurture over nature.

Still, his attitude makes me smile. "I'd like nothing better."

I find a wheelchair parked outside his room and plop him in it, reminding him that it will be easier on his trick knee (he has no such thing). But he smiles contentedly and, in no time, we're merrily wheeling our way through the antiseptic halls of his nursing home.

"Where to?" he calls, the wisps of his remaining hair waving in the breeze.

"I found a new place. I think you'll like it."

We wind through the antiseptic hallways, the rubber wheels of the wheelchair squeaking loudly with each turn on the polished tile floor. We make the last turn and I stop the chair to show him our destination.

"Whaddya think?"

He turns and looks at me sourly. "The cafeteria? This place sucks balls."

So much for hoping even the most repeated experience is new to a man with no memory.

I wheel him to an empty table and promise to return with two drinks. Given his disappointment, I feel like I owe him something, so I fill two plastic cups with Diet Coke and ice and top them off surreptitiously with the contents of a flask I stashed in the Chevelle's glove compartment that morning. Walking back to our table, I see Dad and laugh. His arms are folded across his chest and a sullen frown is etched on his face. In the time it took me to grab our drinks, he devolved from an elderly patient to a petulant child.

If you like your loved ones with wildly irrational swings of emotion, Alzheimer's is the disease for you.

I place one of the cups in front of him.

"What's that?" he snaps.

"I told you. A drink."

"Looks like Coke."

I take a sip and smile. "Yeah, but it tastes like something entirely different."

Arms still folded, he leans over and smells it. His eyes widen in surprise. "Kevin," he whispers with a wicked smile, "what did you do?" My name's not Kevin, but I let it go. At least he's smiling again.

He takes a sip, cackles wildly and then, catching himself, looks over his shoulders conspiratorially. "Do you think they know?" he whispers.

"I think we're safe. But if anyone comes over, let me do the talking."

He nods furiously then brings the cup back to his lips and slurps. We sit for a few minutes and enjoy our drinks in silence. As a familiar warmth washes over me, Dad looks at me, his eyes clear for the first time all visit.

"Sean?" he whispers. "Is this happening?"

I can feel my throat tighten and my eyes water. When Alzheimer's first started making its mark with Dad, he would occasionally ask whether something was really happening, looking to me as the definitive arbiter of what was real and what was fantasy. I never asked the question I was dying to have answered: if I told him something wasn't really happening, would he know the difference? Instead, I would simply nod and tell him, "Yes, Dad, this is happening." It always seemed enough for him. He would relax and nod, comfortable in the knowledge that the disease didn't have complete hold of him yet.

I repeat the mantra once more and his smile returns, though this time I see it in his eyes as well as his mouth. He's here, in earnest, sharing a drink with his son, even if our biological link is just as tenuous as his grasp on reality.

But before I can smile back, his eyes cloud over and the disease races back to reassert its dominance. He scowls and looks at me suspiciously.

"Why are you here? Did Hanneran send you?"

I don't answer, mostly because I'd rather sip my drink and appreciate the moment we just shared, even if fleeting. But also because I don't know who the hell Hanneran is.

What a fucking pernicious disease.

"You want to head back?" I ask. "Mom will get nervous if we're out too long."

He nods and stands to go. But as he sees his half empty cup on the table, he looks up at me, confused.

"Bring it with us. You could use a roadie."

He takes my word for it and grabs the cup. I ease him back into the wheelchair and help him wedge the cup securely between his legs. I wheel him out of the cafeteria and we make our way back through the maze of polished linoleum hallways. We pass the nursing station and I nod to Julius, who responds with a wary smile. Practically on cue, Dad sees the cup between his legs, seemingly for the first time, grabs it and take a sip.

"HEY," he yells in pleasant surprise, "DID YOU KNOW THERE'S HOOCH IN HERE?"

I look at Julius and shrug. Guilty as charged.

"You do know alcohol makes it worse, right?" he asks.

"You think it can get worse than this?"

He doesn't even pause. "You really want me to answer that?"

No, I don't. But seeing my dad guzzle the rest of his drink like it's the last drop of water on Earth, I realize I don't care much either.

We make it back to his room and I park the wheelchair in front of the TV. I flip it on and *America Ninja Warrior* flickers to life. Dad smiles. If this show, in which competitors race across preposterously diabolical obstacle courses, ever goes off the air, Julius better put my dad on suicide watch. I know I should leave but I'm nearly as hooked as my old man, and I soon find myself getting wound up when one of the competitors can't climb the aptly named Warped Wall, a fifteen-foot curved wall that has become a staple in all of the courses.

"Not even close," I say, shaking my head.

"Rookie," Dad scoffs.

We wait through another interminable backstory about a truck driver who dedicated his life to the "sport" after losing his wife to cancer. Neither of us is impressed. Everyone on this show has a sob story.

"Get on with it, already," Dad mumbles.

The trucker is a crowd favorite but Dad shoots me a knowing look.

"Ten bucks he doesn't make it up the Salmon Ladder." Another staple, the Salmon Ladder is a pull-up bar on steroids, where competitors must pull themselves up with enough force to launch up a series of rungs twelve inches apart. Just looking at it makes me feel inadequate.

I take the bet – which is surprisingly easy when you're betting money neither guy has – and we both watch with glee when the trucker falls into the water by the third rung.

"Put it on my tab," I say with a laugh.

"Between that and the tuition you still owe me, you're in pretty deep."

He didn't pay a dime for college – I wanted nothing to do

with my family or their money after the Jenny Nieb debacle –
but there's no use pointing that out now. Besides, he's got
nothing on the rest of the money I owe.

"You've got no idea."

He turns to look at me. "You in trouble, son?"

Hearing him call me 'son' makes my chest tighten. "I'll be
alright," I lie.

He chuckles to himself. "You used to always say that."

"When?"

"As a kid. Whenever you skinned your knee or had trouble
in school, we'd offer to help and you'd give us that little shrug
and say, 'I'll be alright.'"

"I don't remember that."

"If there's one thing this shitty-ass disease has taught me,
Sean, it's that just because you don't remember something
doesn't mean it didn't happen."

I'm floored. "Yeah, well, it's nothing I can't handle."

"You used to say that, too. But you know what?"

"What?"

"You were usually wrong."

I laugh out loud. Son of a bitch has me cold, Alzheimer's
and all.

The laughter fades and we turn our attention back to the
show. Another competitor has fallen off the Salmon Ladder and
needs help climbing out of the water below.

"There's no shame in asking for help," Dad says.

I swallow hard. "Problem is, I'm not sure where to start."

"Don't overthink it. Just solve one thing at a time."

"That's easy to say. It's just..." I trail off as a competitor in
neon yellow spandex starts on the course. "Did things ever get
so bad that you couldn't see the point of living anymore?"

My father turns and looks at me, shaking his head in disbelief. "Are you fucking kidding me? How about every goddamn morning?"

Right. Probably not the guy to complain to.

"Sean, I'm barely me anymore. The times I know what's going on are so fleeting that they're starting to feel less real than my fantasies. But here's one thing I truly believe. You're a fuckup, but you've always been a good kid at heart. I don't know what you've gotten yourself into, but you'll do the right thing in the end. You just have to have the courage to go and do it."

"That's the problem. I'm not sure I do anymore."

"That's horse shit. You can do anything you want."

We both go quiet and I can feel tears sliding down my cheeks. I didn't realize just how much I miss my dad. The crowd on TV roars and I look up to see the guy in yellow spandex making it through the Salmon Ladder.

"Hey," he says brightly. "Remember when you hid in the mountains for over a year and fought off those Russian invaders?"

My laughter comes out as a snort. My face is now covered in tears and snot. "Dad, that was Patrick Swayze in *Red Dawn*."

What can I say? We're a Swayze family. Always have been, always will be.

"Okay, how about the time you survived on that deserted island with only a volleyball to keep you company?"

"Tom Hanks in *Cast Away*."

He scrunches his face and thinks.

"What about when you convinced that girl to give you her underwear to show your friends at the school dance?"

"That was Anthony Michael Hall in *Sixteen Candles*."

"Oh really? And I suppose that wasn't you who cooked the single greatest meal that Parisian food critic ever ate?"

"Christ, Dad," I laugh. "That was a cartoon. And the main character was a rat."

There's a heaviness to his silence as he mines his brain for what's real and what's not. He's pissed. I don't blame him.

"Dad?"

"What?"

"How come almost all your movie references are thirty years old?"

He considers this. "I think that's when my brain stopped giving a shit."

I pull him towards me and kiss the top of his head. On TV, the guy in neon yellow spandex is climbing up a 35-foot plexiglass chute using nothing but his hands and feet pressed up against the walls. He looks like a spider trying to escape a test tube.

It dawns on me that both my dad and I know how he feels.

36

I pull into the driveway a little after six. I smile as I see that Fogel has lived up to his end of the bargain. Officer Bieber is sitting in a black and white across the street. I wave and he flips me off in return. All in all, it's the basis for a solid working relationship. I fire off the text I promised Fogel and then see the garage door open followed by Alex and the girls piling into her car. Seeing the Chevelle, Julia comes clomping towards me in her Uggs, tulle peaking out from beneath her coat, her smile as wide as the ocean.

"You made it!" I'm barely out of the car as she runs over to me and jumps into my arms. I bend down and envelop her in my arms.

"Wouldn't miss it."

Remembering herself, she shrieks and backs up. "My makeup!"

"Still looks great." She's got so much eye makeup on, she looks less like a ten-year-old and more like a dancer out by the airport. But I figure it's time to play the supportive dad for once.

I stand and wave to Claire, who is too much of a teenager to go to the trouble of uncrossing her arms and wave back. Still, I'd like to think there's a hint of a smile beneath her sullen pout. I want to apologize for this morning and shake her of the image of a pathetic, broken man lying in a pool of his own vomit, but before I can say anything, she snaps at Julia.

"Come on. We're gonna be late."

I look at Alex, who only rolls her eyes. A big sister has to boss someone around. "You coming?" she asks.

"What happened to this – 'cocktard' was it? – getting his own ride."

She winces. "Not my finest moment."

"Nor mine," I admit. "Hasn't been for a long time."

"Bus is leaving," she says impatiently.

"I'll be right behind you," I answer, waving them on.

She looks at me quizzically. "Are you sober?"

"Trying something new," I nod.

"I'm not sure it suits you." Without another word, she puts the car in reverse and pulls out of the garage. Julia waves madly from the backseat and I blow her a kiss. Funny thing, life. In the midst of the worst kind of chaos, the small moments are sometimes the best.

I run upstairs to wash my face and change out of my suit. I consider getting the gun out from under the bed and hiding it somewhere out of the house in case Fogel and Ramirez decide to make good on the search warrant, but decide to trust them and leave the gun where it is. I'm turning over new leaves left and right.

I grab my wallet and keys and hustle downstairs, stopping at the pantry long enough to house half a box of Cheez-Its. Crunching merrily, with orange detritus flaking down my chin, I grab a Gatorade out of the fridge and head out to the car. Twelve minutes later, I pull into Henry Wadsworth Longfellow Junior High and gulp down the rest of the Gatorade. I can't resist bringing all 450 horses to a screeching halt next to an uptight couple climbing out of a Tesla. Just to be a dick, I rev the engine a few times. Savor the flavor of an internal combustion engine, asshats.

I climb out of the car and leave the horrified couple behind to join the throngs of proud parents streaming into the lobby. Once inside, I see a quote on the wall.

We judge ourselves by what we are capable of doing, while others judge us by what we have already done.

H.W. Longfellow

Dear God, I hope not.

I follow the hordes to the auditorium and am pleasantly surprised to find Alex sitting a third of the way down holding a seat for me. She slides over to the empty seat so Claire doesn't have to sit next to me (I guess there's only so much a fourteen-year-old can bear). For a second, just as my ass hits the warm, institutional wooden seat, we are the picture of a fully functioning family – right until Alex grimaces, hands me a breath mint and tells me I smell like something that came out of a vending machine. I start to respond but the lights come down, which is probably for the best. She's not far off.

As much as I'd like to be the proud father and say the recital is amazing and my daughter is the second coming of Margot Fonteyn (Google her – you'll thank me later), I think we both know I'd be lying. Truth is, it is needles in the eyeball painful. Don't get me wrong – it's cute, with aspiring young ballerinas flitting about slightly out of time to the music, their tulle skirts bouncing and spinning like undercooked meringues. And, yes, my heart skips a few beats whenever Julia joins the rows of prepubescent girls jumping and twirling across the stage. Of course, I think she's the best up there, but that doesn't mean I'm punching her ticket to Julliard just yet. Fact is, there's not a legitimate dancer in the bunch, but it's a sugary sweet performance that leaves not a dry eye in the house. I sneak a look and see more than a few fathers with lumps in their throats at the loss of innocence that is right around the corner. It's at once awful and wonderful and heartbreaking, and I adore every minute of it.

Of course, no minute can possibly match the one in which a particularly chubby classmate of Julia's decides to throw caution to the wind and go for it with a Grand Jeté (I know – the sheer audacity!). Surprising absolutely no one, she can't get full extension and, after struggling a moment too long to gain the classic midair pose, she flubs the landing and crashes to the floor in a heap. The crowd gasps but the precocious – if untalented – girl pops up, gathers herself and gamely goes on with the show. She owns the place, eight hundred voices screaming in full-throated support of her.

Waiting in the lobby afterward – as Alex holds a bouquet of flowers and strains to catch a glimpse of Julia – I realize sadly that none of this can continue. Not that any of it is real, mind you. In Alex's mind, reality is a husband who never lived up to his potential and has slowly thrown his life away, one bottle at a time. In my daughters' minds, it is a drunk father who passes out each night so he doesn't have to suffer the carping of her shrewish mother. One pleasant night at the junior high ballet can't possibly erase all of that. And yet, as I look at Claire, standing next to her mother bouncing on her toes as she, too, looks for her baby sister, I see nothing but happiness. For a moment anyway, she is a fairly normal fourteen-year-old kid, reveling in the joy of her sister's accomplishment, sharing the laughter of the families around her. I couldn't be happier, for her or for me.

I've been anesthetizing myself against life for so long that I'm surprised to discover there are tears sliding down my cheeks. As

Julia comes bounding down the hall, accepting the flowers with unapologetic shrieks of glee and hugging her mother and sister in turn, I am overcome with a bewildering mixture of pride, sadness, fear and joy. Standing in the middle of the lobby, surrounded by other happy, noisy, boisterous and messy families, I am sobbing. I want so badly to be able to deserve having these girls in my life but I know I never will.

Alex, still holding both girls, looks up and meets my gaze. Smiling sadly, she beckons me over and I join their embrace.

For a moment, I feel whole.

And just as quickly, the spell is broken. Julia wriggles away from her clingy parents and runs off to congratulate and commiserate with a gaggle of her friends. Claire likewise disengages, seeking the solace of her iPhone rather than be subject to another awkward display of affection from her parents. With nothing else to do, Alex and I turn and walk out of the lobby and across the parking lot slowly. The screams of other children and the impatient calls of their mothers and fathers – begging them to "Just come to the car, already!" – fade away and all I can hear is the crunch of crumbling asphalt beneath our feet.

Without a word, Alex turns and heads to her car, leaving me to walk to mine. Now, the only footsteps I hear are mine.

FRIDAY

37

S omething is different. I'm not sure how exactly, but even without opening my eyes, this morning feels unlike any day in recent memory.

Alex stirs next to me and I wonder if she feels it too.

I open my eyes and sit up. Something is definitely amiss but I can't quite place it.

I swing my legs to the floor and get out of bed. I feel...what's the word?

Fine.

Yes, that's it. Fine.

I don't sway or swoon or shake or shimmy. I am neither lying in piss nor rushing to the bathroom to vomit. My torso isn't bathed in sweat, my head isn't pounding and my stomach isn't on the verge of mutiny.

So, this is what sobriety feels like.

I head to the bathroom for a shit, shower and shave and emerge fifteen minutes later feeling refreshed. I pick out my best charcoal suit and match it with a silver Zegna tie that I have previously reserved only for funerals. I figure overseeing the napalming of my career qualifies. I look in the mirror and for the first time in days, I don't recoil in horror. Sure, the eye sockets are still repulsive, having progressed from black to forest green. And my nose is still tough to look at, though now it's down from engorged to merely bulbous. But the swelling in the rest of my face has subsided and the blood in my eyeballs has receded so at least I no longer resemble a villain out of a Marvel flick. I don't look terrific, but at least I'm beginning to look human.

Walking out of the closet, I bump into Alex, who is just getting out of bed.

"Holy hell."

"I know, I know. Like putting lipstick on a pig."

"No! I mean it in a good way. You look almost human."

"I'm as surprised as anyone."

"What's going on?"

I wonder to explain it to her. "You remember what we talked about the other night?"

"The dumpster fire that is your career?"

"Exactly. I'm going to try to do something about it today."

"By dressing up?"

"By getting up in front of a huge group of people and telling the truth."

"Is that wise?"

"Almost assuredly not. But fuck it, it's time to do something."

"I'm sorry. Is this the same Sean Reilly without a proactive bone in his body?"

"The very same."

"What gives?"

"I guess I finally figured out I don't like to be kicked around."

"Except in bed."

"Naturally."

I may be thrown off by the sobriety, but it almost looks like she's proud of me. Then she catches herself and scrunches up her face.

"What?"

"If you're going into battle, you may want to fix that face a little."

"Still grotesque?"

"No, but a little work around the margins could still do wonders."

She leads me back to the bathroom where, after hanging my suit jacket on the back of the door and sitting me down on the toilet, she goes to work. I close my eyes and try not to squirm in the flurry of foundations, bases, primers and concealers. Lots and lots of concealers. Really, more concealers than anything else. But after brushing and sponging and buffing and smoothing, she tells me to open my eyes. When I look in the mirror, I almost don't recognize the person looking back at me. My face, while askew, is no longer monstrous.

"Wow!"

"It should do the job."

"Are you kidding? It's terrific!"

"That's why God created Maybelline."

"Seriously, Alex, thank you. You fixed my face."

"I'm not sure I'd go that far."

"Well, it's definitely better. Thank you."

"You're welcome."

I pause, turning my face away from the mirror to look at her directly. "Huh."

"What?"

"Is this what normal married couples sound like?"

She smiles. "How would I know?"

"Fair point."

I thank her again and promise to try to see her at Claire's game tonight. She kicks me out of the bathroom, giving me the chance to rummage under the bed. I find what I'm looking for and pull the shoebox (Jimmy Choo, naturally) out from under the bed and open it. Sure enough, hidden under Robbie Mueller's love letters is Mac's gun. I pull it out, open the cylinder and see that Alex didn't remove the bullets. I wonder how well she slept the last two nights knowing there was a loaded gun three feet under her head. I shake the bullets out of the gun and slam the cylinder back in place, feeling like a bit of a badass until I realize that I don't have the first clue what to do with a gun. I try sticking it in my waistband at the small of my back but, as soon as I take a step, it falls down my ass, through my right pant leg and clunks the outside of my ankle. Ignoring the pain, I pick up the gun and try the front of my pants, tucking it in gingerly lest it inadvertently fires and blasts apart my already dysfunctional reproductive organ, notwithstanding the fact that I removed the bullets not five seconds ago (I never claimed to be rational). This, too, however, fails for as soon as I take another step, the gun wriggles loose, grazing my scrotum before knocking my left kneecap and landing with a thud on my left instep.

To recap: my entire lower body is now in some measure of agony and I haven't even taken two steps. At this rate, I'll be in a coma before leaving the bedroom. In the end, I decide to just hold the gun in my hand as I walk out of my bedroom and down the hall (but don't think for a moment I don't stop in every doorway along the way to point my gun and clear the room, *Die Hard* style. I rock that shit.).

When I walk downstairs and into the kitchen, Claire is packing her lunch and Julia is eating breakfast.

"Fi fo early?" Julia asks, her mouth full of cereal, milk dripping down her chin.

"Beg your pardon?"

She swallows and tries again. "Why so early?"

"What do you mean?"

"She means," Claire interrupts in the grating tone reserved for teenagers and schoolmarms, "we haven't seen you dressed this early in months."

"Big day at the office. Trying to get off on the right foot."

"Well," she says, "you look good."

I look at her expectantly, waiting for the insult to drop. It never comes. Instead, she smiles at me impishly and stuffs an apple in her bag. Like I said, something is decidedly different today.

"Hey," I say, grabbing my wallet and keys, "I don't know when I'll be home tonight and there's a decent chance I'll be—" I pause, searching for an innocuous synonym for 'arrested.' "—detained. But I'm going to do everything I can to make it to your game."

She doesn't look up. "Okay, whatever."

"Claire." She looks up. "I mean it."

"Okay," she says softly. Her eyes are watery and my heart fills up so much I'm afraid it will burst.

I was about to leave but now I think better of it. I sit on one of the stools at the island. "Listen, you two. I know I've been about the crappiest father imaginable."

"No argument here." Soft-spoken Claire is gone. Back is the surly teen with a solid shot to the groin. It's oddly comforting to have her back.

"And I know me and your mom haven't exactly been getting along these last few—"

"Years." She lands another one.

"I was going to say months, but okay, let's call it years. And I know that's made your lives really hard."

"Try shitty." Three in a row. She's going for a new record.

"Alright, shitty. I know this probably doesn't mean a hell of a lot, but I wanted to tell you both how sorry I am. And how much I love you."

Julia puts her spoon down and looks at me with eyes as big as the moon. "Are you and mom getting divorced?"

"I don't know, sweetheart," I answer, my voice breaking. "I can't answer that. But whether we do or we don't, you have to promise me you'll remember something."

I look at her and she nods, tears welling in her eyes like they are in mine. I look at Claire and she nods as well.

"None of this is your fault. The fighting and the yelling, none of it has ever been about you. It's been about two adults struggling to be the people we always wanted to be, only to find out that neither of us actually liked who we'd become. But that will never excuse us putting you guys in the middle of it. That," I say, my voice cracking, "is unforgivable and I'll never be able to say sorry enough. Just know that – no matter what happens – I will always love you, more than anything else in this world. Can you remember that for me?"

For the second time in two nights – and the second time in as long as I can remember – I find myself hugging both girls, tears streaming down my face.

We pull back from each other and start giggling at the messes that we have all become. I hold on to each of them, trying to preserve the moment for as long as I can, until Claire flashes a smile.

"Dad."

"Yes, Claire?"

"Would you mind terribly if I fixed your face?"

At this, the three of us burst into laughter. I'm late but the jackwagons in marketing can wait. I need to sit patiently while my eldest daughter touches up my makeup.

38

"Have you seen it out there?"

Williams is breathless. We are in the green room, which is a glorified name for a small area someone has curtained off behind the CareFest stage and outfitted with a loveseat and three generic hotel-issue desk chairs. On the other side of the large curtain, the crowd begins to take its seat as adult contemporary rock pulses through the speakers.

"Packed house," I say with a nod.

"Biggest one yet." He's on cloud nine.

"We had to set up overflow room with closed circuit TV."

"You're shitting me."

"I shit you not."

"How the hell did you build a crowd like this?" Tim asks, nearly as ebullient as Williams.

I shrug. "A fair amount of external interest popped up late."

"That's great! Any idea what sparked it?"

"This week's activities probably helped."

Williams claps me on the shoulder. "Great work."

I shrug again. "I'm all about the company."

"Is the guy from the *Times* here?"

I nod. "As soon as I get confirmation, we'll get going. After the opening program, there will be an intermission. I'll introduce you to Marcus so the two of you can go upstairs and talk. The afternoon session is mostly clinical panels, which I think Marcus will want to skip."

"That makes two of us."

I turn to Tim. "You ready for your panel?"

He nods. "Mr. Williams does the keynote then I join him on stage for the town hall." He says it like he's reading from a script.

"That's right. I'll be moderating and we've planted a few questions in the crowd, so it should go smoothly. But remember, there's always a chance we get a wildcard. If we do, just answer the question as best you can and we'll move on. Whole thing shouldn't last more than 30 minutes."

"Got it."

I give one last look to Williams. "You ready?"

"I've been running through my lines all night and again this morning. Let's do this."

The sweat on his forehead belies his confidence. I love watching pompous assholes venture out of their comfort zone. It almost never ends well.

"Alright, I'll get this rolling."

Williams and Tim turn to take their seats. Halfway there, Williams stops to turn around.

"Sean?"

"Yeah?"

"Great work. You really came through for us on this one."

"Let's get through this and then we'll talk."

On cue, my phone buzzes. It's Marcus.

Ok. I'm at this shitshow. Just sat
down – front row, stage right

Great. We're about to start

Why am I here?

Because u love me. And
because the least u can
do before screwing us
is let us go on record

Are we finally on the record?

Yes. Print anything u
see and hear today

Anything?

Anything.

Sounds promising

Buckle up

I call Naomi. "You in position?"

"Good to go. You?"

"Marcus is here. Tim and Williams are ready."

"Guess we didn't get all dressed up for nothing."

"Count to fifty, then cue the lights and let's light this candle."

"Sean?"

"Yeah?"

"You shouldn't try to sound tough. You end up sounding like a dork."

She hangs up before she can hear my laughter.

I count to fifty and try to get my breathing under control.

It's not too late, Sean. You can still back out.

The lights dim and the music goes silent.

Fuck, too late.

On cue, the Voice of God rains down from on high.

"Ladies and gentlemen, welcome to this year's CareFest, brought to you by Infirmus. Please take a moment to silence all cell phones and turn your attention to the main stage for your host in this exploration of high quality patient care, Mister Sean Reilly."

Hank, a thirty-something former A/V club president with greasy hair and a wispy mustache who, while not gallivanting about Middle Earth as his warlock avatar, is backstage coordinator for Infirmus corporate events, walks me to the break in the curtain.

"Remember," he whispers, "twelve steps to your spot. Go much further and you'll fall off the front of the stage." With a clap on the back, he sends me out. "Go get 'em."

I take a deep breath and walk through the opening. Instantly blinded by three spotlights, I plaster a smile on my face and count my steps, trusting that Hank isn't some twisted fuck who gets off sending unsuspecting corporate speakers tumbling off the edge of the stage. I get to twelve and hit my mark without falling into the abyss, so I nod to the crowd and try to ignore the thirty-foot screens projecting my image on either side of the stage. Instead, I walk the stage, taking in the applause and trying my best to look like Steve Jobs.

You know, before he died.

The clapping subsides and I dive in.

"Thank you very much. Ladies and gentlemen, it is my honor to welcome you to this year's CareFest, a celebration of patient care here at Infirmus."

More applause. Jesus, this is easy. Say something nice and people applaud. No wonder Hollywood types get addicted to the spotlight. I make a mental note to look into acting lessons –

because the world needs another middle age actor with an addiction problem.

"We have something special planned for you this year. As in years past, clinicians and caregivers will take the stage to describe the cutting edge techniques they are putting to work to improve patient outcomes here at Infirmus. As you'll soon see, we are doing things here that no one else is."

The crowd – mostly Infirmus employees – applauds once more. I make a point not to look in Marcus' direction, though I have no doubt he is rolling his eyes and laughing.

"But this year," I continue, "we wanted to do something different. Let me show you what I mean. I understand we have one or two Infirmus employees in the audience today, am I right?"

The crowd erupts. I smile and politely quiet them with my hands.

"Okay! Why don't we show our guests how we start every meeting here at Infirmus? Sound good?"

More cheers.

"Alright! Here we go. Infirmus folks, I have a question. Who comes first?"

"Patients come first!"

My shoulders drop and I shake my head in embarrassment, milking the moment for all it's worth. "I'm sorry, the acoustics in here must not be good." I pause for the obligatory laughter. "I could have sworn you said something, but couldn't quite make it out. Let's try that again ... Who comes first?"

"PATIENTS COME FIRST!"

I stagger back, mugging for the crowd. "Woah! Now, THAT I heard!"

And the crowd erupts again. I clap my hands in approval and let the audience bask in its own self-satisfaction, misplaced though it may be.

"That's right!" I shout eagerly, feeding their pride. "Patients come first, which is why we are proud today to bring you the voice of the patient. In just a little bit, you will hear firsthand from patients and families, telling you how Infirmus has impacted their lives. By the time they finish ... well, let's just say I can't wait to see your reaction.

"But before that, we have some housekeeping items. First, I want to let you know that this is the biggest audience we have ever had at CareFest—"

Another roar of applause. Jesus, these guys are easy. I'm starting to wonder if I could get a round of applause just by dropping my pants.

"—so big, in fact, that we had to create an overflow room where even more people are watching on closed circuit TV. We also have some distinguished members of the press here who want to learn more about how we do what we do. That's right, folks. Word has gotten out about what's going on here at Infirmus. And I, for one, couldn't be happier about giving them a behind the scenes look on what we're doing."

The crowd applauds once more and I clap along with them. I catch sight of Tim in the front row, grinning wildly and relishing the moment. He catches my eye and gives me an exuberant thumbs-up.

"Finally," I continue, "I want to say a word of thanks. It takes a lot to put on an event like this, so to everyone who is running around backstage trying to make me look good – which I know takes a lot of work." Lots of good-natured laughter. Everyone loves a self-deprecating host. "And to everyone else who helped put this event together – there are simply too many to be named – thank you. There is simply no way we could have done this without you."

I sneak a sip of water from a glass at the lectern while the audience applauds themselves.

"With that, it's time to get going. Ladies and gentlemen, it is my distinct privilege to introduce the man who makes this all possible. A little over a decade ago, an idealistic young man working at a small hospital in Boston had a vision: to create a world-class national healthcare system. People said it couldn't be done. They told him, 'Don't you know, young man, that all healthcare is local?' He didn't listen. And a good thing, too, because without him, the world wouldn't have Infirmus—"

Wait for it.

"—and we wouldn't have jobs!"

A standing ovation from the crowd. This emceeing gig is a piece of cake, I'm telling you.

"One man had the courage to do what no one else thought possible. One man had the audacity to build what no one else deemed feasible. One man – one man – took a small local hospital and built it into a national healthcare system. One man is why we are all here today. Ladies and gentlemen, it is my honor to welcome that man to the stage, Mr. Vern Williams."

The crowd jumps to its feet and thunders its approval as a generic Fleetwood Mac song pumps through the speakers (bland enough not to offend and white enough so everyone can clap along. Barely.). Williams emerges from behind the curtain and raises his arms like he's just won the presidency. He strides to me confidently, his teeth nearly blinding in the spotlights, and shakes my hand vigorously.

"Terrific work, Sean," he whispers in my ear. "Absolutely magnificent."

"Least I could do," I respond, but he never hears me. He's too busy walking to the edge of the stage, basking in the adulation of the crowd. This is his moment, a lifetime in the making.

I walk offstage and the first person I see is Naomi.

"Christ, lay it on thick enough?"

I nod towards the front of the stage. "There's no such thing as far as he's concerned."

She walks to a dark corner and I follow.

"Are they here?" I ask when we're out of earshot of the stagehands.

She nods. "Our guest speakers are upstairs trying to relax in your office. Diane will bring them down when they're on."

"How are they doing?"

"Nervous as hell, but they're holding it together."

"They wanted to make a splash. This is their chance."

"I don't think they expected it to happen this quickly."

"What can I say? I'm a miracle worker."

She rolls her eyes. "Let's see how the rest of the day goes."

"Questions all set?"

She nods. "Already in the hands of several like-minded employees. After you take a few softballs, call on microphone four and five in that order. Things should go downhill from there."

"Got it."

"And two local TV affiliates are here with cameras. That's my list. What about you?"

"Marcus is in the front row, enduring Williams' speech as we speak."

"So it's Williams, the panel and then the guests of honor. That's it?"

"What?" I ask. "You want more?"

"I'm just wondering what will happen then."

"Most likely, I'll be hauled offstage, drawn and quartered. Which reminds me, you'll have to deal with getting Marcus out of the building when all hell breaks loose."

"I'll handle it."

"Thanks."

"You need anything else?"

"Nope. Just do me a favor and hang around the soundboard in back just to keep an eye on things."

"Why?"

I look at her sideways. "Really?"

She realizes her mistake. "Got it. And you?"

"I'll go back to being the world's greatest emcee and number one Infirmus fan."

"Who knew you were such a great actor?"

"Sometimes, I surprise even myself."

Without warning, Naomi grabs my shoulders and kisses me, a long, soft, tender kiss unlike anything she's given me before. As she pulls away slowly, my stomach flutters.

"What was that for?" I whisper.

"I'm wasn't sure when – or if – I'd have the chance."

"To do what?"

"Say thank you."

"Well remind me to put you in my debt more often."

She smiles. "I mean it, Sean. Thanks for everything."

She leans in for what I think is another kiss, but then she squeezes my crotch at the last second.

"Knock 'em dead out there," she whispers in my ear. Between her breath in my ear and her hand on my junk, I am suddenly in no position to be seen in public. She nibbles my earlobe, then turns and walks away, hips swaying seductively. Damn if she's not the sexiest thing in the world.

I swallow hard and walk uncomfortably back to my spot next to Hank.

"Ninety seconds," he says.

As I readjust to try to hide things downstairs, I can hear Naomi's full-throated laugh somewhere in the dark, followed quickly by a chorus of angry shushes from irate stagehands. To reduce blood flow, I conjure the most non-sexual thoughts I can, but nothing seems to be working, so I finally jam my hand down my pants and rearrange things as best I can. Hank gives me a sideways glance but I throw him a confident nod, which seems to mollify him. I button my jacket for added camouflage and listen to Williams wrap up.

"... which is why, on behalf of our stockholders, I want to say thank you. Thank you, thank you, thank you. You've done what it takes – quarter after quarter, year after year – to deliver record earnings. You've controlled expenses and maximized revenues, giving us one of the best P/E ratios in healthcare and sending our stock price through the roof."

I cover my face with my hands. What a buffoon. He's talking to a roomful of caregivers – none of whom hold any stock, let alone know what the hell a P/E ratio is – and all he can talk about is how rich they've made him and the other investors. He has yet to mention patients. In fact, he's a walking, talking billboard for why the American healthcare system is in the toilet. He's a P.R. person's nightmare.

I can't wait to hear more.

"Some of you may know I like cars – really fast, really expensive cars. In fact, you may have seen my Ferrari parked out front when you walked in here this morning."

Did you hear that, people? Vern Williams has a really expensive car. And a huge dick.

"They are beautiful machines, each one of them hand crafted. And when you start the engine – well, I don't think there's a more beautiful sound in the world."

No question. The sound of waves crashing, birds chirping – even a baby cooing – all pale in comparison to the deafening roar of an internal combustion engine.

"But, as with any machine, parts wear. Components break down. Without a dedicated mechanic to make the necessary repairs, the engine will never hum. The car will never run. None of that beauty –

none of that power – is possible without the grease monkeys working under the hood."

Please say it, please say it, please say it…

"Just like you."

He did it! Oh, Christ Almighty, this couldn't be going any better. Marcus must be shitting his pants trying to figure out how to reconfigure his article to incorporate this entire speech verbatim. With my face still buried in my hands, I can feel my shoulders start to shake. Hank puts a sympathetic hand on my shoulder, but I don't have the heart to tell him that I'm covering my face covered not because I'm mortified, but because I don't want him to see me laughing.

"You are the grease monkeys that make this company run. With your care, dedication and focus, you fix our patients so they can live their lives. But also – and this is critical – so our bottom line can really hum."

And there it is. Patient care is nice, but only insofar as it gooses our profit. Ladies and gentlemen, I give you the American healthcare system.

"So once again, on behalf of the board and all of the stockholders…"

I'm almost on. Trying to compose myself, I wipe the tears off my cheeks and take a couple of deep breaths. Hank gives me a sympathetic look.

"It wasn't that bad."

"Thanks," I answer, trying my best not to laugh in his face.

After Williams' third "thank you," I walk through the curtain, unable to erase the ridiculous smile from my face. I meet Williams center stage as he revels in what he doesn't realize is polite applause from an otherwise mortified audience. We shake hands and he is beaming, his teeth brighter than ever.

"Unbelievable," I whisper to him.

"I nailed it, right?"

He's beside himself with joy. I'm not sure I've ever seen anyone more unjustifiably proud of himself.

He claps me on the shoulder and waives to the audience once more. As he skips offstage, I nearly swallow my tongue when a man in the front row whispers to no one in particular, "Where the fuck is *my* Ferrari?"

"Vern Williams, ladies and gentlemen," I say, hoping it comes out not quite as mockingly as it sounds in my head. The applause comes to an abrupt halt and I plow on. "Now, we're going to mix things up a little bit. Rather bring a bunch of people up here to talk at you, we thought it would be more constructive to engage in a bit of dialogue and have our company leaders answer questions and talk about what *you* want to talk about. So, while my friends here get the stage set up—"

I wave to the stagehands who are placing three chairs just behind me.

"—let me introduce the three members of senior management that will be participating in our town hall discussion. The first needs no introduction – Vern Williams, chief executive officer of Infirmus."

Williams returns to the stage, still beaming, and takes his seat. A few sad claps greet him.

"Next up is the man responsible for clinical operations for the company and one of the key drivers of everything we are celebrating here at CareFest—" Not to mention the only person of color on the entire management team. "—our chief medical officer, Dr. Carmelo Alvarez."

A handsome man with dark skin, bright eyes and jet-black hair strides onstage. He waves to the crowd – now applauding with considerably more vigor – adjusts his impeccably tailored suit and takes his seat next to Williams.

"Finally, a man some of you may not know but who is instrumental in setting the course and direction for this company. As General Counsel and Chief Administrative Officer, he helps ensure that every hospital, dialysis clinic and outpatient surgery center in this company operates smoothly. Whenever a patient walks into an Infirmus facility, you can be sure that this gentleman is working behind the scenes to ensure they have a positive experience. Please welcome Mr. Tim Dwyer.

Tim walks center stage and waves to the crowd. For a brief moment, he, too, appears drunk with the approval of the crowd, but as he turns his back to the audience, he shoots me a quizzical look. He knows my introduction was over the top and I can see in his eyes that he's trying to piece together why.

"The format is straight-forward," I explain as the three panelists take their seats center stage. "There are several microphones set up throughout the convention hall. If you have any questions for these gentlemen about our care model and the outcomes we have been able to achieve, please feel free to line up and we will call on you in turn. For any of you unable to reach a microphone, just raise your hand and one of our staff will bring a handheld microphone to you.

"With that, let's begin. I believe our first question will come from microphone number one. Go ahead, ma'am."

A woman I recognize as a secretary friendly with Diane takes the cue and asks a benign question about patient education and whether patient preferences are taken into account in treatment decisions. Not surprisingly, Williams and Tim defer to Dr. Alvarez, who launches into a rambling description of how Infirmus is incorporating shared decision-making concepts into its care model. It's all bullshit, of course – Infirmus physicians adhere to strict cost-based formularies that dictate treatment regimens for every condition, regardless of patients' preferences – but it makes good copy. I can practically hear Marcus yawning.

As Alvarez drones on, I sneak a look at Tim, who is staring

right at me. He is still trying to figure out what I'm up to, and I realize now that I may not have thought this plan through. Telling the truth is all well and good in concept, but there's good reason the truth has been obscured for so long: the people doing the obscuring have a lot to lose in its revelation. Crossing powerful people has always been a risky proposition, but never more so than when their money and reputation are threatened.

Pretending to listen to Dr. Alvarez beat his answer to death, I wonder whether I should pull back. It's not too late; I could avoid microphones four and five entirely, and bump our guest speakers from the program. I could give the crowd an early break, thank Marcus for his time and tell him to print whatever story he wants. Nothing I've set in motion is irreversible just yet; I could still play the role of good corporate soldier and do what I've always done, which is lay low and survive.

But what would laying low get me? The status quo is what drove me to try to kill myself in the first place. Why perpetuate a scenario in which I don't want to even live? I know I'm a pussy, but isn't it entirely next level cowardice to pass on the opportunity to change something so vile you were willing to kill yourself to be rid of it?

The target is in my sights.

All I have to do is pull the trigger.

Trouble is, last time I was in this position, I ended up shooting a plant.

"Sean?"

My heart is pounding and I can hear the rush of blood in my ears.

"Sean?"

I look up and see thousands of expectant stares coming my direction. The convention center is silent, save for an embarrassed cough from the back. I turn to the panel and see a bewildered Vern Williams looking at me, urging me to say something.

"Earth to Sean," Tim says genially, "come in, Sean." The crowd laughs. He has them on his side.

"My apologies," I stammer, the awkward foil to Tim's hero. "Guess I was somewhere else there for a moment."

"Any chance we can trouble you to come back to the discussion?" The laughter turns derisive.

I clear my throat.

"Sean? You okay, buddy?"

And in that moment, it dawns on me just how clueless I have been. Tim isn't my buddy. He's not even close to a friend. This entire week, with each new discovery, I had assumed Williams was the bad guy. But while he the face of the company that made billions at the expense of patients, only someone with cunning, finesse and elegance could weave the kind of complex web of fraud and deception necessary to make it come to fruition. Williams was a blunt instrument, a man with a vision but without the intellect and subtlety to bring it to life. Tim was different. He had the genius necessary to put all the pieces together. Seeing him in this moment, watching his smile slide almost imperceptibly from benevolent protector to malevolent mastermind, I realize my mistake. He orchestrated this entire fraud. He moved the pieces around the board. He was the one who made sure I would be the one to take the fall the moment he walked into my office Monday morning. I knew I was a patsy. I just didn't realize it was for Tim's hustle and not Williams'.

Until now.

I pause to let the nervous laughter subside and take a breath.

More laughter. I take a breath.

"Never better, Tim," I say confidently, looking directly at him. "In fact, I believe we have someone waiting at microphone four."

I hold his gaze as a young man steps forward at microphone four. It takes me a second to place the voice and then I realize where I've heard it before: it belongs to the same man who begged me not to kick him out of the Widows' Summit.

I guess Randall J. Simon found his conscience after all.

"Thank you. I appreciate the opportunity to speak at this event celebrating the patient perspective. It's a shame, therefore, that this company consistently puts profits ahead of patient care."

The crowd murmurs as the panelists shift uncomfortably in their seats.

"Is there a question?" Tim snaps.

"Yes, sir, there is. I'd like to get the panel's thoughts on a forthcoming report from the state of Missouri detailing how Infirmus puts patient care at risk due to unsafe staffing levels."

"Where did you get this information?" Williams barks without thinking.

"From you, sir. I was ordered to try to quash the report."

The murmur grows to a rumble as a smattering of applause breaks out. All, it appears, is not well in the house of Infirmus.

The three panelists huddle briefly, whispering fervently over who should field it and how they should answer. Throughout the conversation, Tim is staring at me, fuming.

Finally, Dr. Alvarez assumes the mantle of sacrificial lamb and addresses Randall's question. "While we cannot comment on specific personnel issues, I can assure you that all of the company's staffing levels are in strict compliance with state and local regulations."

"What about in the several dozen states with no such regulations?" Randall asks. He's gone from domesticated pet to rabid dog with a bone. Tim must be out of his mind that someone on his own staff is exhibiting the temerity to challenge him publicly. As I suppress the urge to tell him to get used to it, spotlights from the local television cameras scan the crowd, searching for the panel's interlocutor. Randall is undeterred. "How does the company set staffing levels there?"

"Always in accordance with our mission," Alvarez says smoothly, finding his footing, "patients first."

"Our next question," I say, feigning urgency for the sake of stagecraft, "comes from microphone five."

A young woman Naomi urged me to steal from marketing steps forward. "As you know, our social workers are among this company's biggest asset. They do everything from counsel patients about treatment options to help families with care plans. They also play the unfortunate role of grief counselor to families who have lost a loved one. Too often, however, our social workers are being asked to play a different role: financial advisor. Can the panel answer why social workers are being forced to spend more and more of their time not on counseling, but on helping patients apply for financial assistance for high cost insurance plans, even though many of these patients are perfectly happy with their existing coverage?"

The crowd rumbles once more. A woman in back yells, "Greed, that's why!"

The television cameras are having a field day filming crowd reaction and the three panelists' growing discomfort. I opt for a little misdirection.

"How about we go to a different microphone?" I offer.

"Answer the damn question!" shouts a man, ten rows deep.

Tim flashes his best corporate smile, the one that exudes gravitas and understanding. It must kill on Wall Street road-shows. "Sean, it's a great question, one that deserves an answer."

"Crook!" comes another yell from the back.

Tim doesn't miss a beat. "One of the hardest aspects of our broken healthcare system is that it's just too darn expensive. For too many Americans, this means high quality care is out of reach. From the outset, Infirmus has made it our mission to make sure every American – no matter their socioeconomic status – has access to the highest quality care. So while money is not something most of us like to talk about, we make sure that our social workers and financial counselors are trained to help patients with the financial aspects of their care. For those who have the right coverage, no help is needed. But for others who may have inadequate coverage – or no coverage at all – our staff works with them to find organizations, including charities, that can help. We make no apologies for working with these folks because it's the right thing to do for our patients."

"And your profits!" shouts a man in front.

"I think we have time for one more question," I interject, making a show of being the corporate stooge. Judging from the panelists' faces, it's working on everyone other than Tim. "Let's try microphone two."

A woman in her mid-fifties I have never seen before clears her throat nervously. She's not a plant but I quickly discover she doesn't need to be.

"I have been a nurse for over thirty years," she begins. "For me, nursing isn't a career as much as it is a calling. I always knew I could make more doing something else, but the satisfaction I get caring for other people is reward enough. Or at least, I thought it was until today." She pauses to catch her breath and seems surprised when the crowd gives her an ovation. She pushes on. "I don't need much – I really don't – but I have to say, I am appalled by what I have heard here today. Day in and day out, we hear how this company is about the patients. We even shout, 'Patients First,' for Christ's sake – oh!" she exclaims, catching herself. "Excuse me."

The crowd laughs as she turns a bright shade of crimson. But far from ridiculing her, they are on her side. Someone in the back shouts, "You go, girl!" The woman gathers herself and continues.

"Minutes after being led in a cheer of 'Patients First,' we are subjected to the highest ranking officer of this company bragging about his Ferrari and how much money we've made him. Now, I don't need a Ferrari—"

Much more laughter now, all at Williams' expense.

"—but I do expect to be treated fairly. So I guess my question is simple: Mr. Williams, have you no shame, sir?"

The applause is thunderous. The three panelists sit dumbfounded, trying to figure out how a day of celebration has turned so quickly into a corporate scandal. The television camera operators swivel from stage to audience and back again, recording it all for the five, six and eleven o'clock news. The crowd is mutinous and to think, this is only the appetizer.

I spare Williams the need to answer and thank the crowd for their questions, saying we need to move on to the next item on the agenda or else run out of time. The boos that rain down on me sound sweeter than any applause ever could.

"I know, I know," I say, trying to placate the crowd. "I understand your disappointment. But I am positive you will enjoy our next two speakers even more." The panelists hustle offstage, ignoring the barbs from several hecklers in the crowd ("Suck it, Williams!" being my personal favorite). As the stagehands scurry about to clear the stage, I wait patiently for the catcalls to subside. Gradually, the audience takes their seats and silence returns.

"Thank you, ladies and gentlemen. Your passion for patient care is evident. That's what makes you special and why it has been such an honor to work with you. You heard it in the last question – caring for people is not a career; it's a calling.

"I told you at the outset that this year's program will be different than years past. I'm not going to introduce our next two speakers – I'll let them tell you their stories in their own words. But what I can tell you is their message is very different than anything you've heard on this stage before. And I think you'll agree that their perspective is one that desperately needs to be heard."

I turn and walk to the side of the stage, my footsteps echoing in the dead quiet. For a moment, the stage is barren. No says a word. No one takes a breath. I reach the wings and nod to Naomi, who in turn hugs two women next to her, then wordlessly departs. I reach out and take the hand of each woman, trying to gauge their nerves, but all I see in their eyes is resolve. I smile faintly.

"You're on."

They both smile and squeeze my hand. Then, without a word, they start the long walk towards the empty spotlight at center stage. Hearing my single set of footsteps transform into two, the crowd's anticipation rises. A young woman, perhaps a girl, coughs as the footsteps continue their advance. Gradually, their cadence slows. Chairs creak as the crowd leans forward, straining to see what comes next. Finally, without a word, the two widows fill the empty spotlight.

"Hello, my name is Meg Wheeler."

"And I am Michelle Swanson."

"And our husbands," they say in unison, "were Infirmus patients."

"Tragically," Mrs. Wheeler continues alone, "they both died while in your care. And we are here to tell their stories."

Cameras flash and the audience murmurs anxiously. The two women stand patiently as the television cameramen scramble to get a better shot. I look across to the far side of the stage and see Williams, Tim and Dr. Alvarez hustling out of the green room, angling for a better look. They confer urgently, and though I cannot hear them, it is plain from their crimson faces and wild gesticulations that they do not like what they see.

Gradually, the murmur of the crowd – but not their excitement – fades so the younger widow can continue.

"My husband was thirty-two years old when he was admitted to one of your hospitals for knee reconstruction surgery. Keith was an eternal kid, playing sports whenever he could, whether it was basketball, softball, mountain biking or skiing. He was a wonderful man, a gracious husband, a loving father and an unbelievable friend. There's not a day that goes by when I don't break down in tears because I've lost the only man I'll ever love."

Unable to continue, she covers her mouth with her hand, stifling a sob. The entire audience is rapt as Michelle Swanson leans over, puts a comforting hand on the other woman's shoulder and whispers in her ear. Soon, the younger widow takes a deep breath, looks the older woman in the eye and nods.

"Keith always told me," she continues, "that a life without struggle isn't worth living, so it was no surprise when, after blowing out his knee on that damn basketball court, he immediately opted for surgery and six months of rehab. 'It's only pain,' he told me the morning of the surgery. 'I think I can handle that.'

"But what he couldn't handle was the incompetence of the people who were supposed to care for him. First, the surgeon operated on the wrong knee. Then, after reconstructing a perfectly good knee, the doctors and nurses caring for him failed to recognize that my husband had contracted an infection during surgery, sending him into septic shock." Several in the audience groan. "The post-op team didn't report his spiking fever or skyrocketing respiratory rate, so no one ordered a blood work-up. By the time anyone figured out was wrong, it was too late. Keith was gone."

She stops and Michelle Swanson picks up the thread.

"My husband's name was Doug Swanson, which, ironically, is the reason he is no longer with us. He wasn't even a patient at Infirmus, but that didn't stop your company from killing him."

There is a commotion across the stage a. After a flurry of pointing and whisper screams, Williams takes one hand and slashes it violently across his throat. For a moment, it's not clear if he is wants someone to end the speech or Mrs. Swanson's life (if I had to guess, I think he would accept either). Then, Tim grabs the first stagehand he can find and, with the same slashing gesture, makes clear that he wants the lights and sound cut immediately. The pimply-faced young man, startled by the appearance of so many well-dressed irate men, frantically points at Hank, who by this time has also left his perch at the green room to get a better view of the goings on. Hank, knowing full well who butters his bread, straightens up at the appearance of the CEO and his henchmen, and listens dutifully as they bark orders and point furiously from the widows to the lights to the speakers. Catching on to their urgency, he speaks into his headset and waits for an answer.

Mrs. Swanson, meanwhile, doesn't miss a beat. "Doug had kidney failure and had recently suffered a heart attack. It wasn't a big one, but he had to be admitted to a rehab hospital. Still, the doctors said he was doing well and was just a few days away from being able to come home. The day before he died, he was transported by ambulance to his regular dialysis center, same as always, and everything went smoothly. They took him back to the rehab hospital and he went to bed, not knowing that would be the last night of his life.

"The next day, an ambulance picked him up again for dialysis, even though he wasn't scheduled for treatment until the following day. Now, Doug was no fool, and he kept telling the ambulance driver and the staff at his rehab center that they had the wrong man. No one listened, though, and before long, Doug was dropped off at one of your facilities for treatment. At this point, Doug was upset – I mean, wouldn't you be?"

The audience laughs. It's a horrible story but she has them eating out of her hand.

"So he starts yellin' and fussin' and carryin' on about how this isn't his dialysis center and they must have the wrong man, which, of course, they did. It turns out that the rehab hospital had another patient named Doug Swanson who needed dialysis, only he was an eighty-three year old white man who looked nothing like my husband."

The audience gasps, knowing what is coming.

"It was *that* Doug Swanson who should have been dialyzed that day, not my husband. But no one at your dialysis center seemed to care. Mind you, they'd been treating the white Doug Swanson for the better part of twelve years, but I guess they couldn't be bothered to take notice. They simply ignored my Doug's fussin' and fightin', strapped him into his chair and dialyzed him until he died, right there in your clinic."

She pauses, then delivers the killer.

"Patients first, my ass."

At this, Tim's exhortations to Hank only intensify. Hank responds by shouting once more into his headset but it's clear that no one on the other end can either hear him or respond. Hank, who looks like he wants to curl up in a ball and cry, tries to explain to his interrogators that the controls for the lights and sound are in the rear of the convention hall and that the problem cannot be solved backstage. Tim – fully cognizant of the disaster facing him, what with the two widows accusing the company of negligent homicide, and at its own event, no less – assumes the full measure of his six foot two inches and leans into Hank, no doubt explaining the precariousness of his own position should he not end this abomination, *tout de suite.*

Suitably motivated, Hank tries the headset again, albeit at a considerably higher volume and pitch for, though I cannot make out the words, I can certainly hear his anguished cries.

Seemingly receiving no reply, he taps furiously on his earpiece and shrieks into the microphone.

"IS ANYBODY THERE?"

That one I can definitely make out.

With one look at Tim, who has graduated from irate to murderous, Hank eschews the headset and opts for a less technological, but more reliable, approach. Grabbing the pimply-faced colleague who got him into this mess in the first place, he screams something unintelligible into the poor boy's ear and then throws him deeper into the wings. A second later, I see the young man sprint up the far aisle to the control booth in the back of the convention hall.

As the two widows continue their devastating indictment of the company, the stagehand reaches the control booth. He waves his hands frantically, jumps up and down and points to the stage, all to no avail. The spotlight stays tight on the widows and the speakers continue to project the women's voices to the rapt audience. One glance at the soundboard – even from this distance – and the reason is clear. The bald man with a bushy mustache who controls the sound and lights sits motionless, his forehead glistening, jaw clenched and face as white as a sheet. He looks to be in severe physical distress. Naomi, I see with a smile, sits next to him, impassive. I look back at the young stagehand who is transfixed, eyes locked on something below my sightline. I watch blood drain from his face, his pallor soon matching his colleague's. Finally, he turns away and trudges slowly back down the aisle. He has bad news to deliver and it's clear he doesn't know how to do it.

Just then, Tim catches my eye. A look of defiance flashes across his face, followed quickly by a silent plea for help. I tilt my head and smile sadly. There's nothing I can do to stop it, I tell him without a word, nor would I even if I could.

My treachery complete, he becomes apoplectic, looking

around frantically for a way to end this disaster. He lunges towards the widows but Hank, seeing the malevolence in Tim's eyes, finds courage I never would have anticipated and grabs the older man. I watch, transfixed, as the two struggle offstage, the crowd too engrossed in the widows' story to notice.

Then, all hell breaks loose.

The doors at the back of the hall slam open, startling the crowd and causing several women to shriek in surprise. Light streams into the convention center as Mrs. Swanson stops midsentence and watches men and women in dark jackets file through each door, one halting every twenty feet to form a phalanx along the aisles and at every exit. The only people who seem not to notice are Williams and Tim, as the former grabs a handheld mic from a table backstage and the latter continues to grapple with Hank. It is only when an imposing figure with a crew cut and sunglasses hustles backstage that Williams and Tim see the bright yellow letters emblazoned on the back of his and every other agent's jacket.

F.B.I.

For a moment, nothing moves (with the notable exception of my bowels). Tim and Special Agent Sunglasses stare at each other, each daring the other to blink.

Then, Tim doesn't just blink; he panics.

He releases Hank who, now off balance, teeters for a moment before crashing to the floor. Free from Hank's clutches, Tim makes a break for it, which might have been a decent decision about ninety seconds ago. As it is, he makes it about ten feet before crashing headlong into another agent, who calmly and adroitly spins Tim and slams him face first against the cinderblock backstage wall before cuffing him and whispering what I can only imagine are his *Miranda* rights in his ear.

I'm enjoying the scene immensely until an agent of my own grabs my arm and wrenches it behind me. I squawk in pain as cold metal slams down on my wrist, only to have my other arm subjected to the same process. I am spun around and find myself staring at a pleasant looking man in his twenties who, were he not informing me that I was under arrest for violations of the RICO Act, Securities Exchange Act and several other sections of the United States Code I've never heard of, might be the kind of guy I would point out to Claire as a model future husband. And while his cuffing technique could use some work, he is courteous and respectful as he informs me that I have the right to remain silent and anything I say can and will be used against me in a court of law. All in all, I'm not sure I could have drawn a nicer arresting officer.

Williams, however, is having a significantly different experience. Even in the face of disaster, there is no flight or capitulation in him. Still armed with the handheld microphone, he rushes the stage, avoiding Special Agent Sunglasses with a spin move that should be the envy of every NFL tailback. Waving one arm, he screams into the microphone, beseeching the crowd to hear him out. The widows, bemused, step aside and let chief executive's wild ravings speak for themselves. They couldn't articulate the moral depravity of this place any better.

"WAIT!" he screams. "They have it all wrong! It didn't happen like that! These two money-grubbing whores are the ones to blame!" The crowd gasps. Oblivious, he plows on. "They and hundreds like them sue this company every year. And for what? Money, plain and simple. This isn't about justice or fairness. It's about money! People die for lots of reasons – because they're old, they're sick or sometimes because they're just unlucky. But that doesn't mean we should have to pay for it! And it doesn't mean that these two women should get rich. Because the fact is, *we* didn't do anything wrong!"

With his hand outstretched, he takes a step forward beseeching the crowd to recognize that he is one of them.

"We're the good guys," he says, his voice a step lower, "don't you see that? We take care of this country's loved ones. We see people at their weakest and we heal them. We're not like these ... these *vultures*," he says, practically spitting at the widows. "We're better than that. We always have been. And we always—"

"YOU'RE THE VULTURE!" shrieks a woman in the fifth row.

And just like that, the spell is broken. The crowd rises as one and shouts him down, reducing this once titan of American healthcare into a meek and hollowed out man. Williams tries to speak but Special Agent Sunglasses steps forward and, looking at the soundboard, moves his finger across his throat. The sound controller, liberated from whatever spell Naomi had cast, cuts Williams' microphone, not that it matters since the crowd is drowning out anything he is saying, with or without amplification.

Special Agent Sunglasses takes the microphone from Williams and places him under arrest. Williams puts up a last flurry of resistance and, to the delight of the crowd and the television cameras, the much younger federal agent wrenches Williams' arms together behind his back and cuffs his wrists. As he frog marches Williams towards my side of the stage and recites the *Miranda* rights, the crowd rises in a thunderous ovation. No matter how the legal machinations turn out, one thing is certain: Williams' career is over.

I look to my left and see a familiar face.

"Detective Fogel," I say, "good of you to make it."

He smiles. "Wouldn't miss it for the world. Besides, I have to arrest these assholes on state charges before the feds take all the credit."

The special agent walks Williams directly in front of me and turns to Fogel.

"Is this Reilly?"

Fogel nods and Williams watches dumbfounded as the agent takes a key from his pocket and unlocks my cuffs. He then hands Williams, still cuffed, to the junior agent who had arrested me.

"You!" Williams seethes as our eyes meet. "Why the fuck would you do this?"

It's a fair question and, as I hold his gaze, I'm not sure how to answer him. I've gone through so many emotions this week but, standing here in front of a seething and blood-thirsty Williams, I realize that most of all, I'm angry. Angry at the way these fuckers treated me and angry at the way they treated others. Williams and Tim tried to make me a patsy, a fall guy in case their greed was exposed, and I beat them to it. They're cocksuckers of the highest order and they deserve to burn.

But more than that, it's the way they took advantage of those who needed our help that makes me fume. Patients weren't people to be cared for; they were chattel, objects to be manipulated in order to maximize shareholder return and executive compensation. That's not healthcare. That's exploitation. So yeah, I wanted to tear this place down to the ground, and take the Two Horsemen of the Apocalypse down with it. If that makes me a nihilist, so be it. All I know is that this motherfucker with the perfect teeth is about to know pain and that gives me joy.

"Like the sign says," I answer finally. "'Don't fuck with Daddy.'"

His eyes widen in anger, but the junior agent whisks him away before he can respond. I watch with serene satisfaction as he is marched past the throng of reporters, who thrust microphones at him and shout questions they know he will never answer, the television cameras capturing every glorious moment.

Fogel waits until Williams is ushered out a side door and then introduces me to Special Agent Sunglasses.

"Sean, this is Special Agent Tucker of the FBI."

I'm not sure of the proper greeting to someone who just oversaw my arrest and that of most of the people I work with, so I opt for a simple nod. He nods in return but makes no other effort to communicate, so we end up staring at each other like a couple of jackasses. We are spared further awkwardness when a woman with dark hair and beautiful almond shaped eyes wearing a designer suit walks up, practically bouncing on air.

"This is fucking great," she gushes breathlessly.

"And this," Fogel says, "is Cindy Friedman, Deputy Associate Regional Director of Enforcement of the SEC."

"That's a mouthful," I say to her.

"It tends to catch people's attention," she says pleasantly, in stark contrast to Special Agent Tucker.

"I'm sure it does. S, E and C aren't three letters that most people want to hear, at least not in that order."

"Not everyone. Just those who have been up to no good."

"Present company excluded, I hope."

"We'll see." She at least has the decency to accompany her cryptic remark with an honest to goodness smile. It's something at least.

"I'm sorry," I say. "I didn't quite catch your name. It's Cindy..."

"Friedman."

I can't hide my surprise. "That's not what I would have expected."

"What? You don't hang out with many Chinese Jews?"

"No," I say with a laugh. "Clearly, I need to get out more."

"Your people have what you need?" Tucker asks. Holy shit, it speaks.

"Are you kidding?" she gushes. "This is a fucking gold mine. I wasn't sure to believe you last night, but after a first pass through the files upstairs, we're going to have to bring in another team."

"That bad?"

"Depends on your perspective. Great for me, bad for the people who work here. They're going to go to jail for a long, long, time." Catching herself, she looks at me. "Sorry."

"Not at all. Just happy to oblige."

Before she can answer, Naomi walks up beside me. She is nearly as breathless as the SEC agent. I make introductions. Fogel and Friedman shake Naomi's hand but Tucker, true to form, merely nods. This guy has a three-foot rod up his ass.

"I wasn't sure you guys were coming," I say to the various representatives of law enforcement.

"Neither was I," admits Fogel. "But after I got your text last night, things started moving pretty quickly."

"That document was remarkable," Friedman says, referring to the memo that Marcus sent me that I forwarded on to Fogel. "I never thought a U.S. healthcare company would put in writing that it puts profits over patients, but I guess that's why Infirmus is something special."

"We never claimed to be smart."

"Once we saw that document," Tucker adds, "this became something much more than the allegations of a disgruntled employee."

"Wait a second," Naomi interrupts, turning to me. "You did all this?"

I shrug. Before I can answer, Fogel explains. "Sean and I had been, uh, discussing other matters. In the course of those conversations, he let me know that he suspected illegal activity here at Infirmus."

"That's being polite," Friedman says. "This is nothing short of a massive conspiracy to commit securities fraud."

"To say nothing of Medicare fraud, racketeering and possibly involuntary manslaughter," Tucker adds. "Once Fogel explained the allegations and showed us the document, we had enough to get a warrant. From there, things moved pretty quickly. We raided one of your west coast hospitals and had a dozen agents comb through their files all night. They've already come up with enough evidence to keep prosecutors busy for a couple of years."

"Sean?" Naomi asks, struggling to catch up.

I shrug again. It's becoming my go-to move. "I told you I was going to let the truth come out."

"I thought you were talking about letting the widows tell their stories. I never expected ... all this."

"That was a nice touch," Fogel says. "I imagine Tucker and I will be speaking to those women soon."

"They'd like nothing more," I say with a smile.

Deputy Associate Regional Director Friedman can't contain herself any longer. "Mr. Reilly," she says, bouncing in her shoes as she shakes my hand, "it's been a pleasure, but I have to get back upstairs."

She tells Fogel and Tucker she will be in touch and then practically sprints back to the elevator.

"She's a ball of fire," I say to no one in particular.

"She's a little excited," Tucker agrees.

"She should be," adds Fogel. "Tucker, too. You've given them enough to get a significant promotion."

"We're going to be busy," Tucker acknowledges.

"So what happens now?" I ask.

"You're free to go. I won't process your arrest, but that doesn't mean you're out of the woods just yet. Either of you," he says ominously, turning towards Naomi.

"She has nothing to do with this."

"I'm glad to hear that, but I'll let our investigation do the talking."

I start to object but Tucker stops me.

"Listen, Mr. Reilly, we appreciate the tip and the evidence you've shown us. So far, everything we've seen tracks with the story Fogel told us last night. But we've got a job to do. And if we find out you're dirty..." He pauses, searching for the right words. "You need to understand you could go to jail."

"No turning state's evidence?"

"You kind of fucked yourself on that one. Thanks to you, we're already gathering all the evidence we'll ever need."

"Didn't think that one all the way through, now did I?"

He shrugs. "I can tell the U.S. Attorneys how you helped us, Sean, but I can't guarantee they won't go after you in a court of law."

"I understand," I say with a sigh. "I knew the risks when I started this."

He looks at me closely. "Did you?"

"Not entirely," I admit with a smile. "But I figured, what the hell."

He gives me a smile of his own, then shakes my hand again and turns to go.

"Hey," I say, stopping him. "One more question."

"Shoot."

"Why did you let him go on like that?"

"Who?"

"Williams. I thought you'd cut his mic immediately, but you let him yammer on to the crowd for awhile."

"Oh, that. He wasn't under arrest yet. Anything he said could still be used against him in a court of law. So I figured, what the hell."

He flashes a smile and walks off. I watch him bark orders at a fellow agent to make sure all exits are cordoned off, lest any executive manage to sneak out undetected. Against my better instincts, I find myself liking the man.

I look towards the front of the stage and see the two widows, right where they should be, swarmed by reporters as they tell their story. I watch them for a moment, happy that, no matter what else may come, at least the world will know what they have endured. As if reading my mind, Mrs. Swanson turns and sees me watching them. As her partner in crime answers a reporter's question, she smiles and mouths two words in my direction.

Thank you.

I spread my arms and smile, saying thank you in return. Then she turns around and fields a question of her own.

I turn back to Naomi and Detective Fogel.

"I'm impressed," she says, "even if you kept me in the dark. Asshole."

I laugh. "Couldn't have done it without you."

"Of course not."

"Hey, that reminds me. What the hell were you doing to the guy at the control board? I've never seen anyone in such agony."

She smiles. "Not much. Just squeezing his ball bag."

Fogel and I burst out laughing.

"You must have hands like a vice. He looked like he was about to hurl."

"He was. I kept telling him to breathe."

"The poor man didn't move an inch."

"Would you?"

"Are you kidding? You're one mean bitch."

Now it's her turn to burst out laughing. "That's exactly what he whispered when the kid came up to tell him to cut the sound!"

"I should probably leave," Fogel says with a smile, "before someone asks me to arrest you for assault."

"Before you do," I say, "there's something else we need to discuss."

"I thought you'd never ask."

Naomi throws her hands up and turns to go. "I'll leave you two to your secrets."

"Can you do me a favor first?" I ask.

"Depends. What is it?"

"Find Marcus and meet me in the parking lot. I'll be there right after I talk to Detective Fogel."

"Sure thing."

The detective and I walk past the widows, up the aisle and out of the convention hall.

"Where's Ramirez?" I ask as we walk into the lobby.

"Sitting this one out. He seems to think you don't like him."

"What gave him that idea?"

"Your overt hostility had something to do with it."

We skirt a gaggle of FBI agents speaking into their wrists, trying to look important, and walk outside. When we get to the curb, he sees Mac's Chevelle parked in a handicapped spot.

"Do I need to cite you for parking in a handicapped zone?" he asks as we walk over to it.

"You'll never make it stick," I answer, tossing the keys to him. "It's not my car."

"What's the matter? Don't like the classics?"

"She's great, but she was never really my style."

"And the gun?"

"Check the seat."

He leans down and looks through the passenger window to see a rumpled brown paper bag sitting on the front seat.

He looks at me, incredulous. "You left a gun sitting on the front seat?"

"It's not loaded," I protest. "And I locked the car."

He looks at me, a smile creeping across his face. "You'd make a shitty cop, you know that?"

"I'd be better than Ramirez."

"Anyone is better than Ramirez."

I burst out laughing. We both do. Fogel catches himself and says, "You can't tell him I said that. You can't tell *anyone* I said that."

"Don't worry. Your secret is safe."

"Anything else I need to know?"

"Actually, yeah. I assume you're going to run tests on the gun?"

"Yeah," he says slowly, wondering where this is going.

"Well, obviously my fingerprints are all over it."

"Obviously."

"And so are my wife's."

"Okay," he says, still curious where I'm headed.

"And if you test the, uh, barrel..."

"Yes..."

"Well, you might find it has recently been fired."

"I see."

"I, uh, did the firing."

"You did."

"I did."

"And did anyone get hurt?"

"No. No! God, no."

"Of course not." His tone is decidedly calmer than mine.

"I didn't shoot at anyone, if that's what you're asking."

"That is what I'm asking."

"I was just showing Alex the gun."

"Uh huh."

"And it went off."

"Uh huh."

"And, well, the thing of it is, I shot a plant."

"A plant."

"A spathiphyllum, actually."

"I hear they're lovely."

"They are. Wonderful houseplants."

"Which is why you shot it."

"I didn't mean to. I was just—"

"Showing Alex the gun."

"Exactly!"

"Exactly."

"So you see."

"I see what?"

"That while I shot the gun, I didn't actually shoot anyone."

"Non-flora, that is."

"Exactly."

I fidget while Fogel watches me curiously. I am profoundly uncomfortable.

"I'd like to amend what I said earlier," he says finally. "You'd be a shitty cop, but you'd be an even shittier criminal."

"Hey," I say defensively, "aren't you the guy who thought I was in league with Mac?"

"That's a black mark on my record. No doubt about it. I was dead wrong."

"Yeah, well, you don't have to be so certain about it. I mean, I could be a bad dude."

"Sean," he says, now laughing in my face, "you may be a lot of things, but a bad dude ain't one of them."

"From where I stand," I mumble, "I'm not sure I'd agree with you."

He looks at me sympathetically. "Don't be so hard on yourself. Everyone fucks up. It's what you do after you fuck up that defines you. And what you did today takes stones."

"Thanks."

He claps his hands. "Alright. I've got the car. I've got the gun. Anything else I should know before I take you home?"

"Yeah. Check the glove box. You'll see a bank receipt and a disgusting Wendy's wrapper."

"So?"

"So? Have your guys do their CSI shit and I bet you'll be able to tie Mac to the car with whatever disgusting DNA he left on the wrapper. And who knows? Maybe you'll get lucky and the bank receipt will be his personal account."

He seems impressed. "That's pretty good."

I smile. "Who's the shitty cop, now?"

We shake hands and he returns inside, presumably to make sure Tucker doesn't hog all the glory. I inhale deeply and look around. It's a beautiful sunny day and I have nowhere to be. For a moment, I'm not sure what to do next.

"You guys put on quite a show," says a familiar voice.

"You liked it?" I answer, turning to see Naomi and Marcus walking towards me.

"It was great theater. Although," he says, his face growing darker, "it certainly takes the bite out of my so-called scoop."

"Yeah," I respond sheepishly. "Sorry about that."

"Not even a heads up?"

"Everything came together late last night," I say, scrambling. "Plus, I couldn't risk word getting out."

He glares at me and I feel my stomach turn. A perfect morning is about to turn ugly. Then, just as quickly, he breaks into a smile. "Just pulling your leg."

"You're not angry?"

"Are you kidding? I'm pissed! But it's not like you owed me anything. I was trying to take your company down and you along with it. You outplayed me. All I can do is tip my hat."

"If it's any consolation, I didn't mean to ruin your story."

"You didn't," he says with a wave. "I'll reframe it as a behind the scenes piece – 'How one of America's biggest healthcare companies went astray,' that sort of thing. I'll still win the Pulitzer."

"You don't lack confidence, I'll give you that."

"And you don't lack balls.

Naomi laughs. "If you only knew."

"I'm not kidding. This took guts to pull off."

I shrug. "I just got out of the way and let two courageous women tell their story. Not much more to it than that."

"There's way more to it and you know it. You blew the whistle knowing it could bring a pile of shit crashing down on your head."

"Put it that way," Naomi says, "and he doesn't sound all that smart."

"I said he had balls, not a brain."

"Hey," I protest, "I played you, didn't I?"

"Therein lies your genius," Marcus concedes. "You sounded so full of shit, I never knew what to believe." We start walking across the parking lot and Marcus turns to me. "So what's next?"

"Truthfully, I have no idea. It's funny. Things were so bad on Monday that I wanted to kill myself. But I'm way more screwed up today than I was then."

"How so?"

"My life already sucked, and that was before I faced the possibility of imprisonment, not to mention several hundred grand in legal fees. I'm not welcome here and home's not much better. I'm not sure I have anyplace to go."

"We don't need to start taking belts and shoelaces away from you, do we, Sean?" Marcus seems unsure whether he should worry or call bullshit again.

"Nah," I decide. "I just need to think of what to do with these balls you think I have."

"You could always try your hand as a reporter."

I stop cold. "You're shitting me."

"Not at all. You know how the game is played and how to cut through the bullshit. And after today, you've certainly got a knack for the theatrical."

"Marcus, I don't know if you've noticed, but the press isn't exactly thriving these days."

"Neither are you."

"Point taken."

"Listen, I didn't say you'd make a lot of money. I just said it would be something to do."

"I can't even write that well."

"Who said anything about writing? You took what could have been a boring story about healthcare economics and made it dramatic. Between that spot of yours on local news plus today's extravaganza, you created a multimedia narrative. There aren't a lot of people who can do that."

"Naomi did most of it."

"So bring her along."

"And do what? Are you suggesting I go on TV?"

"Holy shit, no. She could go on camera but you've got a face made for radio. You should become a producer. Follow the story, that's what you're good at. There are plenty of ways these days to get it out there."

"Look, Marcus, even if this made sense – which it doesn't – I wouldn't know where to start."

"That's easy. I know plenty of people. I could make some calls."

I am flabbergasted. "You'd do that? For me?"

"I didn't say I'd marry you. Just introduce you to people."

"I don't know what to say."

"Well, that's a first." He reaches out and shakes first my hand then Naomi's. "It's been a pleasure. Something tells me I haven't seen the last of either of you." I smile as I watch him turn and walk towards his rental car.

"Hey Marcus!" I call after him.

"Yeah?" he says, turning around.

"You still looking for a statement from the company for your article?"

"No," he says with a laugh. "I think the picture of Williams being hauled off in cuffs says it all. But Sean?"

"Yeah?"

"Let me know if things get too hot for you once the article is out."

"I'll be fine," I say, not really believing it.

"Well, if you need it, I can have some friends push a few articles out there in your defense. Just say the word."

"Thanks, Marcus. I appreciate it."

"Least I can do."

Naomi and I watch as he climbs into his generic subcompact, redlines the engine and screeches out of the parking lot.

"What now?" I ask.

"What, taking down a Fortune 500 company and getting a Pulitzer prize-winning reporter on your side aren't enough for you?"

I look at her with a sheepish smile. "It is pretty cool, isn't it?"

"The coolest," she says as she wraps her arms around me and gives me a kiss. Slowly, she pulls back and I see a sadness in her eyes.

"This is it for us, isn't it?" I ask.

"Yeah," she says softly, "I think it is."

"I'm going to miss you."

"No, you won't."

"I'll miss your body," I offer.

"Goddamn right, you will," she says with a wicked smile. She kisses me once more before turning and walking towards her car.

Knowing I can't tear my eyes away, she puts a little extra sway in her hips and a little more wiggle in her ass. Laughing, I make a mental note to get my shit together. Then I make a mental note to have as many gin and tonics as possible tonight.

I am aware these mental notes may be at cross-purposes.

39

My shoes click-clack along the linoleum floor as I follow the screech of the whistle to what I hope is Julia's game. My backpack clinks as I sling it higher on my shoulder and check my watch. With any luck, I've only missed the first few minutes. I turn a corner past a homemade banner — "LET'S GO HAWKS" — when I hear a crowd erupt and an announcer bellow.

"REILLY FOR THREEEEEEEEEE!!"

Reilly? As in Claire Reilly?

My phone buzzes and I check the text. It's Fogel.

U were right. Mac's DNA was
all over the burger wrapper

I text him back.

I'd hate to see him eat

No shit. But it gets better

That bank receipt was a deposit
slip for Mac's account. Turns out
our drug dealer is quite the
fiscal conservative

How so?

He rolls most of his drug
money into CDs

HA!

They make less than 2% but
I guess he likes the security

Does this mean
I'm off the hook?

It does with me

THANK YOU!!

No thank you. You made
me look like a hero

Sure you don't want to be
a detective?

I hear Ramirez is looking
for a partner

Smiling and pocketing the phone, I pick up the pace and

hustle through a door underneath enormous red and black letters:

THE HAWK'S NEST

The gym is by no means at capacity, but it is surprisingly full for a girls' junior varsity basketball game. There's a timeout on the floor and I see Claire and her teammates huddled with the coach on the far sideline. I scan the crowd for a familiar face. I see Alex but no Julia, only a little gremlin next to my wife with red and black face paint screaming bloody murder. I hustle along the sideline before the teams retake the court and climb the stands to join Alex.

"Hey," I say, gasping for air and putting the backpack at my feet.

"Didn't think you'd make it."

"Me neither. Where's Jules?"

The diminutive fanatic next to Alex turns and screams, "HEY DAD!"

"Holy crow! Julia?"

"Yeah! Mom let me paint my face. Like it?"

"You kidding? You look great!" I turn to Alex. "Really?"

She shrugs. "It's a playoff game. Gotta support the team."

"Since when do JV teams have playoffs?"

"No idea."

"Wasn't like this when I was a kid."

"They didn't have electricity when you were a kid."

"Touché."

The teams jog back on to the court. Claire is on the floor, guarding the inbounder.

"How's she doing?" I ask, without looking at Alex.

"Leading scorer so far."

I turn to Alex. "Are you shitting me?"

"Dad, you do know there's a ten-year-old present?"

"Sorry, Jules."

"She's only, like, the best one on the team."

I look at Alex. "Really?" I whisper.

"Welcome to your daughter's life," she says. I can't tell if she's pissed, but she seems to be smiling.

The visiting team scrambles to inbound the ball, but the Hawks' defense is suffocating. Claire relentlessly hounds the inbounder, who panics as the referee calls out "Four." She heaves the ball as far as she can to no one in particular. It's a footrace and the Hawks' point guard, a slight but lightning quick freshman, swoops in to steal the ball. She looks back down court and sees Claire who, as soon as the ball was released, sprinted to the wing, just outside the three-point line. Claire doesn't even have to call for the ball; the point guard fires a pass to her, which Claire catches and, in one smooth motion, turns and shoots.

Swish.

The crowd erupts once more as the announcer yells what I gather has become a regular refrain, "REILLY FOR THREEEEEEE!"

"Jesus. When did she get so good?"

Alex laughs as Julia screams her approval along with the rest of the crowd.

We sit down and the game settles into a rhythm, with the visiting team struggling to penetrate the Hawks' stifling defense, only to watch helplessly as the hometown girls score with ease. By the time the coach rests Claire in the second quarter, she leads all scorers in points and assists.

I pull two water bottles out of the backpack and hand one to Alex.

"What's this?"

"Try it," I say, taking a long sip from mine.

She unscrews the cap and sniffs, her nose wrinkling. "Sean," she whispers, "it's illegal to have alcohol in school."

"After today, I'll take my chances." I take another healthy sip of gin and tonic and sigh contentedly. Alex, looking around furtively, takes a small sip and giggles.

"I have to say," she whispers. "This is a much better way to watch the game." We clink bottles and have another sip.

By the third quarter, the Hawks have put the game out of reach. Julia has left us, joining a pack of middle school friends to lay waste to the snack bar. I pull out two more water bottles from the backpack and offer one to Alex.

"Another?" she asks, her face flushed.

"If you're gonna go, go large."

"Okay," she says, taking the bottle warily. "But we're going to share this one."

"Twist my arm."

I look across the court and see Claire laughing with her teammates on the bench as the second stringers continue the onslaught on the court. Sullen around the house, she is radiant here in her element. There is no hint of teenaged angst as she laughs with unencumbered joy, her eyes shining.

"She's beautiful," Alex says, following my gaze.

"You almost can't tell how much we fucked her up."

"We didn't fuck her up, Sean."

"I keep thinking about what you said earlier today. You think she'll ever be able to recover from the other morning?"

"That was bad," she concedes. "But you have to stop being so full of yourself."

"Excuse me?"

"You always think you're responsible for everything. Don't you think people can screw themselves up all on their own?"

"Well that's comforting."

"What I mean is, you're not the only thing going on in all of our lives. That means you're not to blame for everything. But it also means you can't fix everything, either."

I sip my drink and try not to grow depressed at this.

"You ever think about, you know, getting your shit together? Maybe drinking a little less?"

"Let's see. Today, I exposed one of the biggest cases of fraud in American healthcare and got a drug dealer arrested. I think my shit is reasonably together."

"That's not what I mean and you know it." When I don't answer, she pushes on. "You're a fucking mess, Sean. You're a drunk, an absentee father and a shitty-ass husband."

I sigh. "You really want to do this now? Here, in front of all these people?"

"What am I supposed to do, Sean? Wait for you to get drunk and pass out?"

"You ever think I do that because I can't bear the thought of hearing you carp at me anymore?"

She takes a deep breath and tries to maintain her composure.

"Of course," she says softly. "I know I'm at least as much to blame for our marriage falling apart as you are. It's just..." She looks across the court at Claire, who is standing on the bench, cheering like mad as a third stringer makes a ten-foot jumper. Then I see her eyes wander to Julia, who is surrounded by friends at the snack bar as she sticks out her tongue and dances a silly jig. "They need us, Sean."

"Who?"

"The girls."

I snort with laughter and sip my drink. "They haven't needed me since they were in diapers."

"That's not true."

"Of course it is. Just ask them."

"They miss you, Sean," she whispers, trying to hold it together.

"They say it all the time."

I try not to cry by focusing on the game. Down by thirty, the visiting team is still battling. Their point guard pushes the ball on a fast break, then pulls up from the top of the arc and drains a three pointer. As the opposing team's parents erupt with applause, it's hard not to join in.

"We can't abandon them," Alex is saying.

"I'm not suggesting we abandon them," I answer softly. "I'm saying you and I don't work together. We haven't for a long time."

"Don't you think they'll consider us failures if we split up?"

"I think we're way past that point," I say, laughing. "I've lost my job, I'm facing federal prosecution and we're in debt up to our eyeballs. By any definition, we're the paragon of failure."

She laughs reluctantly. "I guess we have fucked up pretty severely."

"There are meth addicts in better shape than us."

She sips her drink, deep in thought. I try again.

"Listen, Alex. I love the girls and I don't want to do anything that's going to hurt them, but the fact is, we have to make some major changes."

"Like?"

"Declaring bankruptcy for one. And selling the houses. Things are going to get very painful, very quickly."

"I know," she says, barely above a whisper.

She turns to watch the game but I press on. If I don't get this out now, I'm worried I never will.

"Alex, face facts. We can't make it as husband and wife. I think we proved that a long time ago. But that doesn't mean we can't still be good parents to our kids – or, in my case, *start* being a good parent."

"So you want to get a divorce?" Even with all of the acrimony and bitterness we've thrown each other's way, her voice still cracks at the thought of divorce. It's almost enough to make me want to stay with her.

Almost.

"I don't want to, but I think we both know it's for the best."

She stews on this for a moment. "You're probably right."

"You know I am."

"The worst part is, splitting up may be more expensive than being together. It means two apartments, two sets of furniture, two of everything."

"You could always kill yourself."

I whip my head around, ready to tear into her, and then I see her smile. She's kidding. We're joking around. This is new territory. I have to get used to this.

"Sorry to say, I've opted for career suicide instead."

"So killing yourself isn't the answer?"

"Oh, it might be the answer," I say, causing her to choke on her drink. "Just not for me."

"Too much of a candy-ass to go through with it?" she coughs.

"No. I've been told I'm quite courageous."

"By whom?"

"A Pulitzer prize-winning reporter. And he should know. He's been in the shit."

"So your bravery is going to carry you through this shitty existence?"

"That and the fact that so people depend on me."

"I'm sorry?" She keeps choking on her drink. She should have that checked out.

"You heard me."

"Like who?"

"You, the girls."

"Well, the girls, anyway."

Now it's my turn to choke. Maybe there's something wrong with this gin. Or maybe it's not safe to laugh and drink at the same time.

"There's also my dad," I sputter, trying to recover.

She looks at me kindly. "It's about time you realized that. You're all he's got. Your brother certainly isn't going to help out."

"Kevin deserves a pass." I look across the gym and watch Claire lead the bench in a cheer. I've never seen her happier. "It's time to put old grudges to rest."

Her eyebrows shoot up. "You have a new lease on life *and* you're forgiving past slights. What the hell's gotten into you?"

"It's easy to be magnanimous when you're invincible."

"I beg your pardon?"

"Yes, Alex. As it turns out, I'm invincible."

"Is that right?"

"Apparently so. I've driven a car at high speed into a bridge abutment, drank enough booze to sink a ship and ingested enough sedatives to kill a walrus and, yet, here I am. Still standing."

"Well, sitting."

"Yeah, but you get the point." I sip my drink and make a note to bring booze to all school events from now on. Even PTA meetings would be tolerable with the warm haze that's enveloped me.

"Invincible, huh? That's quite a superpower."

"I know."

"What are you going to do with it? Call the Avengers? Be a force for good in the universe?"

"I was thinking of something a little more local."

"Crime fighting? I hear Spider-Man is looking for a partner."

"That might be tough, especially as I may soon be doing between five and ten upstate."

"Some kind of superhero – a guy who can't be killed so he can lead the shittiest life imaginable."

"Tell me about it."

"Well, at least pick out a name. Every superhero needs a catchy name. It's practically the law."

"I've been toying with The Shitstorm."

"Not bad."

"Or Captain Contemptible."

"How about The Invincible Dolt?"

I smile. "I like that one."

I sip my drink and watch contentedly as time expires and girls from both teams storm the court. The season is over for one and the playoffs have just begun for the other, but both teams pile on each other, laughing and screaming in delight. For a moment, at least, having won or lost seems far less important than just having played the game.

I think I'm finally starting to understand what that feels like.

Made in the USA
Middletown, DE
05 August 2020